*EVERYMAN, I will go with thee,*

*and be thy guide,*

*In thy most need to go by thy side*

## WILLIAM MAKEPEACE THACKERAY

Born at Calcutta in 1811. Came to England in 1817; educated at Cambridge. Soon abandoned law and entered journalism in 1832–3. Died on 24th December 1863.

W. M. THACKERAY

# The English Humourists
# Charity and Humour
# The Four Georges

INTRODUCTION BY

M. R. RIDLEY, M.A.

DENT: LONDON
EVERYMAN'S LIBRARY
DUTTON: NEW YORK

© Introduction, J. M. Dent & Sons Ltd, 1968
Made in Great Britain
at the
Aldine Press · Letchworth · Herts
for
J. M. DENT & SONS LTD
Aldine House · Bedford Street · London
First included in Everyman's Library 1912
Last reprinted 1968

NO. 610

SBN: 460 00610 x

# CONTENTS

# INTRODUCTION

AFTER some years of hard and competent work in contemporary journalism, largely for *Fraser's Magazine* and *Punch*, Thackeray wrote *Vanity Fair* in monthly numbers during 1847 and 1848. It was slow to take hold while appearing monthly, but as soon as it came out as a book it gripped the public taste and Thackeray's reputation was established. He reinforced it with *Pendennis* in the two following years. He was now, in all probability, financially secure, so long as the vein of novel-writing did not peter out, but periodical novel-writing, especially to a temperamentally indolent man who is always behindhand with his monthly stint, is an exacting job; sudden illness, as he found while engaged on *Pendennis*, was always liable to be catastrophic to the smooth progress of the work; and the demands on his purse were heavy. So he looked round for some means of livelihood which would be reasonably lucrative and yet give him a chance of recouping his energies for the next novel. He turned to lecturing and to the writing of burlesques; one of the latter was that masterpiece *Rebecca and Rowena*, and for the lectures he turned to the century he knew so well and composed those on the *English Humourists of the Eighteenth Century*. These he delivered in London during the summer of 1851, later in the year in towns up and down England, in 1852 and 1853 in America. When they were prepared for publication in 1854 they were copiously annotated by James Hannay.

Before the delivery of the first Thackeray was desperately nervous. One of his audience, who had arrived early, found him 'standing like a forlorn, disconsolate

vii

giant in the middle of the room, gazing about him. "Oh, Lord!" he exclaimed as he shook hands with me "I'm sick at my stomach with fright."' His nervousness was not unnatural. He was not a practised lecturer; the precedents for literary men lecturing had not been numerous since Coleridge and Hazlitt; the financial success of the lectures was very important to him; and his audience, though many of them were his friends, and so kindly disposed, were also highly critical, with more than adequate knowledge, and not at all disposed to be content with the platitudinous, the ill-arranged or the second-rate.

In the event the reception of the lectures was all that any lecturer could wish for; Charlotte Brontë describes it as a furore. I am not sure that we, reading them a hundred years later, are inclined to think that they merited so warm a reception. We grant that they have moments of rare penetration, flashes of excellent insight; but we are apt to feel that they are sometimes thrown together rather haphazardly, and present disconnectedly some vivaciously ill-considered verdicts. But at least we can make sure that we keep in mind what it is that Thackeray is trying to do. He is not trying to entertain us by drawing our attention to a number of funny books. 'It is of the men and of their lives, rather than of their books, that I ask permission to speak to you; and in doing so, you are aware that I cannot hope to entertain you with a merely humourous or facetious story. . . . The men regarding whose lives and stories your kind presence here shows that you have curiosity and sympathy, appeal to a great number of our other faculties besides our mere sense of ridicule. The humourous writer professes to awaken and direct your love, your pity, your kindness—your scorn for untruth, pretention, imposture—your tenderness for the weak, the poor, the oppressed, the unhappy. To the best of his means and ability he comments on all the ordinary actions and passions of life almost. He takes upon himself to be the week-day preacher, so to speak.' We have been warned.

If he was to take his dozen figures in chronological order—as on the whole he did—he would have to start with Prior. But Prior clearly did not carry the guns for an effective opening salvo, and Thackeray wisely selected for his first lecture the enigmatic and exciting figure of Swift. I cannot feel that he made more than a fumbling presentation of him. In the first place, to all of his audience except those to whom the life and works of Swift were already familiar, much of the lecture must have been almost unintelligible. Quite early in the lecture the question is shot at us: 'Would we have liked to live with him?' We have not been given any data for answering the question, so Thackeray answers it for us: 'If you had been his inferior in parts, his equal in mere social station, he would have bullied, scorned, and insulted you; if, undeterred by his great reputation, you had met him like a man, he would have quailed before you, and not had the pluck to reply, and gone home, and years after written a foul epigram about you—watched for you in a sewer, and come out to assail you with a coward's blow and a dirty bludgeon.' A meaner picture could hardly be drawn. Yet there are others, 'a lonely eagle chained behind the bars', 'a vast genius, a magnificent genius, wonderfully bright, and dazzling, and strong— to seize, to know, to see, to flash upon falsehood and scorch it into perdition, to penetrate into the hidden motives, and expose the black thoughts of men—an awful, an evil spirit'. Swift, it seems to me, is continually eluding his observer, who as a result is continually trying to control a kaleidoscope into some sort of coherent unity. He cannot see the white anger that blazes behind the *Modest Proposal*, and so can see in it only a bitter and revolting joke. And I do not think that he gets the last book of *Gulliver* into any sort of perspective: 'The meaning of it is', he says, 'that man is utterly wicked, desperate, and imbecile, and his passions are so monstrous, and his boasted powers so mean, that he is and deserves to be the slave of brutes.'

His own tenderness of heart allowed him to be more

perceptive about Swift's relations with Stella, though I fancy he thought his feelings more marital than they were, and found it easier than we do to excuse the behaviour to Vanessa. But all in all what we have is less a portrait than a series of sketches of the sitter in very different poses. Admittedly he had chosen a uniquely testing sitter, but his own despondent verdict after the first lecture, 'The truth is the lectures won't do', was perhaps not so wide of the mark as the later lectures showed it to be.

The lecture on Swift was, perhaps deliberately, something of a *tour de force*, to launch the series, a violently impressionistic effort which did not come off. It did not suggest that the lecturer was going to be a particularly safe guide to the truth about other subjects; but it did suggest that he might be entertaining, and would certainly have stimulating and provocative ideas. But with Congreve and Addison he moved into calmer waters, under skies less lowering with storms and rent with lightnings. He achieved a manner wholly adapted to his purpose, his subjects were entirely amenable to his control, and, with the one exception of Sterne, sympathetic.

There is a clear picture of Congreve: a commissioner of hackney-coaches, with a place in the Pipe Office, a post in the Custom House, and the patronage of Lord Halifax, all for the writing of the first of his comedies, *The Old Bachelor*. Dryden acknowledged his excellence and London was at his feet. There is a brilliant sketch of the comedy of the time. 'She was a disreputable, darling, laughing, painted French baggage, that Comic Muse. She came over from the Continent with Charles (who chose many more of his female friends there) at the Restoration—a wild dishevelled Laïs, with eyes bright with wit and wine—a saucy Court-favourite that sat at the King's knees, and laughed in his face, and when she showed her bold cheeks at her chariot-window, had some of the noblest and most famous people of the land bowing round her wheel. She was kind and popular enough, that daring Comedy, that audacious poor Nell: she was gay

and generous, kind, frank as such people can afford to
be! and the men who lived with her and laughed with
her, took her pay and drank her wine, turned out when
the Puritans hooted her, to fight and defend her. But the
jade was indefensible, and it is pretty certain her servants
knew it.' And Thackeray goes on to deal with the utter
artificiality which underlies the brilliance, and he concludes with a curt dismissal: 'A touch of Steele's tenderness is worth all his [Congreve's] finery; a flash of Swift's
lightning, a beam of Addison's pure sunshine, and his
tawdry playhouse taper is invisible. But the ladies loved
him, and he was undoubtedly a pretty fellow.'

The portrait of Addison has the same intimacy, but
engagingly more warmth. Thackeray frankly loves
Addison, and lays his finger firmly on what matters
about him. 'It is not for his reputation as the great
author of "Cato" and the "Campaign", or for his merits
as Secretary of State, or for his rank and high distinction
as my Lady Warwick's husband, or for his eminence as an
Examiner of political questions on the Whig side, or a
Guardian of British liberties, that we admire Joseph
Addison. It is as a Tatler of small talk and a Spectator
of mankind, that we cherish and love him, and owe as
much pleasure to him as to any human being that ever
wrote. He came in that artificial age, and began to speak
with his noble, natural voice. . . . Addison wrote his
papers as gaily as if he was going out for a holiday.
When Steele's *Tatler* first began his prattle, Addison,
then in Ireland, caught at his friend's notion, poured
in paper after paper, and contributed the stores of his
mind, the sweet fruits of his reading, the delightful
gleanings of his daily observation, with a wonderful
profusion, and as it seemed, an almost endless fecundity.
He was six-and-thirty years old: full and ripe. . . . He
had not done much as yet. . . . But with his friend's
discovery of the *Tatler*, Addison's calling was found,
and the most delightful talker in the world began to
speak.'

And he says a characteristic goodbye to this writer

whom he loved and venerated. He quotes from Addison's great hymn, and then: 'It seems to me those verses shine like the stars. They shine out of a great deep calm. When he turns to Heaven, a Sabbath comes over that man's mind: and his face lights up from it with a glory of thanks and prayer. His sense of religion stirs through his whole being. In the fields, in the town: looking at the birds in the trees: at the children in the streets: in the morning or in the moonlight: over his books in his own room: in a happy party at a country merry-making or a town assembly, good-will and peace to God's creatures, and love and awe of him who made them, fill his pure heart and shine from his kind face. If Swift's life was the most wretched, I think Addison's was one of the most enviable. A life prosperous and beautiful— a calm death—an immense fame and affection afterwards for his happy and spotless name.'

For his next subject Thackeray changes his method of approach. Hitherto the main figure has taken the stage after a very brief preamble; here we have a long discussion on the Muse of History, followed by a sketch of a highwayman, and then by an account of the career of Lord Mohun; finally, to complete eleven pages of prologue, two pages on an odd periodical called the *British Apollo*, a farrago of answers to questions on all topics in heaven and earth, of poems and of articles. After which there steals in, rather surreptitiously, 'a thick-set, square-faced, black-eyed, soft-hearted little Irish boy'. He is developed as follows: 'Besides being very kind, lazy, and good-natured, this boy went invariably into debt with the tart-woman; ran out of bounds, and entered into pecuniary, or rather promissory, engagements with the neighbouring lollipop vendors and piemen—exhibited an early fondness and capacity for drinking mum and sack, and borrowed from all his comrades who had money to lend'. This apparently authoritative sketch is immediately followed by the engaging admission: 'I have no sort of authority for the statements here made of Steele's early life; but if the child is father of the man . . . Dick Steele the schoolboy must have been one of the most generous, good-for-nothing, amiable little creatures that ever . . .' Thackeray, like all men of proper feelings, has evidently a very soft spot in his heart for this lovable scapegrace, who clutched so often the fringes of fortune and yet could never grasp it. He contrasts his warm zest for life with 'Swift's savage indignation and Addison's lonely serenity', and finds it more congenial than either. And this contrast tempts him into something nearer to ordinary literary criticism than is usual in the lectures: he takes a passage on death from each writer and compares them. And his conclusion to the comparison is: 'I own to liking Dick Steele the man, and Dick Steele the author, much better than much better men and much better authors.'

Being now half way through his course, Thackeray had dealt with only four of his dozen humorists, and was beginning to feel a trifle hurried. The results were by no means wholly unfortunate, since there was a gain in concentration. In the lecture on Prior, Gay and Pope the first two are handled with a perfectly adequate and very pleasant lightness of touch. The aroma and charm of each are indicated, and no extravagant claims are made for either. Gay's poems, in particular, are recommended, with a happy choice of epithet, to 'any man fond of lazy literature'. And then on to 'the greatest name on our list—the highest among the poets, the highest among the English wits and humourists with whom we have to rank him . . . the greatest literary *artist* that England has seen. He polished, he refined, he thought; he took thoughts from other works to adorn and complete his own; borrowing an idea or a cadence from another poet as he would a figure or a simile from a flower, or a river, stream, or any object which struck him in his walk, or contemplation of nature'. There is Thackeray on Plagiarism. He is saying: 'If you are great enough (and perhaps shameless enough), you will not be blamed, but applauded, for stealing from your fellow-craftsman.'

The only blemishes on a brilliant study of Pope seem to me one or two touches which are almost impossible to reconcile with the whole picture: one is the savage attack on Dennis which Addison disowned: 'It is so dirty that it has been printed in Swift's works too.' Another is the venom with which he gloats over the poor miseries of Grub Street. Any man may show inconsistencies, but when we remember those displays we find it hard to accept quite as he meant them the picture of Pope's devotion to his mother and that of his death, 'the departure of that high soul'.

It was characteristic of Thackeray to include an artist among his humorists. He had a good deal of rough and ready skill with a pencil himself, and knew that a moral could be drawn in other media than words. 'Hogarth's art', he says, 'is quite simple; he speaks popular parables to interest simple hearts, and to inspire them with pleasure or pity or warning and terror. Not one of his tales but is as easy as "Goody Two-Shoes"; it is the moral of Tommy was a naughty boy and the master flogged him, and Jacky was a good boy and had plum-cake, which pervades the whole works of the homely and famous English moralist.' There follow excellent summaries of *Marriage à la Mode* and *The Rake's Progress* and a note on 'the portrait of his own honest face, of which the bright blue eyes shine out from the canvas and give you an idea of that keen and brave look with which Wiliam Hogarth regarded the world'.

Hogarth's 'kindred humourist', Smollett, has to be content with the merest sketch, 'manly, kindly, honest and irascible; worn and battered, but brave and full of heart, after a long struggle against a hard fortune', but Fielding gets fuller treatment. I am not sure that the portrait of him is not the best thing in the lectures, drawn with the firmest strokes and the most consistent. 'He has an admirable natural love of truth, the keenest instinctive antipathy to hypocrisy, the happiest satirical gift of laughing it to scorn. His wit is wonderfully wise and detective; it flashes upon a rogue and lightens up a rascal like a policeman's lantern. . . . He may have low tastes, but not a mean mind; he admires with all his heart good and virtuous men, stoops to no flattery, bears no rancour, disdains all disloyal arts, does his public duty uprightly, is fondly loved by his family, and dies at his work.'

The reaction of the reader, and one may guess of the audience, to the observations on Sterne depends no doubt on one's view of Sterne. If one regards him as a sniggerer, one is pleased to see him put firmly in his place: ' There is not a page in Sterne's writing but has something that were better away, a latent corruption—a hint, as of an impure presence.' If one regards him as refreshingly piquant, one will think Thackeray obtusely unfair. But as to what he had to say about Goldsmith there can, I think, be no two opinions. It is not easy to estimate coolly and praise without softness a writer whose prime qualities were to be kindly to all men and beloved by all his friends; but Thackeray achieves it. The one surprising omission is due, one may imagine, rather to his audience than to himself. There is no mention of Goldsmith's comedies; if it were not for allusions to Kelly and Colman's actors one would hardly be aware that he had written any. Clearly for Thackeray's audience Goldsmith was the author of *The Vicar of Wakefield* and *The Deserted Village* and not of *She Stoops to Conquer*.

In 1855 Thackeray prepared and delivered in America his lectures on the *Four Georges*. They were very successful, as they were when he delivered them again after he came back to England. And we may think the popular verdict justified so long as we remember what their author says of them: ' We may peep here and there into that bygone world of the Georges, see what they and their Courts were like; glance at the people round about them; look at past manners, fashions, pleasures, and contrast them with our own. . . . I have been taken to task for not having given grave historical treatises, which it was never my intention to attempt.' They are indeed agreeable chats rather than historical treatises, and should be read as such if they are to be enjoyed. Thackeray was not into his stride in the first, and there are twenty mortal pages about the early Hanoverians and the Königsmarcks, who are hardly relevant, and certainly not interesting, even at the gossip level, before we get to George I. And he is not much of a figure when he does arrive, with his two rather comic German mistresses, Maypole and Elephant, his German *entourage*, and his passion for getting back to Hanover as often as he could. But Thackeray, seizing the chance of a bitter side-slash at his *bête noire* Marlborough, does his best for him. 'He was not a lofty monarch, certainly: he was not a patron of the fine arts: but he was not a hypocrite, he was not revengeful, he was not extravagant. Though a despot in Hanover, he was a moderate ruler in England. His aim was to leave it to itself, as much as possible, and to live out of it as much as he could. His heart was in Hanover.'

Of George II the lecturer has little good to say. All that can be set on the credit side is physical courage, which he showed at Oudenarde and Dettingen (though at the latter in rather ridiculous circumstances) and the fact that he was able to retain throughout his life the devotion of 'the most lovely and accomplished princess of Germany'. In the king's sordid court there is no one whom Thackeray can admire but Lady Suffolk, and he finally dismisses the king as 'one who had neither dignity, learning, morals, nor wit—who tainted a great society by a bad example; who, in youth, manhood, old age, was gross, low, and sensual'.

When he comes to George III Thackeray is in his element. He moves through those sixty years of 'magnificent times and voluptuous people' as though he belonged among them, and he is the perfect cicerone. But it is a strange scene through which he conducts us, since 'around a young king, himself of the most exemplary life and undoubted piety, lived a court society as dissolute as our country ever knew'. And the contrast between king and court makes the task of the cicerone very difficult, so difficult that even on its own lines this, as a piece of history, is the least satisfactory of the four lectures. Thackeray's respect for the man, and his sense of the pathos of the last years, blinds him to his patent weaknesses as king, and the portrait remains incomplete.

When he comes to paint George IV there is no respect for the subject to inhibit the freedom of the brushwork. All that hampers him is that he finds he is trying to paint a cipher; 'you find you have nothing—nothing but a coat and a wig and a mask smiling below it—nothing but a great simulacrum'. To relieve his own feelings and ours he paints three or four great gentlemen, Scott, Southey, Collingwood, Heber, but for the period and its ruler the dismissal is contemptuously terse: '*He* the first gentleman of Europe! There is no stronger satire on the proud English society of that day, than that they admired George.'

Here then are Thackeray's lectures. They are not, as a whole, the best of Thackeray, since the form was not one which wholly suited him, but they are full of touches of Thackeray at his best, so that no lover of Thackeray can read them without very keen pleasure.

M. R. RIDLEY.

1968.

# SELECT BIBLIOGRAPHY

WORKS. *The Yellowplush Correspondence*, 1837; *Catherine*, 1838; *The Paris Sketch-book*, 1840; *The Second Funeral of Napoleon*, 1841; *The Irish Sketch-book*, 1843; *Barry Lyndon*, 1844; *Notes of a Journey from Cornhill to Grand Cairo*, 1846; *The Book of Snobs*, 1846; *Vanity Fair*, 1847–8; *Pendennis*, 1848–50; *Rebecca and Rowena*, 1849; *The English Humourists*, 1851; *Henry Esmond*, 1852; *The Newcomes*, 1853–5; *The Rose and the Ring*, 1854; *The Four Georges*, 1855; *The Virginians*, 1857–9; *Lovel the Widower*, 1860; *Philip*, 1861–2; *Denis Duval*, 1863 (not completed).

COLLECTED WORKS. *Thackeray's Works* (Library Edition), 22 vols., 1867–9; *Thackeray's Works* (Oxford Edition), 17 vols., 1908.

BIOGRAPHY AND CRITICISM. A. Trollope, *Thackeray*, 1879; W. C. Brownell, *Victorian Prose Masters*, 1902; C. Saintsbury, *A Consideration of Thackeray*, 1931; H. N. Wethered, *The Art of Thackeray*, 1938; J. W. Dodds, *Thackeray, a Critical Portrait*, 1941; G. N. Ray, *The Buried Life*, 1952, *The Uses of Adversity*, 1955, *The Age of Wisdom*, 1958; G. Tillotson, *Thackeray the Novelist*, 1954, 1963; J. Loofbourow, *Thackeray and the Form of Fiction*, 1965.

BIBLIOGRAPHY. H. S. Van Duzer, *A Thackeray Library. A Complete Thackeray Bibliography*, 1919. For articles, etc., identified as Thackeray's since the latter date *see* G. N. Ray, *Letters and Private Papers of W. M. Thackeray* (Appendix XII), 1945–6, and *The Times Literary Supplement*, 1 Jan. 1949.

# THE ENGLISH HUMOURISTS
## OF THE
# EIGHTEENTH CENTURY

# THE ENGLISH HUMOURISTS
## *of the*
### EIGHTEENTH CENTURY

## SWIFT

IN treating of the English humourists of the past age, it is of the men and of their lives, rather than of their books, that I ask permission to speak to you ; and in doing so, you are aware that I cannot hope to entertain you with a merely humourous or facetious story. Harlequin without his mask is known to present a very sober countenance, and was himself, the story goes, the melancholy patient whom the doctor advised to go and see Harlequin*—a man full of cares and perplexities like the rest of us, whose Self must always be serious to him, under whatever mask or disguise or

---

\* The anecdote is frequently told of our performer Rich.

uniform he presents it to the public. And as all of you here must needs be grave when you think of your own past and present, you will not look to find, in the histories of those whose lives and feelings I am going to try and describe to you, a story that is otherwise than serious, and often very sad. If Humour only meant laughter, you would scarcely feel more interest about humourous writers than about the private life of poor Harlequin just mentioned, who possesses in common with these the power of making you laugh. But the men regarding whose lives and stories your kind presence here shows that you have curiosity and sympathy, appeal to a great number of our other faculties besides our mere sense of ridicule. The humourous writer professes to awaken and direct your love, your pity, your kindness—your scorn for untruth, pretention, imposture—your tenderness for the weak, the poor, the oppressed, the unhappy. To the best of his means and ability he comments on all the ordinary actions and passions of life almost. He takes upon himself to be the week-day preacher, so to speak. Accordingly, as he finds, and speaks, and feels the truth best, we regard him, esteem him — sometimes love him. And, as his business is to mark other people's lives and peculiarities, we moralise upon *his* life when he has gone—and yesterday's preacher becomes the text for to-day's sermon.

Of English parents, and of a good English family of clergymen,* Swift was born in Dublin in 1667,

* He was from a younger branch of the Swifts of Yorkshire. His grandfather, the Reverend Thomas Swift, vicar of Goodrich, in Here-fordshire, suffered for his loyalty in Charles I.'s time. That gentleman married Elizabeth Dryden, a member of the family of the poet. Sir Walter Scott gives, with his characteristic minuteness in such points, the exact relationship between these famous men. Swift was 'the son of Dryden's second cousin.' Swift, too, was the enemy of Dryden's reputation. Witness the 'Battle of the Books' :—' The difference was greatest among the horse,' says he of the moderns, ' where every private

seven months after the death of his father, who had
come to practise there as a lawyer.  The boy went to
school at Kilkenny, and afterwards to Trinity College,
Dublin, where he got a degree with difficulty, and
was wild, and witty, and poor.  In 1688, by the
recommendation of his mother, Swift was received into
the family of Sir William Temple, who had known
Mrs. Swift in Ireland.  He left his patron in 1694,
and the next year took orders in Dublin.  But he
threw up the small Irish preferment which he got and
returned to Temple, in whose family he remained
until Sir William's death in 1699.  His hopes of
advancement in England failing, Swift returned to
Ireland, and took the living of Laracor.  Hither he
invited Hester Johnson,* Temple's natural daughter,
with whom he had contracted a tender friendship
while they were both dependents of Temple's.  And
with an occasional visit to England, Swift now passed
nine years at home.

In 1709 he came to England, and, with a brief visit
to Ireland, during which he took possession of his
deanery of Saint Patrick, he now passed five years in
England, taking the most distinguished part in the
political transactions which terminated with the death
of Queen Anne.  After her death, his party disgraced,

trooper pretended to the command, from Tasso and Milton to Dryden
and Withers.'  And in *Poetry, a Rhapsody*, he advises the poetaster to—

> 'Read all the Prefaces of Dryden,
>   For these our critics much confide in,
>   Though merely writ, at first for filling,
>   To raise the volume's price a shilling.'

'Cousin Swift, you will never be a poet,' was the phrase of Dryden to
his kinsman, which remained alive in a memory tenacious of such
matters.

* 'Miss Hetty' she was called in the family—where her face, and
her dress, and Sir William's treatment of her, all made the real fact
about her birth plain enough.  Sir William left her a thousand pounds.

and his hopes of ambition over, Swift returned to
Dublin, where he remained twelve years. In this
time he wrote the famous 'Drapier's Letters' and
'Gulliver's Travels.' He married Hester Johnson
(Stella), and buried Esther Vanhomrigh (Vanessa),
who had followed him to Ireland from London, where
she had contracted a violent passion for him. In 1726
and 1727 Swift was in England, which he quitted for
the last time on hearing of his wife's illness. Stella
died in January 1728, and Swift not until 1745,
having passed the last five of the seventy-eight years
of his life with an impaired intellect and keepers to
watch him.*

You know, of course, that Swift has had many
biographers; his life has been told by the kindest and
most good-natured of men, Scott, who admires but
can't bring himself to love him; and by stout old
Johnson,† who, forced to admit him into the company

---

\* Sometimes, during his mental affliction, he continued walking
about the house for many consecutive hours; sometimes he remained
in a kind of torpor. At times he would seem to struggle to bring into
distinct consciousness, and shape into expression, the intellect that lay
smothering under gloomy obstruction in him. A pier-glass falling by
accident, nearly fell on him. He said he wished it had! He once
repeated slowly several times, 'I am what I am.' The last thing he
wrote was an epigram on the building of a magazine for arms and stores,
which was pointed out to him as he went abroad during his mental
disease :—

> 'Behold a proof of Irish sense :
> Here Irish wit is seen :
> When nothing's left that's worth defence,
> They build a magazine !'

† Besides these famous books of Scott's and Johnson's, there is a
copious 'Life' by Thomas Sheridan (Doctor Johnson's 'Sherry'),
father of Richard Brinsley, and son of that good-natured, clever Irish
Doctor Thomas Sheridan, Swift's intimate, who lost his chaplaincy by
so unluckily choosing for a text on the King's birthday, 'Sufficient for
the day is the evil thereof!' Not to mention less important works,
there is also the *Remarks on the Life and Writings of Doctor Jonathan*

ot poets, receives the famous Irishman, and takes off
his hat to him with a bow of surly recognition, scans
him from head to foot, and passes over to the other
side of the street. Doctor Wilde of Dublin,* who
has written a most interesting volume on the closing
years of Swift's life, calls Johnson 'the most malignant
of his biographers': it is not easy for an English
critic to please Irishmen—perhaps to try and please
them. And yet Johnson truly admires Swift: Johnson does not quarrel with Swift's change of politics, or
doubt his sincerity of religion: about the famous
Stella and Vanessa controversy the Doctor does not
bear very hardly on Swift. But he could not give the
Dean that honest hand of his; the stout old man puts
it into his breast, and moves off from him.†

Would we have liked to live with him ? That is

Swift, by that polite and dignified writer, the Earl of Orrery. His
Lordship is said to have striven for literary renown, chiefly that he
might make up for the slight passed on him by his father, who left his
library away from him. It is to be feared that the ink he used to wash
out that stain only made it look bigger. He had, however, known
Swift, and corresponded with people who knew him. His work (which
appeared in 1751) provoked a good deal of controversy, calling out,
among other *brochures*, the interesting *Observations on Lord Orrery's
Remarks*, &c., of Doctor Delany.

  * Doctor Wilde's book was written on the occasion of the remains of
Swift and Stella being brought to the light of day—a thing which
happened in 1835, when certain works going on in St. Patrick's
Cathedral, Dublin, afforded an opportunity of their being examined.
One hears with surprise of these skulls 'going the rounds' of houses,
and being made the objects of *dilettante* curiosity. The larynx of Swift
was actually carried off! Phrenologists had a low opinion of his
intellect from the observations they took.

  Doctor Wilde traces the symptoms of ill-health in Swift, as detailed
in his writings from time to time. He observes, likewise, that the skull
gave evidence of 'diseased action' of the brain during life—such as
would be produced by an increasing tendency to 'cerebral congestion.'

  † 'He [Doctor Johnson] seemed to me to have an unaccountable
prejudice against Swift; for I once took the liberty to ask him if Swift
had personally offended him, and he told me he had not.'—BOSWELL's
*Tour to the Hebrides.*

a question which, in dealing with these people's works, and thinking of their lives and peculiarities, every reader of biographies must put to himself. Would you have liked to be a friend of the great Dean ? I should like to have been Shakspeare's shoeblack—just to have lived in his house, just to have worshipped him—to have run on his errands, and seen that sweet serene face. I should like, as a young man, to have lived on Fielding's staircase in the Temple, and after helping him up to bed perhaps, and opening his door with his latch-key, to have shaken hands with him in the morning, and heard him talk and crack jokes over his breakfast and his mug of small beer. Who would not give something to pass a night at the club with Johnson, and Goldsmith, and James Boswell, Esquire, of Auchinleck ? The charm of Addison's companionship and conversation has passed to us by fond tradition—but Swift ? If you had been his inferior in parts (and that, with a great respect for all persons present, I fear is only very likely), his equal in mere social station, he would have bullied, scorned, and insulted you ; if, undeterred by his great reputation, you had met him like a man, he would have quailed before you,* and not had the pluck to reply, and gone home,

---

* Few men, to be sure, dared this experiment, but yet their success was encouraging. One gentleman made a point of asking the Dean whether his Uncle Godwin had not given him his education. Swift, who hated *that* subject cordially, and indeed, cared little for his kindred, said sternly, ' Yes ; he gave me the education of a dog.' ' Then, sir,' cried the other, striking his fist on the table, ' you have not the gratitude of a dog !'

Other occasions there were when a bold face gave the Dean pause, even after his Irish almost-royal position was established. But he brought himself into greater danger on a certain occasion, and the amusing circumstances may be once more repeated here. He had unsparingly lashed the notable Dublin lawyer, Mr. Sergeant Bettesworth,—

and years after written a foul epigram about you—
watched for you in a sewer, and come out to assail
you with a coward's blow and a dirty bludgeon.  If
you had been a lord with a blue riband, who flattered
his vanity, or could help his ambition, he would have
been the most delightful company in the world.  He
would have been so manly, so sarcastic, so bright, odd,
and original, that you might think he had no object
in view but the indulgence of his humour, and that
he was the most reckless simple creature in the world.
How he would have torn your enemies to pieces for
you ! and made fun of the Opposition !   His servility
was so boisterous that it looked like independence ;*
he would have done your errands, but with the air of
patronising you ; and after fighting your battles,
masked, in the street or the press, would have kept on
his hat before your wife and daughters in the drawing-
room, content to take that sort of pay for his
tremendous services as a bravo.†

> ' Thus at the bar, the booby Bettesworth,
>   Though half-a-crown o'erpays his sweat's worth
>   Who knows in law nor text nor margent,
>   Calls Singleton his brother-serjeant ! '

The Serjeant, it is said, swore to have his life.   He presented himself
at the Deanery.   The Dean asked his name.   ' Sir, I am Serjeant
Bett-es-worth.'
   ' *In what regiment, pray ?* ' asked Swift.
   A guard of volunteers formed themselves to defend the Dean at this
time.
   * ' But, my Hamilton, I will never hide the freedom of my sentiments from you.   I am much inclined to believe that the temper of my
friend Swift might occasion his English friends to wish him happily and
properly promoted at a distance.   His spirit, for I would give it the
softest name, was ever untractable.   The motions of his genius were
often irregular.   He assumed more the air of a patron than of a friend.
He affected rather to dictate than advise.'—*Orrery.*
   † ' . . . An anecdote, which, though only told by Mrs. Pilkington,
is well attested, bears, that the last time he was in London he went to
dine with the Earl of Burlington, who was but newly married.   The

He says as much himself in one of his letters to Bolingbroke :—'All my endeavours to distinguish myself were only for want of a great title and fortune, that I might be used like a lord by those who have an opinion of my parts; whether right or wrong is no great matter. And so the reputation of wit and great learning does the office of a blue riband or a coach and six.'*

Could there be a greater candour? It is an outlaw, who says, 'These are my brains; with these I'll win titles and compete with fortune. These are my bullets; these I'll turn into gold;' and he hears the sound of coaches and six, takes the road like Macheath, and makes society stand and deliver. They are all on their knees before him. Down go my Lord Bishop's apron, and his Grace's blue riband, and my Lady's

Earl, it is supposed, being willing to have a little diversion, did not introduce him to his lady nor mention his name. After dinner said the Dean, "Lady Burlington, I hear you can sing; sing me a song." The lady looked on this unceremonious manner of asking a favour with distaste, and positively refused. He said, "She should sing, or he would make her. Why, madam, I suppose you take me for one of your poor English hedge-parsons; sing when I bid you." As the Earl did nothing but laugh at this freedom, the lady was so vexed that she burst into tears and retired. His first compliment to her when he saw her again was, "Pray, madam, are you as proud and ill-natured now as when I saw you last?" To which she answered with great good-humour, "No, Mr. Dean; I'll sing for you if you please." From which time he conceived a great esteem for her.'—Scott's *Life*. '. . . He had not the least tincture of vanity in his conversation. He was, perhaps, as he said himself, too proud to be vain. When he was polite, it was in a manner entirely his own. In his friendships he was constant and undisguised. He was the same in his enmities.'—*Orrery*.

* 'I make no figure but at Court, where I affect to turn from a lord to the meanest of my acquaintances.'—*Journal to Stella*.

'I am plagued with bad authors, verse and prose, who send me their books and poems, the vilest I ever saw; but I have given their names to my man, never to let them see me.'—*Journal to Stella*.

The following curious paragraph illustrates the life of a courtier :—

'Did I ever tell you that the Lord Treasurer hears ill with the left ear, just as I do? . . . I dare not tell him that I am so, *for fear he should think that I counterfeited to make my court !* '—*Journal to Stella*.

brocade petticoat in the mud. He eases the one of a living, the other of a patent place, the third of a little snug post about the Court, and gives them over to followers of his own. The great prize has not come yet. The coach with the mitre and crozier in it, which he intends to have for *his* share, has been delayed on the way from Saint James's ; and he waits and waits until nightfall, when his runners come and tell him that the coach has taken a different road, and escaped him. So he fires his pistols into the air with a curse, and rides away into his own country. *

---

* The war of pamphlets was carried on fiercely on one side and the other ; and the Whig attacks made the Ministry Swift served very sore. Bolingbroke laid hold of several of the Opposition pamphleteers, and bewails their 'factitiousness' in the following letter :—

'*Bolingbroke to the Earl of Strafford.*

'WHITEHALL : *July 23rd*, 1712.

'IT is a melancholy consideration that the laws of our country are too weak to punish effectually those factitious scribblers, who presume to blacken the brightest characters, and to give even scurrilous language to those who are in the first degrees of honour. This, my Lord, among others, is a symptom of the decayed condition of our Government, and serves to show how fatally we mistake licentiousness for liberty. All I could do was to take up Hart, the printer, to send him to Newgate, and to bind him over upon bail to be prosecuted ; this I have done ; and if I can arrive at legal proof against the author, Ridpath, he shall have the same treatment.'

Swift was not behind his illustrious friend in this virtuous indignation. In the history of the four last years of the Queen, the Dean speaks in the most edifying manner of the licentiousness of the press and the abusive language of the other party :—

'It must be acknowledged that the bad practices of printers have been such as to deserve the severest animadversion from the public. . . . The adverse party, full of rage and leisure since their fall, and unanimous in their cause, employ a set of writers by subscription, who are well versed in all the topics of defamation, and have a style and genius levelled to the generality of their readers. . . . However the mischiefs of the press were too exorbitant to be cured by such a remedy as a tax upon small papers, and a Bill for a much more effectual regulation of it was brought into the House of Commons, but so late in the session that there was no

Swift's seems to me to be as good a name to point a
moral or adorn a tale of ambition as any hero's that
ever lived and failed. But we must remember that
the morality was lax—that other gentlemen besides
himself took the road in his day—that public society
was in a strange disordered condition, and the State

time to pass it for there always appeared an unwillingness to cramp
overmuch the liberty of the press.'

But to a clause in the proposed Bill, that the names of authors should
be set to every printed book, pamphlet, or paper, his Reverence objects
altogether ; for, says he, 'besides the objection to this clause from the
practice of pious men, who, in publishing excellent writings for the
service of religion, have chosen, *out of an humble Christian spirit, to
conceal their names,* it is certain that all persons of true genius or knowledge have an invincible modesty and suspicion of themselves upon first
sending their thoughts into the world.'

This ' invincible modesty' was no doubt the sole reason which induced
the Dean to keep the secret of the *Drapier's Letters* and a hundred
humble Christian works of which he was the author. As for the
Opposition, the Doctor was for dealing severely with them. He writes
to Stella :—

*Journal. Letter XIX.*

'LONDON : *March* 25*th*, 1710-11.

'. . . We have let Guiscard be buried at last, after showing him
pickled in a trough this fortnight for twopence apiece ; and the fellow
that showed would point to his body and say, " See gentlemen, this is
the wound that was given him by his Grace the Duke of Ormond ;" and
" This is the wound," &c. ; and then the show was over, and another set
of rabble came in. 'Tis hard that our laws would not suffer us to hang
his body in chains, because he was not tried ; and in the eye of the law
every man is innocent till then. . . .

*Journal. Letter XXVII.*

'LONDON : *July* 25*th*, 1711.

'I was this afternoon with Mr. Secretary at his office, and helped to
hinder a man of his pardon, who was condemned for a rape. The
Under-Secretary was willing to save him ; but I told the Secretary he
could not pardon him without a favourable report from the Judge ;
besides, he was a fiddler, and consequently a rogue, and deserved hanging
for something else, and so he shall swing.'

# SWIFT

13

was ravaged by other condottieri. The Boyne was
being fought and won, and lost—the bells rung in
William's victory, in the very same tone with which
they would have pealed for James's. Men were loose
upon politics, and had to shift for themselves. They,
as well as old beliefs and institutions, had lost their
moorings and gone adrift in the storm. As in the
South Sea Bubble, almost everybody gambled; as in
the Railway mania—not many centuries ago—almost
every one took his unlucky share: a man of that time,
of the vast talents and ambition of Swift, could scarce
do otherwise than grasp at his prize, and make his
spring at his opportunity. His bitterness, his scorn,
his rage, his subsequent misanthropy are ascribed by
some panegyrists to a deliberate conviction of mankind's unworthiness, and a desire to amend them by
castigation. His youth was bitter, as that of a great
genius bound down by ignoble ties, and powerless in a
mean dependence; his age was bitter,* like that of a
great genius, that had fought the battle and nearly
won it, and lost it, and thought of it afterwards,
writhing in a lonely exile. A man may attribute to
the gods, if he likes, what is caused by his own fury,
or disappointment, or self-will. What public man—
what statesman projecting a *coup*—what king determined on an invasion of his neighbour—what satirist
meditating an onslaught on society or an individual,
can't give a pretext for his move? There was a
French General the other day who proposed to march
into this country and put it to sack and pillage, in
revenge for humanity outraged by our conduct at
Copenhagen: there is always some excuse for men of
the aggressive turn. They are of their nature warlike,
predatory, eager for fight, plunder, dominion.†

* It was his constant practice to keep his birthday as a day of mourning.
† 'These devils of Grub Street rogues, that write the *Flying Post* and

As fierce a beak and talon as ever struck—as strong a wing as ever beat, belonged to Swift. I am glad, for one, that fate wrested the prey out of his claws, and cut his wings and chained him. One can gaze, and not without awe and pity, at the lonely eagle chained behind the bars.

That Swift was born at No. 7 Hoey's Court, Dublin, on the 30th November, 1667, is a certain fact, of which nobody will deny the sister island the honour and glory ; but, it seems to me, he was no more an Irishman than a man born of English parents at Calcutta is a Hindoo.* Goldsmith was an Irishman,

*Medley* n one paper, will not be quiet. They are always mauling Lord Treasurer, Lord Bolingbroke, and me. We have the dog under prosecution, but Bolingbroke is not active enough ; but I hope to swinge him. He is a Scotch rogue, one Ridpath. They get out upon bail, and write on. We take them again, and get fresh bail ; so it goes round.'— *Journal to Stella.*

* Swift was by no means inclined to forget such considerations ; and his English birth makes its mark, strikingly enough, every now and then in his writings. Thus in a letter to Pope (Scott's *Swift*, vol. xix. p. 97) he says :—

'We have had your volume of letters. . . . Some of those who highly value you, and a few who knew you personally, are grieved to find you make no distinction between the English gentry of this kingdom, and the savage old Irish (who are only the vulgar, and some gentlemen who live in the Irish parts of the kingdom) : but the English colonies, who are three parts in four, are much more civilised than many counties in England, and speak better English, and are much better bred.'

And again, in the fourth Drapier's Letter, we have the following :—

' A short paper, printed at Bristol, and reprinted here, reports Mr. Wood to say " that he wonders at the impudence and insolence of the Irish in refusing his coin." When, by the way, it is the true English people of Ireland who refuse it, although we take it for granted that the Irish will do so too whenever they are asked.'—Scott's *Swift*, vol. vi. p. 453.

He goes further, in a good-humoured satirical paper, *On Barbarous Denominations in Ireland*, where (after abusing, as he was wont, the Scotch cadence, as well as expression) he advances to the '*Irish Brogue*,' and speaking of the 'censure' which it brings down, says :—

' And what is yet worse, it is too well known that the bad consequence of this opinion affects those among us who are not the least liable to such reproaches farther than the misfortune of being born in Ireland,

# SWIFT

and always an Irishman : Steele was an Irishman, and
always an Irishman : Swift's heart was English and
in England, his habits English, his logic eminently
English ; his statement is elaborately simple ; he shuns
tropes and metaphors, and uses his ideas and words
with a wise thrift and economy, as he used his money :
with which he could be generous and splendid upon
great occasions, but which he husbanded when there
was no need to spend it.   He never indulges in needless extravagance of rhetoric, lavish epithets, profuse
imagery.  He lays his opinion before you with a grave
simplicity and a perfect neatness.*  Dreading ridicule
too, as a man of his humour—above all, an Englishman of his humour—certainly would, he is afraid to
use the poetical power which he really possessed ; one
often fancies in reading him that he dares not be
eloquent when he might ; that he does not speak
above his voice, as it were, and the tone of society.

although of English parents, and whose education has been chiefly in
that kingdom.'—Scott's *Swift*, vol. vii. p. 149.
   But, indeed, if we are to make *anything* of Race at all, we must call
that man an Englishman whose father comes from an old Yorkshire
family, and his mother from an old Leicestershire one !
   * 'The style of his conversation was very much of a piece with that
of his writings, concise and clear and strong.  Being one day at a
Sheriff's feast, who amongst other toasts called out to him, "Mr.
Dean, The Trade of Ireland !" he answered quick : "Sir, I drink no
memories !" . . .
   'Happening to be in company with a petulant young man who prided
himself on saying pert things . . . and who cried out—"You must
know, Mr. Dean, that I set up for a wit !"  "Do you so ?" says the
Dean.  "Take my advice, and sit down again !"
   'At another time, being in company, where a lady whisking her long
train [long trains were then in fashion] swept down a fine fiddle and
broke it ; Swift cried out—

   "Mantua væ miseræ nimium vicina Cremonæ !"'

—Dr. Delany : *Observations upon Lord Orrery's 'Remarks, &c., on
Swift.'*  London, 1754.

His initiation into politics, his knowledge of business, his knowledge of polite life, his acquaintance with literature even, which he could not have pursued very sedulously during that reckless career at Dublin, Swift got under the roof of Sir William Temple. He was fond of telling in after life what quantities of books he devoured there, and how King William taught him to cut asparagus in the Dutch fashion. It was at Shene and at Moor Park, with a salary of twenty pounds and a dinner at the upper servants' table, that this great and lonely Swift passed a ten years' apprenticeship— wore a cassock that was only not a livery—bent down a knee as proud as Lucifer's to supplicate my Lady's good graces, or run on his honour's errands.* It was here, as he was writing at Temple's table, or following his patron's walk, that he saw and heard the men who had governed the great world—measured himself with them, looking up from his silent corner, gauged their brains, weighed their wits, turned them, and tried them, and marked them. Ah! what platitudes he must have heard! what feeble jokes! what pompous common-places! what small men they must have seemed under those enormous periwigs, to the swarthy, uncouth, silent Irish secretary. I wonder whether it ever struck Temple, that that Irishman was his master? I suppose that dismal conviction did not present itself under the ambrosial wig, or Temple could never have lived with Swift. Swift sickened, rebelled, left the service—ate humble pie and came back again; and so for ten years went on, gathering learning, swallowing scorn, and submitting with a stealthy rage to his fortune.

Temple's style is the perfection of practised and

* 'Don't you remember how I used to be in pain when Sir William Temple would look cold and out of humour for three or four days, and I used to suspect a hundred reasons? I have plucked up my spirits since then, faith; he spoiled a fine gentleman.'—*Journal to Stella.*

easy good breeding. If he does not penetrate very deeply into a subject, he professes a very gentlemanly acquaintance with it; if he makes rather a parade of Latin, it was the custom of his day, as it was the custom for a gentleman to envelop his head in a periwig and his hands in lace ruffles. If he wears buckles and square-toed shoes, he steps in them with a consummate grace, and you never hear their creak, or find them treading upon any lady's train or any rival's heels in the Court crowd. When that grows too hot or too agitated for him, he politely leaves it. He retires to his retreat of Shene or Moor Park; and lets the King's party and the Prince of Orange's party battle it out among themselves. He reveres the Sovereign (and no man perhaps ever testified to his loyalty by so elegant a bow); he admires the Prince of Orange; but there is one person whose ease and comfort he loves more than all the princes in Christendom, and that valuable member of society is himself, Gulielmus Temple, Baronettus. One sees him in his retreat: between his study-chair and his tulip-beds,* clipping

* ' . . The Epicureans were more intelligible in their notion, and fortunate in their expression, when they placed a man's happiness in the tranquillity of his mind and indolence of body: for while we are composed of both, I doubt both must have a share in the good or ill we feel. As men of several languages say the same things in very different words, so in several ages, countries, constitutions of laws and religion, the same thing seems to be meant by very different expressions: what is called by the Stoics apathy, or dispassion: by the sceptics, indisturbance; by the Molinists, quietism; by common men, peace of conscience —seems all to mean but great tranquillity of mind . . . For this reason Epicurus passed his life wholly in his garden; there he studied, there he exercised, there he taught his philosophy; and, indeed, no other sort of abode seems to contribute so much to both the tranquillity of mind and indolence of body, which he made his chief ends. The sweetness of the air, the pleasantness of smell, the verdure of plants, the cleanness and lightness of food, the exercise of working or walking: but, above all, the exemption from cares and solicitude, seems equally to favour and improve both contemplation and health, the enjoyment of sense and imagination, and thereby the quiet and ease both of the

his apricots and pruning his essays,—the statesman, the ambassador no more ; but the philosopher, the Epicurean, the fine gentleman and courtier at St James's as at Shene ; where, in place of kings and fair ladies, he pays his court to the Ciceronian majesty ; or walks a minuet with the Epic Muse ; or dallies by the south wall with the ruddy nymph of gardens.

Temple seems to have received and exacted a prodigious deal of veneration from his household, and to have been coaxed, and warmed, and cuddled by the people round about him, as delicately as any of the plants which he loved. When he fell ill in 1693, the household was aghast at his indisposition ; mild Dorothea his wife, the best companion of the best of men—

'Mild Dorothea, peaceful, wise and great,
   Trembling beheld the doubtful hand of fate.'

As for Dorinda, his sister,—

'Those who would grief describe, might come and trace
   Its watery footsteps in Dorinda's face.

body and mind. . . . Where Paradise was, has been much debated, and little agreed ; but what sort of place is meant by it may perhaps easier be conjectured. It seems to have been a Persian word, since Xenophon and other Greek authors mention it as what was much in use and delight among the kings of those eastern countries. Strabo describing Jericho : "Ibi est palmetum, cui immixtæ sunt etiam aliæ stirpes hortenses, locus ferax palmis abundans, spatio stadiorum centum, totus irriguus : ibi est Regis Balsami paradisus."—*Essay on Gardens.*

In the same famous essay Temple speaks of a friend, whose conduct and prudence he characteristically admires :—

'. . . I thought it very prudent in a gentleman of my friends in Staffordshire, who is a great lover of his garden, to pretend no higher, though his soil be good enough, than to the perfection of plums ; and in these (by bestowing south walls upon them) he has very well succeeded, which he could never have done in attempts upon peaches and grapes ; and *a good plum is certainly better than an ill peach.*'

To see her weep, joy every face forsook,
And grief flung sables on each menial look.
The humble tribe mourned for the quickening soul,
That furnished spirit and motion through the whole.'

Isn't that line in which grief is described as putting the menials into a mourning livery, a fine image? One of the menials wrote it, who did not like that Temple livery nor those twenty-pound wages. Cannot one fancy the uncouth young servitor, with downcast eyes, books and papers in hand, following at his honour's heels in the garden walk; or taking his honour's orders as he stands by the great chair, where Sir William has the gout, and his feet all blistered with moxa? When Sir William has the gout or scolds it must be hard work at the second table;* the Irish

* SWIFT'S THOUGHTS ON HANGING.

*(Directions to Servants).*

'To grow old in the office of a footman is the highest of all indignities; therefore, when you find years coming on without hopes of a place at Court, a command in the army, a succession to the stewardship, an employment in the revenue (which two last you cannot obtain without reading and writing), or running away with your master's niece or daughter, I directly advise you to go upon the road, which is the only post of honour left you : there you will meet many of your old comrades, and live a short life and a merry one, and make a figure at your exit, wherein I will give you some instructions.

'The last advice I give you relates to your behaviour when you are going to be hanged : which, either for robbing your master, for housebreaking, or going upon the highway, or in a drunken quarrel by killing the first man you meet ; may very probably be your lot, and is owing to one of these three qualities : either a love of good fellowship, a generosity of mind, or too much vivacity of spirits. Your good behaviour on the article will concern your whole community : deny the fact with all solemnity of imprecations : a hundred of your brethren, if they can be admitted, will attend about the bar, and be ready upon demand to give you a character before the court ; let nothing prevail on you to confess, but the promise of a pardon for discovering your comrades : but I suppose all this to be in vain : for if you escape now, your fate will be the same another day. Get a speech to be written by the best author of Newgate : some of your kind wenches will provide you with a holland shirt and

secretary owned as much afterwards; and when he came to dinner, how he must have lashed and growled and torn the household with his gibes and scorn! What would the steward say about the pride of them Irish schollards—and this one had got no great credit even at his Irish college, if the truth were known—and what a contempt his Excellency's own gentleman must have had for Parson Teague from Dublin! (The valets and chaplains were always at war. It is hard to say which Swift thought the more contemptible.) And what must have been the sadness, the sadness and terror, of the house-keeper's little daughter with the curling black ringlets and the sweet smiling face, when the secretary who teaches her to read and write, and whom she loves and reverences above all things—above mother, above mild Dorothea, above that tremendous Sir William in his square toes and periwig,—when *Mr. Swift* comes down from his master with rage in his heart, and has not a kind word even for little Hester Johnson?

Perhaps, for the Irish secretary, his Excellency's condescension was even more cruel than his frowns. Sir William *would* perpetually quote Latin and the ancient classics *à propos* of his gardens and his Dutch statues, and *plates-bandes*, and talk about Epicurus and Diogenes Laertius, Julius Cæsar, Semiramis, and the gardens of the Hesperides, Mæcenas, Strabo describing Jericho, and the Assyrian kings. *Apropos* of beans, he would mention Pytha-

white cap, crowned with a crimson or black ribbon : take leave cheerfully of all your friends in Newgate : mount the cart with courage : fall on your knees ; lift up your eyes ; hold a book in your hands, although you cannot read a word ; deny the fact at the gallows ; kiss and forgive the hangman, and so farewell : you shall be buried in pomp at the charge of the fraternity : the surgeon shall not touch a limb of you ; and your fame shall continue until a successor of equal renown succeeds in your place. . .'

goras's precept to abstain from beans, and that this precept probably meant that wise men should abstain from public affairs. *He* is a placid Epicurean ; *he* is a Pythagorean philosopher ; *he* is a wise man—that is the deduction. Does not Swift think so ? One can imagine the downcast eyes lifted up for a moment, and the flash of scorn which they emit. Swift's eyes were as azure as the heavens ; Pope says nobly (as everything Pope said and thought of his friend was good and noble), ' His eyes are as azure as the heavens, and have a charming archness in them.' And one person in that household, that pompous, stately, kindly Moor Park, saw heaven nowhere else.

But the Temple amenities and solemnities did not agree with Swift. He was half-killed with a surfeit of Shene pippins ; and in a garden-seat which he devised for himself at Moor Park, and where he devoured greedily the stock of books within his reach, he caught a vertigo and deafness which punished and tormented him through life. He could not bear the place or the servitude. Even in that poem of courtly condolence, from which we have quoted a few lines of mock melancholy, he breaks out of the funereal procession with a mad shriek, as it were, and rushes away crying his own grief, cursing his own fate, foreboding madness, and forsaken by fortune, and even hope.

I don't know anything more melancholy than the letter to Temple, in which, after having broke from his bondage, the poor wretch crouches piteously towards his cage again, and deprecates his master's anger. He asks for testimonials for orders.

'The particulars required of me are what relate to morals and learning ; and the reasons of quitting your honour's family—that is, whether the last was occasioned

by any ill action.   They are left entirely to your honour's
mercy, though in the first I think I cannot reproach myself for anything further than for *infirmities*.   This is all I
dare at present beg from your honour, under circumstances
of life not worth your regard : what is left me to wish
(next to the health and prosperity of your honour and
family) is that Heaven would one day allow me the
opportunity of leaving my acknowledgments at your feet.
I beg my most humble duty and service be presented to
my ladies, your honour's lady and sister.'

Can prostration fall deeper ?   could a slave bow
lower ? *

Twenty years afterwards Bishop Kennet, describing
the same man, says :—

* ' He continued in Sir William Temple's house till the death of that
great man.'—*Anecdotes of the Family of Swift*, by the Dean.

' It has since pleased God to take this good and great person to himself.'—*Preface to Temple's Works*.

On all *public* occasions, Swift speaks of Sir William in the same tone
But the reader will better understand how acutely he remembered the
indignities he suffered in his household, from the subjoined extracts from
the *Journal to Stella:*—

' I called at Mr. Secretary the other day, to see what the d——— ailed
him on Sunday : I made him a very proper speech ; told him I observed
he was much out of temper, that I did not expect he would tell me the
cause, but would be glad to see he was in better ; and one thing I warned
him of—never to appear cold to me, for I would not be treated like a
school-boy : that I had felt too much of that in my life already'
(*meaning Sir William Temple*), &c., &c.—*Journal to Stella.*

' I am thinking what a veneration we used to have for Sir William
Temple because he might have been Secretary of State at fifty ; and here
is a young fellow hardly thirty in that employment.'—*Ibid.*

' The Secretary is as easy with me, as Mr. Addison was.   I have
often thought what a splutter Sir William Temple makes about being
Secretary of State.'—*Ibid.*

' Lord Treasurer has had an ugly fit of the rheumatism, but is now
quite well.   I was playing at *one-and-thirty* with him and his family the
other night.   He gave us all twelvepence a piece to begin with ; it put
me in mind of Sir William Temple.'—*Ibid.*

' I thought I saw Jack Temple [*nephew to Sir William*] and his wife
pass by me to-day in their coach ; but I took no notice of them.   I am
glad I have wholly shaken off that family.'—*S. to S.*, Sept. 1710.

'Dr. Swift came into the coffee-house and had a bow
from everybody but me. When I came to the ante-
chamber [at Court] to wait before prayers, Dr. Swift was
the principal man of talk and business. He was soliciting
the Earl of Arran to speak to his brother, the Duke of
Ormond, to get a place for a clergyman. He was
promising Mr. Thorold to undertake, with my Lord
Treasurer, that he should obtain a salary of £200 per
annum as member of the English Church at Rotterdam.
He stopped F. Gwynne, Esquire, going into the Queen
with the red bag, and told him aloud, he had something to
say to him from my Lord Treasurer. He took out his
gold watch, and telling the time of day, complained that
it was very late. A gentleman said he was too fast.
"How can I help it," says the Doctor, "if the courtiers
give me a watch that won't go right?" Then he instructed
a young nobleman, that the best poet in England was Mr.
Pope (a papist), who had begun a translation of Homer
into English, for which he would have them all subscribe :
"For," says he, "he shall not begin to print till I have a
thousand guineas for him."* Lord Treasurer, after
leaving the Queen, came through the room, beckoning
Doctor Swift to follow him—both went off just before
prayers.'

There's a little malice in the Bishop's 'just before
prayers.'

This picture of the great Dean seems a true one,
and is harsh, though not altogether unpleasant. He
was doing good, and to deserving men, too, in the
midst of these intrigues and triumphs. His journals

* 'Swift must be allowed,' says Doctor Johnson, 'for a time, to
have dictated the political opinions of the English nation.'

A conversation on the Dean's pamphlets excited one of the Doctor's
liveliest sallies. 'One, in particular, praised his *Conduct of the Allies*.
—JOHNSON : 'Sir, his *Conduct of the Allies* is a performance of very little
ability. . . . Why, sir, Tom Davies might have written the *Conduct of
the Allies* !"'—BOSWELL's *Life of Johnson*.

and a thousand anecdotes of him relate his kind acts
and rough manners. His hand was constantly
stretched out to relieve an honest man—he was
cautious about his money, but ready. If you were in
a strait, would you like such a benefactor? I think I
would rather have had a potato and a friendly word
from Goldsmith than have been beholden to the
the Dean for a guinea and a dinner.* He insulted a
man as he served him, made women cry, guests look
foolish, bullied unlucky friends, and flung his bene-
factions into poor men's faces. No; the Dean was
no Irishman—no Irishman ever gave but with a kind
word and a kind heart.

It is told, as if it were to Swift's credit, that the
Dean of Saint Patrick's performed his family devotions
every morning regularly, but with such secrecy that
the guests in his house were never in the least aware
of the ceremony. There was no need surely why a
Church dignitary should assemble his family privily in
a crypt, and as if he was afraid of heathen persecution.

* 'Whenever he fell into the company of any person for the first
time, it was his custom to try their tempers and disposition by some
abrupt question that bore the appearance of rudeness. If this were well
taken, and answered with good-humour, he afterwards made amends
by his civilities. But if he saw any marks of resentment, from alarmed
pride, vanity, or conceit, he dropped all further intercourse with the
party. This will be illustrated by an anecdote of that sort related by
Mrs. Pilkington. After supper, the Dean having decanted a bottle of
wine, poured what remained into a glass, and seeing it was muddy,
presented it to Mr. Pilkington to drink it. "For," said he, "I always
keep some poor parson to drink the foul wine for me." Mr. Pilkington,
entering into his humour, thanked him, and told him "he did not know
the difference, but was glad to get a glass at any rate." "Why, then,"
said the Dean, "you shan't, for I'll drink it myself. Why, —— take
you, you are wiser than a paltry curate whom I asked to dine with me
a few days ago; for upon my making the same speech to him, he said
he did not understand such usage, and so walked off without his
dinner. By the same token, I told the gentleman who recommended
him to me that the fellow was a blockhead, and I had done with him.'"
—SHERIDAN's *Life of Swift*.

But I think the world was right, and the bishops who advised Queen Anne when they counselled her not to appoint the author of the 'Tale of a Tub' to a bishopric, gave perfectly good advice. The man who wrote the arguments and illustrations in that wild book, could not but be aware what must be the sequel of the propositions which he laid down. The boon companion of Pope and Bolingbroke, who chose these as the friends of his life, and the recipients of his confidence and affection, must have heard many an argument, and joined in many a conversation over Pope's port, or St. John's burgundy, which would not bear to be repeated at other men's boards.

I know of few things more conclusive as to the sincerity of Swift's religion than his advice to poor John Gay to turn clergyman, and look out for a seat on the Bench. Gay, the author of the 'Beggar's Opera'—Gay the wildest of the wits about town—it was this man that Jonathan Swift advised to take orders—to invest in a cassock and bands—just as he advised him to husband his shillings and put his thousand pounds out at interest. The Queen, and the bishops, and the world, were right in mistrusting the religion of that man.*

* ' From the Archbishop of Cashell

'CASHELL : *May 31st*, 1735.

'DEAR SIR,—I have been so unfortunate in all my contests of late that I am resolved to have no more, especially where I am likely to be overmatched; and as I have some reason to hope what is past will be forgotten, I confess I did endeavour in my last to put the best colour I could think of upon a very bad cause. My friends judge right of my idleness; but, in reality, it has hitherto proceeded from a hurry and confusion, arising from a thousand unlucky unforeseen accidents rather than mere sloth. I have but one troublesome affair now upon my hands, which, by the help of the prime serjeant, I hope soon to get rid of; and then you shall see me a true Irish bishop. Sir James Ware has made a very useful collection of the memorable actions of my predecessors. He tells me, they were born in such a town of England or Ireland; were

I am not here, of course, to speak of any man's
religious views, except in so far as they influence his
literary character, his life, his humour. The most
notorious sinners of all those fellow-mortals whom it
is our business to discuss—Harry Fielding and Dick
Steele—were especially loud, and I believe really
fervent, in their expressions of belief; they belaboured
freethinkers, and stoned imaginary atheists on all sorts
of occasions, going out of their way to bawl their own
creed, and persecute their neighbour's, and if they

consecrated such a year; and if not translated, were buried in the
Cathedral Church, either on the north or south side. Whence I con-
clude, that a good bishop has nothing more to do than to eat, drink,
grow, fat, rich, and die; which laudable example I propose for the
remainder of my life to follow; for to tell you the truth, I have for these
four or five years past met with so much treachery, baseness, and
ingratitude among mankind, that I can hardly think it incumbent on any
man to endeavour to do good to so perverse a generation.

'I am truly concerned at the account you give me of your health.
Without doubt a southern ramble will prove the best remedy you can
take to recover your flesh; and I do not know, except in one stage,
where you can choose a road so suited to your circumstances, as from
Dublin hither. You have to Kilkenny a turnpike and good inns, at
every ten or twelve miles' end. From Kilkenny hither is twenty long
miles, bad road, and no inns at all: but I have an expedient for you.
At the foot of a very high hill, just midway, there lives in a neat thatched
cabin, a parson, who is not poor; his wife is allowed to be the best little
woman in the world. Her chickens are the fattest, and her ale the best
in all the country. Besides, the parson has a little cellar of his own, of
which he keeps the key, where he always has a hogshead of the best
wine that can be got, in bottles well corked, upon their sides; and he
cleans, and pulls out the cork better, I think, than Robin. Here I
design to meet you with a coach; if you be tired, you shall stay all
night; if not, after dinner, we will set out about four, and be at Cashell
by nine; and by going through fields and bye-ways, which the parson
will show us, we shall escape all the rocky and stony roads that lie
between this place and that, which are certainly very bad. I hope you
will be so kind as to let me know a post or two before you set out, the
very day you will be at Kilkenny, that I may have all things prepared
for you. It may be, if you ask him, Cope will come: he will do nothing
for me. Therefore, depending upon your positive promise, I shall add
no more arguments to persuade you, and am, with the greatest truth,
your most faithful and obedient servant,

'THEO. CASHELL.'

sinned and stumbled, as they constantly did with debt, with drink, with all sorts of bad behaviour, they got upon their knees and cried 'Peccavi' with a most sonorous orthodoxy. Yes; poor Harry Fielding and poor Dick Steele were trusty and undoubting Church of England men; they abhorred Popery, Atheism, and wooden shoes and idolatries in general; and hiccupped Church and State with fervour.

But Swift? *His* mind had had a different schooling, and possessed a very different logical power. *He* was not bred up in a tipsy guardroom, and did not learn to reason in a Covent Garden tavern. He could conduct an argument from beginning to end. He could see forward with a fatal clearness. In his old age, looking at the 'Tale of a Tub,' when he said, 'Good God, what a genius I had when I wrote that book!' I think he was admiring, not the genius, but the consequences to which the genius had brought him—a vast genius, a magnificent genius, a genius wonderfully bright, and dazzling, and strong,—to seize, to know, to see, to flash upon falsehood and scorch it into perdition, to penetrate into the hidden motives, and expose the black thoughts of men,—an awful, an evil spirit.

Ah, man! you, educated in Epicurean Temple's library, you whose friends were Pope and St. John—what made you to swear to fatal vows, and bind yourself to a life-long hypocrisy before the Heaven which you adored with such real wonder, humility, and reverence? For Swift's was a reverent, was a pious spirit—for Swift could love and could pray. Through the storms and tempests of his furious mind, the stars of religion and love break out in the blue, shining serenely, though hidden by the driving clouds and the maddened hurricane of his life.

It is my belief that he suffered frightfully from the

consciousness of his own scepticism, and that he had
bent his pride so far down as to put his apostasy out
to hire.* The paper left behind him, called 'Thoughts
on Religion,' is merely a set of excuses for not pro-
fessing disbelief. He says of his sermons that he
preached pamphlets: they have scarce a Christian
characteristic; they might be preached from the steps
of a synagogue, or the floor of a mosque, or the box
of a coffee-house almost. There is little or no cant—
he is too great and too proud for that; and, in so far
as the badness of his sermons goes, he is honest. But
having put that cassock on, it poisoned him; he was
strangled in his bands. He goes through life, tearing,
like a man possessed with a devil. Like Abudah in
the Arabian story, he is always looking out for the
Fury, and knows that the night will come and the
inevitable hag with it. What a night, my God, it
was! what a lonely rage and long agony—what a
vulture that tore the heart of that giant!† It is
awful to think of the great sufferings of this great
man. Through life he always seems alone, somehow.
Goethe was so. I can't fancy Shakspeare otherwise.
The giants must live apart. The kings can have no
company. But this man suffered so; and deserved so
to suffer. One hardly reads anywhere of such a pain.

The 'sæva indignatio' of which he spoke as lacerat-
ing his heart, and which he dares to inscribe on his
tombstone—as if the wretch who lay under that stone

* 'Mr. Swift lived with him [Sir William Temple] some time, but
resolving to settle himself in some way of living, was inclined to take
orders. However, although his fortune was very small, he had a scruple
of entering into the Church merely for support.'—*Anecdotes of the Family
of Swift*, by the Dean.

† 'Dr. Swift had a natural severity of face, which even his smiles
could scarce soften, or his utmost gaiety render placid and serene; but
when that sternness of visage was increased by rage, it is scarce possible to
imagine looks or features that carried in them more terror and austerity.
—*Orrery.*

waiting God's judgment had a right to be angry—
breaks out from him in a thousand pages of his writing,
and tears and rends him.  Against men in office, he
having been overthrown ; against men in England, he
having lost his chance of preferment there, the furious
exile never fails to rage and curse.  Is it fair to call
the famous 'Drapier's Letters' patriotism ?  They
are masterpieces of dreadful humour and invective :
they are reasoned logically enough too, but the proposition is as monstrous and fabulous as the Lilliputian
island.  It is not that the grievance is so great, but
there is his enemy—the assault is wonderful for its
activity and terrible rage.  It is Samson with a bone
in his hand, rushing on his enemies and felling them :
one admires not the cause so much as the strength,
the anger, the fury of the champion.  As is the case
with madmen, certain subjects provoke him, and
awaken his fits of wrath.  Marriage is one of these ;
in a hundred passages in his writings he rages against
it ; rages against children ; an object of constant
satire, even more contemptible in his eyes than a lord's
chaplain, is a poor curate with a large family.  The
idea of this luckless paternity never fails to bring down
from him gibes and foul language.  Could Dick Steele,
or Goldsmith, or Fielding, in his most reckless
moment of satire, have written anything like the
Dean's famous 'Modest Proposal' for eating children ?
Not one of these but melts at the thoughts of childhood, fondles and caresses it.  Mr. Dean has no such
softness, and enters the nursery with the tread and
gaiety of an ogre.*  'I have been assured,' says he in

* 'LONDON : *April* 10*th*, 1713.

'Lady Masham's eldest boy is very ill : I doubt he will not live ; and
she stays at Kensington to nurse him, which vexes us all.  She is so
excessively fond, it makes me mad.  She should never leave the Queen,
but leave everything, to stick to what is so much the interest of the
public, as well as her own.   . .'—*Journal.*

the 'Modest Proposal,' 'by a very knowing American
of my acquaintance in London, that a young healthy
child, well nursed, is, at a year old, a most delicious,
nourishing, and wholesome food, whether stewed,
roasted, baked, or boiled ; and I make no doubt it will
equally serve in a *ragoût*.' And taking up this pretty
joke, as his way is, he argues it with perfect gravity
and logic. He turns and twists this subject in a score
of different ways ; he hashes it ; and he serves it up
cold ; and he garnishes it ; and relishes it always. He
describes the little animal as 'dropped from its dam,'
advising that the mother should let it suck plentifully
in the last month, so as to render it plump and fat for
a good table ! 'A child,' says his Reverence, 'will
make two dishes at an entertainment for friends ;
and when the family dines alone, the fore or hind
quarter will make a reasonable dish,' and so on ; and
the subject being so delightful that he can't leave it,
he proceeds to recommend, in place of venison for
squires' tables, 'the bodies of young lads and maidens
not exceeding fourteen or under twelve.' Amiable
humourist ! laughing castigator of morals ! There
was a process well known and practised in the Dean's
gay days ; when a lout entered the coffee-house, the
wags proceeded to what they called 'roasting' him.
This is roasting a subject with a vengeance. The
Dean had a native genius for it. As the 'Almanach
des Gourmands' says, 'On naît rôtisseur.'

And it was not merely by the sarcastic method that
Swift exposed the unreasonableness of loving and
having children. In 'Gulliver,' the folly of love and
marriage is urged by graver arguments and advice.
In the famous Lilliputian kingdom, Swift speaks with
approval of the practice of instantly removing children
from their parents and educating them by the State ;
and amongst his favourite horses, a pair of foals are

stated to be the very utmost a well-regulated equine couple would permit themselves. In fact, our great satirist was of opinion that conjugal love was unadvisable, and illustrated the theory by his own practice and example—God help him!—which made him about the most wretched being in God's world.*

The grave and logical conduct of an absurd proposition, as exemplified in the cannibal proposal just mentioned, is our author's constant method through all his works of humour. Given a country of people six inches or sixty feet high, and by the mere process of the logic, a thousand wonderful absurdities are evolved, at so many stages of the calculation. Turning to the First Minister who waited behind him with a white staff near as tall as the mainmast of the 'Royal Sovereign,' the King of Brobdingnag observes how contemptible a thing human grandeur is, as represented by such a contemptible little creature as Gulliver. 'The Emperor of Lilliput's features are strong and masculine' (what a surprising humour there is in this description!) — 'The Emperor's features,' Gulliver says, 'are strong and masculine, with an Austrian lip, an arched nose, his complexion olive, his countenance erect, his body and limbs well proportioned, and his deportment majestic. He is taller *by the breadth of my nail* than any of his Court, which alone is enough to strike an awe into beholders.'

What a surprising humour there is in these descriptions! How noble the satire is here! how just and honest! How perfect the image! Mr. Macaulay has quoted the charming lines of the poet where the king of the pigmies is measured by the same standard. We have all read in Milton of the spear that was like

* 'My health is somewhat mended, but at best I have an ill head and an aching heart.'—*In May* 1710.

'the mast of some great ammiral;' but these images are surely likely to come to the comic poet originally. The subject is before him. He is turning it in a thousand ways. He is full of it. The figure suggests itself naturally to him, and comes out of his subject, as in that wonderful passage, when Gulliver's box having been dropped by the eagle into the sea, and Gulliver having been received into the ship's cabin, he calls upon the crew to bring the box into the cabin, and put it on the table, the cabin being only a quarter the size of the box. It is the *veracity* of the blunder which is so admirable. Had a man come from such a country as Brobdingnag, he would have blundered so.

But the best stroke of humour, if there be a best in that abounding book, is that where Gulliver, in the unpronounceable country, describes his parting from his master the horse.*

---

* Perhaps the most melancholy satire in the whole of the dreadful book is the description of the very old people in the ' Voyage to Laputa.' At Lugnag, Gulliver hears of some persons who never die, called the Struldbrugs, and expressing a wish to become acquainted with men who must have so much learning and experience, his colloquist describes the Struldbrugs to him.

' He said : They commonly acted like mortals, till about thirty years old, after which, by degrees, they grew melancholy and dejected, increasing in both till they came to fourscore.   This he learned from their own confession : for otherwise there not being above two or three of that species born in an age, they were too few to form a general observation by.   When they came to fourscore years, which is reckoned the extremity of living in this country, they had not only all the follies and infirmities of other old men, but many more, which arose from the dreadful prospect of never dying.   They were not only opinionative, peevish, covetous, morose, vain, talkative, but incapable of friendship, and dead to all natural affection, which never descended below their grandchildren. Envy and impotent desires are their prevailing passions.   But those objects against which their envy seems principally directed, are the vices of the younger sort and the deaths of the old.   By reflecting on the former, they found themselves cut off from all possibility of pleasure ; and whenever they see a funeral, they lament, and repine that others are gone to a harbour of rest, to which they themselves never can hope to

'I took,' he says, 'a second leave of my master, but as I was going to prostrate myself to kiss his hoof, he did me the honour to raise it gently to my mouth. I am not ignorant how much I have been censured for mentioning this last particular. Detractors are pleased to think it improbable that so illustrious a person should descend to

arrive. They have no remembrance of anything but what they learned and observed in their youth and middle age, and even that is very imperfect. And for the truth of particulars of any fact, it is safer to depend on common tradition than upon their best recollections. The least miserable among them appear to be those who turn to dotage, and entirely lose their memories ; these meet with more pity and assistance, because they want many bad qualities which abound in others.

'If a Struldbrug happen to marry one of his own kind, the marriage is dissolved of course, by the courtesy of the kingdom, as soon as the younger of the two comes to be fourscore. For the law thinks it a reasonable indulgence that those who are condemned, without any fault of their own, to a perpetual continuance in the world, should not have their misery doubled by the load of a wife.

'As soon as they have completed the term of eighty years, they are looked on as dead in law ; their heirs immediately succeed to their estates, only a small pittance is reserved for their support ; and the poor ones are maintained at the public charge. After that period, they are held incapable of any employment of trust or profit, they cannot purchase lands or take leases, neither are they allowed to be witnesses in any cause, either civil or criminal, not even for the decision of meers and bounds.

'At ninety they lose their teeth and hair ; they have at that age no distinction of taste, but eat and drink whatever they can get without relish or appetite. The diseases they were subject to still continue, without increasing or diminishing. In talking, they forget the common appellation of things, and the names of persons, even of those who are their nearest friends and relations. For the same reason, they can never amuse themselves with reading, because their memory will not serve to carry them from the beginning of a sentence to the end ; and by this defect they are deprived of the only entertainment whereof they might otherwise be capable.

'The language of this country being always upon the flux, the Struldbrugs of one age do not understand those of another ; neither are they able, after two hundred years, to hold any conversation (further than by a few general words) with their neighbours, the mortals ; and thus they lie under the disadvantage of living like foreigners in their own country.

'This was the account given me of the Struldbrugs, as near as I can remember. I afterwards saw five or six of different ages, the youngest not above two hundred years old, who were brought to me at several times by some of my friends ; but although they were told "that I was

give so great a mark of distinction to a creature so inferior as I. Neither have I forgotten how apt some travellers are to boast of extraordinary favours they have received. But if these censurers were better acquainted with the noble and courteous disposition of the Houyhnhnms they would soon change their opinion.'

The surprise here, the audacity of circumstantial evidence, the astounding gravity of the speaker, who is not ignorant how much he has been censured, the nature of the favour conferred, and the respectful exultation at the receipt of it, are surely complete; it is truth topsy-turvy, entirely logical and absurd.

As for the humour and conduct of this famous fable, I suppose there is no person who reads but must admire; as for the moral, I think it horrible, shameful, unmanly, blasphemous; and giant and great as this Dean is, I say we should hoot him. Some of this audience mayn't have read the last part of *Gulliver*, and to such I would recall the advice of the venerable *Mr. Punch* to persons about to marry, and say 'Don't.' When Gulliver first lands among the

a great traveller, and had seen all the world" they had not the least curiosity to ask me a question; only desired I would give them slums-kudask, or a token of remembrance; which is a modest way of begging, to avoid the law, that strictly forbids it, because they are provided for by the public, although indeed with a very scanty allowance.

'They are despised and hated by all sorts of people; when one of them is born, it is reckoned ominous, and their birth is recorded very particularly; so that you may know their age by consulting the register, which, however, has not been kept above a thousand years past, or at least has been destroyed by time or public disturbances. But the usual way of computing how old they are, is by asking them what kings or great persons they can remember, and then consulting history; for infallibly the last prince in their mind did not begin his reign after they were fourscore years old.

'They were the most mortifying sight I ever beheld, and the women more horrible than the men; besides the usual deformities in extreme old age, they acquired an additional ghastliness, in proportion to their number of years, which is not to be described; and among half-a-dozen, I soon distinguished which was the eldest, although there was not above a century or two between them.'—*Gulliver's Travels.*

Yahoos, the naked howling wretches clamber up trees and assault him, and he describes himself as 'almost stifled with the filth which fell about him.' The reader of the fourth part of 'Gulliver's Travels' is like the hero himself in this instance. It is Yahoo language : a monster gibbering shrieks, and gnashing imprecations against mankind — tearing down all shreds of modesty, past all sense of manliness and shame ; filthy in word, filthy in thought, furious, raging, obscene.

And dreadful it is to think that Swift knew the tendency of his creed—the fatal rocks towards which his logic desperately drifted.    That last part of 'Gulliver' is only a consequence of what has gone before ; and the worthlessness of all mankind, the pettiness, cruelty, pride, imbecility, the general vanity, the foolish pretension, the mock greatness, the pompous dulness, the mean aims, the base successes—all these were present to him ; it was with the din of these curses of the world, blasphemies against Heaven, shrieking in his ears, that he began to write his dreadful allegory—of which the meaning is that man is utterly wicked, desperate, and imbecile, and his passions are so monstrous, and his boasted powers so mean, that he is and deserves to be the slave of brutes, and ignorance is better than his vaunted reason. What had this man done ? what secret remorse was rankling at his heart ? what fever was boiling in him, that he should see all the world bloodshot ?   We view the world with our own eyes, each of us ; and we make from within us the world we see.   A weary heart gets no gladness out of sunshine ; a selfish man is sceptical about friendship, as a man with no ear doesn't care for music.   A frightful self-consciousness it must have been, which looked on mankind so darkly through those keen eyes of Swift.

A remarkable story is told by Scott, of Delany, who interrupted Archbishop King and Swift in a conversation which left the prelate in tears, and from which Swift rushed away with marks of strong terror and agitation in his countenance, upon which the Archbishop said to Delany, 'You have just met the most unhappy man on earth; but on the subject of his wretchedness you must never ask a question.'

The most unhappy man on earth;—*Miserrimus*— what a character of him! And at this time all the great wits of England had been at his feet. All Ireland had shouted after him, and worshipped him as a liberator, a saviour, the greatest Irish patriot and citizen. Dean Drapier Bickerstaff Gulliver—the most famous statesmen and the greatest poets of his day had applauded him and done him homage; and at this time, writing over to Bolingbroke from Ireland, he says, 'It is time for me to have done with the world, and so I would if I could get into a better before I was called into the best, *and not die here in a rage, like a poisoned rat in a hole.*'

We have spoken about the men, and Swift's behaviour to them; and now it behoves us not to forget that there are certain other persons in the creation who had rather intimate relations with the great Dean.*

* The name of Varina has been thrown into the shade by those of the famous Stella and Vanessa; but she had a story of her own to tell about the blue eyes of young Jonathan. One may say that the book of Swift's Life opens at places kept by these blighted flowers! Varina must have a paragraph.

She was a Miss Jane Waryng, sister to a college chum of his. In 1696, when Swift was nineteen years old, we find him writing a love-letter to her, beginning 'Impatience is the most inseparable quality of a lover.' But absence made a great difference in his feelings; so, four years afterwards, the tone is changed. He writes again, a very curious letter, offering to marry her, and putting the offer in such a way that nobody could possibly accept it.

After dwelling on his poverty, &c., he says conditionally, 'I shall be blessed to have you in my arms, without regarding whether your person

Two women whom he loved and injured are known by every reader of books so familiarly that if we had seen them, or if they had been relatives of our own, we scarcely could have known them better. Who hasn't in his mind an image of Stella? Who does not love her? Fair and tender creature : pure and affectionate heart! Boots it to you, now that you have been at rest for a hundred and twenty years, not divided in death from the cold heart which caused yours, whilst it beat, such faithful pangs of love and grief—boots it to you now, that the whole world loves and deplores you? Scarce any man, I believe, ever thought of that grave, that did not cast a flower of pity on it, and write over it a sweet epitaph. Gentle lady, so lovely, so loving, so unhappy! you have had countless champions; millions of manly hearts mourning for you. From generation to generation we take up the fond tradition of your beauty, we watch and follow your tragedy, your bright morning love and purity, your constancy, your grief, your sweet martyrdom. We know your legend by heart. You are one of the saints of English story.

And if Stella's love and innocence are charming to contemplate, I will say that, in spite of ill-usage, in spite of drawbacks, in spite of mysterious separation and union, of hope delayed and sickened heart—in the teeth of Vanessa, and that little episodical aberration which plunged Swift into such woeful pitfalls and quagmires of amorous perplexity—in spite of the verdicts of most women, I believe, who, as far as my experience and conversation go, generally take

be beautiful, or your fortune large. Cleanliness in the first, and competency in the second, is all I ask for!'

The editors do not tell us what became of Varina in life. One would be glad to know that she met with some worthy partner and lived long enough to see her little boys laughing over Lilliput, without any *arrière pensée* of a sad character about the great Dean!

Vanessa's part in the controversy,—in spite of the tears which Swift caused Stella to shed, and the rocks and barriers which fate and temper interposed, and which prevented the pure course of that true love from running smoothly—the brightest part of Swift's story, the pure star in that dark and tempestuous life of Swift's, is his love for Hester Johnson. It has been my business, professionally of course, to go through a deal of sentimental reading in my time, and to acquaint myself with love-making, as it has been described in various languages, and at various ages of the world; and I know of nothing more manly, more tender, more exquisitely touching, than some of these brief notes, written in what Swift calls 'his little language' in his journal to Stella.* He writes to her night and morning often. He never sends away a letter to her but he begins a new one on the same day. He can't bear to let go her kind little hand, as it were. He knows that she is thinking of him, and longing for him far away in Dublin yonder. He takes her letters from under his pillow and talks to them, familiarly, paternally, with fond epithets and pretty caresses—as he would to the sweet and artless creature who loved him. 'Stay,' he writes one morning—it is the 14th of December, 1710—'Stay, I will answer some of your letters this morning in bed. Let me see. Come

* A sentimental Champollion might find a good deal of matter for his art, in expounding the symbols of the 'Little Language.' Usually, Stella is 'M.D.,' but sometimes her companion, Mrs. Dingley, is included in it. Swift is 'Presto;' also P.D.F.R. We have 'Good-night, M.D.; Night, M.D.; Little M.D.; Stellakins; pretty Stella; Dear, roguish, impudent, pretty M.D.' Every now and then he breaks into rhyme, as—

> 'I wish you both a merry new year,
> Roast-beef, mince-pies, and good strong beer,
> And me a share of your good cheer,
> That I was there, as you were here,
> And you are a little saucy dear.'

and appear, little letter! Here I am, says he, and
what say you to Stella this morning fresh and fasting?
And can Stella read this writing without hurting her
dear eyes?' he goes on, after more kind prattle and
fond whispering. The dear eyes shine clearly upon
him then—the good angel of his life is with him and
blessing him. Ah, it was a hard fate that wrung from
them so many tears, and stabbed pitilessly that pure
and tender bosom. A hard fate: but would she have
changed it? I have heard a woman say that she
would have taken Swift's cruelty to have had his
tenderness. He had a sort of worship for her whilst
he wounded her. He speaks of her after she is gone;
of her wit, of her kindness, of her grace, of her beauty,
with a simple love and reverence that are indescribably
touching; in contemplation of her goodness his hard
heart melts into pathos; his cold rhyme kindles and
glows into poetry, and he falls down on his knees, so
to speak, before the angel whose life he had embittered,
confesses his own wretchedness and unworthiness, and
adores her with cries of remorse and love:—

> When on my sickly couch I lay,
> Impatient both of night and day,
> And groaning in unmanly strains,
> Called every power to ease my pains,
> Then Stella ran to my relief,
> With cheerful face and inward grief,
> And though by Heaven's severe decree
> She suffers hourly more than me,
> No cruel master could require
> From slaves employed for daily hire,
> What Stella, by her friendship warmed,
> With vigour and delight performed.
> Now, with a soft and silent tread,
> Unheard she moves about my bed:
> My sinking spirits now supplies

With cordials in her hands and eyes.
Best pattern of true friends ! beware
You pay too dearly for your care
If, while your tenderness secures
My life, it must endanger yours :
For such a fool was never found
Who pulled a palace to the ground,
Only to have the ruins made
Materials for a house decayed.'

One little triumph Stella had in her life—one dear little piece of injustice was performed in her favour, for which I confess, for my part, I can't help thanking fate and the Dean. *That other person* was sacrificed to her—that—that young woman, who lived five doors from Doctor Swift's lodgings in Bury Street, and who flattered him, and made love to him in such an outrageous manner—Vanessa was thrown over.

Swift did not keep Stella's letters to him in reply to those he wrote to her.* He kept Bolingbroke's, and

* The following passages are from a paper begun by Swift on the evening of the day of her death, Jan. 28, 1727-8 :—

'She was sickly from her childhood, until about the age of fifteen ; but then she grew into perfect health, and was looked upon as one of the most beautiful, graceful, and agreeable young women in London— only a little too fat. Her hair was blacker than a raven, and every feature of her face in perfection.

'. . . Properly speaking'—he goes on, with a calmness which, under the circumstances, is terrible—'she has been dying six months ! . . .

'Never was any of her sex born with better gifts of the mind, or who more improved them by reading and conversation. . . . All of us who had the happiness of her friendship agreed unanimously, that in an afternoon's or evening's conversation she never failed before we parted of delivering the best thing that was said in the company. Some of us have written down several of her sayings, or what the French call *bons mots*, wherein she excelled beyond belief.'

The specimens on record, however, on the Dean's paper, called ' Bon Mots de Stella,' scarcely bear out this last part of the panegyric. But the following prove her wit :—

' A gentleman who had been very silly and pert in her company, at last began to grieve at remembering the loss of a child lately dead. A bishop sitting by comforted him—that he should be easy, because "the

Pope's, and Harley's, and Peterborough's : but Stella
'very carefully,' the Lives say, kept Swift's. Of
course : that is the way of the world : and so we cannot tell what her style was, or of what sort were the
little letters which the Doctor placed there at night,
and bade to appear from under his pillow of a morning.
But in Letter IV. of that famous collection he
describes his lodging in Bury Street, where he has the
first floor, a dining-room and bed-chamber, at eight
shillings a week ; and in Letter VI. he says 'he has
visited a lady just come to town,' whose name somehow is not mentioned ; and in Letter VIII. he enters
a query of Stella's—'What do you mean "that boards
near me, that I dine with now and then"? What
the deuce ! You know whom I have dined with
every day since I left you, better than I do.' Of
course she does. Of course Swift has not the slightest
idea of what she means. But in a few letters more it
turns out that the Doctor has been to dine 'gravely'
with a Mrs. Vanhomrigh : then that he has been to
'his neighbour :' then that he has been unwell, and
means to dine for the whole week with his neighbour !
Stella was quite right in her previsions. She saw from
the very first hint what was going to happen ; and

child was gone to heaven." "No, my Lord," said she ; "that is it
which most grieves him, because he is sure never to see his child there."
'When she was extremely ill, her physician said, "Madam, you are
near the bottom of the hill, but we will endeavour to get you up again."
She answered, "Doctor, I fear I shall be out of breath before I get up to
the top."
'A very dirty clergyman of her acquaintance, who affected smartness
and repartees, was asked by some of the company how his nails came to
be so dirty. He was at a loss ; but she solved the difficulty by saying,
"The Doctor's nails grew dirty by scratching himself."
'A Quaker apothecary sent her a viai, corked ; it had a broad brim,
and a label of paper about its neck. "What is that?"—said she—"my
apothecary's son !" The ridiculous resemblance, and the suddenness
of the question, set us all a-laughing.'—*Swift's Works*, Scott's ed.,
vol. ix. 295-6.

scented Vanessa in the air.* The rival is at the
Dean's feet. The pupil and teacher are reading
together, and drinking tea together, and going to
prayers together, and learning Latin together, and
conjugating *amo, amas, amavi* together. The 'little
language' is over for poor Stella. By the rule of
grammar and the course of conjugation, doesn't *amavi*
come after *amo* and *amas?*

The loves of Cadenus and Vanessa† you may peruse in Cadenus's own poem on the subject, and in
poor Vanessa's vehement expostulatory verses and
letters to him ; she adores him, implores him, admires
him, thinks him something godlike, and only prays to
be admitted to lie at his feet.‡ As they are bringing

* 'I am so hot and lazy after my morning's walk, that I loitered at
Mrs. Vanhomrigh's, where my best gown and periwig was, and *out of
more listlessness dine there, very often ;* so I did to-day.' —*Journal to
Stella.*

Mrs. Vanhomrigh, 'Vanessa's' mother, was the widow of a Dutch
merchant who held lucrative appointments in King William's time.
The family settled in London in 1709, and had a house in Bury Street,
St. James's—a street made notable by such residents as Swift and
Steele ; and, in our own time, Moore and Crabbe.

† 'Vanessa was excessively vain. The character given of her by
Cadenus is fine painting, but in general fictitious. She was fond of
dress ; impatient to be admired ; very romantic in her turn of mind ;
superior, in her own opinion, to all her sex ; full of pertness, gaiety,
and pride ; not without some agreeable accomplishments, but far from
being either beautiful or genteel ; . . . happy in the thoughts of being
reported Swift's concubine, but still aiming and intending to be his
wife.' —*Lord Orrery.*

‡ 'You bid me be easy, and you would see me as often as you could.
You had better have said, as often as you can get the better of your
inclinations so much ; or as often as you remember there was such a
one in the world. If you continue to treat me as you do, you will not
be made uneasy by me long. It is impossible to describe what I have
suffered since I saw you last : I am sure I could have borne the rack
much better than those killing killing words of yours. Sometimes I
have resolved to die without seeing you more ; but those resolves, to
your misfortune, did not last long ; for there is something in human
nature that prompts one so to find relief in this world I must give way
to it, and beg you would see me, and speak kindly to me : for I am
sure you'd not condemn any one to suffer what I have done, could you

him home from church, those divine feet of Doctor
Swift's are found pretty often in Vanessa's parlour.
He likes to be admired and adored. He finds Miss
Vanhomrigh to be a woman of great taste and spirit,
and beauty and wit, and a fortune too. He sees her
every day ; he does not tell Stella about the business ;
until the impetuous Vanessa becomes too fond of him,
until the Doctor is quite frightened by the young
woman's ardour, and confounded by her warmth. He
wanted to marry neither of them—that I believe was
the truth ; but if he had not married Stella, Vanessa
would have had him in spite of himself. When he
went back to Ireland, his Ariadne, not content to
remain in her isle, pursued the fugitive Dean. In
vain he protested, he vowed, he soothed, and bullied ;
the news of the Dean's marriage with Stella at last
came to her, and it killed her—she died of that
passion.*

but know it. The reason I write to you is, because I cannot tell it to
you should I see you ; for when I begin to complain, then you are
angry, and there is something in your looks so awful that it strikes me
dumb. Oh! that you may have but so much regard for me left that
this complaint may touch your soul with pity. I say as little as ever
I can ; did you but know what I thought, I am sure it would move you
to forgive me ; and believe I cannot help telling you this and live.'—
*Vanessa.* (M. 1714.)
* 'If we consider Swift's behaviour, so far only as it relates to
women, we shall find that he looked upon them rather as busts than
as whole figures.'—*Orrery.*
'You would have smiled to have found his house a constant seraglio
of very virtuous women, who attended him from morning till night.'—
*Orrery.*
A correspondent of Sir Walter Scott's furnished him with the materials
on which to found the following interesting passage about Vanessa—
after she had retired to cherish her passion in retreat :—
'Marley Abbey, near Celbridge, where Miss Vanhomrigh resided, is
built much in the form of a real cloister, especially in its external
appearance. An aged man (upwards of ninety, by his own account)
showed the grounds to my correspondent. He was the son of Mrs.
Vanhomrigh's gardener, and used to work with his father in the garden
when a boy. He remembered the unfortunate Vanessa well ; and his

And when she died, and Stella heard that Swift had written beautifully regarding her, 'That doesn't

account of her corresponded with the usual description of her person, especially as to her *embonpoint*. He said she went seldom abroad, and saw little company : her constant amusement was reading, or walking in the garden. . . . She avoided company, and was always melancholy, save when Dean Swift was there, and then she seemed happy. The garden was to an uncommon degree crowded with laurels. The old man said that when Miss Vanhomrigh expected the Dean she always planted with her own hand a laurel or two against his arrival. He showed her favourite seat, still called "Vanessa's bower." Three or four trees and some laurels indicate the spot. . . . There were two seats and a rude table within the bower, the opening of which commanded a view of the Liffey. . . . In this sequestered spot, according to the old gardener's account, the Dean and Vanessa used often to sit, with books and writing-materials on the table before them.'—SCOTT's *Swift*, vol. i. pp. 246-7.

'. . . But Miss Vanhomrigh, irritated at the situation in which she found herself, determined on bringing to a crisis those expectations of a union with the object of her affections—to the hope of which she had clung amid every vicissitude of his conduct towards her. The most probable bar was his undefined connection with Mrs. Johnson, which, as it must have been perfectly known to her, had, doubtless, long excited her secret jealousy, although only a single hint to that purpose is to be found in their correspondence, and that so early as 1713, when she writes to him—then in Ireland—"If you are very happy, it is ill-natured of you not to tell me so, *except 'tis what is inconsistent with mine.*" Her silence and patience under this state of uncertainty for no less than eight years, must have been partly owing to her awe for Swift, and partly, perhaps, to the weak state of her rival's health, which, from year to year, seemed to announce speedy dissolution. At length, however, Vanessa's impatience prevailed, and she ventured on the decisive step of writing to Mrs. Johnson herself, requesting to know the nature of that connection. Stella, in reply, informed her of her marriage with the Dean ; and full of the highest resentment against Swift for having given another female such a right in him as Miss Vanhomrigh's inquiries implied, she sent to him her rival's letter of interrogation, and, without seeing him, or awaiting his reply, retired to the house of Mr. Ford, near Dublin. Every reader knows the consequence. Swift, in one of those paroxysms of fury to which he was liable, both from temper and disease, rode instantly to Marley Abbey. As he entered the apartment, the sternness of his countenance, which was peculiarly formed to express the fiercer passions, struck the unfortunate Vanessa with such terror that she could scarce ask whether he would not sit down. He answered by flinging a letter on the table, and, instantly leaving the house, mounted his horse, and returned to Dublin. When Vanessa opened the packet, she only found her own

surprise me,' said Mrs. Stella, 'for we all know the
Dean could write beautifully about a broomstick.' A
woman—a true woman! Would you have had one
of them forgive the other?

In a note in his biography, Scott says that his friend
Doctor Tuke, of Dublin, has a lock of Stella's hair,
enclosed in a paper by Swift, on which are written, in
the Dean's hand, the words: '*Only a woman's hair.*'
An instance, says Scott, of the Dean's desire to veil
his feelings under the mask of cynical indifference.

See the various notions of critics! Do those words
indicate indifference or an attempt to hide feeling?
Did you ever hear or read four words more pathetic?
Only a woman's hair; only love, only fidelity, only
purity, innocence, beauty; only the tenderest heart
in the world stricken and wounded, and passed away
now out of reach of pangs of hope deferred, love
insulted, and pitiless desertion :—only that lock of hair
left; and memory and remorse, for the guilty lonely
wretch, shuddering over the grave of his victim.

And yet to have had so much love, he must have
given some. Treasures of wit and wisdom, and
tenderness, too, must that man have had locked up
in the caverns of his gloomy heart, and shown fitfully
to one or two whom he took in there. But it was
not good to visit that place. People did not remain
there long, and suffered for having been there.* He

letter to Stella. It was her death-warrant. She sunk at once under
the disappointment of the delayed yet cherished hopes which had so
long sickened her heart, and beneath the unrestrained wrath of him for
whose sake she had indulged them. How long she survived this last
interview is uncertain, but the time does not seem to have exceeded
a few weeks.'—*Scott.*

* 'M. Swift est Rabelais dans son bon sens, et vivant en bonne
compagnie. Il n'a pas, à la vérité, la gaité du premier, mais il a toute
la finesse, la raison, le choix, le bon goût qui manquent à notre curé de
Meudon. Ses vers sont d'un goût singulier, et presque inimitable; la
bonne plaisanterie est son partage en vers et en prose; mais pour le bien

shrank away from all affections sooner or later.  Stella
and Vanessa both died near him, and away from him.
He had not heart enough to see them die.  He
broke from his fastest friend, Sheridan ; he slunk away
from his fondest admirer, Pope.  His laugh jars on
one's ear after seven score years.  He was always
alone—alone and gnashing in the darkness, except
when Stella's sweet smile came and shone upon him.
When that went, silence and utter night closed over
him.  An immense genius : an awful downfall and
ruin.  So great a man he seems to me, that thinking
of him is like thinking of an empire falling.  We have
other great names to mention—none, I think, however, so great or so gloomy.

entendre il faut faire un petit voyage dans son pays.'—VOLTAIRE :
*Lettres sur les Anglais.*   Lettre XX.

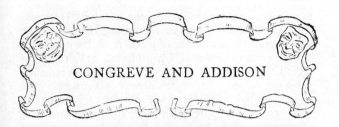

# CONGREVE AND ADDISON

A GREAT number of years ago, before the passing of the Reform Bill, there existed at Cambridge a certain debating club, called the 'Union;' and I remember that there was a tradition amongst the undergraduates who frequented that renowned school of oratory, that the great leaders of the Opposition and Government had their eyes upon the University Debating Club, and that if a man distinguished himself there he ran some chance of being returned to Parliament as a great nobleman's nominee. So Jones of John's, or Thomson of Trinity, would rise in their might, and draping themselves in their gowns, rally round the monarchy, or hurl defiance at priests and kings, with the majesty of Pitt or the fire of Mirabeau, fancying all the while that the great nobleman's emissary was listening to the debate from the back benches, where he was sitting with the family seat in his pocket. Indeed, the legend said that one or two young Cambridge men, orators of the 'Union,' were actually caught up thence, and carried down to Cornwall or Old Sarum, and so into Parliament. And many a young fellow deserted the jogtrot University curriculum, to hang on in the dust behind the fervid wheels of the Parliamentary chariot.

Where, I have often wondered, were the sons of Peers and Members of Parliament in Anne's and George's time? Were they all in the army, or hunt-

ing in the country, or boxing the watch? How was
it that the young gentlemen from the University got
such a prodigious number of places? A lad composed
a neat copy of verses at Christchurch or Trinity, in
which the death of a great personage was bemoaned,
the French king assailed, the Dutch or Prince Eugene
complimented, or the reverse; and the party in power
was presently to provide for the young poet; and a
commissionership, or a post in the Stamps, or the
secretaryship of an Embassy, or a clerkship in the
Treasury, came into the bard's possession. A wonderful fruitbearing rod was that of Busby's. What have
men of letters got in *our* time? Think, not only of
Swift, a king fit to rule in any time or empire—but
Addison, Steele, Prior, Tickell, Congreve, John Gay,
John Dennis, and many others, who got public
employment, and pretty little pickings out of the
public purse.* The wits of whose names we shall

* The following is a *conspectus* of them :—

ADDISON.—Commissioner of Appeals; Under-Secretary of State; Sec-
    retary to the Lord Lieutenant of Ireland; Keeper of the Records in
    Ireland; Lord of Trade; and one of the Principal Secretaries of
    State, successively.
STEELE.— Commissioner of the Stamp Office; Surveyor of the Royal
    Stables at Hampton Court; and Governor of the Royal Company
    of Comedians; Commissioner of 'Forfeited Estates in Scotland.'
PRIOR.—Secretary to the Embassy at the Hague; Gentleman of
    the Bedchamber to King William; Secretary to the Embassy in
    France; Under-Secretary of State; Ambassador to France.
TICKELL.—Under-Secretary of State; Secretary to the Lords Justices of
    Ireland.
CONGREVE.—Commissioner for licensing Hackney-Coaches; Commis-
    sioner for Wine Licenses; place in the Pipe Office; post in the
    Custom House; Secretary of Jamaica.
GAY.—Secretary to the Earl of Clarendon (when Ambassador to
    Hanover).
JOHN DENNIS.—A place in the Custom House.

'En Angleterre . . . les lettres sont plus en honneur qu'ici.'—
VOLTAIRE : *Lettres sur les Anglais.* Lettre XX.

treat in this lecture and two following, all (save one) touched the King's coin, and had, at some period of their lives, a happy quarter-day coming round for them.

They all began at school or college in the regular way, producing panegyrics upon public characters, what were called odes upon public events, battles, sieges, Court marriages and deaths, in which the gods of Olympus and the tragic muse were fatigued with invocations, according to the fashion of the time in France and in England. 'Aid us, Mars, Bacchus, Apollo,' cried Addison, or Congreve, singing of William or Marlborough. 'Accourrez, chastes nymphes du Parnasse,' says Boileau, celebrating the Grand Monarch. 'Des sons que ma lyre enfante marquez-en bien la cadence ; et vous, vents, faites silence ! je vais parler de Louis !' Schoolboys' themes and foundation exercises are the only relics left now of this scholastic fashion. The Olympians are left quite undisturbed in their mountain. What man of note, what contributor to the poetry of a country newspaper, would now think of writing a congratulatory ode on the birth of the heir to a dukedom, or the marriage of a nobleman ? In the past century the young gentlemen of the Universities all exercised themselves at these queer compositions ; and some got fame, and some gained patrons and places for life, and many more took nothing by these efforts of what they were pleased to call their muses.

William Congreve's* Pindaric Odes are still to be found in 'Johnson's Poets,' that now unfrequented poets'-corner, in which so many forgotten bigwigs

* He was the son of Colonel William Congreve, and grandson of Richard Congreve, Esquire, of Congreve and Stretton in Staffordshire —a very ancient family.

have a niche ; but though he was also voted to be one of the greatest tragic poets of any day, it was Congreve's wit and humour which first recommended him to courtly fortune. And it is recorded that his first play, the ' Old Bachelor,' brought our author to the notice of that great patron of English muses, Charles Montague, Lord Halifax—who, being desirous to place so eminent a wit in a state of ease and tranquillity, instantly made him one of the Commissioners for licensing hackney-coaches, bestowed on him soon after a place in the Pipe Office, and likewise a post in the Custom House of the value of £600.

A commissionership of hackney-coaches—a post in the Custom House—a place in the Pipe Office, and all for writing a comedy ! Doesn't it sound like a fable, that place in the Pipe Office ? * ' Ah, l'heureux temps que celui de ces fables ! ' Men of letters there still be : but I doubt whether any Pipe Offices are left. The public has smoked them long ago.

Words, like men, pass current for a while with the public, and, being known everywhere abroad, at length take their places in society ; so even the most secluded and refined ladies here present will have heard

* ' PIPE.—*Pipa*, in law, is a roll in the Exchequer, called also the *great roll.*

' *Pipe Office* is an office in which a person called the *Clerk of the Pipe* makes out leases of Crown lands, by warrant from the Lord Treasurer, or Commissioners of the Treasury, or Chancellor of the Exchequer.

' Clerk of the Pipe makes up all accounts of sheriffs, &c.'—REES : *Cyclopæd.* Art. PIPE.

' *Pipe Office.*—Spelman thinks so called, because the papers were kept in a large *pipe* or cask.

' " These be at last brought into that office of Her Majesty's Exchequer, which we, by a metaphor, do call the *pipe* . . . because the whole receipt is finally conveyed into it by means of divers small *pipes* or quills."—BACON : *The Office of Alienations.*'

[We are indebted to Richardson's *Dictionary* for this fragment of erudition. But a modern man of letters can know little on these points —by experience.]

the phrase from their sons or brothers at school, and
will permit me to call William Congreve, Esquire, the
most eminent literary 'swell' of his age. In my copy
of 'Johnson's Lives' Congreve's wig is the tallest, and
put on with the jauntiest air of all the laurelled
worthies. 'I am the great Mr. Congreve,' he seems
to say, looking out from his voluminous curls. People
called him the great Mr. Congreve.* From the
beginning of his career until the end everybody
admired him. Having got his education in Ireland,
at the same school and college with Swift, he came to
live in the Middle Temple, London, where he luckily
bestowed no attention to the law ; but splendidly
frequented the coffee-houses and theatres, and appeared
in the side-box, the tavern, the Piazza, and the Mall,
brilliant, beautiful, and victorious from the first.
Everybody acknowledged the young chieftain. The
great Mr. Dryden † declared that he was equal to

* 'It has been observed that no change of Ministers affected him in
the least ; nor was he ever removed from any post that was given to him,
except to a better. His place in the Custom House, and his office of
Secretary in Jamaica, are said to have brought him in upwards of twelve
hundred a year.'—*Biog. Brit.* Art. CONGREVE.

† Dryden addressed his 'twelfth epistle' to 'My dear friend, Mr.
Congreve,' on his comedy called the *Double Dealer*, in which he
says :—

> 'Great Jonson did by strength of judgment please ;
> Yet, doubling Fletcher's force, he wants his ease.
> In differing talents both adorned their age ;
> One for the study, t'other for the stage.
> But both to Congreve justly shall submit,
> One match'd in judgment, both o'ermatched in wit.
> In him all beauties of this age we see,' &c. &c.

The *Double Dealer*, however, was not so palpable a hit as the *Old
Bachelor*, but, at first, met with opposition. The critics having fallen
foul of it, our 'Swell' applied the scourge to that presumptuous
body, in the 'Epistle Dedicatory' to the 'Right Honourable Charles
Montague.'

'I was conscious,' said he, 'where a true critic might have put me

Shakspeare, and bequeathed to him his own undisputed poetical crown, and writes of him : 'Mr. Congreve has done me the favour to review the " Æneis " and compare my version with the original. I shall never be ashamed to own that this excellent young man has showed me many faults which I have endeavoured to correct.'

The 'excellent young man' was but three or four and twenty when the great Dryden thus spoke of him : the greatest literary chief in England, the veteran field-marshal of letters, himself the marked man of all Europe, and the centre of a school of wits who daily gathered round his chair and tobacco-pipe at Will's. Pope dedicated his 'Iliad' to him ; * Swift, Addison, Steele, all acknowledge Congreve's rank, and lavish compliments upon him. Voltaire went to wait upon him as on one of the Representatives of Literature ; and the man who scarce praises any other living person

---

upon my defence. I was prepared for the attack . . . but I have not heard anything said sufficient to provoke an answer.'

He goes on—

'But there is one thing at which I am more concerned than all the false criticisms that are made upon me ; and that is, some of the ladies are offended. I am heartily sorry for it ; for I declare, I would rather disoblige all the critics in the world than one of the fair sex. They are concerned that I have represented some women vicious and affected. How can I help it ? It is the business of a comic poet to paint the vices and follies of human kind. . . . I should be very glad of an opportunity to make my compliments to these ladies who are offended But they can no more expect it in a comedy, than *to be tickled by a surgeon when he is letting their blood.*'

* 'Instead of endeavouring to raise a vain monument to myself, let me leave behind me a memorial of my friendship with one of the most valuable men as well as finest writers of my age and country—one who has tried, and knows by his own experience, how hard an undertaking it is to do justice to Homer—and one who, I am sure, seriously rejoices with me at the period of my labours. To him, therefore, having brought this long work to a conclusion, I desire to dedicate it, and to have the honour and satisfaction of placing together in this manner the names of Mr. Congreve and of—A. Pope.'—*Postscript to Translation of the Iliad of Homer*, March 25, 1720.

—who flung abuse at Pope, and Swift, and Steele, and
Addison—the Grub Street Timon, old John Dennis,*
was hat in hand to Mr. Congreve ; and said that when
he retired from the stage, Comedy went with him.

Nor was he less victorious elsewhere. He was
admired in the drawing-rooms as well as the coffee-
houses ; as much beloved in the side-box as on the
stage. He loved, and conquered, and jilted the
beautiful Bracegirdle,† the heroine of all his plays, the
favourite of all the town of her day ; and the Duchess
of Marlborough, Marlborough's daughter, had such
an admiration of him, that when he died she had an
ivory figure made to imitate him,‡ and a large wax
doll with gouty feet to be dressed just as the great
Congreve's gouty feet were dressed in his great lifetime. He saved some money by his Pipe office, and
his Custom House office, and his Hackney-Coach
office, and nobly left it, not to Bracegirdle,§ who

* 'When asked why he listened to the praises of Dennis, he said he
had much rather be flattered than abused. Swift had a particular friendship for our author, and generously took him under his protection in his
high authoritative manner.'—THOS. DAVIES : *Dramatic Miscellanies.*

† 'Congreve was very intimate for years with Mrs Bracegirdle, and
lived in the same street, his house very near hers, until his acquaintance
with the young Duchess of Marlborough. He then quitted that house.
The Duchess showed me a diamond necklace (which Lady Di used afterwards to wear) that cost seven thousand pounds, and was purchased with
the money Congreve left her. How much better would it have been to
have given it to poor Mrs. Bracegirdle.'—DR. YOUNG. *Spence's Anecdotes.*

‡ 'A glass was put in the hand of the statue, which was supposed
to bow to her Grace and to nod in approbation of what she spoke to it.'
—THOS. DAVIES : *Dramatic Miscellanies.*

§ The sum Congreve left Mrs. Bracegirdle was £200, as is said in
the *Dramatic Miscellanies* of Tom Davies ; where are some particulars
about this charming actress and beautiful woman.

She had a 'lively aspect,' says Tom, on the authority of Cibber, and
'such a glow of health and cheerfulness in her countenance, as inspired
everybody with desire.' 'Scarce an audience saw her that were not
half of them her lovers.'

Congreve and Rowe courted her in the persons of their lovers. 'In
Tamerlane, Rowe courted her Selima, in the person of Axalla . . . ;

wanted it, but to the Duchess of Marlborough, who
didn't.*

How can I introduce to you that merry and shameless Comic Muse who won him such a reputation?
Nell Gwynn's servant fought the other footman for
having called his mistress a bad name; and in like
manner, and with pretty little epithets, Jeremy Collier
attacked that godless reckless Jezebel, the English
Comedy of his time, and called her what Nell
Gwynn's man's fellow-servants called Nell Gwynn's
man's mistress. The servants of the theatre, Dryden,
Congreve,† and others, defended themselves with the

Congreve insinuated his addresses in his Valentine to her Angelica, in
*Love for Love;* in his Osmyn to her Almena, in the *Mourning Bride;*
and, lastly, in his Mirabel to her Millamant, in the *Way of the World.*
Mirabel, the fine gentleman of the play, is, I believe, not very distant from
the real character of Congreve.'—*Dramatic Miscellanies*, vol. iii. 1784.

She retired from the stage when Mrs. Oldfield began to be the public
favourite. She died in 1748, in the eighty-fifth year of her age.

* Johnson calls his legacy the 'accumulation of attentive parsimony,
which,' he continues, 'though to her (the Duchess) superfluous and
useless might have given great assistance to the ancient family from
which he descended, at that time, by the imprudence of his relation,
reduced to difficulties and distress.'—*Lives of the Poets.*

† He replied to Collier, in the pamphlet called *Amendments of Mr.
Collier's False and Imperfect Citations*, &c. A specimen or two are subjoined :—

'The greater part of these examples which he has produced are only
demonstrations of his own impurity: they only savour of his utterance,
and were sweet enough till tainted by his breath.

'Where the expression is unblameable in its own pure and genuine
signification, he enters into it, himself, like the evil spirit; he possesses
the innocent phrase, and makes it bellow forth his own blasphemies.

'If I do not return him civilities in calling him names, it is because
I am not very well versed in his nomenclatures. . . . I will only call
him Mr. Collier, and that I will call him as often as I think he shall
deserve it.

'The corruption of a rotten divine is the generation of a sour critic.'

'Congreve,' says Dr. Johnson, 'a very young man, elated with success,
and impatient of censure, assumed an air of confidence and security. . . .
The dispute was protracted through ten years; but at last comedy grew
more modest, and Collier lived to see the reward of his labours in the
reformation of the theatre.'—*Life of Congreve.*

same success, and for the same cause which set Nell's
lacquey fighting. She was a disreputable, daring,
laughing, painted French baggage, that Comic Muse.
She came over from the Continent with Charles (who
chose many more of his female friends there) at the
Restoration—a wild dishevelled Laïs, with eyes bright
with wit and wine—a saucy Court-favourite that sat
at the King's knees, and laughed in his face, and
when she showed her bold cheeks at her chariot-
window, had some of the noblest and most famous
people of the land bowing round her wheel. She was
kind and popular enough, that daring Comedy, that
audacious poor Nell : she was gay and generous, kind,
frank as such people can afford to be ! and the men
who lived with her and laughed with her, took her pay
and drank her wine, turned out when the Puritans
hooted her, to fight and defend her. But the jade
was indefensible, and it is pretty certain her servants
knew it.

There is life and death going on in everything :
truth and lies always at battle. Pleasure is always
warring against self-restraint. Doubt is always crying
Psha ! and sneering. A man in life, a humourist, in
writing about life, sways over to one principle or the
other, and laughs with the reverence for right and the
love of truth in his heart, or laughs at these from the
other side. Didn't I tell you that dancing was a
serious business to Harlequin ? I have read two or
three of Congreve's plays over before speaking of him ;
and my feelings were rather like those, which I dare
say most of us here have had, at Pompeii, looking at
Sallust's house and the relics of an orgy ; a dried
wine-jar or two, a charred supper-table, the breast of a
dancing-girl pressed against the ashes, the laughing
skull of a jester : a perfect stillness round about, as the
cicerone twangs his moral, and the blue sky shines

calmly over the ruin. The Congreve Muse is dead, and her song choked in Time's ashes. We gaze at the skeleton, and wonder at the life which once revelled in its mad veins. We take the skull up, and muse over the frolic and daring, the wit, scorn, passion, hope, desire, with which that empty bowl once fermented. We think of the glances that allured, the tears that melted, of the bright eyes that shone in those vacant sockets ; and of lips whispering love, and cheeks dimpling with smiles, that once covered yon ghastly yellow framework. They used to call those teeth pearls once. See, there's the cup she drank from, the gold-chain she wore on her neck, the vase which held the rouge for her cheeks, her looking-glass, and the harp she used to dance to. Instead of a feast we find a gravestone, and in place of a mistress, a few bones !

Reading in these plays now, is like shutting your ears and looking at people dancing. What does it mean ? the measures, the grimaces, the bowing, shuffling and retreating, the *cavalier seul* advancing upon those ladies—those ladies and men twirling round at the end in a mad galop, after which everybody bows and the quaint rite is celebrated. Without the music we can't understand that comic dance of the last century — its strange gravity and gaiety, its decorum or its indecorum. It has a jargon of its own quite unlike life ; a sort of moral of its own quite unlike life too. I'm afraid it's a Heathen mystery, symbolising a Pagan doctrine ; protesting—as the Pompeians very likely were, assembled at their theatre and laughing at their games ; as Sallust and his friends, and their mistresses protested, crowned with flowers, with cups in their hands—against the new, hard, ascetic, pleasure-hating doctrine whose gaunt disciples, lately passed over from the Asian shores of the Medi-

terranean, were for breaking the fair images of Venus
and flinging the altars of Bacchus down.

I fancy poor Congreve's theatre is a temple of Pagan
delights, and mysteries not permitted except among
heathens.  I fear the theatre carries down that ancient
tradition and worship, as masons have carried their
secret signs and rites from temple to temple.  When
the libertine hero carries off the beauty in the play,
and the dotard is laughed to scorn for having the
young wife : in the ballad, when the poet bids his
mistress to gather roses while she may, and warns her
that old Time is still a-flying : in the ballet, when
honest Corydon courts Phillis under the treillage of
the pasteboard cottage, and leers at her over the head
of grandpapa in red stockings, who is opportunely
asleep ; and when seduced by the invitations of the
rosy youth she comes forward to the footlights, and
they perform on each other's tiptoes that *pas* which
you all know, and which is only interrupted by old
grandpapa awaking from his doze at the pasteboard
châlet (whither he returns to take another nap in case
the young people get an encore) : when Harlequin,
splendid in youth, strength, and agility, arrayed in
gold and a thousand colours, springs over the heads of
countless perils, leaps down the throat of bewildered
giants, and, dauntless and splendid, dances danger
down : when Mr. Punch, that godless old rebel, breaks
every law and laughs at it with odious triumph, out-
wits his lawyer, bullies the beadle, knocks his wife
about the head, and hangs the hangman,—don't you
see in the comedy, in the song, in the dance, in the
ragged little Punch's puppet-show—the Pagan protest ?
Doesn't it seem as if Life puts in its plea and sings its
comment ?  Look how the lovers walk and hold each
other's hands and whisper !  Sings the chorus—
'There is nothing like love, there is nothing like

youth, there is nothing like beauty of your springtime.
Look ! how old age tries to meddle with merry sport !
Beat him with his own crutch, the wrinkled old
dotard ! There is nothing like youth, there is nothing
like beauty, there is nothing like strength. Strength
and valour win beauty and youth. Be brave and
conquer. Be young and happy. Enjoy, enjoy,
enjoy ! Would you know the *Segreto per esser felice ?*
Here it is, in a smiling mistress and a cup of Falernian.'
As the boy tosses the cup and sings his song—hark !
what is that chaunt coming nearer and nearer ?
What is that dirge which *will* disturb us ? The lights
of the festival burn dim—the cheeks turn pale—the
voice quavers — and the cup drops on the floor.
Who's there ? Death and Fate are at the gate, and
they *will* come in.

Congreve's comic feast flares with lights, and round
the table, emptying their flaming bowls of drink, and
exchanging the wildest jests and ribaldry, sit men and
women, waited on by rascally valets and attendants as
dissolute as their mistresses—perhaps the very worst
company in the world. There doesn't seem to be a
pretence of morals. At the head of the table sits
Mirabel or Belmour (dressed in the French fashion
and waited on by English imitators of Scapin and
Frontin). Their calling is to be irresistible, and to
conquer everywhere. Like the heroes of the chivalry
story, whose long-winded loves and combats they were
sending out of fashion, they are always splendid and
triumphant—overcome all dangers, vanquish all
enemies, and win the beauty at the end. Fathers,
husbands, usurers, are the foes these champions contend
with. They are merciless in old age, invariably, and
an old man plays the part in the dramas which the
wicked enchanter or the great blundering giant performs in the chivalry tales, who threatens and grumbles

and resists—a huge stupid obstacle always overcome by the night. It is an old man with a money-box: Sir Belmour his son or nephew spends his money and laughs at him. It is an old man with a young wife whom he locks up: Sir Mirabel robs him of his wife, trips up his gouty old heels, and leaves the old hunks. The old fool, what business has he to hoard his money, or to lock up blushing eighteen? Money is for youth, love is for youth, away with the old people. When Millamant is sixty, having of course divorced the first Lady Millamant, and married his friend Doricourt's granddaughter out of the nursery—it will be his turn; and young Belmour will make a fool of him. All this pretty morality you have in the comedies of William Congreve, Esquire. They are full of wit. Such manners as he observes, he observes with great humour; but ah! it's a weary feast, that banquet of wit where no love is. It palls very soon; sad indigestions follow it, and lonely blank headaches in the morning.

I can't pretend to quote scenes from the splendid Congreve's plays*—which are undeniably bright, witty, and daring—any more than I could ask you to hear the dialogue of a witty bargeman and a brilliant fishwoman exchanging compliments at Billingsgate;

---

* The scene of Valentine's pretended madness in *Love for Love* is a splendid specimen of Congreve's daring manner:—

'*Scandal.* And have you given your master a hint of their plot upon him?

'*Jeremy.* Yes, sir; he says he'll favour it, and mistake her for *Angelica.*

'*Scandal.* It may make us sport.

'*Foresight.* Mercy on us!

'*Valentine.* Husht—interrupt me not—I'll whisper predictions to thee, and thou shalt prophesie;—I am truth, and can teach thy tongue a new trick,—I have told thee what's passed—now I'll tell what's to come:—Dost thou know what will happen to-morrow? Answer me not—for I will tell thee. To-morrow knaves will thrive thro' craft,

but some of his verses—they were amongst the most famous lyrics of the time, and pronounced equal to

and fools thro' fortune : and honesty will go as it did, frost-nipt in a summer suit.   Ask me questions concerning to-morrow.

'*Scandal.*   Ask him, *Mr. Foresight* .

'*Foresight.*   Pray, what will be done at Court ?

'*Valentine.*   *Scandal* will tell you ;—I am truth, I never come there.

'*Foresight.*   In the city ?

'*Valentine.*   Oh, prayers will be said in empty churches at the usual hours.   Yet you will see such zealous faces behind counters as if religion were to be sold in every shop.   Oh, things will go methodically in the city, the clocks will strike twelve at noon, and the horn'd herd buzz in the Exchange at two.   Husbands and wives will drive distinct trades, and care and pleasure separately occupy the family.   Coffee-houses will be full of smoke and stratagem.   And the cropt 'prentice that sweeps his master's shop in the morning, may, ten to one, dirty his sheets before night.   But there are two things, that you will see very strange ; which are, wanton wives with their legs at liberty, and tame cuckolds with chains about their necks.   But hold, I must examine you before I go further ; you look suspiciously.   Are you a husband ?

'*Foresight.*   I am married.

'*Valentine.*   Poor creature !   Is your wife of Covent-garden *Parish* ?

'*Foresight.*   No ; St. Martin's-in-the-Fields.

'*Valentine.*   Alas, poor man !  his eyes are sunk, and his hands shrivelled ; his legs dwindled, and his back bow'd.   Pray, pray for a metamorphosis—change thy shape, and shake off age ; get thee *Medea's* kettle and be boiled anew ; come forth with lab'ring callous hands, and chine of steel, and *Atlas'* shoulders.   Let Taliacotius trim the calves of twenty chairmen, and make thee pedestals to stand erect upon, and look matrimony in the face.   Ha, ha, ha !   That a man should have a stomach to a wedding supper, when the pidgeons ought rather to be laid to his feet !   Ha, ha, ha !

'*Foresight.*   His frenzy is very high now, *Mr. Scandal.*

'*Scandal.*   I believe it is a spring-tide.

'*Foresight.*   Very likely—truly ; you understand these matters.   *Mr. Scandal,* I shall be very glad to confer with you about these things he has uttered.   His sayings are very mysterious and hieroglyphical.

'*Valentine.*   Oh ! why would *Angelica* be absent from my eyes so long ?

'*Jeremy.*   She's here, sir.

'*Mrs. Foresight.*   Now, sister !

'*Mrs Frail.*   O Lord ! what must I say ?

'*Scandal.*   Humour him, madam, by all means.

'*Valentine.*   Where is she ?   Oh ! I see her : she comes, like Riches, Health, and Liberty at once, to a despairing, starving, and abandoned wretch.   Oh—welcome, welcome !

Horace by his contemporaries—may give an idea of his power, of his grace, of his daring manner, his

'*Mrs. Frail.* How d'ye, sir? Can I serve you?

'*Valentine.* Hark'ee—I have a secret to tell you. *Endymion* and the moon shall meet us on *Mount Latmos*, and we'll be married in the dead of night. But say not a word. *Hymen* shall put his torch into a dark lanthorn, that it may be secret; and Juno shall give her peacock poppy-water, that he may fold his ogling tail; and Argus's hundred eyes be shut—ha? Nobody shall know, but *Jeremy*.

'*Mrs. Frail.* No, no; we'll keep it secret; it shall be done presently.

'*Valentine.* The sooner the better. *Jeremy*, come hither—closer—that none may overhear us. *Jeremy*, I can tell you news: *Angelica* is turned nun, and I am turning friar, and yet we'll marry one another in spite of the Pope. Get me a cowl and beads, that I may play my part; for she'll meet me two hours hence in black and white, and a long veil to cover the project, and we won't see one another's faces 'till we have done something to be ashamed of, and then we'll blush once for all.

*Enter* TATTLE.

'*Tattle.* Do you know me, *Valentine?*

'*Valentine.* You!—who are you? No, I hope not.

'*Tattle.* I am *Jack Tattle*. your friend.

'*Valentine.* My friend! What to do? I am no married man, and thou canst not lye with my wife; I am very poor, and thou canst not borrow money of me. Then, what employment have I for a friend?

'*Tattle.* Hah! a good open speaker, and not to be trusted with a secret.

'*Angelica.* Do you know me, *Valentine?*

'*Valentine.* Oh, very well.

'*Angelica.* Who am I?

'*Valentine.* You're a woman, one to whom Heaven gave beauty when it grafted roses on a brier. You are the reflection of Heaven in a pond; and he that leaps at you is sunk. You are all white—a sheet of spotless paper—when you first are born; but you are to be scrawled and blotted by every goose's quill. I know you; for I loved a woman, and loved her so long that I found out a strange thing: I found out what a woman was good for.

'*Tattle.* Ay? pr'ythee, what's that?

'*Valentine.* Why, to keep a secret.

'*Tattle.* O Lord!

'*Valentine.* Oh, exceeding good to keep a secret; for, though she should tell, yet she is not to be believed.

'*Tattle.* Hah! Good again, faith.

'*Valentine.* I would have musick. Sing me the song that I like.'—
CONGREVE: *Love for Love.*

There is a *Mrs. Nickleby*, of the year 1700, in Congreve's comedy of *The Double Dealer*, in whose character the author introduces some

magnificence in compliment, and his polished sarcasm.
He writes as if he was so accustomed to conquer, that

wonderful traits of roguish satire. She is practised on by the gallants
of the play, and no more knows how to resist them than any of the ladies
above quoted could resist Congreve.

'*Lady Plyant.* Oh! reflect upon the horror of your conduct!
Offering to pervert me' [the joke is that the gentleman is pressing the
lady for her daughter's hand, not for her own]—'perverting me from
the road of virtue, in which I have trod thus long, and never made one
trip—not one *faux pas.* Oh, consider it : what would you have to
answer for, if you should provoke me to frailty ! Alas ! humanity is
feeble, Heaven knows ! Very feeble, and unable to support itself.

'*Mellefont.* Where am I ? Is it day ? and am I awake ? Madam——

'*Lady Plyant.* O Lord, ask me the question ! I swear I'll deny it
—therefore don't ask me ; nay, you shan't ask me, I swear I'll deny it.
O Gemini, you have brought all the blood into my face ; I warrant I
am as red as a turkey-cock. O fie, cousin Mellefont !

'*Mellefont.* Nay, madam, hear me ; I mean——

'*Lady Plyant.* Hear you ? No, no ; I'll deny you first ; and hear
you afterwards. For one does not know how one's mind may change
upon hearing—hearing is one of the senses, and all the senses are
fallible. I won't trust my honour, I assure you ; my honour is infallible
and uncomatable.

'*Mellefont.* For Heaven's sake, madam——

'*Lady Plyant.* Oh, name it no more. Bless me, how can you talk
of Heaven, and have so much wickedness in your heart ? May be, you
don't think it a sin. They say some of you gentlemen don't think it a
sin ; but still, my honour, if it were no sin—— But, then, to marry my
daughter for the convenience of frequent opportunities—I'll never consent to that : as sure as can be, I'll break the match.

'*Mellefont.* Death and amazement ! Madam, upon my knees——

'*Lady Plyant.* Nay, nay, rise up ! come, you shall see my good-
nature. I know love is powerful, and nobody can help his passion.
'Tis not your fault ; nor I swear, it is not mine. How can I help it, if
I have charms ? And how can you help it, if you are made a captive ?
I swear it is pity it should be a fault : but, my honour. Well, but your
honour, too—but the sin ! Well, but the necessity. O Lord, here's
somebody coming. I dare not stay. Well, you must consider of your
crime ; and strive as much as can be against it—strive be sure ; but
don't be melancholick—don't despair ; but never think that I'll grant
you anything. O Lord, no ; but be sure you lay aside all thoughts of
the marriage, for though I know you don't love Cynthia, only as a blind
to your passion for me—yet it will make me jealous. O Lord, what did
I say ? Jealous ! No, no, I can't be jealous ; for I must not love you.
Therefore, don't hope ; but don't despair neither. Oh, they're coming ;
I *must* fly.'—*The Double Dealer*, Act ii. sc. v. page 156.

he has a poor opinion of his victims. Nothing's new
except their faces, says he : 'every woman is the
same.' He says this in his first comedy, which he
wrote languidly* in illness, when he was an 'excellent
young man.' Richelieu at eighty could have hardly
said a more excellent thing.

When he advances to make one of his conquests, it
is with a splendid gallantry, in full uniform and with
the fiddles playing, like Grammont's French dandies
attacking the breach of Lerida.

'Cease, cease to ask her name,' he writes of a young
lady at the Wells at Tunbridge, whom he salutes with
a magnificent compliment—

> 'Cease, cease to ask her name,
>     The crowned Muse's noblest theme,
>     Whose glory by immortal fame
>         Shall only sounded be.
>     But if you long to know,
>     Then look round yonder dazzling row :
>     Who most does like an angel show,
>         You may be sure 'tis she.'

Here are lines about another beauty, who perhaps was
not so well pleased at the poet's manner of celebrating
her—

> 'When Lesbia first I saw, so heavenly fair,
>     With eyes so bright and with that awful air,
>     I thought my heart which durst so high aspire
>     As bold as his who snatched celestial fire.

---

* 'There seems to be a strange affectation in authors of appearing
to have done everything by chance. The *Old Bachelor* was written for
amusement in the languor of convalescence. Yet it is apparently composed with great elaborateness of dialogue and incessant ambition of
wit.'—Johnson : *Lives of the Poets.*

But soon as e'er the beauteous idiot spoke,
Forth from her coral lips such folly broke :
Like balm the trickling nonsense heal'd my wound,
And what her eyes enthralled, her tongue unbound.'

Amoret is a cleverer woman than the lovely Lesbia,
but the poet does not seem to respect one much more
than the other; and describes both with exquisite
satirical humour—

'Fair Amoret is gone astray :
    Pursue and seek her every lover.
I'll tell the signs by which you may
    The wandering shepherdess discover.

Coquet and coy at once her air,
    Both studied, though both seem neglected ;
Careless she is with artful care,
    Affecting to seem unaffected.

With skill her eyes dart every glance,
    Yet change so soon you'd ne'er suspect them ;
For she'd persuade they wound by chance,
    Though certain aim and art direct them.

She likes herself, yet others hates
    For that which in herself she prizes ;
And, while she laughs at them, forgets
    She is the thing that she despises.'

What could Amoret have done to bring down such
shafts of ridicule upon her ?   Could she have resisted
the   irresistible Mr. Congreve ?   Could  anybody ?
Could Sabina, when she woke and heard such a bard
singing under her window ?   'See,' he writes—

See ! see, she wakes—Sabina wakes !
    And now the sun begins to rise.
Less glorious is the morn, that breaks
    From his bright beams, than her fair eyes.

With light united, day they give ;
But different fates ere night fulfil :
How many by his warmth will live !
How many will her coldness kill !'

Are you melted ?   Don't you think him a divine
man ?   If not touched by the brilliant Sabina, hear
the devout Selinda—

'Pious Selinda goes to prayers,
If I but ask the favour;
And yet the tender fool's in tears,
When she believes I'll leave her :
Would I were free from this restraint,
Or else had hopes to win her :
Would she could make of me a saint,
Or I of her a sinner !'

What a conquering air there is about these !   What
an irresistible Mr. Congreve it is !   Sinner !  of
course he will be a sinner, the delightful rascal !   Win
her !  of course he will win her, the victorious rogue !
He knows he will : he must—with such a grace, with
such a fashion, with such a splendid embroidered suit.
You see him with red-heeled shoes deliciously turned
out, passing a fair jewelled hand through his dishevelled periwig, and delivering a killing ogle along
with his scented billet.   And Sabina ?   What a
comparison that is between the nymph and the sun !
The sun gives Sabina the *pas*, and does not venture to
rise before her ladyship : the morn's *bright beams* are
less glorious than her *fair eyes* : but before night
everybody will be frozen by her glances : everybody
but one lucky rogue who shall be nameless.   Louis
Quatorze in all his glory is hardly more splendid than
our Phœbus Apollo of the Mall and Spring Gardens.*

* 'Among those by whom it ("Will's") was frequented, Southerne
and Congreve were principally distinguished by Dryden's friendship

When Voltaire came to visit the great Congreve,
the latter rather affected to despise his literary
reputation, and in this perhaps the great Congreve was
not far wrong.* A touch of Steele's tenderness is
worth all his finery; a flash of Swift's lightning, a
beam of Addison's pure sunshine, and his tawdry playhouse taper is invisible. But the ladies loved him, and
he was undoubtedly a pretty fellow.†

. . . But Congreve seems to have gained yet farther than Southerne
upon Dryden's friendship. He was introduced to him by his first play,
the celebrated *Old Bachelor*, being put into the poet's hands to be revised.
Dryden, after making a few alterations to fit it for the stage, returned
it to the author with the high and just commendation, that it was the
best first play he had ever seen.'—Scott's *Dryden*, vol. i. p. 370.

* It was in Surrey Street, Strand (where he afterwards died), that
Voltaire visited him, in the decline of his life.

The anecdote relating to his saying that he wished 'to be visited on
no other footing than as a gentleman who led a life of plainness and
simplicity,' is common to all writers on the subject of Congreve, and
appears in the English version of Voltaire's *Letters concerning the English
Nation*, published in London, 1733, as also in Goldsmith's *Memoir of
Voltaire*. But it is worthy of remark, that it does not appear in the
text of the same Letters in the edition of Voltaire's *Œuvres Complètes* in
the 'Panthéon Littéraire.' Vol. v. of his works. (Paris, 1837.)

'Celui de tous les Anglais qui a porté le plus loin la gloire du théâtre
comique est feu M. Congreve. Il n'a fait que peu de pièces, mais
toutes sont excellentes dans leur genre. . . . . Vous y voyez partout le
langage des honnêtes gens avec des actions de fripon; ce qui prouve qu'il
connaissait bien son monde, et qu'il vivait dans ce qu'on appelle la
bonne compagnie.'—Voltaire: *Lettres sur les Anglais*: Lettre XIX.

† On the death of Queen Mary he published a Pastoral—*The Mourning Muse of Alexis*. Alexis and Menalcas sing alternately in the
orthodox way. The Queen is called Pastora.

> 'I mourn Pastora dead, let Albion mourn,
> And sable clouds her chalky cliffs adorn,'

says Alexis. Among other phenomena, we learn that—

> 'With their sharp nails themselves the Satyrs wound,
> And tug their shaggy beards, and bite with grief the ground'—

(a degree of sensibility not always found in the Satyrs of that period).
. . . It continues—

We have seen in Swift a humourous philosopher,
whose truth frightens one, and whose laughter makes

> ' Lord of these woods and wide extended plains,
>     Stretch'd on the ground and close to earth his face,
>     Scalding with tears the already faded grass.
>
> .    .    .    .    .    .
>
> To dust must all that Heavenly beauty come ?
>     And must Pastora moulder in the tomb ?
>     Ah Death ! more fierce and unrelenting far
>     Than wildest wolves or savage tigers are !
>     With lambs and sheep their hungers are appeased,
>     But ravenous Death the shepherdess has seized.'

This statement that a wolf eats but a sheep, whilst Death eats a
shepherdess—that figure of the ' Great Shepherd ' lying speechless on
his stomach, in a state of despair which neither winds nor floods nor
air can exhibit —are to be remembered in poetry surely ; and this style
was admired in its time by the admirers of the great Congreve !

In the *Tears of Amaryllis for Amyntas* (the young Lord Blandford, the
great Duke of Marlborough's only son), Amaryllis represents Sarah
Duchess !

The tigers and wolves, nature and motion, rivers and echoes, come
into work here again. At the sight of her grief—

> ' Tigers and wolves their wonted rage forego,
>     And dumb distress and new compassion show,
>     Nature herself attentive silence kept,
>     *And motion seemed suspended while she wept !* '

And Pope dedicated the *Iliad* to the author of these lines—and Dryden
wrote to him in his great hand :—

> ' Time, place, and action may with pains be wrought,
>     But Genius must be born and never can be taught.
>     This is your portion, this your native store ;
>     Heaven, that but once was prodigal before,
>     To SHAKSPEARE gave as much, she could not give him more.
>         Maintain your Post : that's all the fame you need,
>     For 'tis impossible you should proceed ;
>     Already I am worn with cares and age,
>     And just abandoning th' ungrateful stage :
>     Unprofitably kept at Heaven's expence,
>     I live a Rent-charge upon Providence :
>     But you, whom every Muse and Grace adorn,
>     Whom I foresee to better fortune born,

one melancholy. We have had in Congreve a humourous observer of another school, to whom the world seems to have no morals at all, and whose ghastly doctrine seems to be that we should eat, drink, and be merry when we can, and go to the deuce (if there be a deuce) when the time comes. We come now to a humour that flows from quite a different heart and spirit—a wit that makes us laugh and leaves us good and happy; to one of the kindest benefactors that society has ever had; and I believe you have divined already that I am about to mention Addison's honoured name.

From reading over his writings, and the biographies which we have of him, amongst which the famous article in the *Edinburgh Review* * may be cited as a

> Be kind to my remains, and oh! defend
> Against your Judgment your departed Friend!
> Let not the insulting Foe my Fame pursue;
> But shade those Lawrels which descend to You:
> And take for Tribute what these Lines express;
> You merit more, nor could my Love do less.'

This is a very different manner of welcome to that of our own day. In Shadwell, Higgons, Congreve, and the comic authors of their time, when gentlemen meet they fall into each other's arms, with 'Jack, Jack, I must buss thee;' or, 'Fore George, Harry, I must kiss thee, lad.' And in a similar manner the poets saluted their brethren. Literary gentlemen do not kiss now; I wonder if they love each other better?

Steele calls Congreve 'Great Sir' and 'Great Author;' says 'Well-dressed barbarians knew his awful name,' and addresses him as if he were a Prince; and speaks of *Pastora* as one of the most famous tragic compositions.

* 'To Addison himself we are bound by a sentiment as much like affection as any sentiment can be which is inspired by one who has been sleeping a hundred and twenty years in Westminster Abbey. . . . After full inquiry and impartial reflection we have long been convinced that he deserved as much love and esteem as can justly be claimed by any of our infirm and erring race.'—*Macaulay*.

'Many who praise virtue do no more than praise it. Yet it is reasonable to believe that Addison's profession and practice were at no great variance; since, amidst that storm of faction in which most of his life

magnificent statue of the great writer and moralist of
the last age, raised by the love and the marvellous skill
and genius of one of the most illustrious artists of our
own : looking at that calm fair face, and clear
countenance—those chiselled features pure and cold, I
can't but fancy that this great man—in this respect,
like him of whom we spoke in the last lecture—was
also one of the lonely ones of the world.   Such men
have very few equals, and they don't herd with those.
It is in the nature of such lords of intellect to be
solitary—they are in the world, but not of it ; and
our minor struggles, brawls, successes, pass under
them.

Kind, just, serene, impartial, his fortitude not tried
beyond easy endurance, his affections not much used,
for his books were his family, and his society was in
public ; admirably wiser, wittier, calmer, and more
instructed than almost every man with whom he met,
how could Addison suffer, desire, admire, feel much ?
I may expect a child to admire me for being taller or
writing more cleverly than she ; but how can I ask
my superior to say that I am a wonder when he
knows better than I ?   In Addison's days you could
scarcely show him a literary performance, a sermon,
or a poem, or a piece of literary criticism, but he felt
he could do better.   His justice must have made him
indifferent.   He didn't praise, because he measured his
compeers by a higher standard than common people
have.*   How was he who was so tall to look up to

was passed, though his station made him conspicuous, and his activity
made him formidable, the character given him by his friends was never
contradicted by his enemies.   Of those with whom interest or opinion
united him, he had not only the esteem but the kindness ; and of others,
whom the violence of opposition drove against him, though he might
lose the love, he retained the reverence.'—*Johnson.*

* 'Addison was perfect good company with intimates, and had something more charming in his conversation that I ever knew in any other
man ; but with any mixture of strangers, and sometimes only with one

any but the loftiest genius? He must have stooped
to put himself on a level with most men. By that
profusion of graciousness and smiles with which
Goethe or Scott, for instance, greeted almost every
literary beginner, every small literary adventurer who
came to his court and went away charmed from the
great king's audience, and cuddling to his heart the
compliment which his literary majesty had paid him—
each of the two good-natured potentates of letters
brought their star and riband into discredit. Everybody had his majesty's orders. Everybody had his
majesty's cheap portrait, on a box surrounded by
diamonds worth twopence apiece. A very great and
just and wise man ought not to praise indiscriminately,
but give his idea of the truth. Addison praises the
ingenious Mr. Pinkethman: Addison praises the
ingenious Mr. Doggett, the actor, whose benefit is
coming off that night: Addison praises Don Saltero:
Addison praises Milton with all his heart, bends his
knee and frankly pays homage to that imperial genius.*
But between those degrees of his men his praise is
very scanty. I don't think the great Mr. Addison
liked young Mr. Pope, the Papist, much; I don't
think he abused him. But when Mr. Addison's men

he seemed to preserve his dignity much, with a stiff sort of silence.'—
POPE  *Spence's Anecdotes.*

* 'Milton's chief talent, and indeed his distinguishing excellence,
lies in the sublimity of his thoughts. There are others of the moderns,
who rival him in every other part of poetry; but in the greatness of his
sentiments he triumphs over all the poets, both modern and ancient,
Homer only excepted. It is impossible for the imagination of man to
distend itself with greater ideas than those which he has laid together
in his first, second, and sixth books.'—*Spectator,* No. 279.

'If I were to name a poet that is a perfect master in all these arts of
working on the imagination, I think Milton may pass for one.'—*Ibid.*
No. 417.

These famous papers appeared in each Saturday's *Spectator,* from
January 19th to May 3rd, 1712. Besides his services to Milton, we may
place those he did to Sacred Music.

abused Mr. Pope, I don't think Addison took his pipe
out of his mouth to contradict them.*

Addison's father was a clergyman of good repute in
Wiltshire, and rose in the Church.† His famous son
never lost his clerical training and scholastic gravity,
and was called 'a parson in a tye-wig' ‡ in London
afterwards at a time when tye-wigs were only worn
by the laity, and the fathers of theology did not think
it decent to appear except in a full bottom. Having
been at school at Salisbury, and the Charterhouse, in
1687, when he was fifteen years old, he went to
Queen's College, Oxford, where he speedily began to
distinguish himself by the making of Latin verses.
The beautiful and fanciful poem of 'The Pigmies
and the Cranes,' is still read by lovers of that sort of

* 'Addison was very kind to me at first, but my bitter enemy afterwards.'—POPE. *Spence's Anecdotes.*

' "Leave him as soon as you can," said Addison to me, speaking of
Pope ; "he will certainly play you some devilish trick else : he has an
appetite to satire." '—LADY WORTLEY MONTAGU. *Spence's Anecdotes.*

† Lancelot Addison, his father, was the son of another Lancelot
Addison, a clergyman in Westmoreland. He became Dean of Lichfield
and Archdeacon of Coventry.

‡ 'The remark of Mandeville, who, when he had passed an evening
in his company, declared that he was "a parson in a tye-wig," can
detract little from his character. He was always reserved to strangers,
and was not incited to uncommon freedom by a character like that of
Mandeville.'—JOHNSON : *Lives of the Poets.*

'Old Jacob Tonson did not like Mr. Addison : he had a quarrel with
him, and, after his quitting the secretaryship, used frequently to say of
him—"One day or other you'll see that man a bishop—I'm sure he
ooks that way ; and indeed I ever thought him a priest in his heart." '—
POPE. *Spence's Anecdotes.*

'Mr. Addison stayed above a year at Blois. He would rise as early
as between two and three in the height of summer, and lie abed till
between eleven and twelve in the depth of winter. He was untalkative
whilst here and often thoughtful : sometimes so lost in thought, that I
have come into his room and stayed five minutes there before he has
known anything of it. He had his masters generally at supper with
him ; kept very little company besides ; and had no amour that I know
of ; and I think I should have known it if he had had any.'—ABBÉ
PHILIPPEAUX OF BLOIS. *Spence's Anecdotes.*

exercise; and verses are extant in honour of King William, by which it appears that it was the loyal youth's custom to toast that sovereign in bumpers of purple Lyæus : many more works are in the Collection, including one on the Peace of Ryswick, in 1697, which was so good that Montague got him a pension of £300 a year, on which Addison set out on his travels.

During his ten years at Oxford, Addison had deeply imbued himself with the Latin poetical literature and had these poets at his fingers' ends when he travelled in Italy.* His patron went out of office, and his pension was unpaid : and hearing that this great scholar, now eminent and known to the literati of Europe (the great Boileau,† upon perusal of Mr. Addison's elegant hexameters, was first made aware that England was not altogether a barbarous nation)— hearing that the celebrated Mr. Addison, of Oxford, proposed to travel as governor to a young gentleman on the grand tour, the great Duke of Somerset proposed to Mr. Addison to accompany his son, Lord Hertford.

Mr. Addison was delighted to be of use to his Grace, and his Lordship his Grace's son, and expressed himself ready to set forth.

His Grace the Duke of Somerset now announced to one of the most famous scholars of Oxford and Europe that it was his gracious intention to allow my Lord Hertford's tutor one hundred guineas per annum. Mr. Addison wrote back that his services were his

* 'His knowledge of the Latin poets, from Lucretius and Catullus down to Claudian and Prudentius, was singularly exact and profound.' —*Macaulay.*

† 'Our country owes it to him, that the famous Monsieur Boileau first conceived an opinion of the English genius for poetry, by perusing the present he made him of the *Musæ Anglicanæ.*'—TICKELL : *Preface to Addison's Works.*

Grace's, but he by no means found his account in the recompense for them. The negotiation was broken off. They parted with a profusion of *congées* on one side and the other.

Addison remained abroad for some time, living in the best society of Europe. How could he do otherwise ? He must have been one of the finest gentlemen the world ever saw : at all moments of life serene and courteous, cheerful and calm.* He could scarcely ever have had a degrading thought. He might have omitted a virtue or two, or many, but could not have committed many faults for which he need blush or turn pale. When warmed into confidence, his conversation appears to have been so delightful that the greatest wits sat rapt and charmed to listen to him. No man bore poverty and narrow fortune with a more lofty cheerfulness. His letters to his friends at this period of his life, when he had lost his Government pension and given up his college chances, are full of courage and a gay confidence and philosophy : and they are none the worse in my eyes, and I hope not in those of his last and greatest biographer (though Mr. Macaulay is bound to own and lament a certain weakness for wine, which the great and good Joseph Addison notoriously possessed, in common with countless gentlemen of his time), because some of the letters are written when his honest hand was shaking a little in the morning after libations to purple Lyæus over-night. He was fond of drinking the healths of his friends : he writes to Wyche,† of Hamburg,

---

* 'It was my fate to be much with the wits ; my father was acquainted with all of them. *Addison was the best company in the world.* I never knew anybody that had so much wit as Congreve.'—LADY WORTLEY MONTAGU. *Spence's Anecdotes.*

† '*Mr. Addison to Mr. Wyche.*

'DEAR SIR,—My hand at present begins to grow steady enough for

gratefully remembering Wyche's ' hoc.' ' I have been
drinking your health to-day with Sir Richard Shirley,'
he writes to Bathurst. 'I have lately had the honour
to meet my Lord Effingham at Amsterdam, where we
have drunk Mr. Wood's health a hundred times in
excellent champagne,' he writes again. Swift* de-

a letter, so the properest use I can put it to is to thank ye honest
gentleman that set it a shaking. I have had this morning a desperate
design in my head to attack you in verse, which I should certainly have
done could I have found out a rhyme to rummer. But though you have
escaped for ye present, you are not yet out of danger, if I can a little
recover my talent at crambo. I am sure, in whatever way I write to
you, it will be impossible for me to express ye deep sense I have of ye
many favours you have lately shown me. I shall only tell you that
Hambourg has been the pleasantest stage I have met with in my
travails. If any of my friends wonder at me for living so long in that
place, I dare say it will be thought a very good excuse when I tell him
Mr. Wyche was there. As your company made our stay at Hambourg
agreeable, your wine has given us all ye satisfaction that we have found
in our journey through Westphalia. If drinking your health will do
you any good, you may expect to be as long-lived as Methuselah, or,
to use a more familiar instance, as ye oldest hoc in ye cellar. I hope ye
two pair of legs that was left a swelling behind us are by this time come
to their shapes again. I can't forbear troubling you with my hearty
respects to ye owners of them, and desiring you to believe me always,
                                                        ' Dear Sir,
                                                            ' Yours,' &c.

' To Mr. Wyche, His Majesty's Resident at
            ' Hambourg, May 1703.'

—*From the Life of Addison,* by Miss AIKIN.   Vol. i. p. 146.
  * It is pleasing to remember that the relation between Swift and
Addison was, on the whole, satisfactory from first to last.  The value of
Swift's testimony, when nothing personal inflamed his vision or warped
his judgment, can be doubted by nobody.
  '*Sept.* 10, 1710.—I sat till ten in the evening with Addison and
Steele.
  ' 11.—Mr. Addison and I dined together at his lodgings, and I sat
with him part of this evening.
  ' 18.—To-day I dined with Mr. Stratford at Mr. Addison's retirement
near Chelsea. . . .  I will get what good offices I can from Mr.
Addison.
  ' 27.—To-day all our company dined at Will Frankland's, with Steele
and Addison, too.
  ' 29.—I dined with Mr. Addison,' &c.—*Journal to Stella.*

scribes him over his cups, when Joseph yielded to a
temptation which Jonathan resisted. Joseph was of
a cold nature, and needed perhaps the fire of wine to
warm his blood. If he was a parson, he wore a tye-wig,
recollect. A better and more Christian man scarcely
ever breathed than Joseph Addison. If he had not
that little weakness for wine—why, we could scarcely
have found a fault with him, and could not have liked
him as we do.*

At thirty-three years of age, this most distinguished wit, scholar, and gentleman was without a
profession and an income. His book of 'Travels'
had failed: his 'Dialogues on Medals' had had no
particular success: his Latin verses, even though
reported the best since Virgil, or Statius at any rate,
had not brought him a Government place, and
Addison was living up three shabby pair of stairs in the
Haymarket (in a poverty over which old Samuel
Johnson rather chuckles), when in these shabby rooms
an emissary from Government and Fortune came and

'Addison inscribed a presentation copy of his travels 'To Doctor
Jonathan Swift, the most agreeable companion, the truest friend, and
the greatest genius of his age.'—(SCOTT. From the information of Mr.
Theophilus Swift.)

'Mr. Addison, who goes over first secretary, is a most excellent
person ; and being my most intimate friend, I shall use all my credit to
set him right in his notions of persons and things.'—*Letters.*

'I examine my heart, and can find no other reason why I write to
you now, besides that great love and esteem I have always had for you.
I have nothing to ask you either for my friend or for myself.'—SWIFT
to ADDISON (1717). SCOTT's *Swift.* Vol. xix. p. 274.

Political differences only dulled for a while their friendly communications. Time renewed them : and Tickell enjoyed Swift's friendship as
a legacy from the man with whose memory his is so honourably connected.

* 'Addison usually studied all the morning; then met his party at
Button's ; dined there, and stayed five or six hours, and sometimes far
into the night. I was of the company for about a year, but found it too
much for me : it hurt my health, and so I quitted it.'—POPE. *Spence's
Anecdotes.*

found him.* A poem was wanted about the Duke of
Marlborough's victory of Blenheim. Would Mr.
Addison write one? Mr. Boyle, afterwards Lord
Carlton, took back the reply to the Lord Treasurer
Godolphin, that Mr. Addison would. When the
poem had reached a certain stage, it was carried to
Godolphin; and the last lines which he read were
these :—

'But, O my Muse! what numbers wilt thou find
To sing the furious troops in battle join'd?
Methinks I hear the drum's tumultuous sound
The victors' shouts and dying groans confound;
The dreadful burst of cannon rend the skies,
And all the thunder of the battle rise.
'Twas then great Marlborough's mighty soul was proved
That, in the shock of charging hosts unmoved,
Amidst confusion, horror, and despair,
Examined all the dreadful scenes of war:
In peaceful thought the field of death surveyed,
To fainting squadrons sent the timely aid,
Inspired repulsed battalions to engage,
And taught the doubtful battle where to rage.
So when an angel, by divine command,
With rising tempests shakes a guilty land
(Such as of late o'er pale Britannia passed),
Calm and serene he drives the furious blast;
And, pleased the Almighty's orders to perform,
Rides in the whirlwind and directs the storm.'

Addison left off at a good moment. That simile
was pronounced to be of the greatest ever produced in
poetry. That angel, that good angel, flew off with
Mr. Addison, and landed him in the place of Com-

* 'When he returned to England (in 1702), with a meanness of
appearance which gave testimony of the difficulties to which he had
been reduced, he found his old patrons out of power, and was, therefore,
for a time, at full leisure for the cultivation of his mind.'—JOHNSON:
Lives of the Poets.

missioner of Appeals—vice Mr. Locke providentially
promoted. In the following year Mr. Addison went
to Hanover with Lord Halifax, and the year after was
made Under-Secretary of State. O angel visits ! you
come 'few and far between' to literary gentlemen's
lodgings ! Your wings seldom quiver at second-floor
windows now !

You laugh ? You think it is in the power of few
writers nowadays to call up such an angel ? Well,
perhaps not ; but permit us to comfort ourselves by
pointing out that there are in the poem of the
'Campaign' some as bad lines as heart can desire ;
and to hint that Mr. Addison did very wisely in not
going farther with my Lord Godolphin than that
angelical simile. Do allow me, just for a little
harmless mischief, to read you some of the lines which
follow. Here is the interview between the Duke and
the King of the Romans after the battle :—

> 'Austria's young monarch, whose imperial sway
> Sceptres and thrones are destined to obey,
> Whose boasted ancestry so high extends
> That in the Pagan Gods his lineage ends,
> Comes from afar, in gratitude to own
> The great supporter of his father's throne.
> What tides of glory to his bosom ran
> Clasped in th' embraces of the godlike man !
> How were his eyes with pleasing wonder fixt,
> To see such fire with so much sweetness mixt !
> Such easy greatness, such a graceful port,
> So turned and finished for the camp or court !'

How many fourth-form boys at Mr. Addison's
school of Charterhouse could write as well as that
now ? The 'Campaign' has blunders, triumphant as
it was ; and weak points like all campaigns.*

* 'Mr. Addison wrote very fluently ; but he was sometimes very slow

In the year 1713 'Cato' came out. Swift has left
a description of the first night of the performance.
All the laurels of Europe were scarcely sufficient for
the author of this prodigious poem.*   Laudations of

and scrupulous in correcting. He would show his verses to several
friends ; and would alter almost everything that any of them hinted at
as wrong.   He seemed to be too diffident of himself ; and too much concerned about his character as a poet ; or (as he worded it) too solicitous
for that kind of praise which, God knows, is but a very little matter
after all !'— POPE.   *Spence's Anecdotes.*

* 'As to poetical affairs,' says Pope in 1713, 'I am content at present
to be a bare looker-on. . . .   Cato was not so much the wonder of Rome
in his days, as he is of Britain in ours ; and though all the foolish
industry possible has been used to make it thought a party play, yet
what the author once said of another may the most properly in the world
be applied to him on this occasion :—

> '"Envy itself is dumb—in wonder lost ;
> And factions strive who shall applaud him most."

'The numerous and violent claps of the Whig party on the one side
of the theatre were echoed back by the Tories on the other ; while the
author sweated behind the scenes with concern to find their applause
proceeding more from the hand than the head. . . .   I believe you have
heard that, after all the applauses of the opposite faction, my Lord
Bolingbroke sent for Booth, who played Cato, into the box, and presented him with fifty guineas in acknowledgment (as he expressed it) for
defending the cause of liberty so well against a perpetual dictator.'—
POPE's *Letters to Sir W. Trumbull.*

*Cato* ran for thirty-five nights without interruption.   Pope wrote the
Prologue, and Garth the Epilogue.

It is worth noticing how many things in *Cato* keep their ground as
habitual quotations ; *e.g.*—

> '.      big with the fate
> Of Cato and of Rome.'

> ''Tis not in mortals to command success ;
> But we'll do more, Sempronius, we'll deserve it.'

> 'Blesses his stars, and thinks it luxury.'

> 'I think the Romans call it Stoicism.'

> 'My voice is still for war.'

> 'When vice prevails, and impious men bear sway,
> The post of honour is a private station.'

Not to mention—

> 'The woman who deliberates is lost.'

Whig and Tory chiefs, popular ovations, compli-
mentary garlands from literary men, translations in all
languages, delight and homage from all—save from
John Dennis in a minority of one. Mr. Addison was
called the 'great Mr. Addison' after this. The Coffee-
house Senate saluted him Divus: it was heresy to
question that decree.

Meanwhile he was writing political papers and advancing in the political profession. He went Secretary
to Ireland. He was appointed Secretary of State in
1717. And letters of his are extant, bearing date some
year or two before, and written to young Lord Warwick,
in which he addresses him as 'my dearest Lord,' and
asks affectionately about his studies, and writes very
prettily about nightingales and birds'-nests, which he
has found at Fulham for his Lordship. Those
nightingales were intended to warble in the ear of
Lord Warwick's mamma. Addison married her
Ladyship in 1716; and died at Holland House three
years after that splendid but dismal union.*

And the eternal—
> 'Plato, thou reasonest well.'

which avenges, perhaps, on the public their neglect of the play!

* 'The lady was persuaded to marry him on terms much like those
on which a Turkish princess is espoused—to whom the Sultan is reported
to pronounce, "Daughter, I give thee this man for thy slave." The
marriage, if uncontradicted report can be credited, made no addition to
his happiness; it neither found them, nor made them, equal. . .
Rowe's ballad of "The Despairing Shepherd" is said to have been
written, either before or after marriage, upon this memorable pair.'—
*Dr. Johnson.*

'I received the news of Mr. Addison's being declared Secretary of
State with the less surprise, in that I knew that post was almost offered
to him before. At that time he declined it, and I really believe that he
would have done well to have declined it now. Such a post as that,
and such a wife as the Countess, do not seem to be, in prudence, eligible
for a man that is asthmatic, and we may see the day when he will be
heartily glad to resign them both.'—LADY WORTLEY MONTAGU to
POPE: *Works, Lord Wharncliffe's edit.*, vol. ii. p. 111.

The issue of this marriage was a daughter, Charlotte Addison, who

But it is not for his reputation as the great author
of 'Cato' and the 'Campaign,' or for his merits as
Secretary of State, or for his rank and high distinction
as my Lady Warwick's husband, or for his eminence
as an Examiner of political questions on the Whig
side, or a Guardian of British liberties, that we admire
Joseph Addison.   It is as a Tatler of small talk and
a Spectator of mankind, that we cherish and love him,
and owe as much pleasure to him as to any human
being that ever wrote.   He came in that artificial
age, and began to speak with his noble, natural voice.
He came, the gentle satirist, who hit no unfair blow ;
the kind judge who castigated only in smiling.   While
Swift went about, hanging and ruthless—a literary
Jeffreys—in Addison's kind court only minor cases
were tried ;  only peccadilloes and small sins against
society :  only a dangerous libertinism in tuckers and
hoops ;* or a nuisance in the abuse of beaux' canes and

inherited, on her mother's death, the estate of Bilton, near Rugby, which
her father had purchased.   She was of weak intellect, and died, un-
married, at an advanced age.

Rowe appears to have been faithful to Addison during his courtship,
for his Collection contains 'Stanzas to Lady Warwick on Mr. Addison's
going to Ireland,' in which her Ladyship is called 'Chloe,' and Joseph
Addison 'Lycidas ;' besides the ballad mentioned by the Doctor, and
which is entitled 'Colin's Complaint.'   But not even the interest attached
to the name of Addison could induce the reader to peruse this composition, though one stanza may serve as a specimen :—

> 'What though I have skill to complain—
> Though the Muses my temples have crowned ;
> What though, when they hear my soft strain,
> The virgins sit weeping around.
>
> Ah, Colin ! thy hopes are in vain ;
> Thy pipe and thy laurel resign :
> Thy false one inclines to a swain
> Whose music is sweeter than thine.'

* One of the most humourous of these is the paper on Hoops, which
the *Spectator* tells us, particularly pleased his friend SIR ROGER :—
Mr. SPECTATOR,—You have diverted the town almost a whole month
at the expense of the country ; it is now high time that you should give

snuff-boxes. It may be a lady is tried for breaking the peace of our sovereign lady Queen Anne, and ogling too dangerously from the side-box; or a Templar for beating the watch, or breaking Priscian's head; or a citizen's wife for caring too much for the puppet-show, and too little for her husband and children: every one of the little sinners brought before him is amusing, and he dismisses each with the pleasantest penalties and the most charming words of admonition.

the country their revenge. Since your withdrawing from this place, the fair sex are run into great extravagances. Their petticoats, which began to heave and swell before you left us, are now blown up into a most enormous concave, and rise every day more and more; in short, sir, since our women know themselves to be out of the eye of the SPECTATOR, they will be kept within no compass. You praised them a little too soon, for the modesty of their head-dresses; for as the humour of a sick person is often driven out of one limb into another, their superfluity of ornaments, instead of being entirely banished, seems only fallen from their heads upon their lower parts. What they have lost in height they make up in breadth, and, contrary to all rules of architecture, widen the foundations at the same time that they shorten the superstructure.

'The women give out, in defence of these wide bottoms, that they are airy and very proper for the season; but this I look upon to be only a pretence and a piece of art, for it is well known we have not had a more moderate summer these many years, so that it is certain the heat they complain of cannot be in the weather; besides, I would fain ask these tender-constituted ladies, why they should require more cooling than their mothers before them?

'I find several speculative persons are of opinion that our sex has of late years been very saucy, and that the hoop-petticoat is made use of to keep us at a distance. It is most certain that a woman's honour cannot be better entrenched than after this manner, in circle within circle, amidst such a variety of outworks of lines and circumvallation. A female who is thus invested in whalebone is sufficiently secured against the approaches of an ill-bred fellow, who might as well think of Sir George Etherege's way of making love in a tub as in the midst of so many hoops.

'Among these various conjectures, there are men of superstitious tempers who look upon the hoop-petticoat as a kind of prodigy. Some will have it that it portends the downfall of the *French* king, and observe, that the farthingale appeared in *England* a little before the ruin of the *Spanish* monarchy. Others are of opinion that it foretells battle and blood-shed, and believe it of the same prognostication as the tail of a blazing star. For my part, I am apt to think it is a sign that multitudes are coming into the world rather than going out of it,' &c. &c.—*Spectator,* No. 127.

Addison wrote his papers as gaily as if he was going out for a holiday. When Steele's *Tatler* first began his prattle, Addison, then in Ireland, caught at his friend's notion, poured in paper after paper, and contributed the stores of his mind, the sweet fruits of his reading, the delightful gleanings of his daily observation, with a wonderful profusion, and as it seemed, an almost endless fecundity. He was six-and-thirty years old : full and ripe. He had not worked crop after crop from his brain, manuring hastily, subsoiling indifferently, cutting and sowing and cutting again, like other luckless cultivators of letters. He had not done much as yet : a few Latin poems—graceful prolusions ; a polite book of travels ; a dissertation on medals, not very deep ; four acts of a tragedy, a great classical exercise ; and the 'Campaign,' a large prize poem that won an enormous prize. But with his friend's discovery of the 'Tatler,' Addison's calling was found, and the most delightful talker in the world began to speak. He does not go very deep : let gentlemen of a profound genius, critics accustomed to the plunge of the bathos, console themselves by thinking that he *couldn't* go very deep. There are no traces of suffering in his writing. He was so good, so honest, so healthy, so cheerfully selfish, if I must use the word. There is no deep sentiment. I doubt, until after his marriage, perhaps, whether he ever lost his night's rest or his day's tranquillity about any woman in his life ;* whereas poor Dick Steele had capacity enough to melt, and to languish, and to sigh, and to cry his honest old eyes out, for a dozen. His writings do not show insight into or reverence for the love of women, which I take to be, one the consequence of the other.

* ' Mr. Addison has not had one epithalamium that I can hear of and must even be reduced, like a poorer and a better poet, Spenser, to, make his own.'—Pope's *Letters.*

He walks about the world watching their pretty
humours, fashions, follies, flirtations, rivalries : and
noting them with the most charming archness.   He
sees them in public, in the theatre, or the assembly, or
the puppet-show ; or at the toy-shop higgling for
gloves and lace ; or at the auction, battling together
over a blue porcelain dragon, or a darling monster in
Japan ; or at church, eyeing the width of their rival's
hoops, or the breadth of their laces, as they sweep
down the aisles.   Or he looks out of his window at
the ' Garter ' in Saint James's Street, at Ardelia's coach,
as she blazes to the drawing-room with her coronet
and six footmen ; and remembering that her father
was a Turkey merchant in the City, calculates how
many sponges went to purchase her earring, and how
many drums of figs to build her coach-box ; or he
demurely watches behind a tree in Spring Garden as
Saccharissa (whom he knows under her mask) trips
out of her chair to the alley where Sir Fopling is
waiting.   He sees only the public life of women.
Addison was one of the most resolute club-men of his
day.   He passed many hours daily in those haunts.
Besides drinking—which, alas ! is past praying for—
you must know it, he owned, too, ladies, that he
indulged in that odious practice of smoking.   Poor
fellow !   He was a man's man, remember.   The only
woman he *did* know, he didn't write about.   I take it
there would not have been much humour in that story.
He likes to go and sit in the smoking-room at the
' Grecian,' or the ' Devil ; ' to pace 'Change and the
Mall *—to mingle in that great club of the world—

* ' I have observed that a reader seldom peruses a book with pleasure
till he knows whether the writer of it be a black or a fair man, of a
mild or a choleric disposition, married or a bachelor ; with other particulars of a like nature, that conduce very much to the right understanding of an author.   To gratify this curiosity, which is so natural
to a reader, I design this paper and my next as prefatory discourses to

sitting alone in it somehow : having good-will and kindness for every single man and woman in it—

my following writings ; and shall give some account in them of the persons that are engaged in this work. As the chief trouble of compiling, digesting, and correcting will fall to my share, I must do myself the justice to open the work with my own history. . . . There runs a story in the family, that when my mother was gone with child of me about three months, she dreamt that she was brought to bed of a judge. Whether this might proceed from a lawsuit which was then depending in the family, or my father's being a justice of the peace, I cannot determine ; for I am not so vain as to think it presaged any dignity that I should arrive at in my future life, though that was the interpretation which the neighbourhood put upon it. The gravity of my behaviour at my very first appearance in the world, and all the time that I sucked, seemed to favour my mother's dream ; for, as she has often told me, I threw away my rattle before I was two months old, and would not make use of my coral till they had taken away the bells from it.

'As for the rest of my infancy, there being nothing in it remarkable, I shall pass it over in silence. I find that during my nonage I had the reputation of a very sullen youth, but was always the favourite of my schoolmaster, who used to say that *my parts were solid and would wear well*. I had not been long at the University before I distinguished myself by a most profound silence ; for during the space of eight years, excepting in the public exercises of the college, I scarce uttered the quantity of a hundred words ; and, indeed, I do not remember that I ever spoke three sentences together in my whole life. . . .

'I have passed my latter years in this city, where I am frequently seen in most public places, though there are not more than half-a-dozen of my select friends that know me. . . . There is no place of general resort wherein I do not often make my appearance ; sometimes I am seen thrusting my head into a round of politicians at "Will's," and listening with great attention to the narratives that are made in these little circular audiences. Sometimes I smoke a pipe at "Child's," and whilst I seem attentive to nothing but the *Postman*, overhear the conversation of every table in the room. I appear on Tuesday night at "St. James's Coffee-house ; " and sometimes join the little committee of politics in the inner-room, as one who comes to hear and improve. My face is likewise very well known at the "Grecian," the "Cocoa-tree," and in the theatres both of Drury Lane and the Haymarket. I have been taken for a merchant upon the Exchange for above these two years ; and sometimes pass for a Jew in the assembly of stock-jobbers at "Jonathan's." In short, wherever I see a cluster of people, I mix with them, though I never open my lips but in my own club.

'Thus I live in the world rather as a "*Spectator*" of mankind than as one of the species ; by which means I have made myself a speculative statesman, soldier, merchant, and artizan, without ever meddling in any practical part in life. I am very well versed in the theory of a husband

having need of some habit and custom binding him to
some few ; never doing any man a wrong (unless it
be a wrong to hint a little doubt about a man's parts,
and to damn him with faint praise) ; and so he looks
on the world and plays with the ceaseless humours of
all of us—laughs the kindest laugh — points our
neighbour's foible or eccentricity out to us with the
most good-natured smiling confidence ; and then,
turning over his shoulder, whispers *our* foibles to our
neighbour. What would Sir Roger de Coverley be
without his follies and his charming little brain-
cracks ? * If the good knight did not call out to the
people sleeping in church, and say 'Amen' with
such a delightful pomposity ; if he did not make
a speech in the assize-court *à propos de bottes*, and
merely to show his dignity to Mr. Spectator : † if he

or a father, and can discern the errors in the economy, business, and
diversions of others, better than those who are engaged in them—as
standers-by discover blots which are apt to escape those who are in the
game. . . . In short, I have acted, in all the parts of my life, as a
looker-on, which is the character I intend to preserve in this paper.'—
*Spectator*, No. 1.

\* 'So effectually, indeed, did he retort on vice the mockery which
had recently been directed against virtue, that, since his time, the open
violation of decency has always been considered, amongst us, the sure
mark of a fool.'—*Macaulay*.

† 'The Court was sat before Sir Roger came ; but, notwithstanding
all the justices had taken their places upon the bench, they made room
for the old knight at the head of them : who for his reputation in the
country took occasion to whisper in the judge's ear that *he was glad his
Lordship had met with so much good weather in his circuit*. I was
listening to the proceedings of the Court with much attention, and
infinitely pleased with that great appearance and solemnity which so
properly accompanies such a public administration of our laws ; when,
after about an hour's sitting, I observed, to my great surprise, in the
midst of a trial, that my friend Sir Roger was getting up to speak. I
was in some pain for him, till I found he had acquitted himself of two or
three sentences, with a look of much business and great intrepidity.

'Upon his first rising, the Court was hushed, and a general whisper
ran among the country people that Sir Roger *was up*. The speech he
made was so little to the purpose, that I shall not trouble my readers
with an account of it, and I believe was not so much designed by the

did not mistake Madam Doll Tearsheet for a lady
of quality in Temple Garden : if he were wiser than
he is : if he had not his humour to salt his life, and
were but a mere English gentleman and game-preserver
—of what worth were he to us ?   We love him for his
vanities as much as his virtues.   What is ridiculous
is delightful in him ; we are so fond of him because
we laugh at him so.   And out of that laughter, and
out of that sweet weakness, and out of those harmless
eccentricities and follies, and out of that touched brain,
and out of that honest manhood and simplicity—we
get a result of happiness, goodness, tenderness, pity,
piety ; such as, if my audience will think their reading
and hearing over, doctors and divines but seldom have
the fortune to inspire.   And why not ?   Is the glory
of Heaven to be sung only by gentlemen in black
coats ?   Must the truth be only expounded in gown
and surplice, and out of those two vestments can
nobody preach it ?   Commend me to this dear preacher
without orders—this parson in the tye-wig.   When
this man looks from the world, whose weaknesses he
describes so benevolently, up to the Heaven which
shines over us all, I can hardly fancy a human face
lighted up with a more serene rapture : a human
intellect thrilling with a purer love and adoration
than Joseph Addison's.   Listen to him : from your
childhood you have known the verses : but who can
hear their sacred music without love and awe ?—

> ' Soon as the evening shades prevail,
>   The moon takes up the wondrous tale,
>   And nightly to the listening earth
>   Repeats the story of her birth ;
>   Whilst all the stars that round her burn,
>   And all the planets in their turn,

knight himself to inform the Court as to give him a figure in my eyes,
and to keep up his credit in the country.'—*Spectator*, No. 122.

Confirm the tidings as they roll,
And spread the truth from pole to pole.
What though, in solemn silence, all
Move round the dark terrestrial ball ;
What though no real voice nor sound
Amid their radiant orbs be found ;
In Reason's ear they all rejoice,
And utter forth a glorious voice,
For ever singing as they shine,
The hand that made us is divine.'

It seems to me those verses shine like the stars. They shine out of a great deep calm. When he turns to Heaven, a Sabbath comes over that man's mind : and his face lights up from it with a glory of thanks and prayer. His sense of religion stirs through his whole being. In the fields, in the town : looking at the birds in the trees : at the children in the streets : in the morning or in the moonlight : over his books in his own room : in a happy party at a country merry-making or a town assembly, good-will and peace to God's creatures, and love and awe of Him who made them, fill his pure heart and shine from his kind face. If Swift's life was the most wretched, I think Addison's was one of the most enviable. A life prosperous and beautiful—a calm death — an immense fame and affection afterwards for his happy and spotless name.*

---

* 'Garth sent to Addison (of whom he had a very high opinion) on his death-bed, to ask him whether the Christian religion was true.' —Dr. Young. *Spence's Anecdotes.*

'I have always preferred cheerfulness to mirth. The latter I consider as an act, the former as an habit of the mind. Mirth is short and transient, cheerfulness fixed and permanent. Those are often raised into the greatest transports of mirth who are subject to the greatest depression of melancholy : on the contrary, cheerfulness, though it does not give the mind such an exquisite gladness, prevents us from falling into any depths of sorrow. Mirth is like a flash of lightning that breaks through a gloom of clouds, and glitters for a moment ; cheerfulness keeps up a kind of daylight in the mind, and fills it with a steady and perpetual serenity.'—Addison : *Spectator*, No. 381.

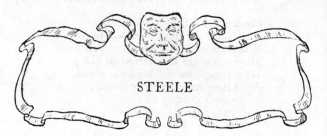

## STEELE

WHAT do we look for in studying the history of a past age? Is it to learn the political transactions and characters of the leading public men? is it to make ourselves acquainted with the life and being of the time? If we set out with the former grave purpose, where is the truth, and who believes that he has it entire? What character of what great man is known to you? You can but make guesses as to character more or less happy. In common life don't you often judge and misjudge a man's whole conduct, setting out from a wrong impression? The tone of a voice, a word said in joke, or a trifle in behaviour—the cut of his hair or the tie of his neckcloth may disfigure him in your eyes, or poison your good opinion; or at the end of years of intimacy it may be your closest friend says something, reveals something which had previously been a secret, which alters all your views about him, and shows that he has been acting on quite a different motive to that which you fancied you knew. And if it is so with those you know, how much more with those you don't know? Say, for example, that I want to understand the character of the Duke of Marlborough. I read Swift's history of the times in which he took a part; the shrewdest of observers and initiated, one would think, into the politics of the age—he hints to me that Marlborough was a coward, and even of doubtful military capacity: he speaks of

Walpole as a contemptible boor, and scarcely mentions, except to flout it, the great intrigue of the Queen's latter days, which was to have ended in bringing back the Pretender. Again, I read Marlborough's Life by a copious archdeacon, who has the command of immense papers, of sonorous language, of what is called the best information; and I get little or no insight into this secret motive which, I believe, influenced the whole of Marlborough's career, which caused his turnings and windings, his opportune fidelity and treason, stopped his army almost at Paris gate, and landed him finally on the Hanoverian side— the winning side: I get, I say, no truth, or only a portion of it, in the narrative of either writer, and believe that Coxe's portrait, or Swift's portrait, is quite unlike the real Churchill. I take this as a single instance, prepared to be as sceptical about any other, and say to the Muse of History, 'O venerable daughter of Mnemosyne, I doubt every single statement you ever made since your ladyship was a Muse! For all your grave airs and high pretensions, you are not a whit more trustworthy than some of your lighter sisters on whom your partisans look down. You bid me listen to a general's oration to his soldiers: Nonsense! He no more made it than Turpin made his dying speech at Newgate. You pronounce a panegyric on a hero: I doubt it, and say you flatter outrageously. You utter the condemnation of a loose character: I doubt it, and think you are prejudiced and take the side of the Dons. You offer me an autobiography: I doubt all autobiographies I ever read; except those, perhaps, of Mr. Robinson Crusoe, Mariner, and writers of his class. *These* have no object in setting themselves right with the public or their own consciences; these have no motive for concealment or half-truths; these call for no more confidence than I can cheerfully give, and do not force me to tax my credulity or to fortify it by evidence. I take up a volume of Doctor Smollett, or a volume of the *Spectator*, and say the fiction carries a greater amount of truth in solution than the volume which purports to be all true. Out of the fictitious book I get the expression of the life of the time; of the manners, of the movement, the dress, the pleasures, the laughter, the ridicules of society—the old times live again, and I travel in the old country of England. Can the heaviest historian do more for me?'

As we read in these delightful volumes of the *Tatler* and *Spectator* the past age returns, the England of our ancestors is revivified. The Maypole rises in the Strand again in London; the churches are thronged with daily worshippers; the beaux are gathering in the coffee-houses; the gentry are going to the Drawing-room; the ladies are thronging to the toy-shops; the chairmen are jostling in the streets; the footmen are running with links before the chariots, or fighting round the theatre doors. In the country I see the young Squire riding to Eton with his servants behind him, and Will Wimble, the friend of the family, to see him safe. To make that journey from the Squire's and back, Will is a week on horseback. The coach takes five days between London and Bath. The Judges and the bar ride the circuit. If my Lady comes to town in her post-chariot, her people carry pistols to fire a salute on Captain Macheath if he should appear, and her couriers ride ahead to prepare apartments for her at the great caravanserais on the road; Boniface receives her under the creaking sign of the 'Bell' or the 'Ram,' and he and his chamberlains bow her up the great stair to the state apartments, whilst her carriage rumbles into the courtyard, where the 'Exeter Fly' is housed that

Bragging of Ramillies
and Malplaquet.

performs the journey in eight days, God willing,
having achieved its daily flight of twenty miles, and
landed its passengers for supper and sleep. The curate
is taking his pipe in the kitchen, where the Captain's
man—having hung up his master's half-pike—is at
his bacon and eggs, bragging of Ramillies and Malplaquet to the townsfolk, who have their club in the
chimney-corner. The Captain is ogling the chamber-
maid in the wooden gallery, or bribing her to know
who is the pretty young mistress that has come in the
coach. The pack-horses are in the great stable, and
the drivers and ostlers carousing in the tap. And in
Mrs. Landlady's bar, over a glass of strong waters, sits
a gentleman of military appearance, who travels with

pistols, as all the rest of the world does, and has a rattling grey mare in the stables which will be saddled and away with its owner half an hour before the 'Fly' sets out on its last day's flight. And some five miles on the road, as the 'Exeter Fly' comes jingling and creaking onwards, it will suddenly be brought to a halt by a gentleman on a grey mare, with a black vizard on his face, who thrusts a long pistol into the coach window, and bids the company to hand out their purses. . . . It must have been no small pleasure even to sit in the great kitchen in those days, and see the tide of humankind pass by. We arrive at places now, but we travel no more. Addison talks jocularly of a difference of manner and costume being quite perceivable at Staines, where there passed a young fellow 'with a very tolerable periwig,' though, to be sure, his hat was out of fashion, and had a Ramillies cock. I would have liked to travel in those days (being of that class of travellers who were proverbially pretty easy *coram latronibus*) and have seen my friend with the grey mare and the black vizard. Alas! there always came a day in the life of that warrior when it was the fashion to accompany him as he passed—without his black mask, and with a nose-gay in his hand, accompanied by halberdiers and attended by the sheriff,—in a carriage without springs, and a clergyman jolting beside him, to a spot close by Cumberland Gate and the Marble Arch, where a stone still records that here Tyburn turnpike stood. What a change in a century; in a few years! Within a few yards of that gate the fields began: the fields of his exploits, behind the hedges of which he lurked and robbed. A great and wealthy city has grown over those meadows. Were a man brought to die there now, the windows would be closed and the inhabitants keep their houses in sickening horror. A hundred years back, people crowded to see that last act of a highwayman's life, and make jokes on it. Swift laughed at him, grimly advising him to provide a Holland shirt and white cap crowned with a crimson or black ribbon for his exit, to mount the cart cheerfully—shake hands with the hangman, and so—farewell. Gay wrote the most delightful ballads, and made merry over the same hero. Contrast these with the writings of our present humourists! Compare those morals and ours—those manners and ours!

We can't tell—you would not bear to be told—the whole truth regarding those men and manners. You could no more suffer in a British drawing-room, under the reign of Queen Victoria, a fine gentleman or fine lady of Queen Anne's time, or hear what they heard and said, than you would receive an ancient Briton. It is as one reads about savages, that one contemplates the wild ways, the barbarous feasts, the terrific pastimes, of the men of pleasure of that age. We have our fine gentlemen, and our 'fast men;' permit me to give you an idea of one particularly fast nobleman of Queen Anne's days, whose biography has been preserved to us by the law reporters.

In 1691, when Steele was a boy at school, my Lord Mohun was tried by his peers for the murder of William Mountford, comedian. In 'Howell's State Trials,' the reader will find not only an edifying account of this exceedingly fast nobleman, but of the times and manners of those days. My Lord's friend, a Captain Hill, smitten with the charms of the beautiful Mrs. Bracegirdle, and anxious to marry her at all hazards, determined to carry her off, and for this purpose hired a hackney-coach with six horses, and a half-dozen of soldiers, to aid him in the storm. The coach with a pair of horses (the four leaders being in

waiting elsewhere) took its station opposite my Lord
Craven's house in Drury Lane, by which door Mrs.
Bracegirdle was to pass on her way from the theatre.
As she passed in company of her mamma and a friend,
Mr. Page, the Captain seized her by the hand, the
soldiers hustled Mr. Page and attacked him sword in
hand, and Captain Hill and his noble friend endeavoured to force Madam Bracegirdle into the coach.
Mr. Page called for help : the population of Drury
Lane rose : it was impossible to effect the capture ;
and bidding the soldiers go about their business, and
the coach to drive off, Hill let go of his prey sulkily,
and waited for other opportunities of revenge. The
man of whom he was most jealous was Will Mountford, the comedian ; Will removed, he thought Mrs.
Bracegirdle might be his : and accordingly the
Captain and his Lordship lay that night in wait for
Will, and as he was coming out of a house in Norfolk
Street, while Mohun engaged him in talk, Hill, in
the words of the Attorney-General, made a pass and
ran him clean through the body.

Sixty-one of my Lord's peers finding him not guilty
of murder, while but fourteen found him guilty, this
very fast nobleman was discharged : and made his appearance seven years after in another trial for murder
—when he, my Lord Warwick, and three gentlemen
of the military profession, were concerned in the fight
which ended in the death of Captain Coote.

This jolly company were drinking together in
'Lockit's' at Charing Cross, when angry words arose
between Captain Coote and Captain French ; whom
my Lord Mohun and my Lord the Earl of Warwick *

---

* The husband of the Lady Warwick who married Addison, and the
father of the young Earl, who was brought to his stepfather's bed to see
'how a Christian could die.' He was amongst the wildest of the nobility
of that day ; and in the curious collection of Chap-Books at the British

and Holland endeavoured to pacify. My Lord Warwick was a dear friend of Captain Coote, lent him a
hundred pounds to buy his commission in the Guards ;
once when the Captain was arrested for thirteen pounds
by his tailor, my Lord lent him five guineas, often
paid his reckoning for him, and showed him other
offices of friendship. On this evening the disputants,
French and Coote, being separated whilst they were
upstairs, unluckily stopped to drink ale again at the
bar of ' Lockit's.' The row began afresh—Coote
lunged at French over the bar, and at last all six
called for chairs, and went to Leicester Fields, where
they fell to. Their Lordships engaged on the side of
Captain Coote. My Lord of Warwick was severely
wounded in the hand, Mr. French also was stabbed,
but honest Captain Coote got a couple of wounds—
one especially, ' a wound in the left side just under
the short ribs, and piercing through the diaphragma,'
which did for Captain Coote. Hence the trials of
my Lords Warwick and Mohun : hence the assemblage of peers, the report of the transaction in which
these defunct fast men still live for the observation of
the curious. My Lord of Warwick is brought to
the bar by the Deputy-Governor of the Tower of
London, having the axe carried before him by the
gentleman gaoler, who stood with it at the bar at
the right hand of the prisoner, turning the edge from

Museum, I have seen more than one anecdote of the freaks of the gay
lord. He was popular in London, as such daring spirits have been in
our time. The anecdotists speak very kindly of his practical jokes.
Mohun was scarcely out of prison for his second homicide, when he
went on Lord Macclesfield's embassy to the Elector of Hanover when
Queen Anne sent the Garter to his Highness. The chronicler of the
expedition speaks of his Lordship as an amiable young man, who had
been in bad company, but was quite repentant and reformed. He and
Macartney afterwards murdered the Duke of Hamilton between them,
in which act Lord Mohun died. This amiable Baron's name was
Charles, and not Henry, as a recent novelist has christened him.

him; the prisoner, at his approach, making three bows, one to his Grace the Lord High Steward, the other to the peers on each hand; and his Grace and the peers returned the salute. And besides these great personages, august in periwigs, and nodding to the right and left, a host of the small come up out of the past and pass before us—the jolly captains brawling in the tavern, and laughing and cursing over their cups—the drawer that serves, the bar-girl that waits, the bailiff on the prowl, the chairmen trudging through the black, lampless streets, and smoking their pipes by the railings, whilst swords are clashing in the garden within. 'Help there! a gentleman is hurt!' The chairmen put up their pipes, and help the gentleman over the railings, and carry him, ghastly and bleeding, to the Bagnio in Long Acre, where they knock up the surgeon—a pretty tall gentleman: but that wound under the short ribs has done for him. Surgeon, lords, captains, bailiffs, chairmen, and gentleman gaoler with your axe, where be you now? The gentleman axeman's head is off his own shoulders; the lords and judges can wag theirs no longer; the bailiff's writs have ceased to run: the honest chairmen's pipes are put out, and with their brawny calves they have walked away into Hades—all is irrecoverably done for as Will Mountford or Captain Coote. The subject of our night's lecture saw all these people—rode in Captain Coote's company of the Guards, very probably—wrote and sighed for Bracegirdle, went home tipsy in many a chair, after many a bottle, in many a tavern—fled from many a bailiff.

In 1709, when the publication of the *Tatler* began, our great-great-grandfathers must have seized upon that new and delightful paper with much such eagerness as lovers of light literature in a later day exhibited

STEELE                    97

when the Waverley novels appeared, upon which the
public rushed, forsaking that feeble entertainment of
which the Miss Porters, the Anne of Swanseas, and
worthy Mrs. Radcliffe herself, with her dreary castles
and exploded old ghosts, had had pretty much the
monopoly.  I have looked over many of the comic
books with which our ancestors amused themselves,
from the novels of Swift's coadjutrix, Mrs. Manley, the
delectable author of the 'New Atlantis,' to the
facetious productions of Tom Durfey, and Tom Brown,
and Ned Ward, writer of the 'London Spy' and
several other volumes of ribaldry.  The slang of the
taverns and ordinaries, the wit of the bagnios, form
the strongest part of the farrago of which these libels
are composed.  In the excellent newspaper collection
at the British Museum, you may see, besides, the
*Craftsmen* and *Postboy* specimens—and queer specimens
they are—of the higher literature of Queen Anne's
time.  Here is an abstract from a notable journal
bearing date Wednesday, October 13th, 1708, and
entitled *The British Apollo; or, curious amusements for
the ingenious, by a society of gentlemen*.  The *British
Apollo* invited and professed to answer questions upon
all subjects of wit, morality, science, and even
religion ; and two out of its four pages are filled with
queries and replies much like some of the oracular
penny prints of the present time.

One of the first querists, referring to the passage
that a bishop should be the husband of one wife, argues
that polygamy is justifiable in the laity.  The society
of gentlemen conducting the *British Apollo* are posed
by this casuist, and promise to give him an answer.
Celinda then wishes to know from 'the gentlemen'
concerning the souls of the dead, whether they shall
have the satisfaction to know those whom they most
valued in this transitory life.  The gentlemen of the

*Apollo* give but poor comfort to poor Celinda. They
are inclined to think not ; for, say they, since every
inhabitant of those regions will be infinitely dearer
than here are our nearest relatives—what have we to
do with a partial friendship in that happy place ? Poor
Celinda ! it may have been a child or a lover whom
she had lost, and was pining after, when the oracle of
*British Apollo* gave her this dismal answer. She has
solved the question for herself by this time, and knows
quite as well as the society of gentlemen.

From theology we come to physics, and Q. asks,
'Why does hot water freeze sooner than cold ?' *Apollo*
replies, 'Hot water cannot be said to freeze sooner
than cold ; but water once heated and cold may be
subject to freeze by the evaporation of the spirituous
parts of the water, which renders it less able to with-
stand the power of frosty weather.'

The next query is rather a delicate one. 'You,
Mr. Apollo, who are said to be the God of Wisdom,
pray give us the reason why kissing is so much in
fashion : what benefit one receives by it, and who was
the inventor, and you will oblige Corinna.' To this
queer demand the lips of Phœbus, smiling, answer :
'Pretty innocent Corinna ! *Apollo* owns that he was
a little surprised by your kissing question, particularly
at that part of it where you desire to know the
benefit you receive by it. Ah ! madam, had you a
lover, you would not come to *Apollo* for a solution ;
since there is no dispute but the kisses of mutual lovers
give infinite satisfaction. As to its invention, 'tis
certain nature was its author, and it began with the
first courtship.'

After a column more of questions, follow nearly two
pages of poems, signed by Philander, Armenia, and
the like, and chiefly on the tender passion ; and the
paper winds up with a letter from Leghorn, an account

of the Duke of Marlborough and Prince Eugene before
Lille, and proposals for publishing two sheets on the
present state of Æthiopia, by Mr. Hill : all of which
is printed for the authors by J. Mayo, at the Printing
Press against Water Lane in Fleet Street. What a
change it must have been—how *Apollo's* oracles must
have been struck dumb—when the *Tatler* appeared,
and scholars, gentlemen, men of the world, men of
genius, began to speak !

Shortly before the Boyne was fought, and young
Swift had begun to make acquaintance with English
Court manners and English servitude, in Sir William
Temple's family, another Irish youth was brought to
learn his humanities at the old school of Charterhouse,
near Smithfield ; to which foundation he had been
appointed by James Duke of Ormond, a governor of
the House, and a patron of the lad's family. The boy
was an orphan, and described, twenty years after, with
a sweet pathos and simplicity, some of the earliest
recollections of a life which was destined to be
chequered by a strange variety of good and evil
fortune.

I am afraid no good report could be given by his
masters and ushers of that thick-set, square-faced,
black-eyed, soft-hearted little Irish boy. He was very
idle. He was whipped deservedly a great number of
times. Though he had very good parts of his own,
he got other boys to do his lessons for him, and only
took just as much trouble as should enable him to
scuffle through his exercises, and by good fortune
escape the flogging-block. One hundred and fifty
years after, I have myself inspected, but only as an
amateur, that instrument of righteous torture still
existing, and in occasional use, in a secluded private
apartment of the old Charterhouse School ; and have
no doubt it is the very counterpart, if not the ancient

and interesting machine itself, at which poor Dick
Steele submitted himself to the tormentors.

Besides being very kind, lazy, and good-natured,
this boy went invariably into debt with the tart-
woman ; ran out of bounds, and entered into pecuniary,
or rather promissory, engagements with the neighbouring lollipop vendors and piemen—exhibited an early
fondness and capacity for drinking mum and sack, and
borrowed from all his comrades who had money to
lend. I have no sort of authority for the statements
here made of Steele's early life ; but if the child is
father of the man, the father of young Steele of
Merton, who left Oxford without taking a degree,
and entered the Life Guards—the father of Captain
Steele of Lucas's Fusiliers, who got his company
through the patronage of my Lord Cutts—the
father of Mr. Steele the Commissioner of Stamps, the
editor of the *Gazette*, the *Tatler*, and *Spectator*, the
expelled Member of Parliament, and the author of
the 'Tender Husband' and the 'Conscious Lovers;'
if man and boy resembled each other, Dick Steele the
schoolboy must have been one of the most generous,
good-for-nothing, amiable little creatures that ever
conjugated the verb *tupto*, I beat, *tuptomai*, I am
whipped, in any school in Great Britain.

Almost every gentleman who does me the honour to
hear me will remember that the very greatest character
which he has seen in the course of his life, and the
person to whom he has looked up with the greatest
wonder and reverence, was the head boy at his school.
The schoolmaster himself hardly inspires such an awe.
The head boy construes as well as the schoolmaster
himself. When he begins to speak the hall is hushed,
and every little boy listens. He writes off copies of
Latin verses as melodiously as Virgil. He is good-
natured, and, his own masterpieces achieved, pours

out other copies of verses for other boys with an
astonishing ease and fluency; the idle ones only
trembling lest they should be discovered on giving in
their exercises, and whipped because their poems were
too good. I have seen great men in my time, but
never such a great one as that head boy of my childhood: we all thought he must be Prime Minister,
and I was disappointed on meeting him in after life
to find he was no more than six feet high.

Dick Steele, the Charterhouse gownboy, contracted
such an admiration in the years of his childhood, and
retained it faithfully through his life. Through the
school and through the world, whithersoever his
strange fortune led this erring, wayward, affectionate
creature, Joseph Addison was always his head boy.
Addison wrote his exercises. Addison did his best
themes. He ran on Addison's messages; fagged for
him and blacked his shoes: to be in Joe's company was
Dick's greatest pleasure; and he took a sermon or a
caning from his monitor with the most boundless
reverence, acquiescence, and affection.*

Steele found Addison a stately College Don at
Oxford, and himself did not make much figure at
this place. He wrote a comedy, which, by the advice
of a friend, the humble fellow burned there; and some
verses, which I dare say are as sublime as other
gentlemen's compositions at that age; but being
smitten with a sudden love for military glory, he
threw up the cap and gown for the saddle and bridle,
and rode privately in the Horse Guards, in the Duke

---

* 'Steele had the greatest veneration for Addison, and used to show
it, in all companies, in a particular manner. Addison, now and then,
used to play a little upon him; but he always took it well.'—POPE.
*Spence's Anecdotes.*
    'Sir Richard Steele was the best-natured creature in the world:
even in his worst state of health, he seemed to desire nothing but to
please and be pleased.'—DR. YOUNG. *Spence's Anecdotes.*

of Ormond's troop—the second—and, probably, with the rest of the gentlemen of his troop, 'all mounted on black horses with white feathers in their hats, and scarlet coats richly laced,' marched by King William, in Hyde Park, in November 1699, and a great show of the nobility, besides twenty thousand people, and above a thousand coaches. 'The Guards had just got their new clothes,' the *London Post* said: 'they are extraordinary grand, and thought to be the finest body of horse in the world.' But Steele could hardly have seen any actual service. He who wrote about himself, his mother, his wife, his loves, his debts, his friends, and the wine he drank, would have told us of his battles if he had seen any. His old patron, Ormond, probably got him his cornetcy in the Guards, from which he was promoted to be a captain in Lucas's Fusiliers, getting his company through the patronage of Lord Cutts, whose secretary he was, and to whom he dedicated his work called the 'Christian Hero.' As for Dick, whilst writing this ardent devotional work, he was deep in debt, in drink, and in all the follies of the town; it is related that all the officers of Lucas's, and the gentlemen of the Guards, laughed at Dick.* And in truth a

---

* 'The gaiety of his dramatic tone may be seen in this little scene between two brilliant sisters, from his comedy *The Funeral, or Grief à la Mode*. Dick wrote this, he said, from "a necessity of enlivening his character," which, it seemed, the *Christian Hero* had a tendency to make too decorous, grave, and respectable in the eyes of readers of that pious piece.

[*Scene draws and discovers* LADY CHARLOTTE, *reading at a table,—* LADY HARRIET, *playing at a glass, to and fro, and viewing herself.*]

'*L. Ha* Nay, good sage sister, you may as well talk to me [*looking at herself as she speaks*] as sit staring at a book which I know you can't attend. Good Dr. Lucas may have writ there what he pleases, but there's no putting Francis, Lord Hardy, now Earl of Brumpton, out of

theologian in liquor is not a respectable object, and a hermit, though he may be out at elbows, must not be in debt to the tailor. Steele says of himself that he

your head, or making him absent from your eyes. Do but look on me, now, and deny it if you can.

*L. Ch.* You are the maddest girl [*smiling*].

*L. Ha.* Look ye, I knew you could not say it and forbear laughing. [*Looking over Charlotte.*]—Oh! I see his name as plain as you do—F-r-a-n, Fran, —c-i-s, cis, Francis, 'tis in every line of the book.

*L. Ch.* [*rising*]. 'Tis in vain, I see, to mind anything in such impertinent company—but, granting 'twere as you say, as to my Lord Hardy—'tis more excusable to admire another than oneself.

*L. Ha.* No, I think not,—yes, I grant you, than really to be vain at one's person, but I don't admire myself,—Pish! I don't believe my eyes to have that softness. [*Looking in the glass.*] They a'n't so piercing : no, 'tis only stuff, the men will be talking.—Some people are such admirers of teeth—Lord, what signifies teeth? [*Showing her teeth.*] A very black-a-moor has as white teeth as I.—No, sister, I don't admire myself, but I've a spirit of contradiction in me : I don't know I'm in love with myself, only to rival the men.

*L. Ch.* Ay, but Mr. Campley will gain ground ev'n of that rival of his, your dear self.

*L. Ha.* Oh, what have I done to you, that you should name that insolent intruder? A confident, opinionative fop. No, indeed, if I am, as a poetical lover of mine sighed and sung of both sexes,

"The public envy and the public care,"

I shan't be so easily catched—I thank him—I want but to be sure I should heartily torment him by banishing him, and then consider whether he should depart this life or not.

*L. Ch.* Indeed, sister, to be serious with you, this vanity in your humour does not at all become you.

*L. Ha.* Vanity! All the matter is, we gay people are more sincere than you wise folks : all your life's an art.—Speak your soul.—Look you there.— [*Hauling her to the glass.*] Are you not struck with a secret pleasure when you view that bloom in your look, that harmony in your shape, that promptitude in your mien?

*L. Ch.* Well, simpleton, if I am at first so simple as to be a little taken with myself, I know it a fault, and take pains to correct it.

*L. Ha.* Pshaw! Pshaw! Talk this musty tale to old Mrs. Fardingale, 'tis too soon for me to think at that rate.

*L. Ch.* They that think it too soon to understand themselves will very soon find it too late.—But tell me honestly, don't you like Campley?

*L. Ha.* The fellow is not to be abhorred, if the forward thing did not think of getting me so easily.—Oh, I hate a heart I can't break

.was always sinning and repenting. He beat his breast and cried most piteously when he *did* repent; but as soon as crying had made him thirsty, he fell to sinning again. In that charming paper in the *Tatler*, in which he records his father's death, his mother's griefs, his own most solemn and tender emotions, he says he is interrupted by the arrival of a hamper of wine, 'the same as is to be sold at Garraway's, next week;' upon the receipt of which he sends for three friends, and they fall to instantly, 'drinking two bottles apiece with great benefit to themselves, and not separating till two o'clock in the morning.'

His life was so. Jack the drawer was always interrupting it, bringing him a bottle from the 'Rose,' or inviting him over to a bout there with Sir Plume and Mr. Diver: and Dick wiped his eyes, which were whimpering over his papers, took down his laced hat, put on his sword and wig, kissed his wife and children, told them a lie about pressing business, and went off to the 'Rose' to the jolly fellows.

While Mr. Addison was abroad, and after he came home in rather a dismal way to wait upon Providence in his shabby lodging in the Haymarket, young Captain Steele was cutting a much smarter figure than that of his classical friend of Charterhouse Cloister and Maudlin Walk. Could not some painter give an interview between the gallant Captain of Lucas's, with his hat cocked, and his lace, and his face too, a trifle tarnished with drink, and that poet, that philosopher, pale, proud, and poor, his friend and monitor

when I please.—What makes the value of dear china, but that 'tis so brittle?—were it not for that, you might as well have stone mugs in your closet.'—*The Funeral*, Act. 2nd.

'We knew the obligations the stage had to his writings [Steele's]; there being scarcely a comedian of merit in our whole company whom his *Tatlers* had not made better by his recommendation of them.'—*Cibber.*

of schooldays, of all days?  How Dick must have
bragged about his chances and his hopes, and the fine
company he kept, and the charms of the reigning
toasts and popular actresses, and the number of bottles
that he and my Lord and some other pretty fellows
had cracked over-night at the ' Devil,' or the ' Garter ' !
Cannot one fancy Joseph Addison's calm smile and
cold grey eyes following Dick for an instant, as he
struts down the Mall to dine with the Guard at Saint
James's, before he turns, with his sober pace and
threadbare suit, to walk back to his lodgings up the
two pair of stairs?  Steele's name was down for promotion, Dick always said himself, in the glorious,
pious, and immortal William's last table-book.
Jonathan Swift's name had been written there by the
same hand too.

Our worthy friend, the author of the ' Christian
Hero,' continued to make no small figure about town
by the use of his wits.*  He was appointed Gazetteer :
he wrote, in 1703, ' The Tender Husband,' his second
play, in which there is some delightful farcical writing,
and of which he fondly owned in after life, and when
Addison was no more, that there were ' many applauded
strokes' from Addison's beloved hand.†  Is it not a

* ' There is not now in his sight that excellent man, whom Heaven
made his friend and superior, to be at a certain place in pain for what he
should say or do.  I will go on in his further encouragement.  The
best woman that ever man had cannot now lament and pine at his
neglect of himself.'—STEELE [of himself] : *The Theatre.* No. 12,
Feb. 1719-20.

† *The Funeral* supplies an admirable stroke of humour,—one which
Sydney Smith has used as an illustration of the faculty in his lectures.

The undertaker is talking to his *employés* about their duty.

' *Sable.* Ha, you !—a little more upon the dismal [*forming their
countenances*] ; this fellow has a good mortal look,—place him near the
corpse : that wainscot-face must be o' top of the stairs ; that fellow's
almost in a fright (that looks as if he were full of some strange misery)
at the end of the hall.  So—But I'll fix you all myself.  Let's have no
laughing now on any provocation.  Look yonder—that hale, well-

pleasant partnership to remember? Can't one fancy Steele full of spirits and youth, leaving his gay company to go to Addison's lodging, where his friend sits in the shabby sitting-room, quite serene, and cheerful, and poor? In 1704, Steele came on the town with another comedy, and behold it was so moral and religious, as poor Dick insisted,—so dull the town thought,—that the 'Lying Lover' was damned.

Addison's hour of success now came, and he was able to help our friend the 'Christian Hero' in such a way, that, if there had been any chance of keeping that poor tipsy champion upon his legs, his fortune was safe, and his competence assured. Steele procured the place of Commissioner of Stamps: he wrote so richly, so gracefully often, so kindly always, with such a pleasant wit and easy frankness, with such a gush of good spirits and good humour, that his early papers may be compared to Addison's own, and are to be read, by a male reader at least, with quite an equal pleasure.*

looking puppy! You ungrateful scoundrel, did not I pity you, take you out of a great man's service, and show you the pleasure of receiving wages? *Did not I give you ten, then fifteen, and twenty shillings a week to be sorrowful?—and the more I give you I think the gladder you are!*'

* ' FROM MY OWN APARTMENT : *Nov.* 16.

'There are several persons who have many pleasures and entertainments in their possession which they do not enjoy; it is, therefore, a kind and good office to acquaint them with their own happiness, and turn their attention to such instances of their good fortune as they are apt to overlook. Persons in the married state often want such a monitor; and pine away their days by looking upon the same condition in anguish and murmuring, which carries with it, in the opinion of others, a complication of all the pleasures of life, and a retreat from its inquietudes.

'I am led into this thought by a visit I made to an old friend who was formerly my schoolfellow. He came to town last week, with his family, for the winter; and yesterday morning sent me word his wife expected me to dinner. I am, as it were, at home at that house, and every member of it knows me for their well-wisher. I cannot, indeed, express the pleasure it is to be met by the children with so much joy

After the *Tatler* in 1711, the famous *Spectator* made its appearance, and this was followed, at various

as I am when I go thither. The boys and girls strive who shall come first, when they think it is I that am knocking at the door; and that child which loses the race to me runs back again to tell the father it is Mr. Bickerstaff. This day I was led in by a pretty girl that we all thought must have forgot me; for the family has been out of town these two years. Her knowing me again was a mighty subject with us, and took up our discourse at the first entrance; after which, they began to rally me upon a thousand little stories they heard in the country, about my marriage to one of my neighbours' daughters: upon which, the gentleman, my friend, said, "Nay; if Mr. Bickerstaff marries a child of any of his old companions, I hope mine shall have the preference: there is Mrs. Mary is now sixteen, and would make him as fine a widow as the best of them. But I know him too well; he is so enamoured with the very memory of those who flourished in our youth, that he will not so much as look upon the modern beauties. I remember, old gentleman, how often you went home in a day to refresh your countenance and dress when Teraminta reigned in your heart. As we came up in the coach, I repeated to my wife some of your verses on her." With such reflections on little passages which happened long ago, we passed our time during a cheerful and elegant meal. After dinner his lady left the room, as did also the children. As soon as we were alone, he took me by the hand: "Well, my good friend," says he, "I am heartily glad to see thee; I was afraid you would never have seen all the company that dined with you to-day again. Do not you think the good woman of the house a little altered since you followed her from the playhouse to find out who she was for me?" I perceived a tear fall down his cheek as he spoke, which moved me not a little. But, to turn the discourse, I said, "She is not, indeed, that creature she was when she returned me the letter I carried from you, and told me, 'She hoped, as I was a gentleman, I would be employed no more to trouble her, who had never offended me; but would be so much the gentleman's friend as to dissuade him from a pursuit which he could never succeed in.' You may remember I thought her in earnest, and you were forced to employ your cousin Will, who made his sister get acquainted with her for you. You cannot expect her to be for ever fifteen." "Fifteen!" replied my good friend. "Ah! you little understand—you, that have lived a bachelor—how great, how exquisite a pleasure there is in being really beloved! It is impossible that the most beauteous face in nature should raise in me such pleasing ideas as when I look upon that excellent woman. That fading in her countenance is chiefly caused by her watching with me in my fever. This was followed by a fit of sickness, which had like to have carried me off last winter. I tell you, sincerely, I have so many obligations to her that I cannot, with any sort of moderation, think of her present state of health. But, as to what you say of fifteen, she gives me every day pleasure beyond what I ever knew in the possession

intervals, by many periodicals under the same editor—
the *Guardian*—the *Englishman*—the *Lover*, whose love
of her beauty when I was in the vigour of youth. Every moment of her
life brings me fresh instances of her complacency to my inclinations, and
her prudence in regard to my fortune. Her face is to me much more
beautiful than when I first saw it ; there is no decay in any feature which
I cannot trace from the very instant it was occasioned by some anxious
concern for my welfare and interests. Thus, at the same time, methinks,
the love I conceived towards her for what she was, is heightened by my
gratitude for what she is. The love of a wife is as much above the
idle passion commonly called by that name, as the loud laughter of
buffoons is inferior to the elegant mirth of gentlemen. Oh ! she is an
inestimable jewel ! In her examination of her household affairs, she
shows a certain fearfulness to find a fault, which makes her servants obey
her like children ; and the meanest we have has an ingenious shame for
an offence not always to be seen in children in other families. I speak
freely to you, my old friend ; ever since her sickness, things that gave
me the quickest joy before turn now to a certain anxiety. As the
children play in the next room, I know the poor things by their steps,
and am considering what they must do should they lose their mother in
their tender years. The pleasure I used to take in telling my boy stories
of battles, and asking my girl questions about the disposal of her baby,
and the gossiping of it, is turned into inward reflection and melancholy."

'He would have gone on in this tender way, when the good lady
entered, and, with an inexpressible sweetness in her countenance, told us,
"she had been searching her closet for something very good to treat
such an old friend as I was." Her husband's eyes sparkled with pleasure
at the cheerfulness of her countenance ; and I saw all his fears vanish
in an instant. The lady observing something in our looks which
showed we had been more serious than ordinary, and seeing her husband
receive her with great concern under a forced cheerfulness, immediately
guessed at what we had been talking of ; and applying herself to me,
said, with a smile, " Mr. Bickerstaff, do not believe a word of what he
tells you ; I shall still live to have you for my second, as I have often
promised you, unless he takes more care of himself than he has done
since his coming to town. You must know he tells me, that he finds
London is a much more healthy place than the country ; for he sees
several of his old acquaintances and schoolfellows are here—*young fellows
with fair, full-bottomed periwigs*. I could scarce keep him this morning
from going out *open-breasted*." My friend, who is always extremely
delighted with her agreeable humour, made her sit down with us. She
did it with that easiness which is peculiar to women of sense ; and to
keep up the good humour she had brought in with her, turned her
raillery upon me. " Mr. Bickerstaff, you remember you followed me
one night from the playhouse ; suppose you should carry me thither to-
morrow night, and lead me in the front box." This put us into a long

was rather insipid—the *Reader*, of whom the public
saw no more after his second appearance—the *Theatre*,
under the pseudonym of Sir John Edgar, which Steele
wrote while Governor of the Royal Company of
Comedians, to which post, and to that of Surveyor of
the Royal Stables at Hampton Court, and to the

field of discourse about the beauties who were the mothers to the present,
and shined in the boxes twenty years ago. I told her "I was glad she
had transferred so many of her charms, and I did not question but her
eldest daughter was within half-a-year of being a toast."

' We were pleasing ourselves with this fantastical preferment of the
young lady, when, on a sudden, we were alarmed with the noise of a
drum, and immediately entered my little godson to give me a point of
war. His mother, between laughing and chiding, would have put him
out of the room ; but I would not part with him so. I found upon conversation with him, though he was a little noisy in his mirth, that the
child had excellent parts, and was a great master of all the learning on
the other side of eight years old. I perceived him a very great historian
in *Æsop's Fables ;* but he frankly declared to me his mind, "that he did
not delight in that learning, because he did not believe they were true ;"
for which reason I found he had very much turned his studies, for about
a twelvemonth past, into the lives of Don Bellianis of Greece, Guy of
Warwick, "the Seven Champions," and other historians of that age. I
could not but observe the satisfaction the father took in the forwardness
of his son, and that these diversions might turn to some profit. I found
the boy had made remarks which might be of service to him during the
course of his whole life. He would tell you the mismanagement of
John Hickerthrift, find fault with the passionate temper in Bevis of
Southampton, and loved Saint George for being the champion of
England ; and by this means had his thoughts insensibly moulded into
the notions of discretion, virtue, and honour. I was extolling his
accomplishments, when his mother told me "that the little girl who led
me in this morning was, in her way, a better scholar than he." " Betty,"
said she, "deals chiefly in fairies and sprights ; and sometimes in a
winter night will terrify the maids with her accounts, until they are
afraid to go up to bed."

' I sat with them until it was very late, sometimes in merry sometimes in serious discourse, with this particular pleasure, which gives the
only true relish to all conversation, a sense that every one of us liked
each other. I went home, considering the different conditions of a
married life and that of a bachelor ; and I must confess it struck me
with a secret concern, to reflect, that whenever I go off I shall leave no
traces behind me. In this pensive mood I return to my family ; that is
to say, to my maid, my dog, my cat, who only can be the better or worse
for what happens to me.'—*The Tatler.*

Commission of the Peace for Middlesex, and to the honour of knighthood, Steele had been preferred soon after the accession of George I.; whose cause honest Dick had nobly fought, through disgrace and danger, against the most formidable enemies, against traitors and bullies, against Bolingbroke and Swift in the last reign. With the arrival of the King, that splendid conspiracy broke up; and a golden opportunity came to Dick Steele, whose hand, alas, was too careless to grip it.

Steele married twice; and outlived his places, his schemes, his wife, his income, his health, and almost everything but his kind heart. That ceased to trouble him in 1729, when he died, worn out and almost forgotten by his contemporaries, in Wales, where he had the remnant of a property.

Posterity has been kinder to this amiable creature; all women especially are bound to be grateful to Steele, as he was the first of our writers who really seemed to admire and respect them. Congreve the Great, who alludes to the low estimation in which women were held in Elizabeth's time, as a reason why the women of Shakspeare make so small a figure in the poet's dialogues, though he can himself pay splendid compliments to women, yet looks on them as mere instruments of gallantry, and destined, like the most consummate fortifications, to fall, after a certain time, before the arts and bravery of the besieger, man. There is a letter of Swift's entitled 'Advice to a very Young Married Lady,' which shows the Dean's opinion of the female society of his day, and that if he despised man he utterly scorned women too. No lady of our time could be treated by any man, were he ever so much a wit or Dean, in such a tone of insolent patronage and vulgar protection. In this performance, Swift hardly takes pains to hide his opinion that a

STEELE 111

woman is a fool: tells her to read books, as if reading
was a novel accomplishment : and informs her that
'not one gentleman's daughter in a thousand has been
brought to read or understand her own natural tongue.'
Addison laughs at women equally ; but, with the
gentleness and politeness of his nature, smiles at them
and watches them, as if they were harmless, half-
witted, amusing, pretty creatures, only made to be
men's playthings. It was Steele who first began to
pay a manly homage to their goodness and understanding, as well as to their tenderness and beauty.* In
his comedies the heroes do not rant and rave about
the divine beauties of Gloriana or Statira, as the
characters were made to do in the chivalry romances
and the high-flown dramas just going out of vogue ;
but Steele admires women's virtue, acknowledges their
sense, and adores their purity and beauty, with an
ardour and strength which should win the good-will
of all women to their hearty and respectful champion.
It is this ardour, this respect, this manliness, which
makes his comedies so pleasant and their heroes such
fine gentlemen. He paid the finest compliment to a
woman that perhaps ever was offered. Of one woman,
whom Congreve had also admired and celebrated,
Steele says, that 'to have loved her was a liberal
education.' 'How often,' he says, dedicating a

* ' As to the pursuits after affection and esteem, the fair sex are happy
in this particular, that with them the one is much more nearly related to
the other than in men. The love of a woman is inseparable from some
esteem of her ; and as she is naturally the object of affection, the woman
who has your esteem has also some degree of your love. A man that
dotes on a woman for her beauty, will whisper his friend, " That creature
has a great deal of wit when you are well acquainted with her." And if
you examine the bottom of your esteem for a woman, you will find you
have a greater opinion of her beauty than anybody else. As to us men, I
design to pass most of my time with the facetious Harry Bickerstaff ;
but William Bickerstaff, the most prudent man of our family, shall be
my executor.'—*Tatler*, No. 206.

volume to his wife, 'how often has your tenderness
removed pain from my sick head, how often anguish
from my afflicted heart! If there are such beings as
guardian angels, they are thus employed. I cannot
believe one of them to be more good in inclination, or
more charming in form, than my wife.' His breast
seems to warm and his eyes to kindle when he meets
with a good and beautiful woman, and it is with his
heart as well as with his hat that he salutes her.
About children, and all that relates to home, he is not
less tender, and more than once speaks in apology of
what he calls his softness. He would have been
nothing without that delightful weakness. It is that
which gives his works their worth and his style its
charm. It, like his life, is full of faults and careless
blunders; and redeemed, like that, by his sweet and
compassionate nature.

We possess of poor Steele's wild and chequered life
some of the most curious memoranda that ever were
left of a man's biography.* Most men's letters, from

---

* The Correspondence of Steele passed after his death into the possession of his daughter Elizabeth, by his second wife, Miss Scurlock, of
Carmarthenshire. She married the Hon. John, afterwards third Lord
Trevor. At her death, part of the letters passed to Mr. Thomas, a grandson of a natural daughter of Steele's; and part to Lady Trevor's next of
kin, Mr. Scurlock. They were published by the learned Nichols—from
whose later edition of them, in 1809, our specimens are quoted.

Here we have him, in his courtship—which was not a very long
one :—

' To Mrs. Scurlock.

' Aug. 30, 1707.

' MADAM,—I beg pardon that my paper is not finer, but I am forced
to write from a coffee-house, where I am attending about business.
There is a dirty crowd of busy faces all around me, talking of money :
while all my ambition, all my wealth, is love! Love which animates
my heart, sweetens my humour, enlarges my soul, and affects every
action of my life. It is to my lovely charmer I owe, that many noble
ideas are continually affixed to my words and actions ; it is the natural
effect of that generous passion to create in the admirer some similitude

Cicero down to Walpole, or down to the great men
of our own time, if you will, are doctored composi-

of the object admired. Thus, my dear, am I every day to improve from
so sweet a companion. Look up, my fair one, to that Heaven which
made thee such ; and join with me to implore its influence on our tender
innocent hours, and beseech the Author of love to bless the rites He has
ordained—and mingle with our happiness a just sense of our transient
condition, and a resignation to His will, which only can regulate our
minds to a steady endeavour to please Him and each other.

'I am for ever your faithful servant,

'RICH. STEELE.'

Some few hours afterwards, apparently, Mistress Scurlock received
the next one—obviously written later in the day !—

'*Saturday night (Aug.* 30, 1707).

' DEAR LOVELY MRS. SCURLOCK,—I have been in very good company,
where your health, under the character of *the woman I loved best*, has
been often drunk ; so that I may say that I am dead drunk for your
sake, which is more than *I die for you.*      RICH. STEELE.'

'*To Mrs. Scurlock.*

'*Sept.* 1, 1707.

' MADAM,—It is the hardest thing in the world to be in love, and yet
attend business. As for me, all who speak to me find me out, and I
must lock myself up, or other people will do it for me.

' A gentleman asked me this morning, " What news from Lisbon ? "
and I answered, " She is exquisitely handsome." Another desired to
know " when I had last been at Hampton Court ? " I replied, " It will
be on Tuesday come se'nnight." Pr'ythee allow me at least to kiss
your hand before that day, that my mind may be in some composure. O
Love !

' " A thousand torments dwell about thee,
   Yet who could live, to live without thee ? "

' Methinks I could write a volume to you ; but all the language on
earth would fail in saying how much, and with what disinterested
passion,                                      I am ever yours,

'RICH. STEELE.'

Two days after this, he is found expounding his circumstances and
prospects to the young lady's mamma. He dates from ' Lord Sunder-
land's office, Whitehall ;' and states his clear income at £1025 per
annum. ' I promise myself,' says he, ' the pleasure of an industrious and
virtuous life, in studying to do things agreeable to you.'

They were married, according to the most probable conjectures, about

tions, and written with an eye suspicious towards
posterity.  That dedication of Steele's to his wife is
an artificial performance, possibly ; at least, it is
written with that degree of artifice which an orator
uses in arranging a statement for the House, or a poet

the 7th Sept.   There are traces of a tiff about the middle of the next
month ; she being prudish and fidgety, as he was impassioned and reckless.   General progress, however, may be seen from the following notes.
The 'house in Bury Street, Saint James's,' was now taken.

'*To Mrs. Steele.*

'*Oct.* 16, 1707.

'DEAREST BEING ON EARTH,—Pardon me if you do not see me till
eleven o'clock, having met a  schoolfellow from India, by whom I am to
be informed on things this night which expressly concern your obedient
husband,                                                RICH. STEELE.'

'*To Mrs. Steele.*

'*Eight o'clock, Fountain Tavern* :
'*Oct.* 22, 1707.

'MY DEAR,—I beg of you not to be uneasy ; for I have done a great
deal of business to-day very successfully, and wait an hour or two about
my *Gazette.*'

'*Dec.* 22, 1707.

'MY DEAR, DEAR WIFE,—I write to let you know I do not come
home to dinner, being obliged to attend some business abroad, of which I
shall give you an account (when I see you in the evening), as becomes
your dutiful and obedient husband.'

'DEVIL TAVERN, TEMPLE BAR :
'*Jan.* 3, 1707-8.

'DEAR PRUE,—I have partly succeeded in my business to day, and in
close two guineas as earnest of more.   Dear Prue, I cannot come home
to dinner.   I languish for your welfare, and will never be a moment
careless more.                         Your faithful husband,' &c.

'*Jan.* 14, 1707-8

'DEAR WIFE,—Mr Edgecombe, Ned Ask, and Mr Lumley have
desired me to sit an hour with them at the " George," in Pall Mall, for
which I desire your patience till twelve o'clock, and that you will go to
bed,' &c.

'GRAY'S INN : *Feb.* 3, 1708.

'DEAR PRUE,—If the man who has my shoemaker's bill calls, let him
be answered that I shall call on him as I come home.   I stay here in

employs in preparing a sentiment in verse or for the
stage. But there are some four hundred letters of
Dick Steele's to his wife, which that thrifty woman
preserved accurately, and which could have been
written but for her and her alone. They contain
details of the business, pleasures, quarrels, reconcilia-
tions of the pair; they have all the genuineness of
conversation; they are as artless as a child's prattle,
and as confidential as a curtain-lecture. Some are
written from the printing-office, where he is waiting
for the proof-sheets of his *Gazette*, or his *Tatler*;
some are written from the tavern, whence he promises

order to get Jonson to discount a bill for me, and shall dine with him for
that end. He is expected at home every minute.
'Your most humble, obedient servant,' &c.

'Tennis-Court Coffee-house : *May* 5, 1708.

'Dear Wife,—I hope I have done this day what will be pleasing to
you; in the meantime shall lie this night at a baker's, one Leg, over
against the "Devil Tavern," at Charing Cross. I shall be able to con-
front the fools who wish me uneasy, and shall have the satisfaction to see
thee cheerful and at ease.

'If the printer's boy be at home, send him hither; and let Mrs.
Todd send by the boy my night-gown, slippers, and clean linen. You
shall hear from me early in the morning,' &c.

Dozens of similar letters follow, with occasional guineas, little parcels
of tea, or walnuts, &c. In 1709 the *Tatler* made its appearance. The
following curious note dates April 7th, 1710 :—

'I enclose to you, ["Dear Prue"] a receipt for the saucepan and spoon,
and a note of £23 of Lewis's, which will make up the £50 I promised
for your ensuing occasion.

'I know no happiness in this life in any degree comparable to the
pleasure I have in your person and society. I only beg of you to add to
your other charms a fearfulness to see a man that loves you in pain and un-
easiness, to make me as happy as it is possible to be in this life. Rising
a little in a morning, and being disposed to a cheerfulness . . . would
not be amiss.'

In another, he is found excusing his coming home, being 'invited to
supper to Mr. Boyle's.' 'Dear Prue,' he says on this occasion, 'do not
send after me, for I shall be ridiculous.'

to come to his wife 'within a pint of wine,' and where he has given a rendezvous to a friend or a money-lender : some are composed in a high state of vinous excitement, when his head is flustered with burgundy, and his heart abounds with amorous warmth for his darling Prue : some are under the influence of the dismal headache and repentance next morning : some, alas, are from the lock-up house where the lawyers have impounded him, and where he is waiting for bail. You trace many years of the poor fellow's career in these letters. In September 1707, from which day she began to save the letters, he married the beautiful Mistress Scurlock. You have his passionate protestations to the lady ; his respectful proposals to her mamma ; his private prayer to Heaven when the union so ardently desired was completed ; his fond professions of contrition and promises of amendment, when, immediately after his marriage, there began to be just cause for the one and need for the other.

Captain Steele took a house for his lady upon their marriage, 'the third door from Germain Street, left hand of Berry Street,' and the next year he presented his wife with a country house at Hampton. It appears she had a chariot and pair, and sometimes four horses : he himself enjoyed a little horse for his own riding. He paid, or promised to pay, his barber fifty pounds a year, and always went abroad in a laced coat and a large black buckled periwig, that must have cost somebody fifty guineas. He was rather a well-to-do gentleman, Captain Steele, with the proceeds of his estates in Barbadoes (left to him by his first wife), his income as a writer of the *Gazette*, and his office of gentleman waiter to His Royal Highness Prince George. His second wife brought him a fortune too. But it is melancholy to relate, that with these houses and chariots and horses and income, the Captain was constantly in want of money, for which his beloved bride was asking as constantly. In the course of a few pages we begin to find the shoemaker calling for money, and some directions from the Captain, who has not thirty pounds to spare. He sends his wife, 'the beautifullest object in the world,' as he calls her, and evidently in reply to applications of her own, which have gone the way of all waste paper, and lighted Dick's pipes, which were smoked a hundred and forty years ago—he sends his wife now a guinea, then a half-guinea, then a couple of guineas, then half a pound of tea; and again no money and no tea at all, but a promise that his darling Prue shall have some in a day or two : or a request, perhaps, that she will send over his night-gown and shaving - plate to the temporary lodging where the nomadic Captain is lying, hidden from the bailiffs. Oh ! that a Christian hero and late Captain in Lucas's should be afraid of a dirty sheriff's officer ! That the pink and pride of chivalry should turn pale before a writ ! It stands to record in poor Dick's own handwriting —the queer collection is preserved at the British Museum to this present day—that the rent of the nuptial house in Jermyn Street, sacred to unutterable tenderness and Prue, and three doors from Bury Street, was not paid until after the landlord had put in an execution on Captain Steele's furniture. Addison sold the house and furniture at Hampton, and, after deducting the sum which his incorrigible friend was indebted to him, handed over the residue of the proceeds of the sale to poor Dick, who wasn't in the least angry at Addison's summary proceeding, and I dare say was very glad of any sale or execution, the result of which was to give him a little ready money. Having a small house in Jermyn Street for which he couldn't pay, and a country house at Hampton on which he had borrowed money, nothing must content Captain Dick but the taking, in 1712, a much finer, larger, and grander house in Bloomsbury Square : where his unhappy landlord got no better satisfaction than his friend in Saint James's, and where it is recorded that Dick giving a grand entertainment, had a half-dozen queer-looking fellows in livery to wait upon his noble guests, and confessed that his servants were bailiffs to a man. 'I fared like a distressed prince,' the kindly prodigal writes, generously complimenting Addison for his assistance in the *Tatler*,—'I fared like a distressed prince, who calls in a powerful neighbour to his aid. I was undone by my auxiliary ; when I had once called him in, I could not subsist without dependence on him.' Poor needy Prince of Bloomsbury ! think of him in his palace with his allies from Chancery Lane ominously guarding him.

All sort of stories are told indicative of his recklessness and his good-humour. One narrated by Doctor Hoadly is exceedingly characteristic ; it shows the life of the time ; and our poor friend very weak, but very kind both in and out of his cups.

'My father,' says Doctor John Hoadly, the Bishop's son, 'when Bishop of Bangor, was, by invitation, present at one of the Whig meetings, held at the "Trumpet," in Shire Lane, when Sir Richard, in his zeal, rather exposed himself, having the double duty of the day upon him, as well to celebrate the immortal memory of King William, it being the 4th November, as to drink his friend Addison up to conversation pitch, whose phlegmatic constitution was hardly warmed for society by that time. Steele was not fit for it. Two remarkable circumstances happened. John Sly, the hatter of facetious memory, was in the house ; and John, pretty mellow, took it into his head to come into the company on his knees, with a tankard of ale in his hand to drink off to the *immortal memory*, and to return in the same manner. Steele, sitting next my father, whispered him—*Do laugh. It is humanity to laugh.* Sir Richard, in the evening, being too much in the same condition, was put into a chair, and sent home. Nothing would serve him but being carried to the Bishop of Bangor's, late as it was. However, the chairmen carried him home, and got him upstairs, when his great complaisance would wait on them downstairs, which he did, and then was got quietly to bed.' *

There is another amusing story which, I believe, that renowned collector, Mr. Joseph Miller, or his successors, have incorporated into their work. Sir Richard Steele, at a time when he was much occupied with theatrical affairs, built himself a pretty private theatre, and before it was opened to his friends and guests, was anxious to try whether the hall was well adapted for hearing. Accordingly he placed himself in the most remote part of the gallery, and begged the carpenter who had built the house to speak up from the stage. The man at first said that he was unaccustomed to public speaking, and did not know what to say to his honour ; but the good-natured knight called out to him to say whatever was uppermost ; and, after a moment, the carpenter began, in a voice perfectly audible : ' Sir Richard Steele !' he said, ' for three months past me and my men has been a working in this theatre, and we've never seen the colour of your honour's money : we will be very much obliged if you'll pay it directly, for until you do we won't drive in another nail.' Sir Richard said

* Of this famous Bishop, Steele wrote,—

'Virtue with so much ease on Bangor sits,
    All faults he pardons, though he none commits.'

that his friend's elocution was perfect, but that he didn't like his subject much.

The great charm of Steele's writing is its naturalness. He wrote so quickly and carelessly that he was forced to make the reader his confidant, and had not the time to deceive him. He had a small share of book-learning, but a vast acquaintance with the world. He had known men and taverns. He had lived with gownsmen, with troopers, with gentlemen ushers of the Court, with men and women of fashion ; with authors and wits, with the inmates of the spunging-houses, and with the frequenters of all the clubs and coffee-houses in the town. He was liked in all company because he liked it ; and you like to see his enjoyment as you like to see the glee of a boxful of children at the pantomime. He was not of those lonely ones of the earth whose greatness obliged them to be solitary ; on the contrary, he admired, I think, more than any man who ever wrote ; and full of hearty applause and sympathy, wins upon you by calling you to share his delight and good-humour. His laugh rings through the whole house. He must have been invaluable at a tragedy, and have cried as much as the most tender young lady in the boxes. He has a relish for beauty and goodness wherever he meets it. He admired Shakespeare affectionately, and more than any man of his time : and according to his generous expansive nature, called upon all his company to like what he liked himself. He did not damn with faint praise : he was in the world and of it ; and his enjoyment of life presents the strangest contrast to Swift's savage indignation and Addison's lonely serenity.*

* Here we have some of his later letters :—

'*To Lady Steele.*

'HAMPTON COURT : *March* 16, 1716-17.

DEAR PRUE,—If you have written anything to me which I should

Permit me to read to you a passage from each writer,
curiously indicative of his peculiar humour : the sub-

have received last night, I beg your pardon that I cannot answer till the
next post. . . . Your son at the present writing is mighty well
employed in tumbling on the floor of the room and sweeping the sand
with a feather. He grows a most delightful child, and very full of play
and spirit. He is also a very great scholar : he can read his primer,
and I have brought down my Virgil. He makes most shrewd remarks
about the pictures. We are very intimate friends and playfellows. He
begins to be very ragged ; and I hope I shall be pardoned if I equip him
with new clothes and frocks, or what Mrs. Evans and I shall think for
his service.'

'*To Lady Steele.*

[Undated.]

'You tell me you want a little flattery from me. I assure you I know
no one who deserves so much commendation as yourself, and to whom
saying the best things would be so little like flattery. The thing speaks
for itself, considering you as a very handsome woman that loves
retirement—one who does not want wit, and yet is extremely sincere ;
and so I could go through all the vices which attend the good qualities
of other people, of which you are exempt. But, indeed, though you
have every perfection, you have an extravagant fault, which almost
frustrates the good in you to me ; and that is, that you do not love to
dress, to appear, to shine out, even at my request, and to make me
proud of you, or rather to indulge the pride I have that you are
mine . . .

'Your most affectionate obsequious husband,
'RICHARD STEELE.

'A quarter of Molly's schooling is paid. The children are perfectly
well.'

'*To Lady Steele.*

'*March* 26, 1717.

'MY DEAREST PRUE,—I have received yours, wherein you give me
the sensible affliction of telling me enow of the continual pain in your
head. . . . When I lay in your place, and on your pillow, I assure you
I fell into tears last night, to think that my charming little insolent
might be then awake and in pain ; and took it to be a sin to go to
sleep.

'For this tender passion towards you, I must be contented that your
*Prueship* will condescend to call yourself my well-wisher. . . .'

At the time when the above later letters were written, Lady Steele
was in Wales, looking after her estate there. Steele, about this time,
was much occupied with a project for conveying fish alive, by which,

ject is the same, and the mood the very gravest. We have said that upon all the actions of man, the most trifling and the most solemn, the humourist takes upon himself to comment. All readers of our old masters know the terrible lines of Swift, in which he hints at his philosophy and describes the end of mankind :*—

'Amazed, confused, its fate unknown,
The world stood trembling at Jove's throne ;
While each pale sinner hung his head,
Jove, nodding, shook the heavens and said:
    "Offending race of human kind,
By nature, reason, learning, blind ;
You who through frailty stepped aside,
And you who never err'd through pride ;
You who in different sects were shamm'd,
And come to see each other damn'd ;
(So some folk told you, but they knew
No more of Jove's designs than you ;)
The world's mad business now is o'er,
And I resent your freaks no more ;
*I* to such blockheads set my wit,
I damn such fools—go, go, you're bit !" '

Addison speaking on the very same theme, but with how different a voice, says, in his famous paper on Westminster Abbey (*Spectator*, No. 26) :

'For my own part, though I am always serious, I do not know what it is to be melancholy, and can therefore take a view of nature in her deep and solemn scenes, with the

---

as he constantly assures his wife, he firmly believed he should make his fortune. It did not succeed, however.

Lady Steele died in December of the succeeding year. She lies buried in Westminster Abbey.

* Lord Chesterfield sends these verses to Voltaire in a characteristic letter.

same pleasure as in her most gay and delightful ones. When I look upon the tombs of the great, every emotion of envy dies within me ; when I read the epitaphs of the beautiful, every inordinate desire goes out ; when I meet with the grief of parents on a tombstone, my heart melts with compassion ; when I see the tomb of the parents themselves, I consider the vanity of grieving for those we must quickly follow.'

(I have owned that I do not think Addison's heart melted very much, or that he indulged very inordinately in the ' vanity of grieving.')

' When,' he goes on, ' when I see kings lying by those who deposed them : when I consider rival wits placed side by side, or the holy men that divided the world with their contests and disputes—I reflect with sorrow and astonishment on the little competitions, factions, and debates of mankind. And, when I read the several dates on the tombs of some that died yesterday, and some six hundred years ago, I consider that great day when we shall all of us be contemporaries, and make our appearance together.'

Our third humourist comes to speak on the same subject. You will have observed in the previous extracts the characteristic humour of each writer— the subject and the contrast—the fact of Death, and the play of individual thought by which each comments on it, and now hear the third writer—death, sorrow, and the grave, being for the moment also his theme.

' The first sense of sorrow I ever knew,' Steele says in the *Tatler*, ' was upon the death of my father, at which time I was not quite five years of age : but was rather amazed at what all the house meant, than possessed of a real understanding why nobody would play with us. I remember I went into the room where his body lay, and my mother sate weeping alone by it. I had my battledore in my hand,

and fell a beating the coffin and calling papa ; for, I know not how, I had some idea that he was locked up there. My mother caught me in her arms, and, transported beyond all patience of the silent grief she was before in, she almost smothered me in her embraces, and told me in a flood of tears, " Papa could not hear me, and would play with me no more : for they were going to put him under ground, whence he would never come to us again." She was a very beautiful woman, of a noble spirit, and there was a dignity in her grief, amidst all the wildness of her transport, which methought struck me with an instinct of sorrow that, before I was sensible what it was to grieve, seized my very soul, and has made pity the weakness of my heart ever since.'

Can there be three more characteristic moods of minds and men ? 'Fools, do you know anything of this mystery ?' says Swift, stamping on a grave, and carrying his scorn for mankind actually beyond it. 'Miserable purblind wretches, how dare you to pretend to comprehend the Inscrutable, and how can your dim eyes pierce the unfathomable depths of yonder boundless heaven ?' Addison, in a much kinder language and gentler voice, utters much the same sentiment : and speaks of the rivalry of wits, and the contests of holy men, with the same sceptic placidity. 'Look what a little vain dust we are,' he says, smiling over the tombstones ; and catching, as is his wont, quite a divine effulgence as he looks heavenward, he speaks, in words of inspiration almost, of ' the Great Day, when we shall all of us be contemporaries, and make our appearance together.'

The third, whose theme is Death, too, and who will speak his word of moral as Heaven teaches him, leads you up to his father's coffin, and shows you his beautiful mother weeping, and himself an unconscious little boy wondering at her side. His own natural tears flow as he takes your hand and confidingly asks your sympathy. 'See how good and innocent and beautiful women are,' he says; 'how tender little children! Let us love these and one another, brother —God knows we have need of love and pardon.' So it is each looks with his own eyes, speaks with his own voice, and prays his own prayer.

When Steele asks your sympathy for the actors in that charming scene of Love and Grief and Death, who can refuse it? One yields to it as to the frank advance of a child, or to the appeal of a woman. A man is seldom more manly than when he is what you call unmanned—the source of his emotion is championship, pity, and courage; the instinctive desire to cherish those who are innocent and unhappy, and defend those who are tender and weak. If Steele is not our friend he is nothing. He is by no means the most brilliant of wits nor the deepest of thinkers: but he is our friend: we love him, as children love with an A, because he is amiable. Who likes a man best because he is the cleverest or the wisest of mankind; or a woman because she is the most virtuous, or talks French or plays the piano better than the rest of her sex? I own to liking Dick Steele the man, and Dick Steele the author, much better than much better men and much better authors.

The misfortune regarding Steele is, that most part of the company here present must take his amiability upon hearsay, and certainly can't make his intimate acquaintance. Not that Steele was worse than his time; on the contrary, a far better, truer, and higher-hearted man than most who lived in it. But things were done in that society, and names were named, which would make you shudder now. What would be the sensation of a polite youth of the present day, if at a ball he saw the young object of his affections

taking a box out of her pocket and a pinch of snuff:
or if at dinner, by the charmer's side, she deliberately
put her knife into her mouth? If she cut her
mother's throat with it, mamma would scarcely be
more shocked. I allude to these peculiarities of
bygone times as an excuse for my favourite Steele,
who was not worse, and often much more delicate than
his neighbours.

There exists a curious document descriptive of the
manners of the last age, which describes most minutely
the amusements and occupations of persons of fashion
in London at the time of which we are speaking:
the time of Swift, and Addison, and Steele.

When Lord Sparkish, Tom Neverout, and Colonel
Alwit, the immortal personages of Swift's polite conversation, came to breakfast with my Lady Smart, at
eleven o'clock in the morning, my Lord Smart was
absent at the levée. His Lordship was at home to
dinner at three o'clock to receive his guests; and we
may sit down to this meal, like the Barmecide's, and
see the fops of the last century before us. Seven of
them sat down at dinner, and were joined by a
country baronet who told them they kept Court hours.
These persons of fashion began their dinner with a
sirloin of beef, fish, a shoulder of veal, and a tongue.
My Lady Smart carved the sirloin, my Lady
Answerall helped the fish, and the gallant Colonel
cut the shoulder of veal. All made a considerable
inroad on the sirloin and the shoulder of veal, with the
exception of Sir John, who had no appetite, having
already partaken of a beefsteak and two mugs of ale,
besides a tankard of March beer, as soon as he got out
of bed. They drank claret, which the master of the
house said should always be drunk after fish; and my
Lord Smart particularly recommended some excellent
cider to my Lord Sparkish, which occasioned some

brilliant remarks from that nobleman. When the host called for wine, he nodded to one or other of his guests, and said, 'Tom Neverout, my service to you.'

After the first course came almond-pudding, fritters, which the Colonel took with his hands out of the dish, in order to help the brilliant Miss Notable ; chickens, black puddings, and soup ; and Lady Smart, the elegant mistress of the mansion, finding a skewer in a dish, placed it in her plate with directions that it should be carried down to the cook and dressed for the cook's own dinner. Wine and small beer were drunk during the second course ; and when the Colonel called for beer, he called the butler Friend, and asked whether the beer was good. Various jocular remarks passed from the gentlefolk to the servants ; at breakfast several persons had a word and a joke for Mrs. Betty, my Lady's maid, who warmed the cream and had charge of the canister (the tea cost thirty shillings a pound in those days). When my Lady Sparkish sent her footman out to my Lady Match to come at six o'clock and play at quadrille, her Ladyship warned the man to follow his nose, and if he fell by the way not to stay to get up again. And when the gentlemen asked the hall porter if his Lady was at home, that functionary replied, with manly waggishness, 'She was at home just now, but she's not gone out yet.'

After the puddings, sweet and black, the fritters and soup, came the third course, of which the chief dish was a hot venison pasty, which was put before Lord Smart, and carved by that nobleman. Besides the pasty, there was a hare, a rabbit, some pigeons, partridges, a goose, and a ham. Beer and wine were freely imbibed during this course, the gentlemen always pledging somebody with every glass which they drank ; and by this time the conversation between

Tom Neverout and Miss Notable had grown so
brisk and lively, that the Derbyshire baronet began
to think the young gentlewoman was Tom's sweetheart ; on which Miss remarked, that she loved Tom
'like pie.'   After the goose, some of the gentlewomen
took a dram of brandy, 'which was very good for the
wholesomes,' Sir John said : and now having had a
tolerably substantial dinner, honest Lord Smart bade
the butler bring up the great tankard full of October
to Sir John.   The great tankard was passed from hand
to hand and mouth to mouth, but when pressed by
the noble host upon the gallant Tom Neverout, he
said, 'No, faith, my Lord ; I like your wine, and
won't put a churl upon a gentleman.   Your honour's
claret is good enough for me.'   And so, the dinner
over, the host said, 'Hang saving, bring us up a
ha'porth of cheese.'

The cloth was now taken away, and a bottle of
burgundy was set down, of which the ladies were
invited to partake before they went to their tea.

When they withdrew, the gentlemen promised to
join them in an hour : fresh bottles were brought :
the 'dead men,' meaning the empty bottles, removed ;
and 'D'you hear, John ! bring clean glasses,' my
Lord Smart said.   On which the gallant Colonel
Alwit said, 'I'll keep my glass ; for wine is the best
liquor to wash glasses in.'

After an hour the gentlemen joined the ladies, and
then they all sat and played quadrille until three
o'clock in the morning, when the chairs and the
flambeaux came, and this noble company went to bed.

Such were manners six or seven score years ago.   I
draw no inference from this queer picture—let all
moralists here present deduce their own.   Fancy the
moral condition of that society in which a lady of
fashion joked with a footman, and carved a sirloin,

and provided besides a great shoulder of veal, a goose, hare, rabbit, chickens, partridges, black puddings, and a ham for a dinner for eight Christians. What —what could have been the condition of that polite world in which people openly ate goose after almond-pudding, and took their soup in the middle of dinner? Fancy a Colonel in the Guards putting his hand into a dish of *beignets d'abricot* and helping his neighbour, a young lady *du monde!* Fancy a noble lord calling out to the servants, before the ladies at his table, 'Hang expense, bring us a ha'porth of cheese!' Such were the ladies of Saint James's—such were the frequenters of 'White's Chocolate-House,' when Swift used to visit it, and Steele described it as the centre of pleasure, gallantry, and entertainment, a hundred and forty years ago!

Dennis, who ran amuck at the literary society of his day, falls foul of poor Steele, and thus depicts him :—

'Sir John Edgar, of the county of —— in Ireland, is of a middle stature, broad shoulders, thick legs, a shape like the picture of somebody over a farmer's chimney—a short chin, a short nose, a short forehead, a broad flat face, and a dusky countenance. Yet with such a face and such a shape, he discovered at sixty that he took himself for a beauty, and appeared to be more mortified at being told that he was ugly, than he was by any reflection made upon his honour or understanding.

'He is a gentleman born, witness himself, of very honourable family; certainly of a very ancient one, for his ancestors flourished in Tipperary long before the English ever set foot in Ireland. He has testimony of this more authentic than the Heralds' Office, or any human testimony. For God has marked him more abundantly than He did Cain, and stamped his native country on his face, his understanding, his writings, his actions, his passions, and, above all, his vanity. The

Hibernian brogue is still upon all these, though long habit and length of days have worn it off his tongue.'*

Although this portrait is the work of a man who was neither the friend of Steele nor of any other man alive, yet there is a dreadful resemblance to the original in the savage and exaggerated traits of the caricature, and everybody who knows him must recognise Dick Steele. Dick set about almost all the undertakings of his life with inadequate means, and, as he took and furnished a house with the most

---

* Steele replied to Dennis in an 'Answer to a Whimsical Pamphlet, called the Character of Sir John Edgar.' What Steele had to say against the cross-grained old Critic discovers a great deal of humour :—

'Thou never didst let the sun into thy garret, for fear he should bring a bailiff along with him. . . .

'Your years are about sixty-five, an ugly vinegar face, that if you had any command you would be obeyed out of fear, from your ill-nature pictured there : not from any other motive. Your height is about some five feet five inches. You see I can give your exact measure as well as if I had taken your dimension with a good cudgel, which I promise you to do as soon as ever I have the good fortune to meet you. . . .

'Your doughty paunch stands before you like a firkin of butter, and your duck legs seem to be cast for carrying burdens.

'Thy works are libels upon others, and satires upon thyself; and while they bark at men of sense, call him fool and knave that wrote them. Thou hast a great antipathy to thy own species ; and hatest the sight of a fool but in thy glass.'

Steele had been kind to Dennis, and once got arrested on account of a pecuniary service which he did him. When John heard of the fact—'Sdeath !' cries John ; 'why did not he keep out of the way as I did ?'

The 'Answer' concludes by mentioning that Cibber had offered Ten Pounds for the discovery of the authorship of Dennis's pamphlet ; on which, says Steele,—'I am only sorry he has offered so much, because the *twentieth part* would have over-valued his whole carcase. But I know the fellow that he keeps to give answers to his creditors will betray him ; for he gave me his word to bring officers on the top of the house that should make a hole through the ceiling of his garret, and so bring him to the punishment he deserves. Some people think this expedient out of the way, and that he would make his escape upon hearing the least noise. I say so too : but it takes him up half-an-hour every night to fortify himself with his old hair trunk, two or three joint-stools, and some other lumber, which he ties together with cords so fast that it takes him up the same time in the morning to release himself.'

generous intentions towards his friends, the most
tender gallantry towards his wife, and with this only
drawback, that he had not wherewithal to pay the
rent when quarter-day came,—so, in his life he proposed to himself the most magnificent schemes of
virtue, forbearance, public and private good, and the
advancement of his own and the national religion;
but when he had to pay for these articles—so difficult
to purchase and so costly to maintain—poor Dick's
money was not forthcoming: and when Virtue called
with her little bill, Dick made a shuffling excuse that
he could not see her that morning, having a headache
from being tipsy over-night; or when stern Duty
rapped at the door with his account, Dick was absent
and not ready to pay. He was shirking at the tavern;
or had some particular business (of somebody's else)
at the ordinary; or he was in hiding, or worse than
in hiding, in the lock-up house. What a situation for
a man !—for a philanthropist—for a lover of right and
truth—for a magnificent designer and schemer!
Not to dare to look in the face the Religion which
he adored and which he had offended: to have to
shirk down back lanes and alleys, so as to avoid the
friend whom he loved and who had trusted him; to
have the house which he had intended for his wife,
whom he loved passionately, and for her Ladyship's
company, which he wished to entertain splendidly, in
the possession of a bailiff's man; with a crowd of
little creditors,—grocers, butchers, and small-coal
men—lingering round the door with their bills and
jeering at him. Alas for poor Dick Steele ! For
nobody else, of course. There is no man or woman
in *our* time who makes fine projects and gives them
up from idleness or want of means. When Duty
calls upon *us*, we no doubt are always at home and
ready to pay that grim tax-gatherer. When *we* are

stricken with remorse and promise reform, we keep
our promise, and are never angry, or idle, or extravagant any more. There are no chambers in *our*
hearts, destined for family friends and affections, and
now occupied by some Sin's emissary and bailiff in
possession. There are no little sins, shabby
peccadilloes, importunate remembrances, or disappointed holders of our promises to reform, hovering
at our steps, or knocking at our door! Of course
not. We are living in the nineteenth century; and
poor Dick Steele stumbled and got up again, and got
into jail and out again, and sinned and repented, and
loved and suffered, and lived and died, scores of years
ago. Peace be with him! Let us think gently of
one who was so gentle: let us speak kindly of one
whose own breast exuberated with human kindness.

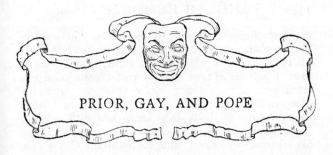

# PRIOR, GAY, AND POPE

MATTHEW PRIOR was one of those famous and lucky
wits of the auspicious reign of Queen Anne, whose
name it behoves us not to pass over. Mat was a
world-philosopher of no small genius, good-nature, and
acumen.\* He loved, he drank, he sang. He

---

\* Gay calls him—'Dear Prior . . . beloved by every muse.'—*Mr.
Pope's Welcome from Greece.*

Swift and Prior were very intimate, and he is frequently mentioned in
the 'Journal to Stella.' 'Mr. Prior,' says Swift, 'walks to make
himself fat, and I to keep myself down. . . . We often walk round the
park together.'

In Swift's works there is a curious tract called *Remarks on the
Characters of the Court of Queen Anne* [Scott's edition, vol. xii.]. The
'Remarks' are not by the Dean; but at the end of each is an addition
in italics from his hand, and these are always characteristic. Thus, to
the Duke of Marlborough, he adds, '*Detestably covetous,*' &c. Prior
is thus noticed—

'*Matthew Prior, Esquire, Commissioner of Trade.*

'On the Queen's accession to the throne, he was continued in his
office; is very well at Court with the Ministry, and is an entire creature
of my Lord Jersey's, whom he supports by his advice; is one of the
best poets in England, but very facetious in conversation. A thin
hollow-looked man, turned of forty years old. *This is near the truth.*'

'Yet counting as far as to fifty his years,
    His virtues and vices were as other men's are.
High hopes he conceived and he smothered great fears,
    In a life party-coloured—half pleasure, half care.

Not to business a drudge, nor to faction a slave,
    He strove to make interest and freedom agree;

describes himself, in one of his lyrics, 'in a little
Dutch chaise on a Saturday night; on his left hand
his Horace, and a friend on his right,' going out of
town from the Hague to pass that evening and the
ensuing Sunday boozing at a Spielhaus with his
companions, perhaps bobbing for perch in a Dutch
canal, and noting down, in a strain and with a grace
not unworthy of his Epicurean master, the charms of
his idleness, his retreat, and his Batavian Chloe.   A
vintner's son in Whitehall, and a distinguished pupil of
Busby of the Rod, Prior attracted some notice by
writing verses at Saint John's College, Cambridge, and,
coming up to town, aided Montagu* in an attack on
the noble old English lion John Dryden; in ridicule
of whose work, 'The Hind and the Panther,' he
brought out that remarkable and famous burlesque,
'The Town and Country Mouse.'  Aren't you all
acquainted with it?  Have you not all got it by
heart?  What! have you never heard of it?  See
what fame is made of!  The wonderful part of the
satire was, that, as a natural consequence of 'The
Town and Country Mouse,' Matthew Prior was
made Secretary of Embassy at the Hague!  I believe
it is dancing, rather than singing, which distinguishes

> In public employments industrious and grave,
>    And alone with his friends, Lord, how merry was he!
>
> Now in equipage stately, now humble on foot,
>    Both fortunes he tried, but to neither would trust;
> And whirled in the round as the wheel turned about,
>    He found riches had wings, and knew man was but dust.'
>                          PRIOR'S *Poems*. [*For my own monument.*]

* 'They joined to produce a parody, entitled *The Town and Country
Mouse*, part of which Mr. Bayes is supposed to gratify his old friends,
Smart and Johnson, by repeating to them. The piece is therefore
founded upon the twice-told jest of the "Rehearsal." . . . There is
nothing new or original in the idea. . . . In this piece, Prior, though
the younger man, seems to have had by far the largest share.'—SCOTT's
*Dryden*, vol. i. p. 330.

the young English diplomatists of the present day; and have seen them in various parts perform that part of their duty very finely.  In Prior's time it appears a different accomplishment led to preferment.  Could you write a copy of Alcaics? that was the question.  Could you turn out a neat epigram or two?  Could you compose 'The Town and Country Mouse'?  It is manifest that, by the possession of this faculty, the most difficult treatise, the laws of foreign nations, and the interests of our own, are easily understood.  Prior rose in the diplomatic service, and said good things that proved his sense and his spirit.  When the apartments at Versailles were shown to him, with the victories of Louis XIV. painted on the walls, and Prior was asked whether the palace of the King of England had any such decorations, 'The monuments of my master's actions,' Mat said, of William, whom he cordially revered, 'are to be seen everywhere except in his own house.'  Bravo, Mat!  Prior rose to be full ambassador at Paris,* where he somehow was cheated out of his ambassadorial plate; and in an heroic poem, addressed by him to her late lamented Majesty, Queen Anne, Mat makes some magnificent allusions to these dishes and spoons, of which Fate had deprived him.  All

---

* 'He was to have been in the same commission with the Duke of Shrewsbury, but that that nobleman,' says Johnson, 'refused to be associated with one so meanly born.  Prior therefore continued to act without a title till the Duke's return next year to England, and then he assumed the style and dignity of ambassador.'

He had been thinking of slights of this sort when he wrote his Epitaph :—

> 'Nobles and heralds, by your leave,
>   Here lies what once was Matthew Prior,
> The son of Adam and of Eve :
>   Can Bourbon or Nassau claim higher?'

But, in this case, the old prejudice got the better of the old joke.

that he wants, he says, is Her Majesty's picture; without that he can't be happy.

'Thee, Gracious Anne, thee present I adore:
Thee, Queen of Peace, if Time and Fate have power
Higher to raise the glories of thy reign,
In words sublimer and a nobler strain
May future bards the mighty theme rehearse.
Here, Stator Jove, and Phœbus, king of verse,
The votive tablet I suspend.'

With that word the poem stops abruptly. The votive tablet is suspended for ever, like Mahomet's coffin. News came that the Queen was dead. Stator Jove and Phœbus, king of verse, were left there, hovering to this day, over the votive tablet. The picture was never got, any more than the spoons and dishes: the inspiration ceased, the verses were not wanted—the ambassador wasn't wanted. Poor Mat was recalled from his embassy, suffered disgrace along with his patrons, lived under a sort of cloud ever after, and disappeared in Essex. When deprived of all his pensions and emoluments, the hearty and generous Oxford pensioned him. They played for gallant stakes—the bold men of those days—and lived and gave splendidly.

Johnson quotes from Spence a legend, that Prior, after spending an evening with Harley, St. John, Pope, and Swift, would go off and smoke a pipe with a couple of friends of his, a soldier and his wife, in Long Acre. Those who have not read his late Excellency's poems should be warned that they smack not a little of the conversation of his Long Acre friends. Johnson speaks slightingly of his lyrics; but with due deference to the great Samuel, Prior's seem to me amongst the easiest, the richest, the most charmingly humorous of English lyrical poems.* Horace is always in his mind; and his song, and his philosophy, his good sense, his happy easy turns and melody, his loves and his Epicureanism, bear a great resemblance to that most delightful and accomplished master. In reading his works one is struck with their modern air, as well as by their happy similarity to the songs of the charming owner of the Sabine farm. In his verses addressed to Halifax, he says, writing of that endless theme to poets, the vanity of human wishes—

'So whilst in fevered dreams we sink,
    And waking, taste what we desire,
    The real draught but feeds the fire,
The dream is better than the drink.

---

* His epigrams have the genuine sparkle :—

'*The Remedy worse than the Disease.*

'I sent for Radcliff; was so ill,
    That other doctors gave me over :
He felt my pulse, prescribed his pill,
    And I was likely to recover.

But when the wit began to wheeze,
    And wine had warmed the politician,
Cured yesterday of my disease,
    I died last night of my physician.'

'Yes, every poet is a fool ;
    By demonstration Ned can show it :
Happy could Ned's inverted rule
    Prove every fool to be a poet.'

'On his death-bed poor Lubin lies,
    His spouse is in despair ;
With frequent sobs and mutual cries
    They both express their care.

"A different cause," says Parson Sly,
    "The same effect may give ;
Poor Lubin fears that he shall die,
    His wife that he may live."'

> Our hopes like towering falcons aim
>   At objects in an airy height :
>   To stand aloof and view the flight,
> Is all the pleasure of the game.'

Would not you fancy that a poet of our own days
was singing ? and in the verses of Chloe weeping and
reproaching him for his inconstancy, where he says—

'The God of us versemen, you know, child, the Sun,
  How, after his journeys, he sets up his rest.
If at morning o'er earth 'tis his fancy to run,
  At night he declines on his Thetis's breast.

So, when I am wearied with wandering all day,
  To thee, my delight, in the evening I come :
No matter what beauties I saw in my way,
  They were but my visits, but thou art my home !

Then finish, dear Chloe, this pastoral war,
  And let us like Horace and Lydia agree :
For thou art a girl as much brighter than her,
  As he was a poet sublimer than me.'

If Prior read Horace, did not Thomas Moore study
Prior ? Love and pleasure finds singers in all days.
Roses are always blowing and fading—to-day as in
that pretty time when Prior sang of them, and of Chloe
lamenting their decay—

> 'She sighed, she smiled, and to the flowers
>   Pointing, the lovely moralist said :
> See, friend, in some few fleeting hours,
>   See yonder what a change is made !
>
> Ah me ! the blooming pride of May
>   And that of Beauty are but one :
> At morn both flourish, bright and gay,
>   Both fade at evening pale and gone.

At dawn poor Stella danced and sung,
　　The amorous youth around her bowed :
At night her fatal knell was rung ;
　　I saw and kissed her in her shroud.

Such as she is who died to-day,
　　Such I, alas, may be to-morrow.
Go, Damon, bid thy Muse display
　　The justice of thy Chloe's sorrow.'

Damon's knell was rung in 1721. May his turf lie
lightly on him ! 'Deus sit propitius huic potatori,' as
Walter de Mapes sang.*　Perhaps Samuel Johnson,

* *Prior to Sir Thomas Hanmer.*

'*Aug.* 4, 1709.

'DEAR SIR,—Friendship may live, I grant you, without being fed
and cherished by correspondence ; but with that additional benefit I am
of opinion it will look more cheerful and thrive better : for in this case,
as in love, though a man is sure of his own constancy, yet his happiness
depends a good deal upon the sentiments of another, and while you and
Chloe are alive, 'tis not enough that I love you both, except I am sure
you both love me again ; and as one of her scrawls fortifies my mind
more against affliction than all Epictetus, with Simplicius's comments
into the bargain, so your single letter gave me more real pleasure than
all the works of Plato. . . . I must return my answer to your very kind
question concerning my health. The Bath waters have done a good
deal towards the recovery of it, and the great specific, *Cape caballum,*
will, I think, confirm it. Upon this head I must tell you that my mare
Betty grows blind, and may one day, by breaking my neck, perfect
my cure : if at Rixham fair any pretty nag that is between thirteen
and fourteen hands presented himself, and you would be pleased to
purchase him for me, one of your servants might ride him to Euston, and
I might receive him there. This, sir, is just as such a thing happens.
If you hear, too, of a Welch widow, with a good jointure, that has her
*goings* and is not very skittish, pray, be pleased to cast your eye on her
for me too. You see, sir, the great trust I repose in your skill and
honour, when I dare put two such commissions in your hand. . . .'—
*The Hanmer Correspondence,* p. 120.

'*From Mr. Prior.*

'PARIS : 1*st*-12*th May*, 1714.

'MY DEAR LORD AND FRIEND,—Matthew never had so great occasion
to write a word to Henry as now : it is noised here that I am soon to

who spoke slightingly of Prior's verses, enjoyed them
more than he was willing to own.    The old moralist

return.   The question that I wish I could answer to the many that ask,
and to our friend Colbert De Torcy (to whom I made your compliments in the manner you commanded) is, what is done for me ; and to
what I am recalled ?   It may look like a bagatelle, what is to become of
a philosopher like me ? but it is not such : what is to become of a
person who had the honour to be chosen, and sent hither as intrusted,
in the midst of a war, with what the Queen designed should make the
peace ; returning with the Lord Bolingbroke, one of the greatest men in
England, and one of the finest heads in Europe (as they say here, if true
or not, *n'importe*) ; having been left by him in the greatest character
(that of Her Majesty's Plenipotentiary), exercising that power conjointly
with the Duke of Shrewsbury, and solely after his departure ; having
here received more distinguished honour than any Minister, except an
Ambassador, ever did, and some which were never given to any but who
had that character ; having had all the success that could be expected ;
having (God be thanked !) spared no pains, at a time when at home the
peace is voted safe and honourable—at a time when the Earl of Oxford
is Lord Treasurer and Lord Bolingbroke First Secretary of State ?   This
unfortunate person, I say, neglected, forgot, unnamed to anything that
may speak the Queen satisfied with his services, or his friends concerned
as to his fortune.

'Mr. de Torcy put me quite out of countenance, the other day, by a
pity that wounded me deeper than ever did the cruelty af the late Lord
Godolphin.   He said he would write to Robin and Harry about me.
God forbid, my Lord, that I should need any foreign intercession, or owe
the least to any Frenchman living, besides the decency of behaviour and
the returns of common civility : some say I am to go to Baden, others
that I am to be added to the Commissioners for settling the commerce·
In all cases I am ready, but in the meantime, *dic aliquid de tribus capellis.*
Neither of these two are, I presume, honours or rewards, neither of them
(let me say to my dear Lord Bolingbroke, and let him not be angry with
me) are what Drift may aspire to, and what Mr. Whitworth, who was
his fellow-clerk, has or may possess.   I am far from desiring to lessen
the great merit of the gentleman I named, for I heartily esteem and love
him ; but in this trade of ours, my Lord, in which you are the general,
as in that of the soldiery, there is a certain right acquired by time and
long service.   You would do anything for your Queen's service, but you
would not be contented to descend, and be degraded to a charge, no way
proportioned to that of Secretary of State, any more than Mr. Ross,
though he would charge a party with a halbard in his hand, would be
content all his life after to be Serjeant.   Was my Lord Dartmouth, from
Secretary, returned again to be Commissioner of Trade, or from Secretary
of War, would Frank Gwyn think himself kindly used to be returned
again to be Commissioner ?   In short, my Lord, you have put me
above myself, and if I am to return to myself, I shall return to something

had studied them as well as Mr. Thomas Moore, and
defended them and showed that he remembered them
very well too, on an occasion when their morality was
called in question by that noted puritan, James
Boswell, Esquire, of Auchinleck.*

In the great society of the wits, John Gay deserved
to be a favourite, and to have a good place.† In his

very discontented and uneasy.  I am sure, my Lord, you will make the
best use you can of this hint for my good.  If I am to have anything, it
will certainly be for Her Majesty's service, and the credit of my friends
in the Ministry, that it be done before I am recalled from home, lest the
world may think either that I have merited to be disgraced, or that ye
dare not stand by me.  If nothing is to be done, *fiat voluntas Dei.*  I
have writ to Lord Treasurer upon this subject, and having implored your
kind intercession, I promise you it is the last remonstrance of this kind
that I will ever make.  Adieu, my Lord, all honour, health, and pleasure
to you.                                        Yours ever, MATT.

'*P.S.*—Lady Jersey is just gone from me.  We drank your healths
together in usquebaugh after our tea : we are the greatest friends alive.
Once more adieu.  There is no such thing as the "Book of Travels"
you mentioned ; if there be, let friend Tilson send us more particular
account of them, for neither I nor Jacob Tonson can find them.  Pray
send Barton back to me, I hope with some comfortable tidings.'—
*Bolingbroke's Letters.*

* 'I asked whether Prior's poems were to be printed entire ; Johnson
said they were.  I mentioned Lord Hales's censure of Prior in his
preface to a collection of sacred poems, by various hands, published by
him at Edinburgh a great many years ago, where he mentions "these
impure tales, which will be the eternal opprobrium of their ingenious
author."  JOHNSON : "Sir, Lord Hales has forgot.  There is nothing in
Prior that will excite to lewdness.  If Lord Hales thinks there is, he
must be more combustible than other people."  I instanced the tale of
"Paulo Purganti and his wife."  JOHNSON : "Sir, there is nothing there
but that his wife wanted to be kissed, when poor Paulo was out of
pocket.  No, sir, Prior is a lady's book.  No lady is ashamed to have
it standing in her library."'—BOSWELL's *Life of Johnson.*

† Gay was of an old Devonshire family, but his pecuniary prospects
not being great, was placed in his youth in the house of a silk-mercer
in London.  He was born in 1688—Pope's year, and in 1712 the Duchess
of Monmouth made him her secretary.  Next year he published his
*Rural Sports,* which he dedicated to Pope, and so made an acquaintance,
which became a memorable friendship.

'Gay,' says Pope, 'was quite a natural man,—wholly without art or
design, and spoke just what he thought and as he thought it.  He dangled
for twenty years about a Court, and at last was offered to be made usher

set all were fond of him.    His success offended nobody.
He missed a fortune once or twice.    He was talked
of for Court favour, and hoped to win it ; but the
Court favour jilted him.    Craggs gave him some
South Sea stock ; and at one time Gay had very nearly
made his fortune.    But Fortune shook her swift
wings and jilted him too : and so his friends, instead
of being angry with him, and jealous of him, were
kind and fond of honest Gay.    In the portraits of the
literary worthies of the early part of the last century,
Gay's face is the pleasantest perhaps of all.    It appears
adorned with neither periwig nor nightcap (the full
dress and *négligé* of learning, without which the painters
of those days scarcely ever portrayed wits), and he
laughs at you over his shoulder with an honest boyish
glee—an artless sweet humour.    He was so kind, so
gentle, so jocular, so delightfully brisk at times, so
dismally woebegone at others, such a natural good
creature, that the Giants loved him.    The great
Swift was gentle and sportive with him,* as the
enormous Brobdingnag maids of honour were with
little Gulliver.    He could frisk and fondle round
Pope,† and sport, and bark, and caper without offend-

to the young princesses.    Secretary Craggs made Gay a present of stock
in the South Sea year ; and he was once worth £20,000, but lost it all
again.    He got about £400 by the first " Beggar's Opera," and £1100
or £1200 by the second.    He was negligent and a bad manager.
Latterly, the Duke of Queensberry took his money into his keeping, and
let him only have what was necessary out of it, and, as he lived with
them, he could not have occasion for much.    He died worth upwards of
£3000.'—Pope.    *Spence's Anecdotes.*

    * 'Mr. Gay is, in all regards, as honest and sincere a man as ever I
knew.'—Swift, *To Lady Betty Germaine*, Jan. 1733.

                † 'Of manners gentle, of affections mild ;
                    In wit a man ; simplicity, a child ;
                    With native humour temp'ring virtuous rage,
                    Form'd to delight at once and lash the age ;
                    Above temptation in a low estate,
                    And uncorrupted e'en among the great :

ing the most thin-skinned of poets and men; and
when he was jilted in that little Court affair of which
we have spoken, his warm-hearted patrons the Duke
and Duchess of Queensberry* (the 'Kitty, beautiful

> A safe companion, and an easy friend,
> Unblamed through life, lamented in thy end.
> These are thy honours; not that here thy bust
> Is mixed with heroes, or with kings thy dust;
> But that the worthy and the good shall say,
> Striking their pensive bosoms, "Here lies Gay."'
>
> <div align="right">Pope's <i>Epitaph on Gay.</i></div>

> 'A hare who, in a civil way,
> Complied with everything like Gay.'
>
> <div align="right"><i>Fables,</i> 'The Hare and many Friends.'</div>

* 'I can give you no account of Gay,' says Pope, curiously, 'since he
was raffled for, and won back by his Duchess.'—*Works, Roscoe's ed.,* vol.
ix. p. 392.

Here is the letter Pope wrote to him when the death of Queen Anne
brought back Lord Clarendon from Hanover, and lost him the Secretaryship of that nobleman, of which he had had but a short tenure.

Gay's Court prospects were never happy from this time.—His dedication of the *Shepherd's Week* to Bolingbroke, Swift used to call the
'original sin' which had hurt him with the house of Hanover :—

'Sept. 23, 1714.

'DEAR MR. GAY,—Welcome to your native soil! welcome to your
friends! thrice welcome to me! whether returned in glory, blest with
Court interest, the love and familiarity of the great, and filled with
agreeable hopes; or melancholy with dejection, contemplative of the
changes of fortune, and doubtful for the future; whether returned a
triumphant Whig or a desponding Tory, equally all hail! equally
beloved and welcome to me! If happy, I am to partake in your elevation; if unhappy, you have still a warm corner in my heart, and a
retreat at Binfield in the worst of times at your service. If you are a
Tory, or thought so by any man, I know it can proceed from nothing
but your gratitude to a few people who endeavoured to serve you,
and whose politics were never your concern. If you are a Whig, as
I rather hope, and as I think your principles and mine (as brother
poets) had ever a bias to the side of liberty, I know you will be an honest
man and an inoffensive one. Upon the whole, I know you are incapable
of being so much of either party as to be good for nothing. Therefore, once more, whatever you are or in whatever state you are, all
hail!

'One or two of your own friends complained they had heard nothing

and young,' of Prior) pleaded his cause with indignation, and quitted the Court in a huff, carrying off with them into their retirement their kind gentle *protégé*. With these kind lordly folks, a real Duke and Duchess, as delightful as those who harboured Don Quixote, and loved that dear old Sancho, Gay lived,

from you since the Queen's death ; I told them no man living loved Mr. Gay better than I, yet I had not once written to him in all his voyage. This I thought a convincing proof how truly one may be a friend to another without telling him so every month. But they had reasons, too, themselves to allege in your excuse, as men who really value one another will never want such as make their friends and themselves easy. The late universal concern in public affairs threw us all into a hurry of spirits : even I, who am more a philosopher than to expect anything from any reign, was borne away with the current, and full of the expectation of the successor. During your journeys, I knew not whither to aim a letter after you ; that was a sort of shooting flying : add to this the demand Homer had upon me, to write fifty verses a day, besides learned notes, all which are at a conclusion for this year. Rejoice with me, O my friend ! that my labour is over ; come and make merry with me in much feasting. We will feed among the lilies (by the lilies I mean the ladies). Are not the Rosalindas of Britain as charming as the Blousa-lindas of the Hague ? or have the two great Pastoral poets of our nation renounced love at the same time ? for Philips, immortal Philips, hath deserted, yea, and in a rustic manner kicked his Rosalind. Dr. Parnell and I have been inseparable ever since you went. We are now at the Bath, where (if you are not, as I heartily hope, better engaged) your coming would be the greatest pleasure to us in the world. Talk not of expenses : Homer shall support his children. I beg a line from you, directed to the Post-house in Bath. Poor Parnell is in an ill state of health.

'Pardon me if I add a word of advice in the poetical way. Write something on the King, or Prince, or Princess. On whatsoever foot you may be with the Court, this can do no harm. I shall never know where to end, and am confounded in the many things I have to say to you, though they all amount but to this, that I am, entirely, as ever,
'Your,' &c.

Gay took the advice 'in the poetical way,' and published 'An Epistle to a Lady, occasioned by the arrival of Her Royal Highness the Princess of Wales.' But though this brought him access to Court, and the attendance of the Prince and Princess at his farce of the 'What d'ye call it ?' it did not bring him a place. On the accession of George II., he was offered the situation of Gentleman Usher to the Princess Louisa (Her Highness being then two years old) ; but 'by this offer,' says Johnson, 'he thought himself insulted.'

and was lapped in cotton, and had his plate of chicken,
and his saucer of cream, and frisked, and barked, and
wheezed, and grew fat, and so ended.\* He became
very melancholy and lazy, sadly plethoric, and only
occasionally diverting in his latter days. But everybody loved him, and the remembrance of his pretty
little tricks ; and the raging old Dean of Saint
Patrick's, chafing in his banishment, was afraid to
open the letter which Pope wrote him announcing the
sad news of the death of Gay.†

Swift's letters to him are beautiful : and having no
purpose but kindness in writing to him, no party aim
to advocate, or slight or anger to wreak, every word
the Dean says to his favourite is natural, trustworthy,
and kindly. His admiration for Gay's parts and
honesty, and his laughter at his weaknesses, were alike
just and genuine. He paints his character in wonderful pleasant traits of jocular satire. 'I writ lately to
Mr. Pope,' Swift says, writing to Gay : 'I wish you
had a little villakin in his neighbourhood ; but you are

* 'Gay was a great eater.—As the French philosopher used to
prove his existence by *Cogito, ergo sum*, the greatest proof of Gay's
existence is, *Edit, ergo est.*'—CONGREVE, *in a letter to Pope. Spence's
Anecdotes.*

† Swift endorsed the letter—'On my dear friend Mr. Gay's death ;
received Dec. 15, but not read till the 20th, by an impulse foreboding
some misfortune.'

'It was by Swift's interest that Gay was made known to Lord Bolingbroke, and obtained his patronage.'—SCOTT's *Swift*, vol. i. p. 156.

Pope wrote on the occasion of Gay's death, to Swift, thus :—

'[*Dec.* 5, 1732.]

' . . One of the nearest and longest ties I have ever had is broken
all on a sudden by the unexpected death of poor Mr. Gay. An in-
flammatory fever hurried him out of this life in three days. . . . He
asked of you a few hours before when in acute torment by the inflamma-
tion in his bowels and breast. . . . His sisters, we suppose, will be his
heirs, who are two widows. . . . Good God ! how often are we to die
before we go quite off this stage ? In every friend we lose a part of
ourselves, and the best part. God keep those we have left ! few are
worth praying for, and one's self the least of all.'

yet too volatile, and any lady with a coach and six horses would carry you to Japan.' 'If your ramble,' says Swift, in another letter, 'was on horseback, I am glad of it, on account of your health ; but I know your arts of patching up a journey between stage-coaches and friend's coaches—for you are as arrant a cockney as any hosier in Cheapside. I have often had it in my head to put it into yours, that you ought to have some great work in scheme, which may take up seven years to finish, besides two or three under-ones that may add another thousand pounds to your stock. And then I shall be in less pain about you. I know you can find dinners, but you love twelvepenny coaches too well, without considering that the interest of a whole thousand pounds brings you but half-a-crown a day.' And then Swift goes off from Gay to pay some grand compliments to her Grace the Duchess of Queensberry, in whose sunshine Mr. Gay was basking, and in whose radiance the Dean would have liked to warm himself too.

But we have Gay here before us, in these letters—lazy, kindly, uncommonly idle ; rather slovenly, I'm afraid ; for ever eating and saying good things ; a little round French abbé of a man, sleek, soft-handed, and soft-hearted.

Our object in these lectures is rather to describe the men than their works ; or to deal with the latter only in as far as they seem to illustrate the character of their writers. Mr. Gay's 'Fables,' which were written to benefit that amiable Prince the Duke of Cumberland, the warrior of Dettingen and Culloden, I have not, I own, been able to peruse since a period of very early youth ; and it must be confessed that they did not effect much benefit upon the illustrious young Prince, whose manners they were intended to mollify, and whose natural ferocity our gentle-hearted

Satirist perhaps proposed to restrain. But the six
pastorals called the 'Shepherd's Week,' and the
burlesque poem of 'Trivia,' any man fond of lazy
literature will find delightful at the present day, and
must read from beginning to end with pleasure.
They are to poetry what charming little Dresden
china figures are to sculpture : graceful, minikin,
fantastic ; with a certain beauty always accompanying
them. The pretty little personages of the pastoral,
with gold clocks to their stockings, and fresh satin
ribbons to their crooks and waistcoats and bodices,
dance their loves to a minuet-tune played on a bird-
organ, approach the charmer, or rush from the false
one daintily on their red-heeled tiptoes, and die of
despair or rapture, with the most pathetic little grins
and ogles ; or repose, simpering at each other, under
an arbour of pea-green crockery ; or piping to pretty
flocks that have just been washed with the best Naples
in a stream of Bergamot. Gay's gay plan seems to
me far pleasanter than that of Philips—his rival and
Pope's—a serious and dreary idyllic cockney ; not
that Gay's 'Bumkinets' and 'Hobnelias' are a whit
more natural than the would-be serious characters of
the other posture-master ; but the quality of this true
humourist was to laugh and make laugh, though
always with a secret kindness and tenderness, to
perform the drollest little antics and capers, but always
with a certain grace, and to sweet music—as you may
have seen a Savoyard boy abroad, with a hurdy-gurdy
and a monkey, turning over head and heels, or clattering and pirouetting in a pair of wooden shoes, yet
always with a look of love and appeal in his bright
eyes, and a smile that asks and wins affection and
protection. Happy they who have that sweet gift of
nature ! It was this which made the great folk and
Court ladies free and friendly with John Gay—which

made Pope and Arbuthnot love him—which melted
the savage heart of Swift when he thought of him—
and drove away, for a moment or two, the dark
frenzies which obscured the lonely tyrant's brain, as
he heard Gay's voice with its simple melody and
artless ringing laughter.

What used to be said about Rubini, *qu'il avait des
larmes dans la voix*, may be said of Gay,* and of one
other humourist of whom we shall have to speak. In
almost every ballad of his, however slight,† in the

* 'Gay, like Goldsmith, had a musical talent. "He could play on the
flute," says Malone, "and was, therefore, enabled to adapt so happily
some of the airs in the *Beggar's Opera.*"— *Notes to Spence.*

> "'Twas when the seas were roaring
>     With hollow blasts of wind,
> A damsel lay deploring
>     All on a rock reclined.
> Wide o'er the foaming billows
>     She cast a wistful look ;
> Her head was crown'd with willows
>     That trembled o'er the brook.
>
> "Twelve months are gone and over,
>     And nine long tedious days ;
> Why did'st thou, venturous lover—
>     Why did'st thou trust the seas ?
> Cease, cease, thou cruel Ocean,
>     And let my lover rest ;
> Ah ! what's thy troubled motion
>     To that within my breast ?
>
> "The merchant, robb'd of pleasure,
>     Sees tempests in despair ;
> But what's the loss of treasure
>     To losing of my dear ?
> Should you some coast be laid on,
>     Where gold and diamonds grow,
> You'd find a richer maiden,
>     But none that loves you so.
>
> "How can they say that Nature
>     Has nothing made in vain ;
> Why, then, beneath the water
>     Should hideous rocks remain ?

'Beggar's Opera'* and in its wearisome continuation
(where the verses are to the full as pretty as in the
first piece, however), there is a peculiar, hinted,
pathetic sweetness and melody. It charms and melts
you. It's indefinable, but it exists; and is the
property of John Gay's and Oliver Goldsmith's best
verse, as fragrance is of a violet, or freshness of a rose.

> No eyes the rocks discover
>   That lurk beneath the deep,
> To wreck the wandering lover,
>   And leave the maid to weep?"
>
> All melancholy lying,
>   Thus wailed she for her dear;
> Repay'd each blast with sighing,
>   Each billow with a tear;
> When o'er the white wave stooping,
>   His floating corpse she spy'd;
> Then like a lily drooping,
>   She bow'd her head and died.'
>            *A Ballad from the 'What d'ye call it?'*

'What can be prettier than Gay's ballad, or, rather, Swift's, Arbuthnot's, Pope's and Gay's, in the "What d'ye call it?" "'Twas when the
seas were roaring"? I have been well informed that they all contributed.'—*Cowper to Unwin,* 1783.

* 'Dr. Swift had been observing once to Mr. Gay, what an odd
pretty sort of thing a Newgate Pastoral might make. Gay was inclined
to try at such a thing for some time, but afterwards thought it would be
better to write a comedy on the same plan. This was what gave rise to
the *Beggar's Opera.* He began on it, and when he first mentioned it
to Swift, the Doctor did not much like the project. As he carried it
on, he showed what he wrote to both of us; and we now and then gave
a correction, or a word or two of advice; but it was wholly of his own
writing. When it was done, neither of us thought it would succeed.
We showed it to Congreve, who, after reading it over, said, "It would
either take greatly, or be damned confoundedly." We were all at the
first night of it, in great uncertainty of the event, till we were very
much encouraged by overhearing the Duke of Argyle, who sat in the
next box to us, say, "It will do—it must do!—I see it in the eyes of
them!" This was a good while before the first act was over, and so
gave us ease soon; for the Duke [besides his own good taste] has a more
particular knack than any one now living in discovering the taste of the
public. He was quite right in this as usual; the good-nature of the
audience appeared stronger and stronger every act, and ended in a
clamour of applause.'—Pope. *Spence's Anecdotes.*

Let me read a piece from one of his letters, which is so famous that most people here are no doubt familiar with it, but so delightful that it is always pleasant to hear :—

'I have just passed part of this summer at an old romantic seat of my Lord Harcourt's, which he lent me. It overlooks a common field, where, under the shade of a haycock, sat two lovers as constant as ever were found in romance—beneath a spreading beech. The name of the one (let it sound as it will) was John Hewet ; of the other Sarah Drew. John was a well-set man, about five-and-twenty ; Sarah a brown woman of eighteen. John had for several months borne the labour of the day in the same field with Sarah ; when she milked, it was his morning and evening charge to bring the cows to her pail. Their love was the talk, but not the scandal, of the whole neighbourhood, for all they aimed at was the blameless possession of each other in marriage. It was but this very morning that he had obtained her parents' consent, and it was but till the next week that they were to wait to be happy. Perhaps this very day, in the intervals of their work, they were talking of their wedding-clothes ; and John was now matching several kinds of poppies and field-flowers to her complexion, to make her a present of knots for the day. While they were thus employed (it was on the last of July) a terrible storm of thunder and lightning arose, that drove the labourers to what shelter the trees or hedges afforded. Sarah, frightened and out of breath, sunk on a haycock ; and John (who never separated from her), sat by her side, having raked two or three heaps together, to secure her. Immediately there was heard so loud a crack, as if heaven had burst asunder. The labourers, all solicitous for each other's safety, called to one another : those that were nearest our lovers, hearing no answer, stepped to the place where they lay : they first saw a little smoke, and after, this faithful pair—John, with one arm about his Sarah's neck, and the other held over her face, as if to screen her from the lightning. They were struck dead, and already grown stiff and cold in this tender posture. There was no mark or discolouring on their bodies—only that Sarah's eyebrow was a little singed, and a small spot between her breasts. They were buried the next day in one grave.'

And the proof that this description is delightful and beautiful is, that the great Mr. Pope admired it so much that he thought proper to steal it and to send it off to a certain lady and wit, with whom he pretended to be in love in those days—my Lord Duke of Kingston's daughter, and married to Mr. Wortley Montagu, then His Majesty's Ambassador at Constantinople.

We are now come to the greatest name on our list —the highest among the poets, the highest among the English wits and humourists with whom we have to rank him. If the author of the ' Dunciad ' be not a humourist, if the poet of the ' Rape of the Lock ' be not a wit, who deserves to be called so ? Besides that brilliant genius and immense fame, for both of which we should respect him, men of letters should admire him as being the greatest literary *artist* that England has seen. He polished, he refined, he thought ; he took thoughts from other works to adorn and complete his own ; borrowing an idea or a cadence from another poet as he would a figure or a simile from a flower, or a river, stream, or any object which struck him in his walk, or contemplation of Nature. He began to imitate at an early age ; * and taught himself

* 'Waller, Spenser, and Dryden were Mr. Pope's great favourites, in the order they are named, in his first reading, till he was about twelve years old.'—POPE. *Spence's Anecdotes.*

'Mr. Pope's father (who was an honest merchant, and dealt in Hollands, wholesale) was no poet, but he used to set him to make English verses when very young. He was pretty difficult in being pleased ; and used often to send him back to new turn them. "These are not good rhimes ;" for that was my husband's word for verses.'—POPE'S MOTHER. *Spence.*

'I wrote things, I'm ashamed to say how soon. Part of an Epic

to write by copying printed books. Then he passed
into the hands of the priests, and from his first clerical
master, who came to him when he was eight years old,
he went to a school at Twyford, and another school
at Hyde Park, at which places he unlearned all that
he had got from his first instructor. At twelve years
old, he went with his father into Windsor Forest,
and there learned for a few months under a fourth
priest. 'And this was all the teaching I ever had,'
he said, 'and God knows it extended a very little
way.'

When he had done with his priests he took to
reading by himself, for which he had a very great
eagerness and enthusiasm, especially for poetry. He
learnt versification from Dryden, he said. In his
youthful poem of 'Alcander,' he imitated every poet,
Cowley, Milton, Spenser, Statius, Homer, Virgil. In
a few years he had dipped into a great number of the
English, French, Italian, Latin, and Greek poets.
'This I did,' he says, 'without any design, except to
amuse myself; and got the languages by hunting after
the stories in the several poets I read, rather than read
the books to get the languages. I followed everywhere

Poem when about twelve. The scene of it lay at Rhodes and some of the
neighbouring islands; and the poem opened under water with a description of the Court of Neptune.'—Pope. *Ibid.*
   'His perpetual application (after he set to study of himself) reduced
him in four year's time to so bad a state of health, that, after trying
physicians for a good while in vain, he resolved to give way to his distemper; and sat down calmly in a full expectation of death in a short
time. Under this thought, he wrote letters to take a last farewell of
some of his more particular friends, and, among the rest, one to the Abbé
Southcote. The Abbé was extremely concerned both for his very ill
state of health and the resolution he said he had taken. He thought
there might yet be hope, and went immediately to Dr. Radcliffe, with
whom he was well acquainted, told him Mr. Pope's case, got full
directions from him, and carried them down to Pope in Windsor Forest.
The chief thing the Doctor ordered him was to apply less, and to ride
every day. The following his advice so restored him to his health.'—
Pope. *Spence.*

as my fancy led me, and was like a boy gathering flowers in the fields and woods, just as they fell in his way. These five or six years I looked upon as the happiest in my life.' Is not here a beautiful holiday picture? The forest and the fairy story-book—the boy spelling Ariosto or Virgil under the trees, battling with the Cid for the love of Chimème, or dreaming of Armida's garden—peace and sunshine round about—the kindest love and tenderness waiting for him at his quiet home yonder—and Genius throbbing in his young heart, and whispering to him, 'You shall be great, you shall be famous; you too shall love and sing; you will sing her so nobly that some kind heart shall forget you are weak and ill formed. Every poet had a love. Fate must give one to you too,'—and day by day he walks the forest, very likely looking out for that charmer. 'They were the happiest days of his life,' he says, when he was only dreaming of his fame : when he had gained that mistress she was no consoler.

That charmer made her appearance, it would seem, about the year 1705, when Pope was seventeen. Letters of his are extant, addressed to a certain Lady M——, whom the youth courted, and to whom he expressed his ardour in language, to say no worse of it, that is entirely pert, odious, and affected. He imitated love-compositions as he had been imitating love-poems just before—it was a sham mistress he courted, and a sham passion, expressed as became it. These unlucky letters found their way into print years afterwards, and were sold to the congenial Mr. Curll. If any of my hearers, as I hope they may, should take a fancy to look at Pope's correspondence, let them pass over that first part of it ; over, perhaps, almost all Pope's letters to women ; in which there is a tone of not pleasant gallantry, and, amidst a profusion of compliments and politenesses, a something which makes one distrust the

little pert, prurient bard. There is very little indeed
to say about his loves, and that little not edifying. He
wrote flames and raptures and elaborate verse and
prose for Lady Mary Wortley Montagu; but that
passion probably came to a climax in an impertinence,
and was extinguished by a box on the ear, or some
such rebuff, and he began on a sudden to hate her
with a fervour much more genuine than that of his
love had been. It was a feeble puny grimace of love,
and paltering with passion. After Mr. Pope had sent
off one of his fine compositions to Lady Mary, he
made a second draft from the rough copy, and
favoured some other friend with it. He was so
charmed with the letter of Gay's that I have just
quoted, that he had copied that and amended it, and
sent it to Lady Mary as his own. A gentleman who
writes letters à deux fins, and after having poured out
his heart to the beloved, serves up the same dish
réchauffé to a friend, is not very much in earnest
about his loves, however much he may be in his
piques and vanities when his impertinence gets its due.

But, save that unlucky part of the 'Pope Correspondence,' I do not know, in the range of our
literature, volumes more delightful.* You live in

* 'Mr. Pope to the Rev. Mr. Broom, Pulham, Norfolk.

'Aug. 29th, 1730.

'DEAR SIR,—I intended to write to you on this melancholy subject,
the death of Mr. Fenton, before yours came, but stayed to have informed
myself and you of the circumstances of it. All I hear is, that he felt a
gradual decay, though so early in life, and was declining for five or six
months. It was not, as I apprehended, the gout in his stomach, but, I
believe, rather a complication first of gross humours, as he was naturally
corpulent, not discharging themselves, as he used no sort of exercise.
No man better bore the approaches of his dissolution (as I am told), or
with less ostentation yielded up his being. The great modesty which
you know was natural to him, and the great contempt he had for all
sorts of vanity and parade, never appeared more than in his last
moments: he had a conscious satisfaction (no doubt) in acting right, in

them in the finest company in the world.  A little
stately, perhaps ; a little *apprêté* and conscious that

feeling himself honest, true, and unpretending to more than his own.
So he died as he lived, with that secret, yet sufficient contentment.

'As to any papers left behind him, I dare say they can be but few ;
for this reason, he never wrote out of vanity, or thought much of the
applause of men.  I know an instance when he did his utmost to conceal
his own merit that way ; and if we join to this his natural love of ease,
I fancy we must expect little of this sort : at least, I have heard of none,
except some few further remarks on Waller (which his cautious integrity
made him leave an order to be given to Mr. Tonson), and perhaps,
though it is many years since I saw it, a translation of the first book of
*Oppian*.  He had begun a tragedy of *Dion*, but made small progress in it.

'As to his other affairs, he died poor but honest, leaving no debts or
legacies, except of a few pounds to Mr. Trumbull and my lady, in token
of respect, gratefulness, and mutual esteem.

'I shall with pleasure take upon me to draw this amiable, quiet,
deserving, unpretending, Christian, and philosophical character in his
epitaph.  There truth may be spoken in a few words ; as for flourish,
and oratory, and poetry, I leave them to younger and more lively writers,
such as love writing for writing's sake, and would rather show their own
fine parts than report the valuable ones of any other man.  So the elegy
I renounce.

'I condole with you from my heart on the loss of so worthy a man
and a friend to us both. . . .

'Adieu ; let us love his memory and profit by his example.  Am very
sincerely, dear sir,                    Your affectionate and real servant.'

'*To the Earl of Burlington.*

'*August* 1714.

'My Lord,—If your mare could speak, she would give you an
account of what extraordinary company she had on the road, which,
since she cannot do, I will.

'It was the enterprising Mr. Lintot, the redoubtable rival of Mr.
Tonson, who, mounted on a stone-horse, overtook me in Windsor Forest.
He said he heard I designed for Oxford, the seat of the Muses, and
would, as my bookseller, by all means accompany me thither.

'I asked him where he got his horse ?  He answered he got it of his
publisher ; " for that rogue, my printer," said he, "disappointed me.  I
hoped to put him in good humour by a treat at the tavern of a brown
fricassée of rabbits, which cost ten shillings, with two quarts of wine,
besides my conversation.  I thought myself cock-sure of his horse, which
he readily promised me, but said that Mr. Tonson had just such another
design of going to Cambridge, expecting there the copy of a new kind of
Horace from Dr. ——— ; and if Mr. Tonson went, he was pre-engaged to
attend him, being to have the printing of the said copy.  So, in short, I

they are speaking to whole generations who are
listening ; but in the tone of their voices—pitched, as

borrowed this stone-horse of my publisher, which he had of Mr.
Oldmixon for a debt. He lent me, too, the pretty boy you see after me.
He was a smutty dog yesterday, and cost me more than two hours to
wash the ink off his face ; but the devil is a fair-conditioned devil, and
very forward in his catechism. If you have any more bags, he shall
carry them."

'I thought Mr. Lintot's civility not to be neglected, so gave the boy
a small bag containing three shirts and an Elzevir Virgil, and, mounting
in an instant, proceeded on the road, with my man before, my courteous
stationer beside, and the aforesaid devil behind.

'Mr. Lintot began in this manner : "Now, damn them ! What if
they should put it into the newspaper how you and I went together to
Oxford ? What would I care ? If I should go down into Sussex, they
would say I was gone to the Speaker ; but what of that ? If my son
were but big enough to go on with the business, by G—d, I would keep
as good company as old Jacob."

'Hereupon, I inquired of his son. "The lad," says he, " has fine
parts, but is somewhat sickly, much as you are. I spare for nothing in
his education at Westminster. Pray, don't you think Westminster to be
the best school in England ? Most of the late Ministry came out of it ;
so did many of this Ministry. I hope the boy will make his fortune."

'"Don't you design to let him pass a year at Oxford ?" "To what
purpose ?" said he. "The Universities do but make pedants, and I
intend to breed him a man of business."

'As Mr. Lintot was talking I observed he sat uneasy on his saddle,
for which I expressed some solicitude. "Nothing," says he. "I can bear
it well enough ; but, since we have the day before us, methinks it would
be very pleasant for you to rest awhile under the woods." When we
were alighted, "See, here, what a mighty pretty Horace I have in my
pocket ? What if you amused yourself in turning an ode till we mount
again ? Lord ! if you pleased, what a clever miscellany might you make
at leisure hours !" "Perhaps I may," said I, "if we ride on : the motion
is an aid to my fancy : a round trot very much awakens my spirits ;
then jog on apace, and I'll think as hard as I can."

'Silence ensued for a full hour ; after which Mr. Lintot lugged the
reins, stopped short, and broke out, "Well, sir, how far have you gone ?"
I answered, seven miles. "Z—ds, sir," said Lintot, "I thought you had
done seven stanzas. Oldisworth, in a ramble round Wimbledon Hill,
would translate a whole ode in half this time. I'll say that for
Oldisworth [though I lost by his Timothy's], he translates an ode of
Horace the quickest of any man in England. I remember Dr. King
would write verses in a tavern, three hours after he could not speak :
and there is Sir Richard, in that rumbling old chariot of his, between
Fleet Ditch and St. Giles's Pound, shall make you half a Job."

"Pray, Mr. Lintot," said I, "now you talk of translators, what is

no doubt they are, beyond the mere conversation key
—in the expression of their thoughts, their various

your method of managing them?" "Sir," replied he, "these are the
saddest pack of rogues in the world : in a hungry fit, they'll swear they
understand all the languages in the universe. I have known one of
them take down a Greek book upon my counter and cry, 'Ah, this is
Hebrew, and must read it from the latter end.' By G—d, I can never
be sure in these fellows, for I neither understand Greek, Latin, French,
nor Italian myself. But this is my way : I agree with them for ten
shillings per sheet, with a proviso that I will have their doings corrected
with whom I please : so by one or the other they are led at last to the
true sense of an author ; my judgment giving the negative to all my
translators." "Then how are you sure these correctors may not impose
upon you?" "Why, I get any civil gentleman (especially any Scotch-
man) that comes into my shop, to read the original to me in English ;
by this I know whether my first translator be deficient, and whether my
corrector merits his money or not.

"'I'll tell you what happened to me last month. I bargained with
S—— for a new version of *Lucretius*, to publish against Tonson's,
agreeing to pay the author so many shillings at his producing so many
lines. He made a great progress in a very short time, and I gave it to
the corrector to compare with the Latin ; but he went directly to
Creech's translation, and found it the same, word for word, all but the
first page. Now, what d'ye think I did? I arrested the translator for
a cheat ; nay, and I stopped the corrector's pay, too, upon the proof that
he had made use of Creech instead of the original."

"'Pray tell me next how you deal with the critics?" "Sir," said he,
"nothing more easy. I can silence the most formidable of them : the
rich ones for a sheet apiece of the blotted manuscript, which cost me
nothing ; they'll go about with it to their acquaintance, and pretend
they had it from the author, who submitted it to their correction : this
has given some of them such an air, that in time they come to be consulted with and dedicated to as the tip-top critics of the town.—As for
the poor critics, I'll give you one instance of my management, by which
you may guess the rest : A lean man, that looked like a very good
scholar, came to me t'other day ; he turned over your Homer, shook his
head, shrugged up his shoulders, and pish'd at every line of it. 'One
would wonder,' says he, 'at the strange presumption of some men ;
Homer is no such easy task as every stripling, every versifier'—— he
was going on when my wife called to dinner. 'Sir,' said I, 'will you
please to eat a piece of beef with me?' 'Mr. Lintot,' said he, 'I
am very sorry you should be at the expense of this great book : I am
really concerned on your account.' 'Sir, I am much obliged to you :
if you can dine upon a piece of beef, together with a slice of pudding'—— 'Mr. Lintot, I do not say but Mr. Pope, if he would condescend to advise with men of learning'—— 'Sir, the pudding is
upon the table, if you please to go in.' My critic complies ; he comes

views and natures, there is something generous, and cheering, and ennobling. You are in the society of men who have filled the greatest parts in the world's story—you are with St. John the statesman ; Peter-

to a taste of your poetry, and tells me in the same breath that the book is commendable, and the pudding excellent.

'"Now, sir," continued Mr. Lintot, "in return for the frankness I have shown, pray tell me, is it the opinion of your friends at Court that my Lord Landsdowne will be brought to the bar or not ?" I told him I heard he would not, and I hoped it, my Lord being one I had particular obligations to.—"That may be," replied Mr. Lintot ; "but by G— if he is not, I shall lose the printing of a very good trial."

'These, my Lord, are a few traits with which you discern the genius of Mr. Lintot, which I have chosen for the subject of a letter. I dropped him as soon as I got to Oxford, and paid a visit to my Lord Carleton, at Middleton. . . . I am,' &c.

'*Dr. Swift to Mr. Pope.*

'*Sept.* 29, 1725.

'I AM now returning to the noble scene of Dublin—into the *grand monde*—for fear of burying my parts ; to signalise myself among curates and vicars, and correct all corruptions crept in relating to the weight of bread-and-butter through those dominions where I govern. I have employed my time (besides ditching) in finishing, correcting, amending, and transcribing my "Travels" [Gulliver's], in four parts complete, newly augmented, and intended for the press when the world shall deserve them, or rather, when a printer shall be found brave enough to venture his ears. I like the scheme of our meeting after distresses and dispersions ; but the chief end I propose to myself in all my labours is to vex the world rather than divert it ; and if I could compass that design without hurting my own person or fortune, I would be the most indefatigable writer you have ever seen without reading. I am exceedingly pleased that you have done with translations ; Lord Treasurer Oxford often lamented that a rascally world should lay you under a necessity of misemploying your genius for so long a time ; but since you will now be so much better employed, when you think of the world, give it one lash the more at my request. I have ever hated all nations, professions, and communities ; and all my love is towards individuals— for instance, I hate the tribe of lawyers, but I love Counsellor Such-a- one and Judge Such-a-one : it is so with physicians (I will not speak of my own trade), soldiers, English, Scotch, French, and the rest. But principally I hate and detest that animal called man—although I heartily love John, Peter, Thomas, and so forth.

'. . . I have got materials towards a treatise proving the falsity of that definition *animal rationale*, and to show it should be only *rationis*

borough the conqueror ; Swift, the greatest wit of all
times ; Gay, the kindliest laugher,—it is a privilege
to sit in that company. Delightful and generous
banquet ! with a little faith and a little fancy any one

*capax. . . .* The matter is so clear that it will admit of no dispute—
nay, I will hold a hundred pounds that you and I agree in the point. . . .

'Mr. Lewis sent me an account of Dr. Arbuthnot's illness, which is
a very sensible affliction to me, who, by living so long out of the world,
have lost that hardness of heart contracted by years and general conversation. I am daily losing friends, and neither seeking nor getting
others. Oh ! if the world had but a dozen of Arbuthnots in it, I would
burn my "Travels" !'

*'Mr. Pope to Dr. Swift.*

'*October* 15, 1725.

'I AM wonderfully pleased with the suddenness of your kind answer.
It makes me hope you are coming towards us, and that you incline
more and more to your old friends. . . . Here is one [Lord Bolingbroke]
who was once a powerful planet, but has now (after long experience
of all that comes of shining) learned to be content with returning to his
first point without the thought or ambition of shining at all. Here is
another [Edward, Earl of Oxford], who thinks one of the greatest
glories of his father was to have distinguished and loved you, and who
loves you hereditarily. Here is Arbuthnot, recovered from the jaws of
death, and more pleased with the hope of seeing you again than of
reviewing a world, every part of which he has long despised but what
is made up of a few men like yourself. . . .

'Our friend Gay is used as the friends of Tories are by Whigs—and
generally by Tories too. Because he had humour, he was supposed to
have dealt with Dr. Swift, in like manner as when any one had learning
formerly, he was thought to have dealt with the devil. . . .

'Lord Bolingbroke had not the least harm by his fall ; I wish he had
received no more by his other fall. But Lord Bolingbroke is the most
improved mind since you saw him, that ever was improved without
shifting into a new body, or being *paullo minus ab angelis.* I have
often imagined to myself, that if ever all of us meet again, after so many
varieties and changes, after so much of the old world and of the old
man in each of us has been altered, that scarce a single thought of the
one, any more than a single atom of the other, remains just the same ;
I have fancied, I say, that we should meet like the righteous in the
millennium, quite in peace, divested of all our former passions, smiling
at our past follies, and content to enjoy the kingdom of the just in
tranquillity.

.       .       .       .       .       .       .       .

'I designed to have left the following page for Dr. Arbuthnot to fill,
but he is so touched with the period in yours to me, concerning him,
that he intends to answer it by a whole letter. . . .'

of us here may enjoy it, and conjure up those great
figures out of the past, and listen to their wit and
wisdom.    Mind that there is always a certain *cachet*
about great men—they may be as mean on many
points as you or I, but they carry their great air—
they speak of common life more largely and generously
than common men do—they regard the world with a
manlier countenance, and see its real features more
fairly than the timid shufflers who only dare to look
up at life through blinkers, or to have an opinion
when there is a crowd to back it.    He who reads these
noble records of a past age, salutes and reverences the
great spirits who adorn it.    You may go home now
and talk with St. John ; you may take a volume
from your library and listen to Swift and Pope.

Might I give counsel to any young hearer, I would
say to him, Try to frequent the company of your
betters.    In books and life that is the most wholesome society ; learn to admire rightly ; the great
pleasure of life is that.    Note what the great men
admired ; they admired great things : narrow spirits
admire basely, and worship meanly.    I know nothing
in any story more gallant and cheering than the love
and friendship which this company of famous men
bore towards one another.    There never has been a
society of men more friendly, as there never was one
more illustrious.    Who dares quarrel with Mr. Pope,
great and famous himself, for liking the society of
men great and famous ? and for liking them for the
qualities which made them so ?    A mere pretty
fellow from White's could not have written the
'Patriot King,' and would very likely have despised
little Mr. Pope, the decrepit Papist, whom the great
St. John held to be one of the best and greatest of
men ; a mere nobleman of the Court could no more
have won Barcelona, than he could have written

Peterborough's letters to Pope,* which are as witty as Congreve: a mere Irish Dean could not have written 'Gulliver;' and all these men loved Pope, and Pope loved all these men.  To name his friends is to name the best men of his time.  Addison had a senate; Pope reverenced his equals.  He spoke of Swift with respect and admiration always.  His admiration for Bolingbroke was so great, that when some one said of his friend, 'There is something in that great man which looks as if he was placed here by mistake,' 'Yes,' Pope answered, 'and when the comet appeared to us a month or two ago, I had

---

* Of the Earl of Peterborough, Walpole says :—'He was one of those men of careless wit and negligent grace, who scatter a thousand *bon-mots* and idle verses, which we painful compilers gather and hoard till the authors stare to find themselves authors.  Such was this lord, of an advantageous figure and enterprising spirit ; as gallant as Amadis and as brave ; but a little more expeditious in his journeys : for he is said to have seen more kings and more postillions than any man in Europe. . . .  He was a man, as his friend said, who would neither live nor die like any other mortal.'

### 'From the Earl of Peterborough to Pope.

'You must receive my letters with a just impartiality, and give grains of allowance for a gloomy or rainy day ; I sink grievously with the weather-glass, and am quite spiritless when oppressed with the thoughts of a birthday or a return.

'Dutiful affection was bringing me to town ; but undutiful laziness, and being much out of order, keep me in the country : however, if alive, I must make my appearance at the birthday. . . .

'You seem to think it vexatious that I shall allow you but one woman at a time either to praise or love.  If I dispute with you upon this point, I doubt every jury will give a verdict against me.  So, sir, with a Mahometan indulgence, I allow your pluralities, the favourite privilege of our church.

'I find you don't mend upon correction ; again I tell you you must not think of women in a reasonable way ; you know we always make goddesses of those we adore upon earth ; and do not all the good men tell us we must lay aside reason in what relates to the Deity ?

'. . . I should have been glad of anything of Swift's.  Pray, when you write to him next, tell him I expect him with impatience, in a place as odd and as much out of the way as himself.            Yours.'

Peterborough married Mrs. Anastasia Robinson, the celebrated singer.

sometimes an imagination that it might possibly be
come to carry him home as a coach comes to one's
door for visitors.' So these great spirits spoke of one
another. Show me six of the dullest middle-aged
gentlemen that ever dawdled round a club table so
faithful and so friendly.

We have said before that the chief wits of this time,
with the exception of Congreve, were what we should
now call men's men. They spent many hours of the
four-and-twenty, a fourth part of each day nearly, in
clubs and coffee-houses, where they dined, drank, and
smoked. Wit and news went by word of mouth ; a
journal in 1710 contained the very smallest portion of
one or the other. The chiefs spoke, the faithful
*habitués* sat round ; strangers came to wonder and
listen. Old Dryden had his headquarters at 'Will's,'
in Russell Street, at the corner of Bow Street : at
which place Pope saw him when he was twelve years
old. The company used to assemble on the first floor
—what was called the dining-room floor in those days
—and sat at various tables smoking their pipes. It is
recorded that the beaux of the day thought it a great
honour to be allowed to take a pinch out of Dryden's
snuff-box. When Addison began to reign, he with a
certain crafty propriety—a policy let us call it—which
belonged to his nature, set up his court, and appointed
the officers of his royal house. His palace was
'Button's,' opposite 'Will's.'* A quiet opposition, a

* 'Button had been a servant in the Countess of Warwick's family,
who, under the patronage of Addison, kept a coffee-house on the south
side of Russell Street, about two doors from Covent Garden. Here it
was that the wits of that time used to assemble. It is said that when
Addison had suffered any vexation from the Countess, he withdrew the
company from Button's house.

'From the coffee-house he went again to a tavern, where he often sat
late and drank too much wine.'—*Dr. Johnson.*

Will's Coffee-house was on the west side of Bow Street, and 'corner
of Russell Street.'—See *Handbook of London.*

silent assertion of empire, distinguished this great man. Addison's ministers were Budgell, Tickell, Philips, Carey; his master of the horse, honest Dick Steele, who was what Duroc was to Napoleon, or Hardy to Nelson: the man who performed his master's bidding, and would have cheerfully died in his quarrel. Addison lived with these people for seven or eight hours every day. The male society passed over their punch-bowls and tobacco-pipes about as much time as ladies of that age spent over spadille and manille.

For a brief space, upon coming up to town, Pope formed part of King Joseph's court, and was his rather too eager and obsequious humble servant.* Dick Steele, the editor of the *Tatler*, Mr. Addison's man, and his own man too—a person of no little figure in the world of letters—patronised the young poet, and set him a task or two. Young Mr. Pope did the task very quickly and smartly (he had been at the feet, quite as a boy, of Wycherley's † decrepit reputation

* 'My acquaintance with Mr. Addison commenced in 1712 : I liked him then as well as I liked any man, and was very fond of his conversation. It was very soon after that Mr. Addison advised me "not to be content with the applause of half the nation." He used to talk much and often to me, of moderation in parties : and used to blame his dear friend Steele for being too much of a party man. He encouraged me in my design of translating the *Iliad*, which was begun that year, and finished in 1718.'—Pope. *Spence's Anecdotes.*

'Addison had Budgell, and I think Philips, in the house with him —Gay they would call one of my *élèves.*—They were angry with me for keeping so much with Dr. Swift and some of the late Ministry.'—Pope. *Spence's Anecdotes.*

† '*To Mr. Blount.*

*Jan.* 21, 1715-16.

'I know of nothing that will be so interesting to you at present as some circumstances of the last act of that eminent comic poet and our friend, Wycherley. He had often told me, and I doubt not he did all his acquaintance, that he would marry as soon as his life was despaired of. Accordingly, a few days before his death, he underwent the ceremony, and joined together those two sacraments which wise men say we should

and propped up for a year that doting old wit): he was anxious to be well with the men of letters, to get a footing and a recognition. He thought it an honour to be admitted into their company; to have the confidence of Mr. Addison's friend Captain Steele. His eminent parts obtained for him the honour of heralding Addison's triumph of 'Cato' with his admirable prologue, and heading the victorious procession as it were. Not content with this act of homage and admiration, he wanted to distinguish himself by assaulting Addison's enemies, and attacked John Dennis with a prose lampoon, which highly offended his lofty patron. Mr. Steele was instructed to write

be the last to receive; for, if you observe, matrimony is placed after extreme unction in our catechism, as a kind of hint of the order of time in which they are to be taken. The old man then lay down, satisfied in the consciousness of having, by this one act, obliged a woman who (he was told) had merit, and shown an heroic resentment of the ill-usage of his next heir. Some hundred pounds which he had with the lady discharged his debts: a jointure of £500 a year made her a recompence; and the nephew was left to comfort himself as well as he could with the miserable remains of a mortgaged estate. I saw our friend twice after this was done—less peevish in his sickness than he used to be in his health; neither much afraid of dying, nor (which in him had been more likely) much ashamed of marrying. The evening before he expired, he called his young wife to the bedside, and earnestly entreated her not to deny him one request—the last he should make. Upon her assurances of consenting to it, he told her: "My dear, it is only this—that you will never marry an old man again." I cannot help remarking that sickness, which often destroys both wit and wisdom, yet seldom has power to remove that talent which we call humour. Mr. Wycherley showed his even in his last compliment; though I think his request a little hard, for why should he bar her from doubling her jointure on the same easy terms?

'So trivial as these circumstances are, I should not be displeased myself to know such trifles when they concern or characterise any eminent person. The wisest and wittiest of men are seldom wiser or wittier than others in these sober moments; at least, our friend ended much in the same character he had lived in; and Horace's rule for play may as well be applied to him as a playwright:—

'"Servetur ad imum
Qualis ab incepto processerit et sibi constet."

'I am,' &c.

to Mr. Dennis, and inform him that Mr. Pope's
pamphlet against him was written quite without Mr.
Addison's approval.*    Indeed, 'The Narrative of Dr.
Robert Norris on the Phrenzy of J. D.' is a vulgar
and mean satire, and such a blow as the magnificent
Addison could never desire to see any partisan of his
strike in any literary quarrel.   Pope was closely allied
with Swift when he wrote this pamphlet.   It is so
dirty that it has been printed in Swift's works, too.
It bears the foul marks of the master hand.   Swift
admired and enjoyed with all his heart the prodigious
genius of the young Papist lad out of Windsor Forest,
who had never seen a university in his life, and came
and conquered the Dons and the doctors with his wit.
He applauded, and loved him, too, and protected him,
and taught him mischief.   I wish Addison could have
loved him better.   The best satire that ever has been
penned would never have been written then ; and one
of the best characters the world ever knew would have
been without a flaw.   But he who had so few equals
could not bear one, and Pope was more than that.
When Pope, trying for himself, and soaring on his
immortal young wings, found that his, too, was a
genius, which no pinion of that age could follow, he
rose and left Addison's company, settling on his own
eminence, and singing his own song.

It was not possible that Pope should remain a
retainer of Mr. Addison ; nor likely that after escaping
from his vassalage and assuming an independent crown,
the sovereign whose allegiance he quitted should view
him amicably.†   They did not do wrong to mislike

* 'Addison, who was no stranger to the world, probably saw the
selfishness of Pope's friendship ; and resolving that he should have the
consequences of his officiousness to himself, informed Dennis by Steele
that he was sorry for the insult.'—JOHNSON.  *Life of Addison.*

† 'While I was heated with what I heard, I wrote a letter to Mr.
Addison, to let him know "that I was not unacquainted with this

each other. They but followed the impulse of nature, and the consequence of position. When Bernadotte became heir to a throne, the Prince Royal of Sweden was naturally Napoleon's enemy. 'There are many passions and tempers of mankind,' says Mr. Addison in the *Spectator*, speaking a couple of years before the little differences between him and Mr. Pope took place, 'which naturally dispose us to depress and vilify the merit of one rising in the esteem of mankind. All those who made their entrance into the world with the same advantages, and were once looked on as his equals, are apt to think the fame of his merits a reflection on their own deserts. Those who were once his equals envy and defame him, because they now see him the superior; and those who were once his superiors, because they look upon him as their equal.' Did Mr. Addison, justly perhaps thinking that, as young Mr. Pope had not had the benefit of a university education, he couldn't know Greek, therefore he couldn't translate Homer, encourage his young friend Mr. Tickell, of Queen's, to translate that poet, and aid him with his own known scholarship and skill?* It was natural that Mr. Addison should doubt of the learning of an amateur Grecian, should have a high opinion of Mr. Tickell, of Queen's, and should help that ingenious young man. It was natural,

behaviour of his; that if I was to speak of him severely in return for it, it should not be in such a dirty way; that I should rather tell him himself fairly of his faults, and allow his good qualities; and that it should be something in the following manner." I then subjoined the first sketch of what has since been called my satire on Addison. He used me very civilly ever after; and never did me any injustice, that I know of, from that time to his death, which was about three years after.'—POPE. *Spence's Anecdotes.*

* 'That Tickell should have been guilty of a villainy seems to us highly improbable; that Addison should have been guilty of a villainy seems to us highly improbable; but that these two men should have conspired together to commit a villainy, seems, to us, improbable in a tenfold degree.'—*Macaulay*

on the other hand, that Mr. Pope and Mr. Pope's
friends should believe that his counter-translation,
suddenly advertised and so long written, though
Tickell's college friends had never heard of it—though,
when Pope first wrote to Addison regarding his scheme,
Mr. Addison knew nothing of the similar project of
Tickell, of Queen's—it was natural that Mr. Pope
and his friends, having interests, passions, and prejudices of their own, should believe that Tickell's
translation was but an act of opposition against Pope,
and that they should call Mr. Tickell's emulation Mr.
Addison's envy—if envy it were.

> 'And were there one whose fires
> True genius kindles and fair fame inspires,
> Blest with each talent and each art to please,
> And born to write, converse, and live with ease ;
> Should such a man, too fond to rule alone,
> Bear, like the Turk, no brother near the throne ;
> View him with scornful yet with jealous eyes,
> And hate, for arts that caused himself to rise ;
> Damn with faint praise, assent with civil leer,
> And, without sneering, teach the rest to sneer :
> Willing to wound, and yet afraid to strike,
> Just hint a fault, and hesitate dislike ;
> Alike reserved to blame as to commend,
> A timorous foe and a suspicious friend ;
> Dreading even fools, by flatterers besieged,
> And so obliging that he ne'er obliged :
> Like Cato give his little senate laws,
> And sit attentive to his own applause ;
> While wits and Templars every sentence raise,
> And wonder with a foolish face of praise ;
> Who but must laugh if such a man there be,
> Who would not weep if Atticus were he ?'

'I sent the verses to Mr. Addison,' said Pope, 'and
he used me very civilly ever after.' No wonder he

did. It was shame very likely more than fear that silenced him. Johnson recounts an interview between Pope and Addison after their quarrel, in which Pope was angry, and Addison tried to be contemptuous and calm. Such a weapon as Pope's must have pierced any scorn. It flashes for ever, and quivers in Addison's memory. His great figure looks out on us from the past—stainless but for that—pale, calm, and beautiful : it bleeds from that black wound. He should be drawn, like Saint Sebastian, with that arrow in his side. As he sent to Gay and asked his pardon, as he bade his stepson come and see his death, be sure he had forgiven Pope, when he made ready to show how a Christian could die.

Pope then formed part of the Addisonian court for a short time, and describes himself in his letters as sitting with that coterie until two o'clock in the morning over punch and burgundy amidst the fumes of tobacco. To use an expression of the present day, the 'pace' of those *viveurs* of the former age was awful. Peterborough lived into the very jaws of death ; Godolphin laboured all day and gambled at night ; Bolingbroke,* writing to Swift, from Dawley,

---

* '*Lord Bolingbroke to the Three Yahoos of Twickenham.*

'*July* 23, 1726.

'Jonathan, Alexander, John, most excellent Triumvirs of Parnassus,—Though you are probably very indifferent where I am, or what I am doing, yet I resolve to believe the contrary. I persuade myself that you have sent at least fifteen times within this fortnight to Dawley farm, and that you are extremely mortified at my long silence. To relieve you, therefore, from this great anxiety of mind, I can do no less than write a few lines to you ; and I please myself beforehand with the vast pleasure which this epistle must needs give you. That I may add to this pleasure, and give further proofs of my beneficent temper, I will likewise inform you, that I shall be in your neighbourhood again by the end of next week : by which time I hope that Jonathan's imagination of business will be succeeded by some imagination more becoming a professor of that divine science, *la bagatelle*. Adieu. Jonathan, Alexander, John, mirth be with you !'

in his retirement, dating his letter at six o'clock in
the morning, and rising, as he says, refreshed, serene,
and calm, calls to mind the time of his London life;
when about that hour he used to be going to bed,
surfeited with pleasure, and jaded with business; his
head often full of schemes, and his heart as often full
of anxiety. It was too hard, too coarse a life for the
sensitive, sickly Pope. He was the only wit of the
day, a friend writes to me, who wasn't fat.* Swift
was fat; Addison was fat; Steele was fat; Gay and
Thomson were preposterously fat—all that fuddling
and punch-drinking, that club and coffee-house
boozing, shortened the lives and enlarged the waistcoats of the men of that age. Pope withdrew in a
great measure from this boisterous London company,
and being put into an independence by the gallant
exertions of Swift † and his private friends, and by the
enthusiastic national admiration which justly rewarded
his great achievement of the 'Iliad,' purchased that
famous villa of Twickenham which his song and life
celebrated; duteously bringing his old parent to live
and die there, entertaining his friends there, and
making occasional visits to London in his little chariot,
in which Atterbury compared him to 'Homer in a
nutshell.'

  'Mr. Dryden was not a genteel man,' Pope quaintly
said to Spence, speaking of the manner and habits of
the famous old patriarch of 'Will's.' With regard to
Pope's own manners, we have the best contemporary

---

* Prior must be excepted from this observation   'He was lank and
lean.'

† Swift exerted himself very much in promoting the *Iliad* subscription; and also introduced Pope to Harley and Bolingbroke. Pope
realised by the *Iliad* upwards of £5000, which he laid out partly in
annuities, and partly in the purchase of his famous villa. Johnson
remarks that 'it would be hard to find a man so well entitled to notice
by his wit, that ever delighted so much in talking of his money.'

authority that they were singularly refined and polished. With his extraordinary sensibility, with his known tastes, with his delicate frame, with his power and dread of ridicule, Pope could have been no other than what we call a highly-bred person.* His closest friends, with the exception of Swift, were among the delights and ornaments of the polished society of their age.    Garth,† the accomplished and benevolent, whom Steele has described so charmingly, of whom Codrington said that his character was 'all beauty,' and whom Pope himself called the best of Christians without knowing it ; Arbuthnot,‡ one of the wisest, wittiest,

* 'His (Pope's) voice in common conversation was so naturally musical, that I remember honest Tom Southerne used always to call him "the little nightingale." '—*Orrery.*

† Garth, whom Dryden calls 'generous as his Muse,' was a York-shireman. He graduated at Cambridge, and was made M.D. in 1691. He soon distinguished himself in his profession, by his poem of the 'Dispensary,' and in society, and pronounced Dryden's funeral oration. He was a strict Whig, a notable member of the 'Kit-Cat,' and a friendly, convivial, able man. He was knighted by George I., with the Duke of Marlborough's sword. He died in 1718.

‡ 'Arbuthnot was the son of an episcopal clergyman in Scotland, and belonged to an ancient and distinguished Scotch family. He was educated at Aberdeen ; and, coming up to London—according to a Scotch practice often enough alluded to—to make his fortune, first made himself known by *An Examination of Dr. Woodward's Account of the Deluge.* He became physician successively to Prince George of Denmark and to Queen Anne. He is usually allowed to have been the most learned, as well as one of the most witty and humourous members of the Scriblerus Club. The opinion entertained of him by the humourists of the day is abundantly evidenced in their correspondence. When he found himself in his last illness, he wrote thus, from his retreat at Hampstead, to Swift :—

' " HAMPSTEAD : *Oct.* 4, 1734.

' 'MY DEAR AND WORTHY FRIEND,—You have no reason to put me among the rest of your forgetful friends, for I wrote two long letters to you, to which I never received one word of answer. The first was about your health ; the last I sent a great while ago, by one De la Mar. I can assure you with great truth that none of your friends or acquaint-ance has a more warm heart towards you than myself. I am going out

most accomplished, gentlest of mankind ; Bolingbroke,
the Alcibiades of his age ; the generous Oxford ; the

of this troublesome world, and you, among the rest of my friends, shall
have my last prayers and good wishes.

'" . . I came out to this place so reduced by a dropsy and an
asthma, that I could neither sleep, breathe, eat, nor move. I most
earnestly desired and begged of God that He would take me. Contrary
to my expectation, upon venturing to ride (which I had forborne for
some years), I recovered my strength to a pretty considerable degree,
slept, and had my stomach again. . .   What I did, I can assure you
was not for life, but ease ; for I am at present in the case of a man that
was almost in harbour, and then blown back to sea—who has a reasonable hope of going to a good place, and an absolute certainty of leaving
a very bad one. Not that I have any particular disgust at the world ;
for I have as great comfort in my own family and from the kindness of
my friends as any man ; but the world, in the main, displeases me, and
I have too true a presentiment of calamities that are to befall my
country. However, if I should have the happiness to see you before I
die, you will find that I enjoy the comforts of life with my usual cheerfulness. I cannot imagine why you are frightened from a journey to
England : the reasons you assign are not sufficient—the journey, I am
sure, would do you good. In general, I recommend riding, of which I
have always had a good opinion, and can now confirm it from my own
experience.

'" My family give you their love and service. The great loss I
sustained in one of them gave me my first shock, and the trouble I
have with the rest to bring them to a right temper to bear the loss of
a father who loves them, and whom they love, is really a most sensible
affliction to me. I am afraid, my dear friend, we shall never see one
another more in this world. I shall, to the last moment, preserve my
love and esteem for you, being well assured you will never leave the
paths of virtue and honour ; for all that is in this world is not worth
the least deviation from the way. It will be great pleasure to me to
hear from you sometimes ; for none are with more sincerity than I am,
my dear friend, your most faithful friend and humble servant."'

' Arbuthnot,' Johnson says, ' was a man of great comprehension,
skilful in his profession, versed in the sciences, acquainted with ancient
literature, and able to animate his mass of knowledge by a bright and
active imagination ; a scholar with great brilliance of wit ; a wit who,
in the crowd of life, retained and discovered a noble ardour of religious
zeal.'

Dugald Stewart has testified to Arbuthnot's ability in a department
of which he was particularly qualified to judge : ' Let me add, that, in
the list of philosophical reformers, the authors of *Martinus Scriblerus*
ought not to be overlooked. Their happy ridicule of the scholastic
logic and metaphysics is universally known ; but few are aware of the

magnificent, the witty, the famous, and chivalrous
Peterborough : these were the fast and faithful friends
of Pope, the most brilliant company of friends, let us
repeat, that the world has ever seen.   The favourite
recreation of his leisure hours was the society of
painters, whose art he practised.   In his correspondence
are letters between him and Jervas, whose pupil he
loved to be—Richardson, a celebrated artist of his
time, and who painted for him a portrait of his old
mother, and for whose picture he asked and thanked
Richardson in one of the most delightful letters that
ever were penned,*—and the wonderful Kneller, who
bragged more, spelt worse, and painted better than
any artist of his day.†

acuteness and sagacity displayed in their allusions to some of the most
vulnerable passages in Locke's *Essay*.   In this part of the work it is
commonly understood that Arbuthnot had the principal share.'—See
*Preliminary Dissertation to Encyclopædia Britannica*, note to p. 242, and
also note B. B. B., p. 285.

\* ' *To Mr. Richardson.*

'TWICKENHAM, *June* 10, 1733.

'As I know you and I mutually desire to see one another, I hoped
that this day our wishes would have met, and brought you hither.
And this for the very reason, which possibly might hinder you coming,
that my poor mother is dead.   I thank God her death was as easy as
her life was innocent ; and as it cost her not a groan, or even a sigh,
there is yet upon her countenance such an expression of tranquillity,
nay, almost of pleasure, that it is even amiable to behold it.   It would
afford the finest image of a saint expired that ever painting drew ; and
it would be the greatest obligation which even that obliging art could
ever bestow on a friend, if you could come and sketch it for me.   I am
sure, if there be no very prevalent obstacle, you will leave any common
business to do this ; and I hope to see you this evening, as late as you
will, or to-morrow morning as early, before this winter flower is faded.
I will defer her interment till to-morrow night.   I know you love me,
or I could not have written this—I could not (at this time) have written
at all.   Adieu !   May you die as happily !            Yours,' &c.

† ' Mr. Pope was with Sir Godfrey Kneller one day, when his
nephew, a Guinea trader, came in.   "Nephew," said Sir Godfrey, "you
have the honour of seeing the two greatest men in the world."   "I don't

It is affecting to note, through Pope's correspondence,
the marked way in which his friends, the greatest, the
most famous, and wittiest men of the time—generals
and statesmen, philosophers and divines—all have a
kind word and a kind thought for the good simple
old mother, whom Pope tended so affectionately.
Those men would have scarcely valued her, but that
they knew how much he loved her, and that they
pleased him by thinking of her. If his early letters to
women are affected and insincere, whenever he speaks
about this one, it is with a childish tenderness and an
almost sacred simplicity. In 1713, when young Mr.
Pope had, by a series of the most astonishing victories
and dazzling achievements, seized the crown of poetry,
and the town was in an uproar of admiration, or
hostility, for the young chief; when Pope was issuing
his famous decrees for the translation of the 'Iliad;'
when Dennis and the lower critics were hooting and
assailing him; when Addison and the gentlemen of
his court were sneering with sickening hearts at the
prodigious triumphs of the young conqueror; when
Pope, in a fever of victory, and genius, and hope, and
anger, was struggling through the crowd of shouting
friends and furious detractors to his temple of Fame,
his old mother writes from the country, 'My deare,'
says she—'my deare, there's Mr. Blount, of Mapel
Durom, dead the same day that Mr. Inglefield died.
Your sister is well; but your brother is sick. My
service to Mrs. Blount, and all that ask of me. I
hope to hear from you, and that you are well, which
is my daily prayer; and this with my blessing.' The
triumph marches by, and the car of the young con-

know how great you may be," said the Guinea man, " but I don't like
your looks: I have often bought a man much better than both of you
together, all muscles and bones, for ten guineas "'—DR. WARBURTON.
*Spence's Anecdotes.*

queror, the hero of a hundred brilliant victories : the fond mother sits in the quiet cottage at home and says, 'I send you my daily prayers, and I bless you, my deare.'

In our estimate of Pope's character, let us always take into account that constant tenderness and fidelity of affection which pervaded and sanctified his life, and never forget that maternal benediction.*    It accompanied him always : his life seems purified by those artless and heartfelt prayers.  And he seems to have received and deserved the fond attachment of the other members of his family.  It is not a little touching to read in Spence of the enthusiastic admiration with which his half-sister regarded him, and the simple anecdote by which she illustrates her love.  'I think no man was ever so little fond of money.'  Mrs. Rackett says about her brother, 'I think my brother when he was young read more books than any man in the world ;' and she falls to telling stories of his schooldays, and the manner in which his master at Twyford ill-used him.  'I don't think my brother knew what fear was,' she continues ; and the accounts of Pope's friends bear out this character for courage. When he had exasperated the dunces, and threats of violence and personal assault were brought to him, the dauntless little champion never for one instant allowed fear to disturb him, or condescended to take any guard in his daily walks except occasionally his faithful dog to bear him company.  'I had rather die

---

*Swift's mention of him as one

> 'whose filial piety excels
> Whatever Grecian story tells,'

is well known.  And a sneer of Walpole's may be put to a better use than he ever intended it for, *à propos* of this subject.  He charitably sneers, in one of his letters, at Spence's 'fondling an old mother—in imitation of Pope !'

at once,' said the gallant little cripple, 'than live in fear of those rascals.'

As for his death, it was what the noble Arbuthnot asked and enjoyed for himself—a euthanasia—a beautiful end. A perfect benevolence, affection, serenity, hallowed the departure of that high soul. Even in the very hallucinations of his brain, and weaknesses of his delirium, there was something almost sacred. Spence describes him in his last days, looking up and with a rapt gaze as if something had suddenly passed before him. 'He said to me, "What's that?" pointing into the air with a very steady regard, and then looked down and said, with a smile of the greatest softness, "'Twas a vision!"' He laughed scarcely ever, but his companions describe his countenance as often illuminated by a peculiar sweet smile.

'When,' said Spence,* the kind anecdotist whom Johnson despised—'when I was telling Lord Bolingbroke that Mr. Pope, on every catching and recovery of his mind, was always saying something kindly of his present or absent friends; and that this was so surprising, as it seemed to me as if humanity had outlasted understanding, Lord Bolingbroke said, "It has so," and then added, "I never in my life knew a man who had so tender a heart for his particular friends, or a more general friendship for mankind. I have known him these thirty years, and value myself more for that man's love than"—— Here,' Spence says, 'St. John sunk his head and lost his voice in

* Joseph Spence was the son of a clergyman, near Winchester. He was a short time at Eton, and afterwards became a Fellow of New College, Oxford, a clergyman, and professor of poetry. He was a friend of Thomson's, whose reputation he aided. He published an *Essay on the Odyssey* in 1726, which introduced him to Pope. Everybody liked him. His *Anecdotes* were placed, while still in MS., at the service of Johnson and also of Malone. They were published by Mr. Singer in 1820.

tears.' The sob which finishes the epitaph is finer than words. It is the cloak thrown over the father's face in the famous Greek picture, which hides the grief and heightens it.

In Johnson's 'Life of Pope' you will find described, with rather a malicious minuteness, some of the personal habits and infirmities of the great little Pope. His body was crooked, he was so short that it was necessary to raise his chair in order to place him on a level with other people at table.* He was sewed up in a buckram suit every morning, and required a nurse like a child. His contemporaries reviled these misfortunes with a strange acrimony, and made his poor deformed person the butt for many a bolt of heavy wit. The facetious Mr. Dennis, in speaking of him, says, 'If you take the first letter of Mr. Alexander Pope's Christian name, and the first and last letters of his surname, you have A. P. E.' Pope catalogues, at the end of the 'Dunciad,' with a rueful precision, other pretty names, besides Ape, which Dennis called him. That great critic pronounced Mr. Pope a little ass, a fool, a coward, a Papist, and therefore a hater of Scripture, and so forth. It must be remembered that the pillory was a flourishing and popular institution in those days. Authors stood in it in the body sometimes · and dragged their enemies thither morally, hooted them with foul abuse, and assailed them with garbage of the gutter. Poor Pope's figure was an easy one for those clumsy caricaturists to draw. Any

* He speaks of Arbuthnot's having helped him through 'that long disease, my life' But not only was he so feeble as is implied in his use of the 'buckram,' but 'it now appears,' says Mr. Peter Cunningham, 'from his unpublished letters, that, like Lord Hervey, he had recourse to ass's milk for the preservation of his health.' It is to his lordship's use of that simple beverage that he alludes when he says—

'Let Sporus tremble !—A. What, that thing of silk, Sporus, that mere white-curd of ass's milk ?'

stupid hand could draw a hunchback and write Pope
underneath. They did. A libel was published against
Pope, with such a frontispiece. This kind of rude
jesting was an evidence not only of an ill nature, but
a dull one. When a child makes a pun, or a lout
breaks out into a laugh, it is some very obvious
combination of words, or discrepancy of objects, which
provokes the infantine satirist, or tickles the boorish
wag; and many of Pope's revilers laughed not so
much because they were wicked, as because they knew
no better.

Without the utmost sensibility, Pope could not
have been the poet he was; and through his life,
however much he protested that he disregarded their
abuse, the coarse ridicule of his opponents stung and
tore him. One of Cibber's pamphlets coming into
Pope's hands, whilst Richardson the painter was with
him, Pope turned round and said, 'These things are
my diversions;' and Richardson, sitting by whilst
Pope perused the libel, said he saw his features
'writhing with anguish.' How little human nature
changes! Can't one see that little figure? Can't
one fancy one is reading Horace? Can't one fancy
one is speaking of to-day?

The tastes and sensibilities of Pope, which led him
to cultivate the society of persons of fine manners, or
wit, or taste, or beauty, caused him to shrink equally
from that shabby and boisterous crew which formed
the rank and file of literature in his time: and he was
as unjust to these men as they to him. The delicate
little creature sickened at habits and company which
were quite tolerable to robuster men: and in the
famous feud between Pope and the Dunces, and without attributing any peculiar wrong to either, one can
quite understand how the two parties should so hate
each other. As I fancy, it was a sort of necessity that

when Pope's triumph passed, Mr. Addison and his men should look rather contemptuously down on it from their balcony ; so it was natural for Dennis and Tibbald, and Welsted and Cibber, and the worn and hungry pressmen in the crowd below, to howl at him and assail him. And Pope was more savage to Grub Street than Grub Street was to Pope. The thong with which he lashed them was dreadful ; he fired upon that howling crew such shafts of flame and poison, he slew and wounded so fiercely, that in reading the 'Dunciad' and the prose lampoons of Pope, one feels disposed to side against the ruthless little tyrant, at least to pity those wretched folk on whom he was so unmerciful. It was Pope, and Swift to aid him, who established among us the Grub Street tradition. He revels in base descriptions of poor men's want ; he gloats over poor Dennis's garret, and flannel nightcap and red stockings ; he gives instructions how to find Curll's author—the historian at the tallow-chandler's under the blind arch in Petty France, the two translators in bed together, the poet in the cock-loft in Budge Row, whose landlady keeps the ladder. It was Pope, I fear, who contributed, more than any man who ever lived, to depreciate the literary calling. It was not an unprosperous one before that time, as we have seen ; at least there were great prizes in the profession which had made Addison a Minister, and Prior an Ambassador, and Steele a Commissioner, and Swift all but a bishop. The profession of letters was ruined by that libel of the 'Dunciad.' If authors were wretched and poor before, if some of them lived in haylofts, of which their landladies kept the ladders, at least nobody came to disturb them in their straw ; if three of them had but one coat between them, the two remained invisible in the garret, the third, at any rate, appeared

decently at the coffee-house and paid his twopence like
a gentleman.   It was Pope that dragged into light all
this poverty and meanness, and held up those wretched
shifts and rags to public ridicule.   It was Pope that
has made generations of the reading world (delighted
with the mischief, as who would not be that reads it ?)
believe that author and wretch, author and rags,
author and dirt, author and drink, gin, cowheel, tripe,
poverty, duns, bailiffs, squalling children, and clamorous
landladies, were always associated together.   The
condition of authorship began to fall from the days of
the ' Dunciad : ' and I believe in my heart that much
of that obloquy which has since pursued our calling
was occasioned by Pope's libels and wicked wit.
Everybody read those.   Everybody was familiarised
with the idea of the poor devil, the author.   The
manner is so captivating that young authors practise
it, and begin their career with satire.   It is so easy to
write, and so pleasant to read ! to fire a shot that
makes a giant wince, perhaps ; and fancy one's self
his conqueror.   It is easy to shoot—but not as Pope
did.   The shafts of his satire rise sublimely : no poet's
verse ever mounted higher than that wonderful flight
with which the ' Dunciad ' concludes : *—

> ' She comes, she comes ! the sable throne behold
> Of Night primeval and of Chaos old ;
> Before her, Fancy's gilded clouds decay,
> And all its varying rainbows die away ;
> Wit shoots in vain its momentary fires,
> The meteor drops, and in a flash expires.
> As, one by one, at dread Medea's strain
> The sick'ning stars fade off the ethereal plain ;
> As Argus' eyes, by Hermes' wand oppress'd,
> Closed, one by one, to everlasting rest ;—

---

* ' He (Johnson) repeats to us, in his forcible melodious manner, the
concluding lines of the " Dunciad." '—*Boswell.*

Thus, at her fell approach and secret might,
Art after Art goes out, and all is night.
See skulking Truth to her old cavern fled,
Mountains of casuistry heaped o'er her head ;
Philosophy that leaned on Heaven before,
Shrinks to her second cause and is no more.
Religion, blushing, veils her sacred fires,
And, unawares, Morality expires.
Nor public flame, nor private, dares to shine,
Nor human spark is left, nor glimpse divine.
Lo ! thy dread empire, Chaos, is restored,
Light dies before thy uncreating word ;
Thy hand, great Anarch, lets the curtain fall,
And universal darkness buries all.'*

In these astonishing lines Pope reaches, I think, to
the very greatest height which his sublime art has
attained, and shows himself the equal of all poets of all
times. It is the brightest ardour, the loftiest assertion
of truth, the most generous wisdom illustrated by the
noblest poetic figure, and spoken in words the aptest,
grandest, and most harmonious. It is heroic courage
speaking : a splendid declaration of righteous wrath
and war. It is the gage flung down, and the silver
trumpet ringing defiance to falsehood and tyranny,
deceit, dulness, superstition. It is Truth, the
champion, shining and intrepid, and fronting the
great world tyrant with armies or slaves at his back.
It is a wonderful and victorious single combat, in that
great battle which has always been waging since
society began.

In speaking of a work of consummate art one does
not try to show what it actually is, for that were vain ;
but what it is like, and what are the sensations

* 'Mr. Langton informed me that he once related to Johnson (on
the authority of Spence), that Pope himself admired these lines so much
that when he repeated them his voice faltered. "And well it might,
sir," said Johnson, "for they are noble lines." '—*J. Boswell, junior.*

produced in the mind of him who views it. And in considering Pope's admirable career, I am forced into similitudes drawn from other courage and greatness, and into comparing him with those who achieved triumphs in actual war. I think of the works of young Pope as I do of the actions of young Bonaparte or young Nelson. In their common life you will find frailties and meannesses, as great as the vices and follies of the meanest men. But in the presence of the great occasion, the great soul flashes out, and conquers transcendent. In thinking of the splendour of Pope's young victories, of his merit, unequalled as his renown, I hail and salute the achieving genius, and do homage to the pen of a hero.

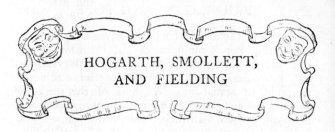

# HOGARTH, SMOLLETT,
# AND FIELDING

I SUPPOSE, as long as novels last and authors aim at
interesting their public, there must always be in the
story a virtuous and gallant hero, a wicked monster
his opposite, and a pretty girl who finds a champion;
bravery and virtue conquer beauty : and vice, after
seeming to triumph through a certain number of pages,
is sure to be discomfited in the last volume, when
justice overtakes him and honest folk come by their
own. There never was perhaps a greatly popular
story but this simple plot was carried through it :
mere satiric wit is addressed to a class of readers and
thinkers quite different to those simple souls who
laugh and weep over the novel. I fancy very few
ladies, indeed, for instance, could be brought to like
'Gulliver' heartily, and (putting the coarseness and
difference of manners out of the question) to relish
the wonderful satire of 'Jonathan Wild.' In that
strange apologue, the author takes for a hero the
greatest rascal, coward, traitor, tyrant, hypocrite, that
his wit and experience, both large in this matter,
could enable him to devise or depict : he accompanies
this villain through all the actions of his life, with a
grinning deference and a wonderful mock respect ;
and doesn't leave him till he is dangling at the gallows,
when the satirist makes him a low bow and wishes the
scoundrel good day.

It was not by satire of this sort, or by scorn and
contempt, that Hogarth achieved his vast popularity

and acquired his reputation.* His art is quite
simple ; † he speaks popular parables to interest

* Coleridge speaks of the 'beautiful female faces' in Hogarth's
pictures, 'in whom,' he says, 'the satirist never extinguished that
love of beauty which belonged to him as a poet.'—*The Friend*.

† ' I was pleased with the reply of a gentleman, who, being asked
which book he esteemed most in his library, answered "Shakspeare :"
being asked which he esteemed next best, replied "Hogarth." His
graphic representations are indeed books : they have the teeming,
fruitful, suggestive meaning of *words*. Other pictures we look at—his
prints we read. . . .

' The quantity of thought which Hogarth crowds into every picture
would almost unvulgarise every subject which he might choose. . . .

' I say not that all the ridiculous subjects of Hogarth have necessarily
something in them to make us like them ; some are indifferent to us,
some in their nature repulsive, and only made interesting by the wonderful skill and truth to nature in the painter : but I contend that there is
in most of them that sprinkling of the better nature, which, like holy
water, chases away and disperses the contagion of the bad. They have
this in them, besides, that they bring us acquainted with the every-day
human face,—they give us skill to detect those gradations of sense and
virtue (which escape the careless or fastidious observer) in the circumstances of the world about us ; and prevent that disgust at common life,
that *tædium quotidianarum formarum*, which an unrestricted passion
for ideal forms and beauties is in danger of producing. In this, as in
many other things, they are analogous to the best novels of Smollett
and Fielding.'—*Charles Lamb*.

' It has been observed that Hogarth's pictures are exceedingly unlike
any other representations of the same kind of subjects—that they form
a class, and have a character peculiar to themselves. It may be worth
while to consider in what this general distinction consists.

' In the first place, they are, in the strictest sense, *historical* pictures :
and if what Fielding says be true, that his novel of *Tom Jones* ought to
be regarded as an epic prose-poem, because it contained a regular
development of fable, manners, character, and passion, the compositions
of Hogarth will, in like manner, be found to have a higher claim to the
title of epic pictures than many which have of late arrogated that
denomination to themselves. When we say that Hogarth treated his
subject historically, we mean that his works represent the manners and
humours of mankind in action, and their characters by varied expression.
Everything in his pictures has life and motion in it. Not only does the
business of the scene never stand still, but every feature and muscle is
put into full play ; the exact feeling of the moment is brought out, and
carried to its utmost height, and then instantly seized and stamped on
the canvas for ever. The expression is always taken *en passant* in a
state of progress or change, and, as it were, at the salient point. . . .
His figures are not like the background on which they are painted :

simple hearts, and to inspire them with pleasure or
pity or warning and terror.    Not one of his tales but
is as easy as 'Goody Two-Shoes ;' it is the moral of
Tommy was a naughty boy and the master flogged
him, and Jacky was a good boy and had plum-cake,
which pervades the whole works of the homely and
famous English moralist.    And if the moral is written
in rather too large letters after the fable, we must remember how simple the scholars and schoolmaster
both were, and like neither the less because they are
so artless and honest.    'It was a maxim of Doctor
Harrison's,' Fielding says, in 'Amelia,'—speaking of
the benevolent divine and philosopher who represents
the good principle in that novel—'that no man can
descend below himself, in doing any act which may
contribute to protect an innocent person, *or to bring a
rogue to the gallows.*'    The moralists of that age had no
compunction, you see ;   they had not begun to be
sceptical about the theory of punishment, and thought
that the hanging of a thief was a spectacle for
edification.    Masters sent their apprentices, fathers
took their children, to see Jack Sheppard or Jonathan
Wild hanged, and it was as undoubting subscribers
to this moral law, that Fielding wrote and Hogarth
painted.    Except in one instance, where, in the mad-
house scene in the 'Rake's Progress,' the girl whom
he has ruined is represented as still tending and weeping
over him in his insanity, a glimpse of pity for his rogues
never seems to enter honest Hogarth's mind.    There's

even the pictures on the wall have a peculiar look of their own.    Again,
with the rapidity, variety, and scope of history, Hogarth's heads have
all the reality and correctness of portraits.    He gives the extremes of
character and expression, but he gives them with perfect truth and
accuracy.    This is, in fact, what distinguishes his compositions from all
others of the same kind, that they are equally remote from caricature
and from mere still life. . . .    His faces go to the very verge of caricature, and yet never (we believe in any single instance) go beyond it.'
—*Hazlitt.*

not the slightest doubt in the breast of the jolly
Draco.

The famous set of pictures called 'Marriage à la
Mode,' and which are now exhibited in the National
Gallery in London, contains the most important and
highly wrought of the Hogarth comedies. The care
and method with which the moral grounds of these
pictures are laid is as remarkable as the wit and skill
of the observing and dexterous artist. He has to
describe the negotiations for a marriage pending
between the daughter of a rich citizen Alderman and
young Lord Viscount Squanderfield, the dissipated
son of a gouty old Earl. Pride and pomposity appear
in every accessory surrounding the Earl. He sits in
gold lace and velvet—as how should such an Earl
wear anything but velvet and gold lace? His coronet
is everywhere: on his footstool, on which reposes one
gouty toe turned out; on the sconces and looking-
glasses; on the dogs; on his lordship's very crutches;
on his great chair of state and the great baldaquin
behind him; under which he sits pointing majestically
to his pedigree, which shows that his race is sprung
from the loins of William the Conqueror, and
confronting the old Alderman from the City, who
has mounted his sword for the occasion, and wears his
Alderman's chain, and has brought a bag full of
money, mortgage deeds and thousand-pound notes,
for the arrangement of the transaction pending
between them. Whilst the steward (a Methodist—
therefore a hypocrite and cheat : for Hogarth scorned
a Papist and a Dissenter) is negotiating between the
old couple, their children sit together, united but
apart. My Lord is admiring his countenance in the
glass, while his bride is twiddling her marriage ring
on her pocket-handkerchief, and listening with rueful
countenance to Counsellor Silvertongue, who has

been drawing the settlements. The girl is pretty, but the painter, with a curious watchfulness, has taken care to give her a likeness to her father; as in the young Viscount's face you see a resemblance to the Earl his noble sire. The sense of the coronet pervades the picture, as it is supposed to do the mind of its wearer. The pictures round the room are sly hints indicating the situation of the parties about to marry. A martyr is led to the fire; Andromeda is offered to sacrifice; Judith is going to slay Holofernes. There is the ancestor of the house (in the picture it is the Earl himself as a young man), with a comet over his head, indicating that the career of the family is to be brilliant and brief. In the second picture the old lord must be dead, for Madam has now the Countess's coronet over her bed and toilet-glass, and sits listening to that dangerous Counsellor Silvertongue, whose portrait now actually hangs up in her room, whilst the counsellor takes his ease on the sofa by her side, evidently the familiar of the house, and the confidant of the mistress. My Lord takes his pleasure elsewhere than at home, whither he returns jaded and tipsy from the 'Rose,' to find his wife yawning in her drawing-room, her whist-party over, and the daylight streaming in; or he amuses himself with the very worst company abroad, whilst his wife sits at home listening to foreign singers, or wastes her money at auctions, or, worse still, seeks amusement at masquerades. The dismal end is known. My Lord draws upon the counsellor, who kills him, and is apprehended whilst endeavouring to escape. My Lady goes back perforce to the Alderman in the City, and faints upon reading Counsellor Silvertongue's dying speech at Tyburn, where the counsellor has been executed for sending his Lordship out of the world. Moral:—Don't listen to evil silver-tongued

counsellors : don't marry a man for his rank, or a
woman for her money : don't frequent foolish auctions
and masquerade balls unknown to your husband :
don't have wicked companions abroad and neglect
your wife, otherwise you will be run through the
body, and ruin will ensue, and disgrace, and Tyburn.
The people are all naughty, and Bogey carries them
all off.  In the ' Rake's Progress,' a loose life is ended
by a similar sad catastrophe.  It is the spendthrift
coming into possession of the wealth of the paternal
miser ;  the prodigal surrounded by flatterers, and
wasting his substance on the very worst company ;
the bailiffs, the gambling-house, and Bedlam for an
end.  In the famous story of ' Industry and Idleness,'
the moral is pointed in a manner similarly clear.
Fair-haired Frank Goodchild smiles at his work,
whilst naughty Tom Idle snores over his loom.
Frank reads the edifying ballads of 'Whittington'
and the ' London 'Prentice,' whilst that reprobate
Tom Idle prefers 'Moll Flanders,' and drinks hugely
of beer.  Frank goes to church of a Sunday, and
warbles hymns from the gallery ; while Tom lies on
a tombstone outside playing at 'halfpenny-under-the
hat ' with street blackguards, and is deservedly caned
by the beadle.  Frank is made overseer of the business, whilst Tom is sent to sea.  Frank is taken into
partnership and marries his master's daughter, sends
out broken victuals to the poor, and listens in his
nightcap and gown, with the lovely Mrs. Goodchild
by his side, to the nuptial music of the City bands and
the marrow-bones and cleavers ; whilst idle Tom,
returned from sea, shudders in a garret lest the officers
are coming to take him for picking pockets.  The
Worshipful Francis Goodchild, Esquire, becomes
Sheriff of London, and partakes of the most splendid
dinners which money can purchase or Alderman

devour; whilst poor Tom is taken up in a night-cellar, with that one-eyed and disreputable accomplice who first taught him to play chuck-farthing on a Sunday. What happens next? Tom is brought up before the justice of his country, in the person of Mr. Alderman Goodchild, who weeps as he recognises his old brother 'prentice, as Tom's one-eyed friend peaches on him, and the clerk makes out the poor rogue's ticket for Newgate. Then the end comes. Tom goes to Tyburn in a cart with a coffin in it; whilst the Right Honourable Francis Goodchild, Lord Mayor of London, proceeds to his Mansion House, in his gilt coach with four footmen and a sword-bearer, whilst the companies of London march in the august procession, whilst the trainbands of the City fire their pieces and get drunk in his honour; and—O crowning delight and glory of all—whilst His Majesty the King looks out from his royal balcony, with his ribbon on his breast, and his Queen and his star by his side, at the corner house of Saint Paul's Churchyard.

How the times have changed! The new Post Office now not disadvantageously occupies that spot where the scaffolding is in the picture, where the tipsy trainband-man is lurching against the post, with his wig over one eye, and the 'prentice-boy is trying to kiss the pretty girl in the gallery. Passed away 'prentice-boy and pretty girl! Passed away tipsy trainband-man with wig and bandolier! On the spot where Tom Idle (for whom I have an unaffected pity) made his exit from this wicked world, and where you see the hangman smoking his pipe as he reclines on the gibbet and views the hills of Harrow or Hampstead beyond, a splendid marble arch, a vast and modern city—clean, airy, painted drab, populous with nursery-maids and children, the abode of wealth and comfort—the elegant, the prosperous, the polite Tyburnia rises, the most respectable district in the habitable globe.

In that last plate of the London Apprentices, in which the apotheosis of the Right Honourable Francis Goodchild is drawn, a ragged fellow is represented in the corner of the simple, kindly piece, offering for sale a broadside, purporting to contain an account of the appearance of the ghost of Tom Idle executed at Tyburn. Could Tom's ghost have made its appearance in 1847, and not in 1747, what changes would have been remarked by that astonished escaped criminal! Over that road which the hangman used to travel constantly, and the Oxford stage twice a week, go ten thousand carriages every day: over yonder road, by which Dick Turpin fled to Windsor, and Squire Western journeyed into town, when he came to take up his quarters at the ' Hercules Pillars ' on the outskirts of London, what a rush of civilisation and order flows now! What armies of gentlemen with umbrellas march to banks, and chambers, and counting-houses ! What regiments of nursery-maids and pretty infantry; what peaceful processions of policemen, what light broughams and what gay carriages, what swarms of busy apprentices and artificers, riding on omnibus-roofs, pass daily and hourly ! Tom Idle's times are quite changed : many of the institutions gone into disuse which were admired in his day. There's more pity and kindness and a better chance for poor Tom's successors now than at that simpler period when Fielding hanged him and Hogarth drew him.

To the student of history, these admirable works must be invaluable, as they give us the most complete and truthful picture of the manners, and even the thoughts, of the past century. We look, and see

pass before us the England of a hundred years ago—
the peer in his drawing-room, the lady of fashion in
her apartment, foreign singers surrounding her, and
the chamber filled with gew-gaws in the mode of that
day; the church, with its quaint florid architecture
and singing congregation; the parson with his great
wig, and the beadle with his cane: all these are represented before us, and we are sure of the truth of
the portrait. We see how the Lord Mayor dines in
state; how the prodigal drinks and sports at the
bagnio; how the poor girl beats hemp in Bridewell;
how the thief divides his booty and drinks his punch
at the night-cellar, and how he finishes his career at
the gibbet. We may depend upon the perfect accuracy
of these strange and varied portraits of the bygone
generation: we see one of Walpole's Members of
Parliament chaired after his election, and the lieges
celebrating the event, and drinking confusion to the
Pretender: we see the grenadiers and trainbands of
the City marching out to meet the enemy; and have
before us, with sword and firelock, and 'White
Hanoverian Horse' embroidered on the cap, the very
figures of the men who ran away with Johnny Cope,
and who conquered at Culloden. The Yorkshire
waggon rolls into the inn-yard; the country parson,
in his jack-boots, and his bands and short cassock,
comes trotting into town, and we fancy it is Parson
Adams, with his sermons in his pocket. The Salisbury
fly sets forth from the old 'Angel'—you see the
passengers entering the great heavy vehicle, up the
wooden steps, their hats tied down with handkerchiefs
over their faces, and under their arms, sword, hanger,
and case-bottle; the landlady—apoplectic with the
liquors in her own bar—is tugging at the bell; the
hunchbacked postillion—he may have ridden the
leaders to Humphrey Clinker—is begging a gratuity;

the miser is grumbling at the bill; Jack of the
'Centurion' lies on the top of the clumsy vehicle,
with a soldier by his side—it may be Smollett's Jack
Hatchway—it has a likeness to Lismahago. You see
the suburban fair and the strolling company of actors;
the pretty milkmaid singing under the windows of
the enraged French musician: it is such a girl as
Steele charmingly described in the *Guardian*, a few
years before this date, singing, under Mr. Ironside's
window in Shire Lane, her pleasant carol of a May
morning. You see noblemen and blacklegs bawling
and betting in the Cockpit: you see Garrick as he
was arrayed in 'King Richard;' Macheath and Polly
in the dresses which they wore when they charmed
our ancestors, and when noblemen in blue ribbons sat
on the stage and listened to their delightful music.
You see the ragged French soldiery, in their white
coats and cockades, at Calais Gate: they are of the
regiment, very likely, which friend Roderick Random
joined before he was rescued by his preserver Monsieur
de Strap, with whom he fought on the famous day of
Dettingen. You see the judges on the bench; the
audience laughing in the pit; the student in the
Oxford Theatre; the citizen on his country walk;
you see Broughton the boxer, Sarah Malcolm the
murderess, Simon Lovat the traitor, John Wilkes the
demagogue, leering at you with that squint which has
become historical, and that face which, ugly as it was,
he said he could make as captivating to woman as the
countenance of the handsomest beau in town. All
these sights and people are with you. After looking
in the 'Rake's Progress' at Hogarth's picture of
Saint James's Palace Gate, you may people the
street, but little altered within these hundred years,
with the gilded carriages and thronging chairmen
that bore the courtiers your ancestors to Queen

Caroline's drawing-room more than a hundred years
ago.

What manner of man* was he who executed these

* Hogarth (whose family name was Hogart) was the grandson of a
Westmoreland yeoman. His father came to London, and was an author
and schoolmaster. William was born in 1698 (according to the
most probable conjecture) in the parish of Saint Martin, Ludgate.
He was early apprenticed to an engraver of arms on plate.
The following touches are from his *Anecdotes of Himself* (Edition of
1833) :—

'As I had naturally a good eye, and a fondness for drawing, shows
of all sorts gave me uncommon pleasure when an infant ; and mimicry,
common to all children, was remarkable in me. An early access to a
neighbouring painter drew my attention from play ; and I was, at every
possible opportunity, employed in making drawings. I picked up an
acquaintance of the same turn, and soon learned to draw the alphabet
with great correctness. My exercises, when at school, were more
remarkable for the ornaments which adorned them, than for the exercise
itself. In the former, I soon found that blockheads with better memories
could much surpass me ; but for the latter I was particularly distinguished. . . .

'I thought it still more unlikely that by pursuing the common
method, and copying *old* drawings, I could ever attain the power of
making *new* designs, which was my first and greatest ambition. I
therefore endeavoured to habituate myself to the exercise of a sort of
technical memory ; and by repeating in my own mind the parts of which
objects were composed, I could by degrees combine and put them down
with my pencil. Thus, with all the drawbacks which resulted from the
circumstances I have mentioned, I had one material advantage over my
competitors, viz., the early habit I thus acquired of retaining in my
mind's eye, without coldly copying it on the spot, whatever I intended
to imitate.

'The instant I became master of my own time, I determined to
qualify myself for engraving on copper. In this I readily got employment ; and frontispieces to books, such as prints to *Hudibras*, in twelves,
&c., soon brought me into the way. But the tribe of booksellers remained as my father had left them. . . which put me upon publishing
on my own account. But here again I had to encounter a monopoly
of printsellers, equally mean and destructive to the ingenious ; for the
first plate I published, called "The Taste of the Town," in which the
reigning follies were lashed, had no sooner begun to take a run, than
I found copies of it in the print-shops, vending at half-price, while the
original prints were returned to me again, and I was thus obliged
to sell the plate for whatever these pirates pleased to give me, as
there was no place of sale but at their shops. Owing to this, and
other circumstances, by engraving, until I was near thirty, I could

portraits—so various, so faithful, and so admirable?
In the National Collection of Pictures most of us have

do little more than maintain myself : *but even then I was a punctual
paymaster.*

' I then married and'——

[But William is going too fast here.  He made a 'stolen union,' on
March 23, 1729, with Jane, daughter of Sir James Thornhill, serjeant-
painter.  For some time Sir James kept his heart and his purse-strings
close, but 'soon after became both reconciled and generous to the
young couple.'—*Hogarth's Works*, by NICHOLS and STEEVENS, vol. i.
p. 44.]

'—commenced painter of small Conversation Pieces, from twelve to
fifteen inches high.  This, being a novelty, succeeded for a few years.'

[About this time Hogarth had summer lodgings at South Lambeth,
and did all kinds of work, 'embellishing' the 'Spring Gardens' at
'Vauxhall,' and the like.  In 1731, he published a satirical plate
against Pope, founded on the well-known imputation against him of his
having satirised the Duke of Chandos, under the name of *Timon*, in
his poem on 'Taste.'  The plate represented a view of Burlington
House, with Pope whitewashing it, and bespattering the Duke of
Chandos's coach.  Pope made no retort, and has never mentioned
Hogarth.]

' Before I had done anything of much consequence in this walk, I
entertained some hopes of succeeding in what the puffers in books call
*The Great Style of History Painting ;* so that without having had a stroke
of this *grand* business before, I quitted small portraits and familiar
conversations, and with a smile at my own temerity, commenced
history-painter, and on a great staircase at St. Bartholomew's Hospital,
painted two Scripture Stories, the "Pool of Bethesda" and the "Good
Samaritan," with figures seven feet high. . . .  But as religion, the
great promoter of this style in other countries, rejected it in England, I
was unwilling to sink into a *portrait manufacturer ;* and, still ambitious
of being singular, dropped all expectations of advantage from that source,
and returned to the pursuit of my former dealings with the public at
large.

' As to portrait-painting, the chief branch of the art by which a
painter can procure himself a tolerable livelihood, and the only one by
which a lover of money can get a fortune, a man of very moderate
talents may have great success in it, as the artifice and address of a
mercer is infinitely more useful than the abilities of a painter.  By the
manner in which the present race of professors in England conduct it,
that also becomes still life.'

.      .      .      .      .      .

' By this inundation of folly and puff' (*he has been speaking of the
success of Vanloo, who came over here in* 1737), 'I must confess I was
much disgusted, and determined to try if by any means I could stem
the torrent, and, *by opposing, end it.*  I laughed at the pretensions of

seen the best and most carefully finished series of his comic paintings, and the portrait of his own honest face, of which the bright blue eyes shine out from the canvas and give you an idea of that keen and brave

these quacks in colouring, ridiculed their productions as feeble and contemptible, and asserted that it required neither taste nor talents to excel their most popular performances. This interference excited much enmity, because, as my opponents told me, my studies were in another way. "You talk," added they, "with ineffable contempt of portrait-painting ; if it is so easy a task, why do not you convince the world, by painting a portrait yourself?" Provoked at this language, I, one day at the Academy in St. Martin's Lane, put the following question : " Supposing any man, at this time, were to paint a portrait as well as Vandyke, would it be seen or acknowledged, and could the artist enjoy the benefit or acquire the reputation due to his performance ? "

'They ask me in reply, if I could paint one as well ; and I frankly answered, I believed I could. . . .

'Of the mighty talents said to be requisite for portrait-painting I had not the most exalted opinion.'

Let us now hear him on the question of the Academy :—

'To pester the three great estates of the empire, about twenty or thirty students drawing after a man or a horse, appears, as must be acknowledged, foolish enough : but the real motive is, that a few bustling characters, who have access to people of rank, think they can thus get a superiority over their brethren, be appointed to places, and have salaries, as in France, for telling a lad when a leg or an arm is too long or too short. . . .

'France, ever aping the magnificence of other nations, has in its turn assumed a foppish kind of splendour sufficient to dazzle the eyes of the neighbouring states, and draw vast sums of money from this country. . . .

'To return to our Royal Academy : I am told that one of their leading objects will be, sending young men abroad to study the antique statues, for such kind of studies may sometimes improve an exalted genius, but they will not create it ; and whatever has been the cause, this same travelling to Italy has, in several instances that I have seen, seduced the student from nature and led him to paint marble figures, in which he has availed himself of the great works of antiquity, as a coward does when he puts on the armour of an Alexander ; for, with similar pretensions and similar vanity, the painter supposes he shall be adored as a second Raphael Urbino.'

We must now hear him on his 'Sigismunda :'—

'As the most violent and virulent abuse thrown on "Sigismunda" was from a set of miscreants, with whom I am proud of having been ever at war—I mean the expounders of the mysteries of old pictures—I have been sometimes told they were beneath my notice. This is true of them individually ; but as they have access to people of rank, who

look with which William Hogarth regarded the world.
No man was ever less of a hero ; you see him before
you, and can fancy what he was—a jovial, honest
London citizen, stout and sturdy ; a hearty, plain-
spoken man,* loving his laugh, his friend, his glass,

seem as happy in being cheated as these *merchants* are in cheating them,
they have a power of doing much mischief to a modern artist.   However mean the vendor of poisons, the mineral is destructive :—to me its
operation was troublesome enough.   Ill nature spreads so fast that now
was the time for every little dog in the profession to bark !'

Next comes a characteristic account of his controversy with Wilkes
and Churchill.

'The stagnation rendered it necessary that I should do some *timed
thing*, to recover my lost time, and stop a gap in my income.   This
drew forth my print of "The Times," a subject which tended to the
restoration of peace and unanimity, and put the opposers of these
humane objects in a light which gave great offence to those who were
trying to foment disaffection in the minds of the populace.   One of the
most notorious of them, till now my friend and flatterer, attacked me
in the *North Briton*, in so infamous and malign a style, that he himself,
when pushed even by his best friends, was driven to so poor an excuse
as to say he was drunk when he wrote it. . . .

'This renowned patriot's portrait, drawn like as I could as to
features, and marked with some indications of his mind, fully answered
my purpose.   The ridiculous was apparent to every eye !   A Brutus !
A saviour of his country with such an aspect—was so arrant a farce,
that though it gave rise to much laughter in the lookers-on, galled both
him and his adherents to the bone. . . .

'Churchill, Wilkes's toad-echo, put the *North Briton* attack into verse,
in an epistle to Hogarth ; but as the abuse was precisely the same,
except a little poetical heightening, which goes for nothing, it made no
impression. . . .   However, having an old plate by me, with some
parts ready, such as the background and a dog, I began to consider how
I could turn so much work laid aside to some account, and so patched
up a print of Master Churchill in the character of a Bear.   The
pleasure and pecuniary advantage which I derived from these two
engravings, together with occasionally riding on horseback, restored me
to as much health as can be expected at my time of life.'

* 'It happened in the early part of Hogarth's life, that a nobleman
who was uncommonly ugly and deformed came to sit to him for his
picture.   It was executed with a skill that did honour to the artist's
abilities ; but the likeness was rigidly observed, without even the
necessary attention to compliment or flattery.   The peer, disgusted at
this counterpart of himself, never once thought of paying for a reflection
that would only disgust him with his deformities.   Some time was
suffered to elapse before the artist applied for his money ; but after-

his roast beef of Old England, and having a proper *bourgeois* scorn for French frogs, for mounseers, and wooden shoes in general, for foreign fiddlers, foreign singers, and, above all, for foreign painters, whom he held in the most amusing contempt.

It must have been great fun to hear him rage against Correggio and the Caracci; to watch him thump the table and snap his fingers, and say, ' Historical painters be hanged ! here's the man that will paint against any of them for a hundred pounds. Correggio's "Sigismunda !" Look at Bill Hogarth's "Sigismunda ;" look at my altar-piece at Saint Mary Redcliffe, Bristol: look at my " Paul before Felix,' and see whether I'm not as good as the best of them.' *

wards many applications were made by him (who had then no need of a banker) for payment, without success. The painter, however, at last hit upon an expedient. . . . It was couched in the following card :—

' " Mr. Hogarth's dutiful respects to Lord ——. Finding that he does not mean to have the picture which was drawn for him, is informed again of Mr. Hogarth's necessity for the money. If, therefore, his Lordship does not send for it, in three days it will be disposed of, with the addition of a tail, and some other little appendages, to Mr. Hare, the famous wild-beast man : Mr. Hogarth having given that gentleman a conditional promise of it, for an exhibition-picture, on his Lordship's refusal."

' This intimation had the desired effect.'—*Works*, by NICHOLS and STEEVENS, vol. i. p. 25.

* ' Garrick himself was not more ductile to flattery. A word in favour of " Sigismunda " might have commanded a proof print or forced an original print out of our artist's hands. . . .

' The following authenticated story of our artist (furnished by the late Mr. Belchier, F.R.S., a surgeon of eminence) will also serve to show how much more easy it is to detect ill-placed or hyperbolical adulation respecting others, than when applied to ourselves. Hogarth, being at dinner with the great Cheselden and some other company, was told that Mr. John Freke, surgeon of St. Bartholomew's Hospital, a few evenings before at Dick's Coffee-house, had asserted that Greene was as eminent in composition as Handel. "That fellow Freke," replied Hogarth, " is always shooting his bolt absurdly, one way or another. Handel is a giant in music; Greene only a light Florimel kind of a composer." "Ay," says our artist's informant, " but at the same time

Posterity has not quite confirmed honest Hogarth's opinion about his talents for the sublime.   Although Swift could not see the difference between tweedle-dee and tweedle-dum, posterity has not shared the Dean's contempt for Handel ; the world has discovered a difference between tweedle-dee and tweedle-dum, and given a hearty applause and admiration to Hogarth, too, but not exactly as a painter of scriptural subjects, or as a rival of Correggio.   It does not take away from one's liking for the man, or from the moral of his story, or the humour of it—from one's admiration for the prodigious merit of his performances, to remember that he persisted to the last in believing that the world was in a conspiracy against him with respect to his talents as an historical painter, and that a set of miscreants, as he called them, were employed to run his genius down.   They say it was Liston's firm belief, that he was a great and neglected tragic actor ; they say that every one of us believes in his heart, or would like to have others believe, that he is something which he is not.   One of the most notorious of the ' miscreants,' Hogarth says, was Wilkes, who assailed him in the *North Briton ;* the other was Churchill, who put the *North Briton* attack into heroic verse, and published his ' Epistle to Hogarth.'   Hogarth replied by that caricature of Wilkes, in which the patriot still figures before us, with his Satanic grin and squint, and by a caricature of Churchill, in which he is represented as a bear with a staff, on which, lie the first, lie the second—lie the tenth, are engraved in unmistakable letters.   There is very little mistake about honest Hogarth's satire : if he has to paint a

Mr. Freke declared you were as good a portrait-painter as Vandyke." " *There* he was right," adds Hogarth, " and so, by G——, I am, give me my time and let me choose my subject." '—*Works*, by NICHOLS and STEEVENS, vol. i. pp. 236, 237

man with his throat cut, he draws him with his head almost off; and he tried to do the same for his enemies in this little controversy. 'Having an old plate by me,' says he, 'with some parts ready, such as the background, and a dog, I began to consider how I could turn so much work laid aside to some account, and so patched up a print of Master Churchill, in the character of a bear; the pleasure and pecuniary advantage which I derived from these two engravings, together with occasionally riding on horseback, restored me to as much health as I can expect at my time of life.'

And so he concludes his queer little book of Anecdotes: 'I have gone through the circumstances of a life which till lately passed pretty much to my own satisfaction, and I hope in no respect injurious to any other man. This I may safely assert, that I have done my best to make those about me tolerably happy, and my greatest enemy cannot say I ever did an intentional injury. What may follow, God knows.'*

A queer account still exists of a holiday jaunt taken by Hogarth and four friends of his, who set out like the redoubted Mr. Pickwick and his companions, but just a hundred years before those heroes; and made an excursion to Gravesend, Rochester, Sheerness, and adjacent places.† One of the gentlemen noted down the proceedings of the journey, for which Hogarth and a brother artist made drawings. The book is chiefly curious at this moment from showing the citizen life of those days, and the rough jolly style of merriment, not of the five companions merely, but of

* Of Hogarth's kindliness of disposition, the story of his rescue of the drummer-girl from the ruffian at Southwark Fair is an illustration: and in this case virtue was not its own reward, since her pretty face afterwards served him for a model in many a picture.

† He made this excursion in 1732, his companions being John Thornhill (son of Sir James), Scott the landscape painter, Tothall, and Forrest.

thousands of jolly fellows of their time.  Hogarth and his friends, quitting the 'Bedford Arms,' Covent Garden, with a song, took water to Billingsgate, exchanging compliments with the bargemen as they went down the river.  At Billingsgate Hogarth made a 'caracatura' of a facetious porter, called the Duke of Puddledock, who agreeably entertained the party with the humours of the place.  Hence they took a Gravesend boat for themselves; had straw to lie upon, and a tilt over their heads, they say, and went down the river at night, sleeping and singing jolly choruses.

They arrived at Gravesend at six, when they washed their faces and hands, and had their wigs powdered.  Then they sallied forth for Rochester on foot, and drank by the way three pots of ale.  At one o'clock they went to dinner with excellent port, and a quantity more beer, and afterwards Hogarth and Scott played at hopscotch in the town hall.  It would appear that they slept most of them in one room, and the chronicler of the party describes them all as waking at seven o'clock, and telling each other their dreams.  You have rough sketches by Hogarth of the incidents of this holiday excursion.  The sturdy little painter is seen sprawling over a plank to a boat at Gravesend; the whole company are represented in one design, in a fisherman's room, where they had all passed the night.  One gentleman in a nightcap is shaving himself; another is being shaved by the fisherman; a third, with a handkerchief over his bald pate, is taking his breakfast; and Hogarth is sketching the whole scene.

They describe at night how they returned to their quarters, drank to their friends, as usual, emptied several cans of good flip, all singing merrily.

It is a jolly party of tradesmen engaged at high jinks.  These were the manners and pleasures of

Hogarth, of his time very likely, of men not very refined, but honest and merry. It is a brave London citizen, with John Bull habits, prejudices, and pleasures.*

Of SMOLLETT's associates and manner of life the author of the admirable 'Humphrey Clinker' has given us an interesting account in that most amusing of novels.†

* 'Doctor Johnson made four lines once, on the death of poor Hogarth, which were equally true and pleasing; I know not why Garrick's were preferred to them :—

> ' " The hand of him here torpid lies,
>     That drew th' essential forms of grace;
>     Here, closed in death, th' attentive eyes,
>     That saw the manners in the face."

'Mr. Hogarth, among the variety of kindnesses shown to me when I was too young to have a proper sense of them, was used to be very earnest that I should obtain the acquaintance, and if possible the friendship, of Doctor Johnson; whose conversation was, to the talk of other men, like Titian's painting compared to Hudson's, he said : "but don't you tell people now that I say so," continued he, "for the connoisseurs and I are at war, you know; and because I hate *them*, they think I hate *Titian*—and let them !"... Of Dr. Johnson, when my father and he were talking about him one day, "That man," says Hogarth, "is not contented with believing the Bible; but he fairly resolves, I think, to believe nothing *but* the Bible. Johnson," added he, "though so wise a fellow, is more like King David than King Solomon, for he says in his haste, *All men are liars*." '—*Mrs. Piozzi.*

Hogarth died on the 26th of October, 1764. The day before his death, he was removed from his villa at Chiswick to Leicester Fields, 'in a very weak condition, yet remarkably cheerful.' He had just received an agreeable letter from Franklin. He lies buried at Chiswick.

† 'To Sir Watkin Phillips, Bart., of Jesus College, Oxon.

'DEAR PHILLIPS,—In my last, I mentioned my having spent an evening with a society of authors, who seemed to be jealous and afraid of one another. My uncle was not at all surprised to hear me say I was disappointed in their conversation. "A man may be very entertaining and instructive upon paper," said he, " and exceedingly dull in common discourse. I have observed, that those who shine most in private company are but secondary stars in the constellation of genius. A small stock of ideas is more easily managed, and sooner displayed, than a great quantity crowded together. There is very seldom anything

I have no doubt that this picture by Smollett is as faithful a one as any from the pencil of his kindred humourist, Hogarth.

extraordinary in the appearance and address of a good writer ; whereas a dull author generally distinguishes himself by some oddity or extravagance. For this reason I fancy that an assembly of grubs must be very diverting."

'My curiosity being excited by this hint, I consulted my friend Dick Ivy, who undertook to gratify it the very next day, which was Sunday last. He carried me to dine with S——, whom you and I have long known by his writings. He lives in the skirts of the town ; and every Sunday his house is open to all unfortunate brothers of the quill, whom he treats with beef, pudding, and potatoes, port, punch, and Calvert's entire butt beer. He has fixed upon the first day of the week for the exercise of his hospitality, because some of his guests could not enjoy it on any other, for reasons that I need not explain. I was civilly received in a plain, yet decent habitation, which opened backwards into a very pleasant garden, kept in excellent order ; and, indeed, I saw none of the outward signs of authorship either in the house or the landlord, who is one of those few writers of the age that stand upon their own foundation, without patronage, and above dependence. If there was nothing characteristic in the entertainer, the company made ample amends for his want of singularity.

'At two in the afternoon, I found myself one of ten messmates seated at table ; and I question if the whole kingdom could produce such another assemblage of originals. Among their peculiarities, I do not mention those of dress, which may be purely accidental. What struck me were oddities originally produced by affectation, and afterwards confirmed by habit. One of them wore spectacles at dinner, and another his hat flapped ; though (as Ivy told me) the first was noted for having a seaman's eye when a bailiff was in the wind ; and the other was never known to labour under any weakness or defect of vision, except about five years ago, when he was complimented with a couple of black eyes by a player, with whom he had quarrelled in his drink. A third wore a laced stocking, and made use of crutches, because, once in his life, he had been laid up with a broken leg, though no man could leap over a stick with more agility. A fourth had contracted such an antipathy to the country, that he insisted upon sitting with his back towards the window that looked into the garden ; and when a dish of cauliflower was set upon the table, he snuffed up volatile salts to keep him from fainting ; yet this delicate person was the son of a cottager, born under a hedge, and had many years run wild among asses on a common. A fifth affected distraction : when spoke to, he always answered from the purpose. Sometimes he suddenly started up, and rapped out a dreadful oath ; sometimes he burst out a laughing ; then he folded his arms, and sighed ; and then he hissed like fifty serpents.

'At first, I really thought he was mad ; and, as he sat near me,

We have before us, and painted by his own hand,
Tobias Smollett, the manly, kindly, honest, and

began to be under some apprehensions for my own safety ; when our
landlord, perceiving me alarmed, assured me aloud that I had nothing
to fear. "The gentleman," said he, "is trying to act a part for which
he is by no means qualified : if he had all the inclination in the world,
it is not in his power to be mad ; his spirits are too flat to be kindled
into phrenzy." "'Tis no bad p-p-puff, however," observed a person in
a tarnished laced coat ; "aff-ffected m-madness w-ill p-pass for w-wit
w-with nine-nineteen out of t-twenty." "And affected stuttering for
humour," replied our landlord ; "though, God knows ! there is no
affinity between them." It seems this wag, after having made some
abortive attempts in plain speaking, had recourse to this defect, by
means of which he frequently extorted the laugh of the company,
without the least expense of genius ; and that imperfection, which he
had at first counterfeited, was now become so habitual, that he could
not lay it aside.

'A certain winking genius, who wore yellow gloves at dinner, had,
on his first introduction, taken such offence at S——, because he looked
and talked, and ate and drank, like any other man, that he spoke
contemptuously of his understanding ever after, and never would repeat
his visit, until he had exhibited the following proof of his caprice. Wat
Wyvil, the poet, having made some unsuccessful advances towards an
intimacy with S——, at last gave him to understand, by a third person,
that he had written a poem in his praise, and a satire against his person :
that if he would admit him to his house, the first should be immediately
sent to press ; but that if he persisted in declining his friendship, he
would publish the satire without delay. S—— replied, that he looked
upon Wyvil's panegyric as, in effect, a species of infamy, and would
resent it accordingly with a good cudgel ; but if he published the satire,
he might deserve his compassion, and had nothing to fear from his
revenge. Wyvil having considered the alternative, resolved to mortify
S—— by printing the panegyric, for which he received a sound drubbing.
Then he swore the peace against the aggressor, who, in order to avoid
a prosecution at law, admitted him to his good graces. It was the
singularity in S——'s conduct on this occasion, that reconciled him to
the yellow-gloved philosopher, who owned he had some genius ; and
from that period cultivated his acquaintance.

'Curious to know upon what subjects the several talents of my fellow-
guests were employed, I applied to my communicative friend Dick Ivy,
who gave me to understand that most of them were, or had been,
understrappers, or journeymen, to more creditable authors, for whom
they translated, collated, and compiled, in the business of bookmaking ;
and that all of them had, at different times, laboured in the service of
our landlord, though they had now set up for themselves in various
departments of literature. Not only their talents, but also their nations
and dialects, were so various, that our conversation resembled the con-

irascible; worn and battered, but still brave and
full of heart, after a long struggle against a hard

fusion of tongues at Babel. We had the Irish brogue, the Scotch
accent, and foreign idiom, twanged off by the most discordant voci-
feration; for as they all spoke together, no man had any chance to be
heard, unless he could bawl louder than his fellows. It must be owned,
however, there was nothing pedantic in their discourse; they carefully
avoided all learned disquisitions, and endeavoured to be facetious : nor
did their endeavours always miscarry; some droll repartee passed, and
much laughter was excited; and if any individual lost his temper so far
as to transgress the bounds of decorum, he was effectually checked
by the master of the feast, who exerted a sort of paternal authority over
this irritable tribe.

'The most learned philosopher of the whole collection, who had
been expelled the university for atheism, has made great progress in a
refutation of Lord Bolingbroke's metaphysical works, which is said to
be equally ingenious and orthodox; but, in the meantime, he has been
presented to the grand jury as a public nuisance for having blasphemed
in an alehouse on the Lord's day. The Scotchman gives lectures on
the pronunciation of the English language, which he is now publishing
by subscription.

'The Irishman is a political writer, and goes by the name of My
Lord Potatoe. He wrote a pamphlet in vindication of a Minister,
hoping his zeal would be rewarded with some place or pension; but
finding himself neglected in that quarter, he whispered about that the
pamphlet was written by the Minister himself, and he published an
answer to his own production. In this he addressed the author under
the title of "your Lordship," with such solemnity, that the public
swallowed the deceit, and bought up the whole impression. The wise
politicians of the metropolis declared they were both masterly performances, and chuckled over the flimsy reveries of an ignorant garretteer, as
the profound speculations of a veteran statesman, acquainted with all the
secrets of the cabinet. The imposture was detected in the sequel, and
our Hibernian pamphleteer retains no part of his assumed importance
but the bare title of "my Lord," and the upper part of the table at the
potatoe-ordinary in Shoe Lane.

'Opposite to me sat a Piedmontese, who had obliged the public with
a humorous satire, entitled *The Balance of the English Poets;* a performance which evinced the great modesty and taste of the author, and,
in particular, his intimacy with the elegancies of the English language.
The sage, who laboured under the ἀγροφοβία, or "horror of green
fields," had just finished a treatise on practical agriculture, though, in
fact, he had never seen corn growing in his life, and was so ignorant of
grain, that our entertainer, in the face of the whole company, made him
own that a plate of hominy was the best rice-pudding he had ever eat.

'The stutterer had almost finished his travels through Europe and
part of Asia, without ever budging beyond the liberties of the King's

fortune. His brain had been busied with a hundred
different schemes : he had been reviewer and
historian, critic, medical writer, poet, pamphleteer.
He had fought endless literary battles ; and braved
and wielded for years the cudgels of controversy.
It was a hard and savage fight in those days, and
a niggard pay. He was oppressed by illness, age,
narrow fortune ; but his spirit was still resolute, and
his courage steady ; the battle over, he could do
justice to the enemy with whom he had been so
fiercely engaged, and give a not unfriendly grasp to

Bench, except in term-time with a tip-staff for his companion ; and as
for little Tim Cropdale, the most facetious member of the whole society,
he had happily wound up the catastrophe of a virgin tragedy, from the
exhibition of which he promised himself a large fund of profit and
reputation. Tim had made shift to live many years by writing novels,
at the rate of five pounds a volume ; but that branch of business is now
engrossed by female authors, who publish merely for the propagation of
virtue, with so much ease, and spirit, and delicacy, and knowledge of
the human heart, and all in the serene tranquillity of high life, that
the reader is not only enchanted by their genius, but reformed by their
morality.

'After dinner, we adjourned into the garden, where I observed Mr.
S—— gave a short separate audience to every individual in a small
remote filbert-walk, from whence most of them dropped off one after
another, without further ceremony.'

Smollett's house was in Lawrence Lane, Chelsea, and is now
destroyed.—See *Handbook of London*, p. 115.

'The person of Smollett was eminently handsome, his features
prepossessing, and, by the joint testimony of all his surviving friends,
his conversation, in the highest degree, instructive and amusing. Of
his disposition, those who have read his works (and who has not ?) may
form a very accurate estimate ; for in each of them he has presented,
and sometimes under various points of view, the leading features of his
own character without disguising the most unfavourable of them. . . .
When unseduced by his satirical propensities, he was kind, generous,
and humane to others ; bold, upright, and independent in his own
character ; stooped to no patron, sued for no favour, but honestly and
honourably maintained himself on his literary labours. . . . He was a
doting father, and an affectionate husband : and the warm zeal with
which his memory was cherished by his surviving friends showed
clearly the reliance which they placed upon his regard.'—*Sir Walter
Scott.*

the hand that had mauled him. He is like one of those Scotch cadets, of whom history gives us so many examples, and whom, with a national fidelity, the great Scotch novelist has painted so charmingly. Of gentle birth * and narrow means, going out from his northern home to win his fortune in the

* Smollett of Bonhill, in Dumbartonshire. *Arms*, azure, a bend, or, between a lion rampant, ppr., holding in his paw a banner, argent, and a bugle-horn, also ppr. *Crest*, an oak-tree, ppr. *Motto*, *Viresco*.

Smollett's father, Archibald, was the fourth son of Sir James Smollett of Bonhill, a Scotch Judge and Member of Parliament, and one of the commissioners for framing the Union with England. Archibald married, without the old gentleman's consent, and died early, leaving his children dependent on their grandfather. Tobias, the second son, was born in 1721, in the old house of Dalquharn in the valley of Leven ; and all his life loved and admired that valley and Loch Lomond beyond all the valleys and lakes in Europe. He learned the 'rudiments' at Dumbarton Grammar School, and studied at Glasgow.

But when he was only ten, his grandfather died, and left him without provision (figuring as the old judge in *Roderick Random* in consequence, according to Sir Walter). Tobias, armed with the *Regicide, a Tragedy* —a provision precisely similar to that with which Doctor Johnson had started, just before—came up to London. The *Regicide* came to no good, though at first patronised by Lord Lyttelton ('one of those little fellows who are sometimes called great men,' Smollett says) ; and Smollett embarked as 'surgeon's mate' on board a line-of-battle ship, and served in the Carthagena expedition, in 1741. He left the service in the West Indies, and, after residing some time in Jamaica, returned to England in 1746.

He was now unsuccessful as a physician, to begin with ; published the satires, *Advice* and *Reproof*, without any luck ; and (1747) married the 'beautiful and accomplished Miss Lascelles.'

In 1748 he brought out his *Roderick Random*, which at once made a 'hit.' The subsequent events of his life may be presented, chronologically, in a bird's-eye view :—

1750. Made a tour to Paris, where he chiefly wrote *Peregrine Pickle*.
1751. Published *Peregrine Pickle*.
1753. Published *Adventures of Ferdinand Count Fathom*.
1755. Published version of *Don Quixote*.
1756. Began the *Critical Review*.
1758. Published his *History of England*.
1763-1766. Travelling in France and Italy : published his *Travels*.
1769. Published *Adventures of an Atom*.
1770. Set out for Italy ; died at Leghorn 21st of October, 1771, in the fifty-first year of his age.

world, and to fight his way, armed with courage, hunger, and keen wits. His crest is a shattered oak-tree, with green leaves yet springing from it. On his ancient coat-of-arms there is a lion and a horn; this shield of his was battered and dinted in a hundred fights and brawls\* through which the stout Scotch-man bore it courageously. You see somehow that he is a gentleman, through all his battling and struggling, his poverty, his hard-fought successes, and his defeats. His novels are recollections of his own adventures; his characters drawn, as I should think, from person-ages with whom he became acquainted in his own career of life. Strange companions he must have had; queer acquaintances he made in the Glasgow college —in the country apothecary's shop; in the gun-room of the man-of-war where he served as surgeon; and in the hard life on shore, where the sturdy adventurer struggled for fortune. He did not invent much, as I

---

\* A good specimen of the old 'slashing' style of writing is presented by the paragraph on Admiral Knowles, which subjected Smollett to prosecution and imprisonment. The admiral's defence on the occasion of the failure of the Rochfort expedition came to be examined before the tribunal of the *Critical Review.*

'He is,' said our author, 'an admiral without conduct, an engineer without knowledge, an officer without resolution, and a man without veracity!'

Three months' imprisonment in the King's Bench avenged this sting-ing paragraph.

But the *Critical* was to Smollett a perpetual fountain of 'hot water.' Among less important controversies may be mentioned that with Grainger, the translator of Tibullus. Grainger replied in a pam-phlet; and in the next number of the *Review* we find him threatened with 'castigation,' as an 'owl that has broken from his mew!'

In Doctor Moore's biography of him is a pleasant anecdote. After publishing the *Don Quixote,* he returned to Scotland to pay a visit to his mother :—

'On Smollett's arrival, he was introduced to his mother with the connivance of Mrs. Telfer (her daughter), as a gentleman from the West Indies, who was intimately acquainted with her son. The better to support his assumed character, he endeavoured to preserve a serious countenance, approaching to a frown; but while his mother's eyes were

fancy, but had the keenest perceptive faculty, and
described what he saw with wonderful relish and
delightful broad humour. I think Uncle Bowling, in
'Roderick Random,' is as good a character as Squire
Western himself; and Mr. Morgan, the Welsh
apothecary, is as pleasant as Doctor Caius. What
man who has made his inestimable acquaintance—
what novel-reader who loves Don Quixote and Major
Dalgetty—will refuse his most cordial acknowledgments to the admirable Lieutenant Lismahago! The
novel of 'Humphrey Clinker' is, I do think, the
most laughable story that has ever been written since
the goodly art of novel-writing began. Winifred
Jenkins and Tabitha Bramble must keep Englishmen
on the grin for ages yet to come; and in their letters
and the story of their loves there is a perpetual fount
of sparkling laughter, as inexhaustible as Bladud's
well.

FIELDING, too, has described, though with a greater
hand, the characters and scenes which he knew and
saw. He had more than ordinary opportunities for

riveted on his countenance, he could not refrain from smiling: she
immediately sprung from her chair, and throwing her arms round his
neck, exclaimed, "Ah, my son! my son! I have found you at last!"
  'She afterwards told him, that if he had kept his austere looks and
continued to *gloom*, he might have escaped detection some time longer,
but "your old roguish smile," added she, "betrayed you at once."'
  'Shortly after the publication of *The Adventures of an Atom*, disease
again attacked Smollett with redoubled violence. Attempts being vainly
made to obtain for him the office of Consul in some part of the Mediter-
ranean, he was compelled to seek a warmer climate, without better
means of provision than his own precarious finances could afford. The
kindness of his distinguished friend and countryman, Dr. Armstrong
(then abroad), procured for Dr. and Mrs. Smollett a house at Monte
Nero, a village situated on the side of a mountain overlooking the sea,
in the neighbourhood of Leghorn, a romantic and salutary abode, where
he prepared for the press the last and, like music "sweetest in the close,"
the most pleasing of his compositions, *The Expedition of Humphrey Clinker*.
This delightful work was published in 1771.'—*Sir Walter Scott*.

becoming acquainted with life. His family and education, first—his fortunes and misfortunes afterwards, brought him into the society of every rank and condition of man. He is himself the hero of his books : he is wild Tom Jones, he is wild Captain Booth ; less wild, I am glad to think, than his predecessor : at least heartily conscious of demerit, and anxious to amend.

When Fielding first came upon the town in 1727, the recollection of the great wits was still fresh in the coffee-houses and assemblies, and the judges there declared that young Harry Fielding had more spirits and wit than Congreve or any of his brilliant successors. His figure was tall and stalwart ; his face handsome, manly, and noble-looking ; to the very last days of his life he retained a grandeur of air, and although worn down by disease, his aspect and presence imposed respect upon the people round about him.

A dispute took place between Mr. Fielding and the captain* of the ship in which he was making his last voyage, and Fielding relates how the man finally went down on his knees, and begged his passenger's pardon. He was living up to the last days of his life, and his spirit never gave in. His vital power must have been immensely strong. Lady Mary Wortley Montagu† prettily characterises Fielding and this

---

* The dispute with the captain arose from the wish of that functionary to intrude on his right to his cabin, for which he had paid thirty pounds. After recounting the circumstances of the apology, he characteristically adds :—

'And here, that I may not be thought the sly trumpeter of my own praises, I do utterly disclaim all praise on the occasion. Neither did the greatness of my mind dictate, nor the force of my Christianity exact this forgiveness. To speak truth, I forgave him from a motive which would make men much more forgiving, if they were much wiser than they are : because it was convenient for me so to do.'

† Lady Mary was his second cousin—their respective grandfathers

capacity for happiness which he possessed, in a little
notice of his death when she compares him to Steele,
who was as improvident and as happy as he was, and
says that both should have gone on living for ever.
One can fancy the eagerness and gusto with which a
man of Fielding's frame, with his vast health and
robust appetite, his ardent spirits, his joyful humour,
and his keen and healthy relish for life, must have
seized and drunk that cup of pleasure which the town
offered to him.   Can any of my hearers remember the
youthful feats of a college breakfast—the meats
devoured and the cups quaffed in that Homeric feast?
I can call to mind some of the heroes of those youthful banquets, and fancy young Fielding from Leyden
rushing upon the feast, with his great laugh, and
immense healthy young appetite, eager and vigorous
to enjoy.   The young man's wit and manners made
him friends everywhere: he lived with the grand
Man's society of those days; he was courted by peers
and men of wealth and fashion.   As he had a paternal

being sons of George Fielding, Earl of Desmond, son of William, Earl
of Denbigh.

In a letter dated just a week before his death, she says :—

'H. Fielding has given a true picture of himself and his first wife in
the characters of *Mr.* and *Mrs. Booth*, some compliments to his own
figure excepted ; and I am persuaded, several of the incidents he
mentions are real matters of fact.   I wonder he does not perceive *Tom
Jones* and *Mr. Booth* are sorry scoundrels. . . .   Fielding has really a
fund of true humour, and was to be pitied at his first entrance into the
world, having no choice, as he said himself, but to be a hackney writer
or a hackney coachman.   His genius deserved a better fate ; but I
cannot help blaming that continued indiscretion, to give it the softest
name, that has run through his life, and I am afraid still remains. . . .
Since I was born no original has appeared excepting Congreve, and
Fielding, who would, I believe, have approached nearer to his excellences,
if not forced by his necessities to publish without correction, and throw
many productions into the world he would have thrown into the fire, if
meat could have been got without money, or money without scribbling.
. . .   I am sorry not to see any more of Peregrine Pickle's performances ; I wish you would tell me his name.'—*Letters and Works* (Lord
Wharncliffe's ed.), vol. iii. pp. 93, 94.

allowance from his father, General Fielding, which, to use Henry's own phrase, any man might pay who would ; as he liked good wine, good clothes, and good company, which are all expensive articles to purchase, Harry Fielding began to run into debt, and borrow money in that easy manner in which Captain Booth borrows money in the novel : was in nowise particular in accepting a few pieces from the purses of his rich friends, and bore down upon more than one of them, as Walpole tells us only too truly, for a dinner or a guinea.   To supply himself with the latter, he began to write theatrical pieces, having already, no doubt, a considerable acquaintance amongst the Oldfields and Bracegirdles behind the scenes.   He laughed at these pieces and scorned them.   When the audience upon one occasion began to hiss a scene which he was too lazy to correct, and regarding which, when Garrick remonstrated with him, he said that the public was too stupid to find out the badness of his work : when the audience began to hiss, Fielding said with characteristic coolness—'They have found it out, have they ?'   He did not prepare his novels in this way, and with a very different care and interest laid the foundations and built up the edifices of his future fame.

Time and shower have very little damaged those. The fashion and ornaments are, perhaps, of the architecture of that age, but the buildings remain strong and lofty, and of admirable proportions— masterpieces of genius and monuments of workman- like skill.

I cannot offer or hope to make a hero of Harry Fielding.   Why hide his faults ?   Why conceal his weaknesses in a cloud of periphrases ?   Why not show him, like him as he is, not robed in a marble toga, and draped and polished in an heroic attitude, but with inked ruffles, and claret stains on his tarnished laced coat, and on his manly face the marks of good fellowship, of illness, of kindness, of care and wine? Stained as you see him, and worn by care and dissipation, that man retains some of the most precious and splendid human qualities and endowments. He has an admirable natural love of truth, the keenest instinctive antipathy to hypocrisy, the happiest satirical gift of laughing it to scorn. His wit is wonderfully wise and detective; it flashes upon a rogue and lightens up a rascal like a policeman's lantern. He is one of the manliest and kindliest of human beings: in the midst of all his imperfections, he respects female innocence and infantine tenderness as you would suppose such a great-hearted, courageous soul would respect and care for them. He could not be so brave, generous, truth-telling as he is, were he not infinitely merciful, pitiful, and tender. He will give any man his purse—he can't help kindness and profusion. He may have low tastes, but not a mean mind; he admires with all his heart good and virtuous men, stoops to no flattery, bears no rancour, disdains all disloyal arts, does his public duty uprightly, is fondly loved by his family, and dies at his work.*

If that theory be—and I have no doubt it is—the right and safe one, that human nature is always pleased with the spectacle of innocence rescued by fidelity, purity, and courage, I suppose that of the heroes of Fielding's three novels, we should like honest

* He sailed for Lisbon, from Gravesend, on Sunday morning, June 30th, 1754; and began *The Journal of a Voyage* during the passage. He died at Lisbon, in the beginning of October of the same year. He lies buried there, in the English Protestant churchyard, near the Estrella Church, with this inscription over him :—

'HENRICUS FIELDING.<br>
LUGET BRITANNIA GREMIO NON DATUM<br>
FOVERE NATUM.'

Joseph Andrews the best, and Captain Booth the second, and Tom Jones the third.*

Joseph Andrews, though he wears Lady Booby's cast-off livery, is, I think, to the full as polite as Tom Jones in his fustian suit, or Captain Booth in regimentals. He has, like those heroes, large calves, broad shoulders, a high courage, and a handsome face. The accounts of Joseph's bravery and good qualities; his voice, too musical to halloo to the dogs; his bravery in riding races for the gentlemen of the county, and his constancy in refusing bribes and temptation, have something affecting in their *naïveté* and freshness, and prepossess one in favour of that handsome young hero. The rustic bloom of Fanny, and the delightful simplicity of Parson Adams, are described with a friendliness which wins the reader of their story; we part from them with more regret than from Booth and Jones.

Fielding, no doubt, began to write this novel in ridicule of 'Pamela,' for which work one can understand the hearty contempt and antipathy which such an athletic and boisterous genius as Fielding's must have entertained. He couldn't do otherwise than laugh at the puny cockney bookseller, pouring out endless volumes of sentimental twaddle, and hold him up to scorn as a mollcoddle and a milksop. *His* genius had been nursed on sack posset, and not on dishes of tea. *His* muse had sung the loudest in tavern choruses, had seen the daylight streaming in over thousands of emptied bowls, and reeled home to chambers on the shoulders of the watchman. Richardson's goddess was attended by old maids and dowagers, and fed on muffins and bohea. ' Milksop !' roars Harry Fielding, clattering at the timid shop-shutters. ' Wretch ! Monster !

* Fielding himself is said by Doctor Warton to have preferred *Joseph Andrews* to his other writings.

Mohock!' shrieks the sentimental author of
'Pamela;'* and all the ladies of his court cackle out
an affrighted chorus. Fielding proposes to write a
book in ridicule of the author, whom he disliked and
utterly scorned and laughed at; but he is himself of so
generous, jovial, and kindly a turn that he begins to
like the characters which he invents, can't help
making them manly and pleasant as well as ridiculous,
and before he has done with them all, loves them
heartily every one.

Richardson's sickening antipathy for Harry Fielding
is quite as natural as the other's laughter and contempt
at the sentimentalist. I have not learned that these
likings and dislikings have ceased in the present day:
and every author must lay his account not only to
misrepresentation, but to honest enmity among critics,
and to being hated and abused for good as well as for
bad reasons. Richardson disliked Fielding's works
quite honestly: Walpole quite honestly spoke of them
as vulgar and stupid. Their squeamish stomachs
sickened at the rough fare and the rough guests
assembled at Fielding's jolly revel. Indeed the cloth
might have been cleaner: and the dinner and the
company were scarce such as suited a dandy. The
kind and wise old Johnson would not sit down with
him.† But a greater scholar than Johnson could

---

* 'Richardson,' says worthy Mrs. Barbauld, in her Memoir of him,
prefixed to his Correspondence, 'was exceedingly hurt at this (*Joseph
Andrews*), the more so as they had been on good terms, and he was very
intimate with Fielding's two sisters. He never appears cordially to have
forgiven it (perhaps it was not in human nature he should), and he always
speaks in his letters with a great deal of asperity of *Tom Jones*, more
indeed than was quite graceful in a rival author. No doubt he himself
thought his indignation was solely excited by the loose morality of the
work and of its author, but he could tolerate Cibber.'

† It must always be borne in mind, that besides that the Doctor
couldn't be expected to like Fielding's wild life (to say nothing of the
fact that they were of opposite sides in politics), Richardson was one of

afford to admire that astonishing genius of Harry
Fielding ; and we all know the lofty panegyric which
Gibbon wrote of him, and which remains a towering
monument to the great novelist's memory. 'Our
immortal Fielding,' Gibbon writes, 'was of the
younger branch of the Earls of Denbigh, who drew
their origin from the Counts of Hapsburgh. The
successors of Charles V. may disdain their brethren of
England, but the romance of "Tom Jones," that
exquisite picture of humour and manners, will outlive
the palace of the Escurial and the Imperial Eagle of
Austria.'

There can be no gainsaying the sentence of this
great judge. To have your name mentioned by
Gibbon, is like having it written on the dome of St.
Peter's. Pilgrims from all the world admire and
behold it.

As a picture of manners, the novel of 'Tom Jones'
is indeed exquisite : as a work of construction, quite a
wonder : the by-play of wisdom ; the power of
observation ; the multiplied felicitous turns and
thoughts ; the varied character of the great Comic
Epic : keep the reader in a perpetual admiration and
curiosity.* But against Mr. Thomas Jones himself

his earliest and kindest friends. Yet Johnson too (as Boswell tells us)
read *Amelia* through without stopping.

* 'Manners change from generation to generation, and with manners
morals appear to change—actually change with some, but appear to
change with all but the abandoned. A young man of the present day
who should act as Tom Jones is supposed to act at Upton, with Lady
Bellaston, &c., would not be a Tom Jones ; and a Tom Jones of the
present day, without perhaps being in the ground a better man, would
have perished rather than submit to be kept by a harridan of fortune.
Therefore, this novel is, and indeed pretends to be, no example of conduct.
But, notwithstanding all this, I do loathe the cant which can recommend
*Pamela* and *Clarissa Harlowe* as strictly moral, although they poison the
imagination of the young with continued doses of *tinct. lyttæ*, while *Tom
Jones* is prohibited as loose. I do not speak of young women ; but a
young man whose heart or feelings can be injured, or even his passions

we have a right to put in a protest, and quarrel with the esteem the author evidently has for that character. Charles Lamb says finely of Jones that a single hearty laugh from him 'clears the air'—but then it is in a certain state of the atmosphere. It might clear the air when such personages as Blifil or Lady Bellaston poison it. But I fear very much that (except until the very last scene of the story), when Mr. Jones enters Sophia's drawing-room, the pure air there is rather tainted with the young gentleman's tobacco-pipe and punch. I can't say that I think Mr. Jones a virtuous character; I can't say but that I think Fielding's evident liking and admiration for Mr. Jones shows that the great humourist's moral sense was blunted by his life, and that here, in Art and Ethics, there is a great error. If it is right to have a hero whom we may admire, let us at least take care that he is admirable : if, as is the plan of some authors (a plan decidedly against their interests, be it said), it is propounded that there exists in life no such being, and therefore that in novels, the picture of life, there should appear no such character ; then Mr. Thomas Jones becomes an admissible person, and we examine his defects and good qualities, as we do those of Parson Thwackum, or Miss Seagrim. But a hero with a flawed reputation ; a hero spunging for a guinea ; a hero who can't pay his landlady, and is obliged to let his honour out to hire, is absurd, and his claim to heroic rank untenable. I protest against Mr. Thomas Jones holding such rank at all. I protest even against his being considered a more than ordinary young fellow, ruddy-cheeked, broad-shouldered, and fond of

excited by this novel, is already thoroughly corrupt. There is a cheerful, sunshiny, breezy spirit, that prevails everywhere, strongly contrasted with the close, hot, day-dreamy continuity of Richardson.'—COLERIDGE. *Literary Remains*, vol. ii. p. 374.

wine and pleasure. He would not rob a church, but that is all ; and a pretty long argument may be debated, as to which of these old types—the spendthrift, the hypocrite, Jones and Blifil, Charles and Joseph Surface—is the worst member of society and the most deserving of censure. The prodigal Captain Booth is a better man than his predecessor Mr. Jones, in so far as he thinks much more humbly of himself than Jones did : goes down on his knees, and owns his weaknesses, and cries out, ' Not for my sake, but for the sake of my pure and sweet and beautiful wife Amelia, I pray you, O critical reader, to forgive me.' That stern moralist regards him from the bench (the judge's practice out of court is not here the question), and says, ' Captain Booth, it is perfectly true that your life has been disreputable, and that on many occasions you have shown yourself to be no better than a scamp —you have been tippling at the tavern, when the kindest and sweetest lady in the world has cooked your little supper of boiled mutton and awaited you all the night ; you have spoilt the little dish of boiled mutton thereby, and caused pangs and pains to Amelia's tender heart.* You have got into debt

* ' Nor was she (Lady Mary Wortley Montagu) a stranger to that beloved first wife, whose picture he drew in his " Amelia," when, as she said, even the glowing language he knew how to employ did not do more than justice to the amiable qualities of the original, or to her beauty, although this had suffered a little from the accident related in the novel—a frightful overturn, which destroyed the gristle of her nose. He loved her passionately, and she returned his affection. . . .

' His biographers seem to have been shy of disclosing that, after the death of this charming woman, he married her maid. And yet the act was not so discreditable to his character as it may sound. The maid had few personal charms, but was an excellent creature, devotedly attached to her mistress, and almost broken-hearted for her loss. In the first agonies of his own grief, which approached to frenzy, he found no relief but from weeping along with her ; nor solace when a degree calmer, but in talking to her of the angel they mutually regretted. This made her his habitual confidential associate, and in process of time he began to think he could not give his children a tenderer mother, or

without the means of paying it. You have gambled
the money with which you ought to have paid your
rent. You have spent in drink or in worse amusements the sums which your poor wife has raised upon
her little home treasures, her own ornaments, and the
toys of her children. But, you rascal! you own
humbly that you are no better than you should be,
you never for one moment pretend that you are anything but a miserable weak-minded rogue. You do
in your heart adore that angelic woman, your wife,
and for her sake, sirrah, you shall have your discharge.
Lucky for you, and for others like you, that in spite
of your failings and imperfections, pure hearts pity
and love you. For your wife's sake you are permitted
to go hence without a remand; and I beg you, by
the way, to carry to that angelical lady the expression
of the cordial respect and admiration of this court.'
Amelia pleads for her husband, Will Booth : Amelia
pleads for her reckless kindly old father, Harry
Fielding. To have invented that character is not
only a triumph of art, but it is a good action. They
say it was in his own home that Fielding knew her
and loved her : and from his own wife that he drew
the most charming character in English fiction.
Fiction ! why fiction ? why not history ? I know
Amelia just as well as Lady Mary Wortley Montagu.
I believe in Colonel Bath almost as much as in Colonel

secure for himself a more faithful housekeeper and nurse. At least,
this was what he told his friends ; and it is certain that her conduct as
his wife confirmed it, and fully justified his good opinion.—*Letters and
Works of Lady Mary Wortley Montagu.* Edited by Lord Wharncliffe.
*Introductory Anecdotes,* vol. i. pp. 80, 81.

Fielding's first wife was Miss Craddock, a young lady from Salisbury,
with a fortune of £1500, whom he married in 1736. About the same
time he succeeded, himself, to an estate of £200 per annum, and on the
joint amount he lived for some time as a splendid country gentleman in
Dorsetshire. Three years brought him to the end of his fortune ; when
he returned to London, and became a student of law.

Gardiner or the Duke of Cumberland. I admire the author of 'Amelia,' and thank the kind master who introduced me to that sweet and delightful companion and friend. 'Amelia' perhaps is not a better story than 'Tom Jones,' but it has the better ethics; the prodigal repents, at least, before forgiveness,—whereas that odious broad-backed Mr. Jones carries off his beauty with scarce an interval of remorse for his manifold errors and shortcomings; and is not half punished enough before the great prize of fortune and love falls to his share. I am angry with Jones. Too much of the plum-cake and rewards of life fall to that boisterous, swaggering young scapegrace. Sophia actually surrenders without a proper sense of decorum; the fond, foolish, palpitating little creature!—'Indeed Mr. Jones,' she says,—'it rests with you to appoint the day.' I suppose Sophia is drawn from life as well as Amelia; and many a young fellow, no better than Mr. Thomas Jones, has carried by a *coup de main* the heart of many a kind girl who was a great deal too good for him.

What a wonderful art! What an admirable gift of nature was it by which the author of these tales was endowed, and which enabled him to fix our interest, to waken our sympathy, to seize upon our credulity, so that we believe in his people—speculate gravely upon their faults or their excellences, prefer this one or that, deplore Jones's fondness for play and drink, Booth's fondness for play and drink, and the unfortunate position of the wives of both gentlemen—love and admire those ladies with all our hearts, and talk about them as faithfully as if we had breakfasted with them this morning in their actual drawing-rooms, or should meet them this afternoon in the Park! What a genius! what a vigour! what a bright-eyed intelligence and observation! what a wholesome hatred for

meanness and knavery ! what a vast sympathy ! what
a cheerfulness ! what a manly relish of life ! what a
love of human kind ! what a poet is here !—watching,
meditating, brooding, creating ! What multitudes of
truth has that man left behind him ! What generations he has taught to laugh wisely and fairly ! What
scholars he has formed and accustomed to the exercise
of thoughtful humour and the manly play of wit !
What a courage he had ! What a dauntless and
constant cheerfulness of intellect, that burned bright
and steady through all the storms of his life and
never deserted its last wreck ! It is wonderful
to think of the pains and misery which the man
suffered ; the pressure of want, illness, remorse
which he endured ! and that the writer was neither
malignant nor melancholy, his view of truth never
warped, and his generous human kindness never
surrendered.*

* In the *Gentleman's Magazine* for 1786, an anecdote is related of
Harry Fielding, 'in whom,' says the correspondent, 'good-nature and
philanthropy in their extreme degree were known to be the prominent
features.' It seems that 'some parochial taxes' for his house in Beau-
fort Buildings had long been demanded by the collector. 'At last,
Harry went off to Johnson, and obtained by a process of literary mortgage the needful sum. He was returning with it, when he met an old
college chum whom he had not seen for many years. He asked the
chum to dinner with him at a neighbouring tavern ; and learning that
he was in difficulties, emptied the contents of his pocket into his. On
returning home he was informed that the collector had been twice for
the money. "Friendship has called for the money and had it," said
Fielding ; "let the collector call again."'
It is elsewhere told of him, that being in company with the Earl of
Denbigh, his kinsman, and the conversation turning upon their relationship, the Earl asked him how it was that he spelled his name 'Fielding,'
and not 'Feilding,' like the head of the house ? 'I cannot tell, my
Lord,' said he, 'except it be that my branch of the family were the first
who knew how to spell.'
In 1748, he was made Justice of the Peace for Westminster and
Middlesex, an office then paid by fees and very laborious, without being
particularly reputable. It may be seen from his own words, in the
Introduction to the 'Voyage,' what kind of work devolved upon him,

In the quarrel mentioned before, which happened on Fielding's last voyage to Lisbon, and when the

and in what a state he was, during these last years ; and still more clearly, how he comported himself through all.

'Whilst I was preparing for my journey, and when I was almost fatigued to death with several long examinations, relating to five different murders, all committed within the space of a week, by different gangs of street-robbers, I received a message from his Grace the Duke of New-castle, by Mr. Carrington. the King's messenger, to attend his Grace the next morning in Lincoln's Inn Fields, upon some business of import-ance : but I excused myself from complying with the message, as, besides being lame, I was very ill with the great fatigues I had lately undergone, added to my distemper.

'His Grace, however, sent Mr. Carrington the very next morning, with another summons ; with which, though in the utmost distress, I immediately complied ; but the Duke happening, unfortunately for me, to be then particularly engaged, after I had waited some time, sent a gentleman to discourse with me on the best plan which could be invented for these murders and robberies, which were every day committed in the streets ; upon which I promised to transmit my opinion in writing to his Grace, who, as the gentleman informed me, intended to lay it before the Privy Council.

'Though this visit cost me a severe cold, I, notwithstanding, set myself down to work, and in about four days sent the Duke as regular a plan as I could form, with all the reasons and arguments I could bring to support it, drawn out on several sheets of paper ; and soon received a message from the Duke, by Mr. Carrington, acquainting me that my plan was highly approved of, and that all the terms of it would be com-plied with.

'The principal and most material of these terms was the immediately depositing £600 in my hands ; at which small charge I undertook to demolish the then reigning gangs, and to put the civil policy into such order, that no such gangs should ever be able for the future to form themselves into bodies, or at least to remain any time formidable to the public.

'I had delayed my Bath journey for some time, contrary to the repeated advice of my physical acquaintances and the ardent desire of my warmest friends, though my distemper was now turned to a deep jaundice ; in which case the Bath waters are generally reputed to be almost infallible. But I had the most eager desire to demolish this gang of villains and cut-throats. . . .

'After some weeks the money was paid at the Treasury, and within a few days after £200 of it had come into my hands, the whole gang of cut-throats was entirely dispersed. . . .

Further on, he says,—

'I will confess that my private affairs at the beginning of the winter had but a gloomy aspect ; for I had not plundered the public or the poor

stout captain of the ship fell down on his knees, and asked the sick man's pardon—'I did not suffer,' Fielding says, in his hearty, manly way, his eyes lighting up as it were with their old fire—'I did not suffer a brave man and an old man to remain a moment in that posture, but immediately forgave him.' Indeed, I think, with his noble spirit and unconquerable generosity, Fielding reminds one of those brave men of whom one reads in stories of English shipwrecks and disasters—of the officer on the African shore, when disease had destroyed the crew, and he himself is seized by fever, who throws the lead with a death-stricken hand, takes the soundings, carries the ship out of the river or off the dangerous coast, and dies in the manly endeavour—of the wounded captain, when the vessel founders, who never loses his heart, who eyes the danger steadily, and has a cheery word for all, until the inevitable fate overwhelms him, and the gallant ship goes down. Such a brave and gentle heart, such an intrepid and courageous spirit, I love to recognise in the manly, the English Harry Fielding.

of those sums which men, who are always ready to plunder both as much as they can, have been pleased to suspect me of taking ; on the contrary, by composing, instead of inflaming, the quarrels of porters and beggars (which I blush when I say hath not been universally practised), and by refusing to take a shilling from a man who most undoubtedly would not have had another left, I had reduced an income of about £500 a year of the dirtiest money upon earth to little more than £300, a considerable portion of which remained with my clerk.'

# STERNE AND GOLDSMITH

ROGER STERNE, Sterne's father, was the second son of a numerous race, descendants of Richard Sterne, Archbishop of York, in the reign of James II.; and children of Simon Sterne, and Mary Jaques, his wife, heiress of Elvington, near York.* Roger was a lieutenant in Handyside's regiment, and engaged in Flanders in Queen Anne's wars. He married the daughter of a noted sutler—'N.B., he was in debt to him,' his son writes, pursuing the paternal biography —and marched through the world with this companion ; she following the regiment and bringing many children to poor Roger Sterne. The captain was an irascible but kind and simple little man, Sterne says, and informs us that his sire was run through the body at Gibraltar, by a brother officer, in a duel which arose out of a dispute about a goose. Roger never entirely recovered from the effects of this rencontre, but died presently at Jamaica, whither he had followed the drum.

Laurence, his second child, was born at Clonmel, in Ireland, in 1713, and travelled for the first ten years of his life, on his father's march, from barrack to transport, from Ireland to England.†

* He came of a Suffolk family—one of whom settled in Nottinghamshire. The famous 'starling' was actually the family crest.

† 'It was in this parish (of Animo, in Wicklow), during our stay, that I had that wonderful escape in falling through a mill-race, whilst the

One relative of his mother's took her and her family
under shelter for ten months at Mullingar ; another
collateral descendant of the Archbishop's housed them
for a year at his castle near Carrickfergus. Larry
Sterne was put to school at Halifax in England, finally
was adopted by his kinsman of Elvington, and parted
company with his father, the Captain, who marched
on his path of life till he met the fatal goose which
closed his career. The most picturesque and delightful parts of Laurence Sterne's writings we owe
to his recollections of the military life. Trim's
montero cap, and Le Fevre's sword, and dear Uncle
Toby's roquelaure are doubtless reminiscences of the
boy, who had lived with the followers of William and
Marlborough, and had beat time with his little feet to
the fifes of Ramillies in Dublin barrack-yard, or
played with the torn flags and halberds of Malplaquet
on the parade-ground at Clonmel.

Laurence remained at Halifax school till he was
eighteen years old. His wit and cleverness appear to
have acquired the respect of his master here ; for
when the usher whipped Laurence for writing his
name on the newly whitewashed school-room ceiling,
the pedagogue in chief rebuked the understrapper, and
said that the name should never be effaced, for Sterne
was a boy of genius, and would come to preferment.

His cousin, the Squire of Elvington, sent Sterne to
Jesus College, Cambridge, where he remained five
years, and, taking orders, got, through his uncle's
interest, the living of Sutton and the prebendary of
York. Through his wife's connections he got the
living of Stillington. He married her in 1741, having
ardently courted the young lady for some years

mill was going, and of being taken up unhurt : the story is incredible,
but known for truth in all that part of Ireland, where hundreds of the
common people flocked to see me.'—*Sterne*

previously. It was not until the young lady fancied herself dying, that she made Sterne acquainted with the extent of her liking for him. One evening when he was sitting with her, with an almost broken heart to see her so ill (the Reverend Mr. Sterne's heart was a good deal broken in the course of his life), she said —'My dear Laurey, I never can be yours, for I verily believe I have not long to live; but I have left you every shilling of my fortune;' a generosity which overpowered Sterne. She recovered: and so they were married, and grew heartily tired of each other before many years were over. 'Nescio quid est materia cum me,' Sterne writes to one of his friends (in dog-Latin, and very sad dog-Latin too); 'sed sum fatigatus et ægrotus de meâ uxore plus quam unquam:' which means, I am sorry to say, 'I don't know what is the matter with me; but I am more tired and sick of my wife than ever.' *

This to be sure was five-and-twenty years after Laurey had been overcome by her generosity, and she by Laurey's love. Then he wrote to her of the delights of marriage, saying, 'We will be as merry and as innocent as our first parents in Paradise, before the arch-fiend entered that indescribable scene. The kindest affections will have room to expand in our retirement: let the human tempest and hurricane rage at a distance, the desolation is beyond the horizon of peace. My L. has seen a polyanthus blow in December? Some friendly wall has sheltered it from the biting wind. No planetary influence shall reach us but that which presides and cherishes the

* 'My wife returns to Toulouse, and proposes to pass the summer at Bagnères. I, on the contrary, go and visit my wife, the Church, in Yorkshire. We all live the longer, at least the happier, for having things our own way; this is my conjugal maxim. I own 'tis not the best of maxims, but I maintain 'tis not the worst.'—Sterne's *Letters*, 20th January, 1764.

sweetest flowers. The gloomy family of care and distrust shall be banished from our dwelling, guarded by thy kind and tutelar deity. We will sing our choral songs of gratitude and rejoice to the end of our pilgrimage. Adieu, my L. Return to one who languishes for thy society !—As I take up my pen, my poor pulse quickens, my pale face glows, and tears are trickling down on my paper as I trace the word L.'

And it is about this woman, with whom he finds no fault but that she bores him, that our philanthropist writes, 'Sum fatigatus et ægrotus'—*Sum mortaliter in amore* with somebody else ! That fine flower of love, that polyanthus over which Sterne snivelled so many tears, could not last for a quarter of a century !

Or rather it could not be expected that a gentleman with such a fountain at command should keep it to *arroser* one homely old lady, when a score of younger and prettier people might be refreshed from the same gushing source.* It was in December, 1767, that

---

* In a collection of ' Seven Letters by Sterne and his Friends ' (printed for private circulation in 1844), is a letter of M. Tollot, who was in France with Sterne and his family in 1764. Here is a paragraph :—

'Nous arrivâmes le lendemain à Montpellier, où nous trouvâmes notre ami Mr. Sterne, sa femme, sa fille, Mr. Huet, et quelques autres Anglaises. J'eus, je vous l'avoue, beaucoup de plaisir en revoyant le bon et agréable Tristram. . . . Il avait été assez longtemps à Toulouse, où il se serait amusé sans sa femme, qui le poursuivit partout, et qui voulait être de tout. Ces dispositions dans cette bonne dame lui ont fait passer d'assez mauvais momens ; il supporte tous ces désagrémens avec une patience d'ange.'

About four months after this very characteristic letter, Sterne wrote to the same gentleman to whom Tollot had written ; and from his letter we may extract a companion paragraph :—

'. . . All which being premised, I have been for eight weeks smitten with the tenderest passion that ever tender wight underwent. I wish, dear cousin, thou could'st conceive (perhaps thou canst without my wishing it) how deliciously I cantered away with it the first month, two up, two down, always upon my *hanches*, along the streets from my hotel to hers, at first once—then twice, then three times a day, till at length I was within an ace of setting up my hobby-horse in her stable for good and all. I might as well, considering how the enemies of the Lord have

the Reverend Laurence Sterne, the famous Shandean,
the charming Yorick, the delight of the fashionable
world, the delicious divine, for whose sermons the
whole polite world was subscribing,* the occupier of
Rabelais's easy chair, only fresh stuffed and more
elegant than when in possession of the cynical old
curate of Meudon,†—the more than rival of the Dean

blasphemed thereupon. The last three weeks we were every hour upon
the doleful ditty of parting ; and thou may'st conceive, dear cousin, how
it altered my gait and air : for I went and came like any louden'd carl,
and did nothing but *jouer des sentimens* with her from sun-rising even to
the setting of the same ; and now she is gone to the south of France :
and to finish the *comédie*, I fell ill, and broke a vessel in my lungs, and
half bled to death. Voilà mon histoire !'
    Whether husband or wife had most of the 'patience d'ange' may be
uncertain ; but there can be no doubt which needed it most !
    * '"Tristram Shandy" is still a greater object of admiration, the man
as well as the book : one is invited to dinner, where he dines, a fortnight
before. As to the volumes yet published, there is much good fun in
them, and humour sometimes hit and sometimes missed. Have you
read his "Sermons," with his own comick figure, from a painting by
Reynolds, at the head of them ? They are in the style I think most proper
for the pulpit, and show a strong imagination and a sensible heart ; but you
see him often tottering on the verge of laughter, and ready to throw his
periwig in the face of the audience.'—GRAY's *Letters* : June 22nd, 1760.
    'It having been observed that there was little hospitality in London
—Johnson : " Nay, sir, any man who has a name, or who has the power
of pleasing, will be very generally invited in London. The man, Sterne,
I have been told, has had engagements for three months." Goldsmith :
" And a very dull fellow." Johnson : " Why, no, sir." '—BOSWELL's
*Life of Johnson.*
    'Her [Miss Monckton's] vivacity enchanted the sage, and they used
to talk together with all imaginable ease. A singular instance happened
one evening, when she insisted that some of Sterne's writings were very
pathetic. Johnson bluntly denied it. "I am sure," said she, "they
have affected me." "Why," said Johnson, smiling, and rolling himself
about—"that is, because, dearest, you're a dunce." When she some time
afterwards mentioned this to him, he said with equal truth and politeness, " Madam, if I had thought so, I certainly should not have said
it." '—*Ibid.*
    † A passage or two from Sterne's Sermons may not be without interest
here. Is not the following, levelled against the cruelties of the Church
of Rome, stamped with the autograph of the author of the *Sentimental
Journey ?*—
    'To be convinced of this, go with me for a moment into the prisons of

of Saint Patrick's, wrote the above-quoted respectable
letter to his friend in London : and it was in April of
the same year that he was pouring out his fond heart
to Mrs. Elizabeth Draper, wife of ' Daniel Draper,
Esquire, Councillor of Bombay, and, in 1775, chief of

the Inquisition—behold *religion* with mercy and justice chained down
under her feet—there, sitting ghastly upon a black tribunal, propped up
with racks, and instruments of torment.—Hark !—what a piteous groan !
—See the melancholy wretch who uttered it, just brought forth to
undergo the anguish of a mock-trial, and endure the utmost pain that a
studied system of *religious cruelty* has been able to invent.   Behold this
helpless victim delivered up to his tormentors.   *His body so wasted with
sorrow and long confinement, you'll see every nerve and muscle as it suffers.*—
Observe the last movement of that horrid engine.—What convulsions it
has thrown him into !   Consider the nature of the posture in which he
now lies stretched.—What exquisite torture he endures by it !—'Tis all
nature can bear.—Good GOD !  see how it keeps his weary soul hanging
upon his trembling lips, willing to take its leave, but not suffered to
depart.   Behold the unhappy wretch led back to his cell—dragg'd out of
it again to meet the flames—and the insults in his last agonies, which
this principle—this principle, that there can be religion without morality
—has prepared for him.'—*Sermon 27th.*

The next extract is preached on a text to be found in Judges xix.
1, 2, 3, concerning a ' certain Levite ' :—

'Such a one the Levite wanted to share his solitude and fill up that
uncomfortable blank in the heart in such a situation : for, notwithstanding all we meet with in books, in many of which, no doubt, there are a
good many handsome things said upon the sweets of retirement, &c. . . .
yet still " it *is not good for man to be alone ;* " nor can all which the cold-
hearted pedant stuns our ears with upon the subject, ever give one answer
of satisfaction to the mind ; in the midst of the loudest vauntings of
philosophy, nature will have her yearnings for society and friendship ; a
good heart wants some object to be kind to—and the best parts of our
blood, and the purest of our spirits, suffer most under the destitution.

' Let the torpid monk seek Heaven comfortless and alone.   God speed
him !   For my own part, I fear I should never so find the way : *let me
be wise and religious, but let me be* MAN ; wherever Thy Providence
places me, or whatever be the road I take to Thee, give me some
companion in my journey, be it only to remark to, " How our shadows
lengthen as our sun goes down ! "—to whom I may say, " How fresh is
the face of Nature ; how sweet the flowers of the field ! how delicious
are these fruits ! " '—*Sermon 18th.*

The first of these passages gives us another drawing of the famous
' Captive.'   The second shows that the same reflection was suggested to
the Reverend Laurence by a text in Judges as by the *fille-de-chambre.*

Sterne's Sermons were published as those of ' Mr. Yorick.'

the factory of Surat—a gentleman very much respected in that quarter of the globe.'

'I got thy letter last night, Eliza,' Sterne writes, 'on my return from Lord Bathurst's, where I dined'—(the letter has this merit in it, that it contains a pleasant reminiscence of better men than Sterne, and introduces us to a portrait of a kind old gentleman)—'I got thy letter last night, Eliza, on my return from Lord Bathurst's; and where I was heard—as I talked of thee an hour without intermission—with so much pleasure and attention, that the good old Lord toasted your health three different times; and now he is in his 85th year, says he hopes to live long enough to be introduced as a friend to my fair Indian disciple, and to see her eclipse all other Nabobesses as much in wealth as she does already in exterior and, what is far better' (for Sterne is nothing without his morality), 'in interior merit. This nobleman is an old friend of mine. You know he was always the protector of men of wit and genius, and has had those of the last century, Addison, Steele, Pope, Swift, Prior, &c., always at his table. The manner in which his notice began of me was as singular as it was polite. He came up to me one day as I was at the Princess of Wales' Court, and said, "I want to know you, Mr. Sterne, but it is fit you also should know who it is that wishes this pleasure. You have heard of an old Lord Bathurst, of whom your Popes and Swifts have sung and spoken so much? I have lived my life with geniuses of that cast; but have survived them; and, despairing ever to find their equals, it is some years since I have shut up my books and closed my accounts; but you have kindled a desire in me of opening them once more before I die: which I now do: so go home and dine with me." This nobleman, I say, is a prodigy, for he has all the wit and promptness of a man of thirty; a disposition to be pleased, and a power to please others, beyond whatever I knew: added to which a man of learning, courtesy, and feeling.

'He heard me talk of thee, Eliza, with uncommon

satisfaction—for there was only a third person, *and of sensibility*, with us : and a most sentimental afternoon till nine o'clock have we passed ! * But thou, Eliza, wert the star that conducted and enlivened the discourse ! And when I talked not of thee, still didst thou fill my mind, and warm every thought I uttered, for I am not ashamed to acknowledge I greatly miss thee. Best of all good girls !—the sufferings I have sustained all night in consequence of thine, Eliza, are beyond the power of words. . . . And so thou hast fixed thy Bramin's portrait over thy writing-desk, and wilt consult it in all doubts and difficulties ?—Grateful and good girl ! Yorick smiles contentedly over all thou dost : his picture does not do justice to his own complacency. I am glad your shipmates are friendly beings' (Eliza was at Deal, going back to the Councillor at Bombay, and indeed it was high time she should be off). 'You could least dispense with what is contrary to your own nature, which is soft and gentle, Eliza ; it would civilise savages—though pity were it thou should'st be tainted with the office. Write to me, my child, thy delicious letters. Let them speak the easy carelessness of a heart that opens itself anyhow, everyhow. Such, Eliza, I write to thee !' (The artless rogue. of course he did !) 'And so I should ever love thee, most artlessly, most affectionately, if Providence permitted thy

* 'I am glad that you are in love : 'twill cure you at least of the spleen, which has a bad effect on both man and woman. I myself must ever have some Dulcinea in my head ; it harmonises the soul ; and in these cases I first endeavour to make the lady believe so, or rather, I begin first to make myself believe that I am in love ; but I carry on my affairs quite in the French way, sentimentally : "L'amour," say they, "n'est rien sans sentiment." Now, notwithstanding they make such a pother about the *word*, they have no precise idea annexed to it. And so much for that same subject called love.'—STERNE's *Letters :* May 23, 1765.

'*P. S.*—My *Sentimental Journey* will please Mrs. J—— and my Lydia' [his daughter, afterwards Mrs. Medalle]—'I can answer for those two. It is a subject which works well, and suits the frame of mind I have been in for some time past. I told you my design in it was to teach us to love the world and our fellow-creatures better than we do—so it runs most upon those gentler passions and affections which aid so much to it.'—*Letters* [1767].

residence in the same section of the globe : for I am all
that honour and affection can make me

'"Thy Bramin."'

The Bramin continues addressing Mrs. Draper
until the departure of the 'Earl of Chatham' Indiaman
from Deal, on the 2nd of April, 1767. He is amiably
anxious about the fresh paint for Eliza's cabin ; he is
uncommonly solicitous about her companions on
board :—

'I fear the best of your shipmates are only genteel by
comparison with the contrasted crew with which thou
beholdest them. So was—you know who—from the same
fallacy which was put upon your judgment when—but I
will not mortify you !'

'You know who' was, of course, Daniel Draper,
Esquire, of Bombay—a gentleman very much respected
in that quarter of the globe, and about whose probable
health our worthy Bramin writes with delightful
candour :—

'I honour you, Eliza, for keeping secret some things
which, if explained, had been a panegyric on yourself.
There is a dignity in venerable affliction which will not
allow it to appeal to the world for pity or redress. Well
have you supported that character, my amiable, my
philosophic friend ! And, indeed, I begin to think you
have as many virtues as my Uncle Toby's widow. Talking
of widows—pray, Eliza, if ever you are such, do not think
of giving yourself to some wealthy Nabob, because I design
to marry you myself. My wife cannot live long, and I
know not the woman I should like so well for her substitute
as yourself. 'Tis true I am ninety-five in constitution, and
you but twenty-five ; but what I want in youth, I will
make up in wit and good-humour. Not Swift so loved
his Stella, Scarron his Maintenon, or Waller his Saccharissa.
Tell me, in answer to this, that you approve and honour
the proposal.'

Approve and honour the proposal! The coward was writing gay letters to his friends this while, with sneering allusions to this poor foolish *Bramine*. Her ship was not out of the Downs and the charming Sterne was at the 'Mount Coffee-house,' with a sheet of gilt-edged paper before him, offering that precious treasure his heart to Lady P——, asking whether it gave her pleasure to see him unhappy? whether it added to her triumph that her eyes and lips had turned a man into a fool?—quoting the Lord's Prayer, with a horrible baseness of blasphemy, as a proof that he had desired not to be led into temptation, and swearing himself the most tender and sincere fool in the world. It was from his home at Coxwould that he wrote the Latin Letter, which, I suppose, he was ashamed to put into English. I find in my copy of the Letters, that there is a note of I can't call it admiration, at Letter 112, which seems to announce that there was a No. 3 to whom the wretched worn-out old scamp was paying his addresses; * and the

* *'To Mrs. H——*

'COXWOULD: *Nov.* 15, 1767.

'Now be a good dear woman, my H——, and execute those commissions well, and when I see you I will give you a kiss—there's for you! But I have something else for you which I am fabricating at a great rate, and that is my "Sentimental Journey," which shall make you cry as much as it has affected me, or I will give up the business of sentimental writing.  .      'I am yours, &c. &c.,

'T. SHANDY.'

*'To the Earl of ——*

'COXWOULD : *Nov.* 28, 1767.

'MY LORD,—'Tis with the greatest pleasure I take my pen to thank your lordship for your letter of inquiry about Yorick : he was worn out, both his spirits and body, with the "Sentimental Journey." 'Tis true, then, an author must feel himself, or his reader will not ; but I have torn my whole frame into pieces by my feelings : I believe the brain stands as much in need of recruiting as the body. Therefore I shall set out for town the twentieth of next month, after having recruited myself a week at York. I might indeed solace myself with

year after, having come back to his lodgings in Bond
Street, with his 'Sentimental Journey' to launch upon
the town, eager as ever for praise and pleasure—as
vain, as wicked, as witty, as false as he had ever been
—death at length seized the feeble wretch, and on the
18th of March, 1768, that 'bale of cadaverous goods,'
as he calls his body, was consigned to Pluto.*   In his
last letter there is one sign of grace—the real affection with which he entreats a friend to be a guardian
to his daughter Lydia.   All his letters to her are artless, kind, affectionate, and *not* sentimental; as a
hundred pages in his writings are beautiful, and full,
not of surprising humour merely, but of genuine love
and kindness.   A perilous trade, indeed, is that of a
man who has to bring his tears and laughter, his
recollections, his personal griefs and joys, his private
thoughts and feelings to market, to write them on

my wife (who is come from France); but, in fact, I have long been a
sentimental being, whatever your lordship may think to the contrary.'
    * 'In February, 1768, Laurence Sterne, his frame exhausted by long
debilitating illness, expired at his lodgings in Bond Street, London.
There was something in the manner of his death singularly resembling
the particulars detailed by *Mrs. Quickly* as attending that of *Falstaff*, the
compeer of *Yorick* for infinite jest, however unlike in other particulars.
As he lay on his bed totally exhausted, he complained that his feet
were cold, and requested the female attendant to chafe them.   She
did so, and it seemed to relieve him.   He complained that the cold
came up higher; and whilst the assistant was in the act of chafing his
ankles and legs, he expired without a groan.   It was also remarkable
that his death took place much in the manner which he himself had
wished; and that the last offices were rendered him, not in his own
house, or by the hand of kindred affection, but in an inn, and by
strangers.
    'We are well acquainted with Sterne's features and personal appear-
ance, to which he himself frequently alludes.   He was tall and thin,
with a hectic and consumptive appearance.'—*Sir Walter Scott.*
    'It is known that Sterne died in hired lodgings, and I have been told
that his attendants robbed him even of his gold sleeve-buttons while he
was expiring.'—*Dr. Ferriar.*
    'He died at No. 41 (now a cheesemonger's), on the west side of Old
Bond Street.'—*Handbook of London.*

paper, and sell them for money. Does he exaggerate his grief, so as to get his reader's pity for a false sensibility? feign indignation, so as to establish a character for virtue? elaborate repartees, so that he may pass for a wit? steal from other authors, and put down the theft to the credit side of his own reputation for ingenuity and learning? feign originality? affect benevolence or misanthropy? appeal to the gallery gods with claptraps and vulgar baits to catch applause?

How much of the paint and emphasis is necessary for the fair business of the stage, and how much of the rant and rouge is put on for the vanity of the actor? His audience trusts him : can he trust himself? How much was deliberate calculation and imposture—how much was false sensibility—and how much true feeling? Where did the lie begin, and did he know where? and where did the truth end in the art and scheme of this man of genius, this actor, this quack? Some time since, I was in the company of a French actor who began after dinner, and at his own request, to sing French songs of the sort called *des chansons grivoises*, and which he performed admirably, and to the dissatisfaction of most persons present. Having finished these, he commenced a sentimental ballad— it was so charmingly sung that it touched all persons present, and especially the singer himself, whose voice trembled, whose eyes filled with emotion, and who was snivelling and weeping quite genuine tears by the time his own ditty was over. I suppose Sterne had this artistical sensibility ; he used to blubber perpetually in his study, and finding his tears infectious, and that they brought him a great popularity, he exercised the lucrative gift of weeping : he utilised it, and cried on every occasion. I own that I don't value or respect much the cheap dribble of those

fountains.  He fatigues me with his perpetual disquiet
and his uneasy appeals to my risible or sentimental
faculties.  He is always looking in my face, watching
his effect, uncertain whether I think him an impostor
or not ; posture-making, coaxing, and imploring me.
'See what sensibility I have—own now that I'm very
clever—do cry now, you can't resist this.'  The
humour of Swift and Rabelais, whom he pretended to
succeed, poured from them as naturally as song does
from a bird ; they lose no manly dignity with it, but
laugh their hearty great laugh out of their broad
chests as nature bade them.  But this man—who can
make you laugh, who can make you cry too—never
lets his reader alone, or will permit his audience
repose ; when you are quiet, he fancies he must rouse
you, and turns over head and heels, or sidles up and
whispers a nasty story.  The man is a great jester,
not a great humourist.  He goes to work systematic-
ally and of cold blood ; paints his face, puts on his
ruff and motley clothes, and lays down his carpet and
tumbles on it.

For instance, take the 'Sentimental Journey,' and
see in the writer the deliberate propensity to make
points and seek applause.  He gets to 'Dessein's
Hotel,' he wants a carriage to travel to Paris, he goes
to the inn-yard, and begins what the actors call
'business' at once.  There is that little carriage (the
*désobligeante.*)

'Four months had elapsed since it had finished its career
of Europe in the corner of Monsieur Dessein's coach-yard,
and having sallied out thence but a vamped-up business at
first, though it had been twice taken to pieces on Mont
Cenis, it had not profited much by its adventures, but by
none so little as the standing so many months unpitied in
the corner of Monsieur Dessein's coach-yard.  Much, indeed, was not to be said for it—but something might—

and when a few words will rescue misery out of her distress, I hate the man who can be a churl of them.'

*Le tour est fait!* Paillasse has tumbled! Paillasse has jumped over the *désobligeante*, cleared it, hood and all, and bows to the noble company. Does anybody believe that this is a real Sentiment? that this luxury of generosity, this gallant rescue of Misery—out of an old cab, is genuine feeling? It is as genuine as the virtuous oratory of Joseph Surface when he begins, 'The man who,' &c. &c., and wishes to pass off for a saint with his credulous, good-humoured dupes.

Our friend purchases the carriage: after turning that notorious old monk to good account, and effecting (like a soft and good-natured Paillasse as he was, and very free with his money when he had it) an exchange of snuff-boxes with the old Franciscan, jogs out of Calais; sets down in immense figures on the credit side of his account the sous he gives away to the Montreuil beggars; and, at Nampont, gets out of the chaise and whimpers over that famous dead donkey, for which any sentimentalist may cry who will. It is agreeably and skilfully done—that dead jackass: like Monsieur de Soubise's cook on the campaign, Sterne dresses it, and serves it up quite tender and with a very piquant sauce. But tears and fine feelings, and a white pocket-handkerchief, and a funeral sermon, and horses and feathers, and a procession of mutes, and a hearse with a dead donkey inside! Psha, mountebank! I'll not give thee one penny more for that trick, donkey and all!

This donkey had appeared once before with signal effect. In 1765, three years before the publication of the 'Sentimental Journey,' the seventh and eighth volumes of 'Tristram Shandy' were given to the world, and the famous Lyons donkey makes his entry in those volumes (pp. 315, 316) :—

'Twas by a poor ass, with a couple of large panniers at his back, who had just turned in to collect eleemosynary turnip-tops and cabbage-leaves, and stood dubious, with his two fore feet at the inside of the threshold, and with his two hinder feet towards the street, as not knowing very well whether he was to go in or no.

'Now 'tis an animal (be in what hurry I may) I cannot bear to strike : there is a patient endurance of suffering wrote so unaffectedly in his looks and carriage which pleads so mightily for him, that it always disarms me, and to that degree that I do not like to speak unkindly to him : on the contrary, meet him where I will, whether in town or country, in cart or under panniers, whether in liberty or bondage, I have ever something civil to say to him on my part ; and, as one word begets another (if he has as little to do as I), I generally fall into conversation with him ; and surely never is my imagination so busy as in framing responses from the etchings of his countenance ; and where those carry me not deep enough, in flying from my own heart into his, and seeing what is natural for an ass to think—as well as a man, upon the occasion. In truth, it is the only creature of all the classes of beings below me with whom I can do this. . . . With an ass I can commune for ever.

' "Come, Honesty," said I, seeing it was impracticable to pass betwixt him and the gate, "art thou for coming in or going out ? "

'The ass twisted his head round to look up the street.

' "Well !" replied I, "we'll wait a minute for thy driver."

'He turned his head thoughtful about, and looked wistfully the opposite way.

' " I understand thee perfectly," answered I : "if thou takest a wrong step in this affair, he will cudgel thee to death. Well ! a minute is but a minute ; and if it saves a fellow-creature a drubbing, it shall not be set down as ill-spent."

'He was eating the stem of an artichoke as this discourse went on, and, in the little peevish contentions between hunger and unsavouriness, had dropped it out of his mouth half-a-dozen times, and had picked it up again. "God help thee, Jack!" said I, "thou hast a bitter breakfast on't —and many a bitter day's labour, and many a bitter blow, I fear, for its wages! 'Tis all, all bitterness to thee— whatever life is to others! And now thy mouth, if one knew the truth of it, is as bitter, I dare say, as soot" (for he had cast aside the stem), "and thou hast not a friend perhaps in all this world that will give thee a macaroon." In saying this, I pulled out a paper of 'em, which I had just bought, and gave him one;—and, at this moment that I am telling it, my heart smites me that there was more of pleasantry in the conceit of seeing *how* an ass would eat a macaroon than of benevolence in giving him one, which presided in the act.

'When the ass had eaten his macaroon, I pressed him to come in. The poor beast was heavy loaded—his legs seemed to tremble under him—he hung rather backwards, and, as I pulled at his halter, it broke in my hand. He looked up pensive in my face: "Don't thrash me with it; but if you will you may." "If I do," said I, "I'll be d——."'

A critic who refuses to see in this charming description wit, humour, pathos, a kind nature speaking, and a real sentiment, must be hard indeed to move and to please. A page or two farther we come to a description not less beautiful—a landscape and figures, deliciously painted by one who had the keenest enjoyment and the most tremulous sensibility:—

''Twas in the road between Nismes and Lunel, where is the best Muscatto wine in all France: the sun was set, they had done their work: the nymphs had tied up their hair afresh, and the swains were preparing for a carousal.

My mule made a dead point. "'Tis the pipe and tambourine," said I—"I never will argue a point with one of your family as long as I live ;" so leaping off his back, and kicking off one boot into this ditch and t'other into that, "I'll take a dance," said I, "so stay you here."

'A sunburnt daughter of labour rose up from the group to meet me as I advanced towards them ; her hair, which was of a dark chestnut approaching to a black, was tied up in a knot, all but a single tress.

'"We want a cavalier," said she, holding out both her hands, as if to offer them. "And a cavalier you shall have," said I, taking hold of both of them. "We could not have done without you," said she, letting go one hand, with self-taught politeness, and leading me up with the other.

'A lame youth, whom Apollo had recompensed with a pipe, and to which he had added a tambourine of his own accord, ran sweetly over the prelude, as he sat upon the bank. "Tie me up this tress instantly," said Nannette, putting a piece of string into my hand. It taught me to forget I was a stranger. The whole knot fell down—we had been seven years acquainted. The youth struck the note upon the tambourine, his pipe followed, and off we bounded.

'The sister of the youth—who had stolen her voice from heaven—sang alternately with her brother. 'Twas a Gascoigne roundelay : "*Viva la joia, fidon la tristessa.*" The nymphs joined in unison, and their swains an octave below them.

'*Viva la joia* was in Nannette's lips, *viva la joia* in her eyes. A transient spark of amity shot across the space betwixt us. She looked amiable. Why could I not live and end my days thus ? "Just Disposer of our joys and sorrows !" cried I, "why could not a man sit down in the lap of content here, and dance, and sing, and say his prayers, and go to heaven with this nut-brown maid ?" Capriciously did she bend her head on one side, and dance up insidious. "Then 'tis time to dance off," quoth I.'

And with this pretty dance and chorus, the volume artfully concludes. Even here one can't give the whole description. There is not a page in Sterne's writing but has something that were better away, a latent corruption—a hint, as of an impure presence.*

Some of that dreary *double entendre* may be attributed to freer times and manners than ours, but not all. The foul satyr's eyes leer out of the leaves constantly : the last words the famous author wrote were bad and wicked—the last lines the poor stricken wretch penned were for pity and pardon. I think of these past writers and of one who lives amongst us now, and am grateful for the innocent laughter and the

* 'With regard to Sterne, and the charge of licentiousness which presses so seriously upon his character as a writer, I would remark that there is a sort of knowingness, the wit of which depends, 1st, on the modesty it gives pain to ; or, 2ndly, on the innocence and innocent ignorance over which it triumphs ; or, 3rdly, on a certain oscillation in the individual's own mind between the remaining good and the encroaching evil of his nature—a sort of dallying with the devil—a fluxionary art of combining courage and cowardice, as when a man snuffs a candle with his fingers for the first time, or better still, perhaps, like that trembling daring with which a child touches a hot tea-urn, because it has been forbidden ; so that the mind has its own white and black angel ; the same or similar amusement as may be supposed to take place between an old debauchee and a prude—the feeling resentment, on the one hand, from a prudential anxiety to preserve appearances and have a character ; and, on the other, an inward sympathy with the enemy. We have only to suppose society innocent, and then nine-tenths of this sort of wit would be like a stone that falls in snow, making no sound, because exciting no resistance ; the remainder rests on its being an offence against the good manners of human nature itself.

'This source, unworthy as it is, may doubtless be combined with wit, drollery, fancy, and even humour ; and we have only to regret the misalliance ; but that the latter are quite distinct from the former, may be made evident by abstracting in our imagination the morality of the characters of Mr. Shandy, my Uncle Toby, and Trim, which are all antagonists to this spurious sort of wit, from the rest of " Tristram Shandy," and by supposing, instead of them, the presence of two or three callous debauchees. The result will be pure disgust. Sterne cannot be too severely censured for thus using the best dispositions of our nature as the panders and condiments for the basest.'—COLERIDGE. *Literary Remains*, vol. i. pp. 141, 142.

sweet and unsullied page which the author of ' David Copperfield' gives to my children.

> ' Jeté sur cette boule,
> Laid, chétif et souffrant ;
> Etouffé dans la foule,
> Faute d'être assez grand :
>
> Une plainte touchante
> De ma bouche sortit.
> Le bon Dieu me dit : Chante,
> Chante, pauvre petit !
>
> Chanter, ou je m'abuse,
> Est ma tâche ici-bas.
> Tous ceux qu'ainsi j'amuse,
> Ne m'aimeront-ils pas ? '

In those charming lines of Béranger, one may fancy described the career, the sufferings, the genius, the gentle nature of GOLDSMITH, and the esteem in which we hold him. Who, of the millions whom he has amused, doesn't love him? To be the most beloved of English writers, what a title that is for a man !* A wild youth, wayward, but full of tenderness and affection, quits the country village, where his boyhood has been passed in happy musing, in idle shelter, in fond longing to see the great world out of doors, and

---

* 'He was a friend to virtue, and in his most playful pages never forgets what is due to it. A gentleness, delicacy, and purity of feeling distinguishes whatever he wrote, and bears a correspondence to the generosity of a disposition which knew no bounds but his last guinea. . . .

'The admirable ease and grace of the narrative, as well as the pleasing truth with which the principal characters are designed, make the "Vicar of Wakefield" one of the most delicious morsels of fictitious composition on which the human mind was ever employed.

'. . . We read the "Vicar of Wakefield" in youth and in age—we return to it again and again, and bless the memory of an author who contrives so well to reconcile us to human nature.'—*Sir Walter Scott.*

STERNE AND GOLDSMITH 241

achieve name and fortune; and after years of dire
struggle, and neglect and poverty, his heart turning
back as fondly to his native place as it had longed
eagerly for change when sheltered there, he writes a
book and a poem, full of the recollections and feelings
of home: he paints the friends and scenes of his youth,
and peoples Auburn and Wakefield with remembrances
of Lissoy. Wander he must, but he carries away a
home-relic with him, and dies with it on his breast.
His nature is truant; in repose it longs for change:
as on the journey it looks back for friends and quiet.
He passes to-day in building an air-castle for to-
morrow, or in writing yesterday's elegy; and he
would fly away this hour, but that a cage and
necessity keep him. What is the charm of his verse,
of his style, and humour? His sweet regrets, his
delicate compassion, his soft smile, his tremulous
sympathy, the weakness which he owns? Your love
for him is half pity. You come hot and tired from
the day's battle, and this sweet minstrel sings to you.
Who could harm the kind vagrant harper? Whom
did he ever hurt? He carries no weapon, save the
harp on which he plays to you; and with which he
delights great and humble, young and old, the captains
in the tents, or the soldiers round the fire, or the
women and children in the villages, at whose porches
he stops and sings his simple songs of love and beauty.
With that sweet story of the 'Vicar of Wakefield'*

* 'Now Herder came,' says Goethe in his autobiography, relating
his first acquaintance with Goldsmith's masterpiece, 'and together with
his great knowledge brought many other aids, and the later publications
besides. Among these he announced to us the "Vicar of Wakefield" as
an excellent work, with the German translation of which he would make
us acquainted by reading it aloud to us himself. . . .
'A Protestant country clergyman is perhaps the most beautiful
subject for a modern idyl; he appears like Melchizedeck, as priest and
king in one person. To the most innocent situation which can be
imagined on earth, to that of a husbandman, he is, for the most part,

he has found entry into every castle and every hamlet in Europe. Not one of us, however busy or hard, united by similarity of occupation as well as by equality in family relationships ; he is a father, a master of a family, an agriculturist, and thus perfectly a member of the community. On this pure, beautiful earthly foundation rests his higher calling ; to him is it given to guide men through life, to take care of their spiritual education, to bless them at all the leading epochs of their existence, to instruct, to strengthen, to console them, and, if consolation is not sufficient for the present, to call up and guarantee the hope of a happier future. Imagine such a man with pure human sentiments, strong enough not to deviate from them under any circumstances, and by this already elevated above the multitude of whom one cannot expect purity and firmness ; give him the learning necessary for his office, as well as a cheerful, equable activity, which is even passionate, as it neglects no moment to do good —and you will have him well endowed. But at the same time add the necessary limitation, so that he must not only pause in a small circle, but may also, perchance, pass over to a smaller ; grant him good-nature, placability, resolution, and everything else praiseworthy that springs from a decided character, and over all this a cheerful spirit of compli- ance, and a smiling toleration of his own failings and those of others,— then you will have put together pretty well the image of our excellent Wakefield.

'The delineation of this character on his course of life through joys and sorrows, the ever-increasing interest of the story, by the combina- tion of the entirely natural with the strange and the singular, make this novel one of the best which have ever been written ; besides this, it has the great advantage that it is quite moral, nay, in a pure sense, Christian —represents the reward of a good-will and perseverance in the right, strengthens an unconditional confidence in God, and attests the final triumph of good over evil ; and all this without a trace of cant or pedantry. The author was preserved from both of these by an elevation of mind that shows itself throughout in the form of irony, by which this little work must appear to us as wise as it is amiable. The author, Dr. Goldsmith, has, without question, a great insight into the moral world, into its strength and its infirmities ; but at the same time he can thank- fully acknowledge that he is an Englishman, and reckon highly the advantages which his country and his nation afford him. The family, with the delineation of which he occupies himself, stands upon one of the last steps of citizen comfort, and yet comes in contact with the highest ; its narrow circle, which becomes still more contracted, touches upon the great world through the natural and civil course of things ; this little skiff floats on the agitated waves of English life, and in weal or woe it has to expect injury or help from the vast fleet which sails around it.

'I may suppose that my readers know this work, and have it in memory ; whoever hears it named for the first time here, as well as

but once or twice in our lives has passed an evening with him, and undergone the charm of his delightful music.

Goldsmith's father was no doubt the good Doctor Primrose, whom we all of us know.\* Swift was yet alive, when the little Oliver was born at Pallas, or Pallasmore, in the county of Longford, in Ireland. In 1730, two years after the child's birth, Charles Goldsmith removed his family to Lissoy, in the county Westmeath, that sweet 'Auburn' which every person who hears me has seen in fancy. Here the kind parson†

he who is induced to read it again, will thank me.'—Goethe. *Truth and Poetry; from my own Life.* (English Translation, vol, i. pp. 378, 379.)

'He seems from infancy to have been compounded of two natures, one bright, the other blundering; or to have had fairy gifts laid in his cradle by the "good people" who haunted his birthplace, the old goblin mansion on the banks of the Inny. He carries with him the wayward elfin spirit, if we may so term it, throughout his career. His fairy gifts are of no avail at school, academy, or college : they unfit him for close study and practical science, and render him heedless of everything that does not address itself to his poetical imagination and genial and festive feelings ; they dispose him to break away from restraint, to stroll about hedges, green lanes, and haunted streams, to revel with jovial companions, or to rove the country like a gipsy in quest of odd adventures. . . . Though his circumstances often compelled him to associate with the poor, they never could betray him into companionship with the depraved. His relish for humour, and for the study of character, as we have before observed, brought him often into convivial company of a vulgar kind ; but he discriminated between their vulgarity and their amusing qualities, or rather wrought from the whole store familiar features of life which form the staple of his most popular writings.'— *Washington Irving.*

\* 'The family of Goldsmith, Goldsmyth, or, as it was occasionally written, Gouldsmith, is of considerable standing in Ireland, and seems always to have held a respectable station in society. Its origin is English, supposed to be derived from that which was long settled at Crayford in Kent.'—Prior's *Life of Goldsmith*

Oliver's father, great-grandfather, and great-great-grandfather were clergymen ; and two of them married clergymen's daughters.

> † 'At church, with meek and unaffected grace,
> His looks adorn'd the venerable place ;
> Truth from his lips prevail'd with double sway,
> And fools who came to scoff remain'd to pray.

brought up his eight children; and loving all the
world, as his son says, fancied all the world loved him.
He had a crowd of poor dependants besides those
hungry children. He kept an open table; round
which sat flatterers and poor friends, who laughed at
the honest rector's many jokes, and ate the produce
of his seventy acres of farm. Those who have seen
an Irish house in the present day can fancy that one
of Lissoy. The old beggar still has his allotted corner
by the kitchen turf; the maimed old soldier still gets
his potatoes and buttermilk; the poor cottier still asks
his honour's charity, and prays God bless his reverence
for the sixpence; the ragged pensioner still takes his
place by right and sufferance. There's still a crowd
in the kitchen, and a crowd round the parlour table,
profusion, confusion, kindness, poverty. If an Irishman comes to London to make his fortune, he has a
half-dozen of Irish dependants who take a percentage
of his earnings. The good Charles Goldsmith* left

> The service past, around the pious man,
> With steady zeal each honest rustic ran;
> E'en children follow'd with endearing wile,
> And pluck'd his gown to share the good man's smile.
> His ready smile a parent's warmth exprest,
> Their welfare pleased him, and their cares distrest;
> To them his heart, his love, his griefs were given,
> But all his serious thoughts had rest in heaven.
> As some tall cliff that lifts its awful form,
> Swells from the vale, and midway leaves the storm,
> Though round its breast the rolling clouds are spread,
> Eternal sunshine settles on its head.'—*The Deserted Village.*

* 'In May this year (1768), he lost his brother, the Rev. Henry
Goldsmith, for whom he had been unable to obtain preferment in the
Church. . . .

'. . . To the curacy of Kilkenny West, the moderate stipend of which,
forty pounds a year, is sufficiently celebrated by his brother's lines. It
has been stated that Mr. Goldsmith added a school, which, after having
been held at more than one place in the vicinity, was finally fixed
at Lissoy. Here his talents and industry gave it celebrity, and under
his care the sons of many of the neighbouring gentry received their

but little provision for his hungry race when death
summoned him; and one of his daughters being
engaged to a Squire of rather superior dignity, Charles
Goldsmith impoverished the rest of his family to
provide the girl with a dowry.

The small-pox, which scourged all Europe at that
time, and ravaged the roses off the cheeks of half the
world, fell foul of poor little Oliver's face, when the
child was eight years old, and left him scarred and dis-
figured for his life. An old woman in his father's
village taught him his letters, and pronounced him a
dunce : Paddy Byrne, the hedge-schoolmaster, took
him in hand : and from Paddy Byrne, he was trans-
mitted to a clergyman at Elphin. When a child was
sent to school in those days, the classic phrase was
that he was placed under Mr. So-and-so's *ferule.* Poor
little ancestors ! It is hard to think how ruthlessly
you were birched ; and how much of needless whipping and tears our small forefathers had to undergo !
A relative—kind uncle Contarine—took the main
charge of little Noll ; who went through his schooldays righteously doing as little work as he could ;
robbing orchards, playing at ball, and making his
pocket-money fly about whenever fortune sent it to
him. Everybody knows the story of that famous
'Mistake of a Night,' when the young schoolboy,
provided with a guinea and a nag, rode up to the

education. A fever breaking out among the boys about 1765, they
dispersed for a time, but re-assembling at Athlone, he continued his
scholastic labours there until the time of his death, which happened,
like that of his brother, about the forty-fifth year of his age. He was
a man of an excellent heart and an amiable disposition.'—Prior's
*Goldsmith.*

> 'Where'er I roam, whatever realms to see,
> My heart, untravell'd, fondly turns to thee :
> Still to my brother turns with ceaseless pain,
> And drags at each remove a lengthening chain.'
> *The Traveller.*

'best house' in Ardagh, called for the landlord's company over a bottle of wine at supper, and for a hot cake for breakfast in the morning; and found, when he asked for the bill, that the best house was Squire Featherstone's, and not the inn for which he mistook it. Who does not know every story about Goldsmith? That is a delightful and fantastic picture of the child dancing and capering about in the kitchen at home, when the old fiddler gibed at him for his ugliness, and called him Æsop; and little Noll made his repartee of 'Heralds proclaim aloud this saying—See Æsop dancing and his monkey playing.' One can fancy a queer pitiful look of humour and appeal upon that little scarred face—the funny little dancing figure, the funny little brogue. In his life, and his writings, which are the honest expression of it, he is constantly bewailing that homely face and person; anon he surveys them in the glass ruefully; and presently assumes the most comical dignity. He likes to deck out his little person in splendour and fine colours. He presented himself to be examined for ordination in a pair of scarlet breeches, and said honestly that he did not like to go into the Church, because he was fond of coloured clothes. When he tried to practise as a doctor, he got by hook or by crook a black velvet suit, and looked as big and grand as he could, and kept his hat over a patch on the old coat: in better days he bloomed out in plum-colour, in blue silk, and in new velvet. For some of those splendours the heirs and assignees of Mr. Filby, the tailor, have never been paid to this day: perhaps the kind tailor and his creditor have met and settled their little account in Hades.*

* 'When Goldsmith died, half the unpaid bill he owed to Mr. William Filby (amounting in all to £79) was for clothes supplied to this nephew Hodson.'—FORSTER'S *Goldsmith*, p. 520.

As this nephew Hodson ended his days (see the same page) 'a

They showed until lately a window at Trinity
College, Dublin, on which the name of O. Goldsmith
was engraved with a diamond. Whose diamond was
it? Not the young sizar's, who made but a poor
figure in that place of learning. He was idle, penniless, and fond of pleasure :* he learned his way early
to the pawnbroker's shop. He wrote ballads, they
say, for the street-singers, who paid him a crown for a
poem, and his pleasure was to steal out at night and
hear his verses sung. He was chastised by his tutor
for giving a dance in his rooms, and took the box on
the ears so much to heart, that he packed up his all,
pawned his books and little property, and disappeared
from college and family. He said he intended to go
to America, but when his money was spent, the young
prodigal came home ruefully, and the good folks there
killed their calf—it was but a lean one—and welcomed
him back.

After college he hung about his mother's house,
and lived for some years the life of a buckeen—passed
a month with this relation and that, a year with one
patron, a great deal of time at the public-house.†
Tired of this life, it was resolved that he should go to
London, and study at the Temple ; but he got no
farther on the road to London and the woolsack than
Dublin, where he gambled away the fifty pounds given

prosperous Irish gentleman,' it is not unreasonable to wish that he had
cleared off Mr. Filby's bill.

* Poor fellow ! He hardly knew an ass from a mule, nor a turkey
from a goose, but when he saw it on the table.'—CUMBERLAND'S
*Memoirs*.

† 'These youthful follies, like the fermentation of liquors, often disturb
the mind only in order to its future refinement : a life spent in phlegmatic apathy resembles those liquors which never ferment, and are
consequently always muddy.'—GOLDSMITH. *Memoir of Voltaire.*

' He [Johnson] said "Goldsmith was a plant that flowered late.
There appeared nothing remarkable about him when he was young." '—
*Boswell.*

to him for his outfit, and whence he returned to the indefatigable forgiveness of home. Then he determined to be a doctor, and uncle Contarine helped him to a couple of years at Edinburgh. Then from Edinburgh he felt that he ought to hear the famous professors of Leyden and Paris, and wrote most amusing pompous letters to his uncle about the great Farheim, Du Petit, and Duhamel du Monceau, whose lectures he proposed to follow. If uncle Contarine believed those letters—if Oliver's mother believed that story which the youth related of his going to Cork, with the purpose of embarking for America, of his having paid his passage-money, and having sent his kit on board; of the anonymous captain sailing away with Oliver's valuable luggage, in a nameless ship, never to return; if uncle Contarine and the mother at Ballymahon believed his stories, they must have been a very simple pair; as it was a very simple rogue indeed who cheated them. When the lad, after failing in his clerical examination, after failing in his plan for studying the law, took leave of these projects and of his parents, and set out for Edinburgh, he saw mother, and uncle, and lazy Ballymahon, and green native turf, and sparkling river for the last time. He was never to look on old Ireland more, and only in fancy revisit her.

'But me not destined such delights to share,
   My prime of life in wandering spent and care,
   Impelled, with steps unceasing, to pursue
   Some fleeting good that mocks me with the view;
   That like the circle bounding earth and skies
   Allures from far, yet, as I follow, flies:
   My fortune leads to traverse realms alone,
   And find no spot of all the world my own.'

I spoke in a former lecture of that high courage

which enabled Fielding, in spite of disease, remorse,
and poverty, always to retain a cheerful spirit and to
keep his manly benevolence and love of truth intact,
as if these treasures had been confided to him for the
public benefit, and he was accountable to posterity for
their honourable employ, and a constancy equally
happy and admirable I think was shown by Goldsmith, whose sweet and friendly nature bloomed
kindly always in the midst of a life's storm, and rain,
and bitter weather.* The poor fellow was never so
friendless but he could befriend some one; never so
pinched and wretched but he could give of his crust,
and speak his word of compassion. If he had but his
flute left, he could give that, and make the children
happy in the dreary London court. He could give
the coals in that queer coal-scuttle we read of to his
poor neighbour : he could give away his blankets in
college to the poor widow, and warm himself as he
best might in the feathers : he could pawn his coat to
save his landlord from gaol : when he was a school-
usher he spent his earnings in treats for the boys, and
the good-natured school-master's wife said justly that
she ought to keep Mr. Goldsmith's money as well as
the young gentlemen's. When he met his pupils in
later life, nothing would satisfy the Doctor but he
must treat them still. 'Have you seen the print of
me after Sir Joshua Reynolds?' he asked of one of
his old pupils. 'Not seen it? not bought it? Sure,
Jack, if your picture had been published, I'd not have

* 'An "inspired idiot," Goldsmith, hangs strangely about him [John-
son]. . . . Yet, on the whole, there is no evil in the "gooseberry-fool,"
but rather much good ; of a finer, if of a weaker sort than Johnson's ;
and all the more genuine that he himself could never become *conscious* of
it,—though unhappily never cease *attempting* to become so : the author
of the genuine "Vicar of Wakefield," nill he will he, must needs fly
towards such a mass of genuine manhood.'—CARLYLE's *Essays* (2nd ed.),
vol. iv. p. 91.

been without it half-an-hour.' His purse and his heart were everybody's, and his friends' as much as his own. When he was at the height of his reputation, and the Earl of Northumberland, going as Lord Lieutenant to Ireland, asked if he could be of any service to Doctor Goldsmith, Goldsmith recommended his brother, and not himself, to the great man. 'My patrons,' he gallantly said, 'are the booksellers, and I want no others.'* Hard patrons they were, and hard work he did ; but he did not complain much : if in his early writings some bitter words escaped him, some allusions to neglect and poverty, he withdrew these expressions when his works were republished, and better days seemed to open for him ; and he did not care to complain that printer or publisher had over-looked his merit, or left him poor. The Court face was turned from honest Oliver, the Court patronised Beattie ; the fashion did not shine on him—fashion adored Sterne.† Fashion pronounced Kelly to be

* 'At present, the few poets of England no longer depend on the great for subsistence ; they have now no other patrons but the public, and the public, collectively considered, is a good and a generous master. It is indeed too frequently mistaken as to the merits of every candidate for favour ; but to make amends it is never mistaken long. A perform-ance indeed may be forced for a time into reputation, but, destitute of real merit, it soon sinks ; time, the touchstone of what is truly valuable, will soon discover the fraud, and an author should never arrogate to himself any share of success till his works have been read at least ten years with satisfaction.

'A man of letters at present, whose works are valuable, is perfectly sensible of their value. Every polite member of the community, by buying what he writes, contributes to reward him. The ridicule, there-fore, of living in a garret might have been wit in the last age, but continues such no longer, because no longer true. A writer of real merit now may easily be rich, if his heart be set only on fortune ; and for those who have no merit, it is but fit that such should remain in merited obscurity.'—GOLDSMITH. *Citizen of the World*, Let. 84.

† Goldsmith attacked Sterne obviously enough, censuring his in-decency, and slighting his wit, and ridiculing his manner, in the 53rd letter in the 'Citizen of the World.'

'As in common conversation,' says he, 'the best way to make the

the great writer of comedy of his day.  A little—not
ill-humour, but plaintiveness—a little betrayal of
wounded pride which he showed, render him not the
less amiable.  The author of the ' Vicar of Wakefield'
had a right to protest when Newbery kept back the
manuscript for two years ; had a right to be a little
peevish with Sterne ; a little angry when Colman's
actors declined their parts in his delightful comedy,
when the manager refused to have a scene painted
for it, and pronounced its damnation before hearing.
He had not the great public with him ; but he had
the noble Johnson, and the admirable Reynolds, and
the great Gibbon, and the great Burke, and the great
Fox—friends and admirers illustrious indeed, as
famous as those who, fifty years before, sat round
Pope's table.

Nobody knows, and I dare say Goldsmith's buoyant
temper kept no account of, all the pains which he
endured during the early period of his literary career.
Should any man of letters in our day have to bear up
against such, Heaven grant he may come out of the
period of misfortune with such a pure kind heart as
that which Goldsmith obstinately bore in his breast.

audience laugh is by first laughing yourself ; so in writing, the properest
manner is to show an attempt at humour, which will pass upon most
for humour in reality.  To affect this, readers must be treated with the
most perfect familiarity ; in one page the author is to make them a low
bow, and in the next to pull them by the nose ; he must talk in riddles,
and then send them to bed in order to dream for the solution,' &c.

Sterne's humourous *mot* on the subject of the gravest part of the
charges, then, as now, made against him, may perhaps be quoted here,
from the excellent, the respectable Sir Walter Scott :—

' Soon after "Tristram" had appeared, Sterne asked a Yorkshire lady
of fortune and condition, whether she had read his book.  "I have not,
Mr. Sterne," was the answer ; "and to be plain with you, I am informed
it is not proper for female perusal."  "My dear good lady," replied the
author, " do not be gulled by such stories ; the book is like your young
heir there " (pointing to a child of three years old, who was rolling on
the carpet in his white tunic) : "he shows at times a good deal that is
usually concealed, but it is all in perfect innocence."'

The insults to which he had to submit are shocking
to read of—slander, contumely, vulgar satire, brutal
malignity perverting his commonest motives and
actions; he had his share of these, and one's anger is
roused at reading of them, as it is at seeing a woman
insulted or a child assaulted, at the notion that a
creature so very gentle and weak, and full of love,
should have had to suffer so.   And he had worse than
insult to undergo—to own to fault and deprecate the
anger of ruffians.   There is a letter of his extant to
one Griffiths, a bookseller, in which poor Goldsmith is
forced to confess that certain books sent by Griffiths
are in the hands of a friend from whom Goldsmith had
been forced to borrow money.   'He was wild, sir,'
Johnson said, speaking of Goldsmith to Boswell with
his great, wise benevolence and noble mercifulness of
heart—'Dr. Goldsmith was wild, sir; but he is so no
more.'   Ah! if we pity the good and weak man who
suffers undeservedly, let us deal very gently with him
from whom misery extorts not only tears, but shame;
let us think humbly and charitably of the human
nature that suffers so sadly and falls so low.   Whose
turn may it be to-morrow!   What weak heart, confident before trial, may not succumb under temptation
invincible?   Cover the good man who has been
vanquished—cover his face and pass on.

For the last half-dozen years of his life, Goldsmith
was far removed from the pressure of any ignoble
necessity: and in the receipt, indeed, of a pretty large
income from the booksellers his patrons.   Had he lived
but a few years more, his public fame would have been
as great as his private reputation, and he might have
enjoyed alive a part of that esteem which his country
has ever since paid to the vivid and versatile genius
who has touched on almost every subject of literature,
and touched nothing that he did not adorn.   Except

in rare instances, a man is known in our profession, and esteemed as a skilful workman, years before the lucky hit which trebles his usual gains, and stamps him a popular author. In the strength of his age, and the dawn of his reputation, having for backers and friends the most illustrious literary men of his time,* fame and prosperity might have been in store for Goldsmith, had fate so willed it, and, at forty-six, had not sudden disease carried him off. I say prosperity rather than competence, for it is probable that no sum could have put order into his affairs or sufficed for his irreclaimable habits of dissipation. It must be remembered that he owed £2000 when he died. 'Was ever poet,' Johnson asked, 'so trusted before?' As has been the case with many another good fellow of his nation, his life was tracked and his substance wasted by crowds of hungry beggars and lazy dependants. If they came at a lucky time (and be sure they knew his affairs better than he did himself, and watched his pay-day), he gave them of his money : if they begged on empty-purse days, he gave them his promissory bills : or he treated them to a tavern where he had credit ; or he obliged them with an order upon honest Mr. Filby for coats, for which he paid as long as he could earn, and until the shears of Filby were to cut for him no more. Staggering under a load of debt and labour, tracked by bailiffs and reproachful creditors,

* 'Goldsmith told us that he was now busy in writing a Natural History ; and that he might have full leisure for it, he had taken lodgings at a farmer's house, near to the six-mile stone in the Edgware Road, and had carried down his books in two returned postchaises. He said he believed the farmer's family thought him an odd character, similar to that in which the *Spectator* appeared to his landlady and her children; he was *The Gentleman*. Mr. Mickle, the translator of the *Lusiad*, and I, went to visit him at this place a few days afterwards. He was not at home ; but having a curiosity to see his apartment, we went in, and found curious scraps of descriptions of animals scrawled upon the wall with a blacklead pencil.'—*Boswell*

running from a hundred poor dependants, whose
appealing looks were perhaps the hardest of all pains
for him to bear, devising fevered plans for the morrow,
new histories, new comedies, all sorts of new literary
schemes, flying from all these into seclusion, and out
of seclusion into pleasure—at last, at five-and-forty,
death seized him and closed his career.*    I have been
many a time in the chambers in the Temple which
were his, and passed up the staircase, which Johnson
and Burke and Reynolds trod to see their friend, their
poet, their kind Goldsmith—the stair on which the
poor women sat weeping bitterly when they heard
that the greatest and most generous of all men was
dead within the black oak door.†    Ah ! it was a
different lot from that for which the poor fellow sighed,
when he wrote with heart yearning for home those
most charming of all fond verses, in which he fancies
he revisits Auburn :—

* 'When Goldsmith was dying, Dr. Turton said to him, " Your pulse
is in greater disorder than it should be, from the degree of fever which
you have ; is your mind at ease ? "    Goldsmith answered it was not.'—
Dr. Johnson (in Boswell).
    'Chambers, you find, is gone far, and poor Goldsmith is gone much
further.    He died of a fever, exasperated, as I believe, by the fear of
distress.    He had raised money and squandered it, by every artifice of
acquisition and folly of expense.    But let not his failings be remembered ;
he was a very great man.'—Dr Johnson to Boswell, July 5th, 1774.
    † 'When Burke was told [of Goldsmith's death] he burst into tears,
Reynolds was in his painting-room when the messenger went to him ;
but at once he laid his pencil aside, which in times of great family
distress he had not been known to do, left his painting-room, and did
not re-enter it that day. . . .
    'The staircase of Brick Court is said to have been filled with
mourners, the reverse of domestic ; women without a home, without
domesticity of any kind, with no friend but him they had come to weep
for ; outcasts of that great, solitary, wicked city, to whom he had never
forgotten to be kind and charitable.    And he had domestic mourners,
too.    His coffin was re-opened at the request of Miss Horneck and her
sister (such was the regard he was known to have for them !) that a
lock might be cut from his hair.    It was in Mrs. Gwyn's possession
when she died, after nearly seventy years.'—FORSTER's Goldsmith.

' Here, as I take my solitary rounds,
Amidst thy tangling walks and ruined grounds,
And, many a year elapsed, return to view
Where once the cottage stood, the hawthorn grew,
Remembrance wakes, with all her busy train,
Swells at my breast, and turns the past to pain.

In all my wanderings round this world of care,
In all my griefs—and God has given my share—
I still had hopes, my latest hours to crown,
Amidst these humble bowers to lay me down ;
To husband out life's taper at the close,
And keep the flame from wasting by repose ;
I still had hopes—for pride attends us still—
Amidst the swains to show my book-learned skill,
Around my fire an evening group to draw,
And tell of all I felt and all I saw ;
And, as a hare, whom hounds and horns pursue,
Pants to the place from whence at first he flew—
I still had hopes, my long vexations past,
Here to return, and die at home at last.

O blest retirement, friend to life's decline !
Retreats from care that never must be mine—
How blest is he who crowns, in shades like these,
A youth of labour with an age of ease ;
Who quits a world where strong temptations try,
And, since 'tis hard to combat, learns to fly !
For him no wretches born to work and weep
Explore the mine or tempt the dangerous deep ;
No surly porter stands in guilty state
To spurn imploring famine from the gate :
But on he moves to meet his latter end,
Angels around befriending virtue's friend ;
Sinks to the grave with unperceived decay,
Whilst resignation gently slopes the way ;
And all his prospects brightening to the last,
His heaven commences ere the world be past.'

In these verses, I need not say with what melody, with what touching truth, with what exquisite beauty of comparison—as indeed in hundreds more pages of the writings of this honest soul—the whole character of the man is told—his humble confession of faults and weakness ; his pleasant little vanity, and desire that his village should admire him ; his simple scheme of good in which everybody was to be happy—no beggar was to be refused his dinner—nobody in fact was to work much, and he to be the harmless chief of the Utopia, and the monarch of the Irish Yvetot. He would have told again, and without fear of their failing, those famous jokes* which had hung fire in London ; he

* 'Goldsmith's incessant desire of being conspicuous in company was the occasion of his sometimes appearing to such disadvantage, as one should hardly have supposed possible in a man of his genius. When his literary reputation had risen deservedly high, and his society was much courted, he became very jealous of the extraordinary attention which was everywhere paid to Johnson. One evening, in a circle of wits, he found fault with me for talking of Johnson as entitled to the honour of unquestionable superiority. "Sir," said he, "you are for making a monarchy of what should be a republic."

'He was still more mortified, when, talking in a company with fluent vivacity, and, as he flattered himself, to the admiration of all present, a German who sat next him, and perceived Johnson rolling himself as if about to speak, suddenly stopped him, saying, "Stay, stay—Toctor Shonson is going to zay zomething." This was no doubt very provoking, especially to one so irritable as Goldsmith, who frequently mentioned it with strong expressions of indignation.

'It may also be observed that Goldsmith was sometimes content to be treated with an easy familiarity, but upon occasions would be consequential and important. An instance of this occurred in a small particular. Johnson had a way of contracting the names of his friends, as Beauclerk, Beau ; Boswell, Bozzy. . . I remember one day, when Tom Davies was telling that Doctor Johnson said—"We are all in labour for a name to *Goldy's* play," Goldsmith seemed displeased that such a liberty should be taken with his name, and said, "I have often desired him not to call me *Goldy*."'

This is one of several of Boswell's depreciatory mentions of Goldsmith —which may well irritate biographers and admirers, and also those who take that more kindly and more profound view of Boswell's own character, which was opened up by Mr. Carlyle's famous article on his book. No wonder that Mr. Irving calls Boswell an 'incarnation of toadyism.

would have talked of his great friends of the Club—of
my Lord Clare and my Lord Bishop, my Lord
Nugent—sure he knew them intimately, and was
hand and glove with some of the best men in town—
and he would have spoken of Johnson and of Burke,
and of Sir Joshua who had painted him—and he would
have told wonderful sly stories of Ranelagh and the
Pantheon, and the masquerades at Madame Cornelis';
and he would have toasted, with a sigh, the Jessamy
Bride—the lovely Mary Horneck.

The figure of that charming young lady forms one
of the prettiest recollections of Goldsmith's life.  She
and her beautiful sister, who married Bunbury, the
graceful and humourous amateur artist of those days,
when Gilray had but just begun to try his powers, were
among the kindest and dearest of Goldsmith's many
friends, cheered and pitied him, travelled abroad with
him, made him welcome at their home, and gave him
many a pleasant holiday.  He bought his finest clothes
to figure at their country-house at Barton—he wrote

And the worst of it is, that Johnson himself has suffered from this habit
of the Laird of Auchinleck's.  People are apt to forget under what
Boswellian stimulus the great Doctor uttered many hasty things :—
things no more indicative of the nature of the depths of his character
than the phosphoric gleaming of the sea, when struck at night, is
indicative of radical corruption of nature !  In truth, it is clear enough
on the whole that both Johnson and Goldsmith *appreciated* each other,
and that they mutually knew it.  They were, as it were, tripped up
and flung against each other, occasionally, by the blundering and silly
gambolling of people in company.

Something must be allowed for Boswell's ' rivalry for Johnson's good
graces ' with Oliver (as Sir Walter Scott has remarked), for Oliver was
intimate with the Doctor before his biographer was,—and, as we all
remember, marched off with him to 'take tea with Mrs. Williams'
before Boswell had advanced to that honourable degree of intimacy.
But, in truth, Boswell—though he perhaps showed more talent in his
delineation of the Doctor than is generally ascribed to him—had not
faculty to take a fair view of *two* great men at a time.  Besides, as Mr.
Forster justly remarks, ' he was impatient of Goldsmith from the first
hour of their acquaintance.'—*Life and Adventures*, p. 292.

them droll verses. They loved him, laughed at him, played him tricks, and made him happy. He asked for a loan from Garrick, and Garrick kindly supplied him, to enable him to go to Barton : but there were to be no more holidays and only one brief struggle more for poor Goldsmith. A lock of his hair was taken from the coffin and given to the Jessamy Bride. She lived quite into our time. Hazlitt saw her an old lady, but beautiful still, in Northcote's painting-room, who told the eager critic how proud she always was that Goldsmith had admired her. The younger Colman has left a touching reminiscence of him (vol. i. 63, 64) :—

'I was only five years old,' he says, 'when Goldsmith took me on his knee one evening whilst he was drinking coffee with my father, and began to play with me, which amiable act I returned, with the ingratitude of a peevish brat, by giving him a very smart slap on the face : it must have been a tingler, for it left the marks of my spiteful paw on his cheek. This infantile outrage was followed by summary justice, and I was locked up by my indignant father in an adjoining room to undergo solitary imprisonment in the dark. Here I began to howl and scream most abominably, which was no bad step towards my liberation, since those who were not inclined to pity me might be likely to set me free for the purpose of abating a nuisance.

' At length a generous friend appeared to extricate me from jeopardy, and that generous friend was no other than the man I had so wantonly molested by assault and battery —it was the tender-hearted Doctor himself, with a lighted candle in his hand and a smile upon his countenance, which was still partially red from the effects of my petulance. I sulked and sobbed as he fondled and soothed, till I began to brighten. Goldsmith seized the propitious moment of returning good-humour, when he put down the candle and began to conjure. He placed three hats, which happened to be in the room, and a shilling under each. The shillings, he told me, were England, France and Spain. "Hey presto cockalorum !" cried the Doctor, and lo, on uncovering the shillings, which had been dispersed each beneath a separate hat, they were all found congregated under one. I was no politician at five years old, and therefore might not have wondered at the sudden revolution which brought England, France, and Spain all under one crown ; but as also I was no conjuror, it amazed me beyond measure. . . . From that time, whenever the Doctor came to visit my father, "I plucked his gown to share the good man's smile ;" a game at romps constantly ensued, and we were always cordial friends and merry playfellows. Our unequal companionship varied somewhat as to sports as I grew older ; but it did not last long : my senior playmate died in his forty-fifth year, when I had attained my eleventh. . . . In all the numerous accounts of his virtues and foibles, his genius and absurdities, his knowledge of nature and ignorance of the world, his "compassion for another's woe" was always predominant ; and my trivial story of his humouring a froward child weighs but as a feather in the recorded scale of his benevolence.'

Think of him reckless, thriftless, vain, if you like —but merciful, gentle, generous, full of love and pity. He passes out of our life, and goes to render his account beyond it. Think of the poor pensioners weeping at his grave ; think of the noble spirits that admired and deplored him ; think of the righteous pen that wrote his epitaph—and of the wonderful and unanimous response of affection with which the world has paid back the love he gave it. His humour delighting us still : his song fresh and beautiful as when first he charmed with it : his words in all our mouths : his very weaknesses beloved and familiar—his benevolent spirit seems still to smile upon us ; to do gentle kindnesses ; to succour with sweet charity : to soothe, caress, and forgive : to plead with the fortunate for the unhappy and the poor.

His name is the last in the list of those men of humour who have formed the themes of the discourses which you have heard so kindly.

Long before I had ever hoped for such an audience, or dreamed of the possibility of the good fortune which has brought me so many friends, I was at issue with some of my literary brethren upon a point—which they held from tradition I think rather than experience—that our profession was neglected in this country ; and that men of letters were ill received and held in slight esteem.    It would hardly be grateful of me now to alter my old opinion that we do meet with good-will and kindness, with generous helping hands in the time of our necessity, with cordial and friendly recognition.    What claim had any one of these of whom I have been speaking, but genius ?    What return of gratitude, fame, affection, did it not bring to all ?

What punishment befell those who were unfortunate among them, but that which follows reckless habits and careless lives ?    For these faults a wit must suffer like the dullest prodigal that ever ran in debt.    He must pay the tailor if he wears the coat ; his children must go in rags if he spends his money at the tavern ; he can't come to London and be made Lord Chancellor if he stops on the road and gambles away his last shilling at Dublin.    And he must pay the social penalty of these follies too, and expect that the world will shun the man of bad habits, that women will avoid the man of loose life, that prudent folks will close their doors as a precaution, and before a demand should be made on their pockets by the needy prodigal. With what difficulty had any one of these men to contend, save that eternal and mechanical one of want of means and lack of capital, and of which thousands of

young lawyers, young doctors, young soldiers and
sailors, of inventors, manufacturers, shopkeepers, have
to complain ?   Hearts as brave and resolute as ever
beat in the breast of any wit or poet, sicken and break
daily in the vain endeavour and unavailing struggle
against life's difficulty.   Don't we see daily ruined
inventors, grey-haired midshipmen, baulked heroes,
blighted curates, barristers pining a hungry life out in
chambers, the attorneys never mounting to their
garrets, whilst scores of them are rapping at the door
of the successful quack below ?   If these suffer, who
is the author, that he should be exempt ?   Let us bear
our ills with the same constancy with which others
endure them, accept our manly part in life, hold our
own, and ask no more.   I can conceive of no kings
or laws causing or curing Goldsmith's improvidence,
or Fielding's fatal love of pleasure, or Dick Steele's
mania for running races with the constable.   You
never can outrun that sure-footed officer—not by any
swiftness or by dodges devised by any genius, however
great ; and he carries off the Tatler to the spunging-
house, or taps the Citizen of the World on the shoulder
as he would any other mortal.

Does society look down on a man because he is an
author ?   I suppose if people want a buffoon they
tolerate him only in so far as he is amusing ; it can
hardly be expected that they should respect him as an
equal.   Is there to be a guard of honour provided for
the author of the last new novel or poem ? how long
is he to reign, and keep other potentates out of possession ?   He retires, grumbles, and prints a lamentation
that literature is despised.   If Captain A. is left out of
Lady B.'s parties, he does not state that the army is
despised : if Lord C. no longer asks Counsellor D. to
dinner, Counsellor D. does not announce that the bar
is insulted.   He is not fair to society if he enters it

with this suspicion hankering about him ; if he is
doubtful about his reception, how hold up his head
honestly, and look frankly in the face that world about
which he is full of suspicion ? Is he place-hunting,
and thinking in his mind that he ought to be made an
Ambassador like Prior, or a Secretary of State like
Addison ? his pretence of equality falls to the ground
at once : he is scheming for a patron, not shaking the
hand of a friend, when he meets the world. Treat
such a man as he deserves ; laugh at his buffoonery,
and give him a dinner and a *bon jour ;* laugh at his
self-sufficiency and absurd assumptions of superiority,
and his equally ludicrous airs of martydom : laugh at
his flattery and his scheming, and buy it, if it's worth
the having. Let the wag have his dinner and the
hireling his pay, if you want him, and make a profound
bow to the *grand homme incompris,* and the boisterous
martyr, and show him the door. The great world,
the great aggregate experience, has its good sense, as
it has its good humour. It detects a pretender, as it
trusts a loyal heart. It is kind in the main : how
should it be otherwise than kind, when it is so wise
and clear-headed ? To any literary man who says,
'It despises my profession,' I say, with all my might
—no, no, no. It may pass over your individual case
—how many a brave fellow has failed in the race and
perished unknown in the struggle !—but it treats you
as you merit in the main. If you serve it, it is not
unthankful ; if you please it, it is pleased ; if you
cringe to it, it detects you, and scorns you if you are
mean ; it returns your cheerfulness with its good
humour ; it deals not ungenerously with your weaknesses ; it recognises most kindly your merits ; it
gives you a fair place and fair play. To any one of
those men of whom we have spoken was it in the
main ungrateful ? A king might refuse Goldsmith a

pension, as a publisher might keep his masterpiece and
the delight of all the world in his desk for two years ;
but it was mistake, and not ill-will. Noble and
illustrious names of Swift, and Pope, and Addison !
dear and honoured memories of Goldsmith and
Fielding ! kind friends, teachers, benefactors ! who
shall say that our country, which continues to bring
you such an unceasing tribute of applause, admiration,
love, sympathy, does not do honour to the literary
calling in the honour which it bestows upon *you* ?

# CHARITY AND HUMOUR

# CHARITY AND HUMOUR *

SEVERAL charitable ladies of this city, to some of whom I am under great personal obligation, having thought that a Lecture of mine would advance a benevolent end which they had in view, I have preferred, in place of delivering a Discourse, which many of my hearers no doubt know already, upon a subject merely literary or biographical, to put together a few thoughts which may serve as a supplement to the former Lectures, if you like, and which have this at least in common with the kind purpose which assembles you here, that they rise out of the same occasion, and treat of charity.

Besides contributing to our stock of happiness, to our harmless laughter and amusement, to our scorn for falsehood and pretension, to our righteous hatred of hypocrisy, to our education in the perception of truth, our love of honesty, our knowledge of life, and shrewd guidance through the world, have not our

---

* This lecture was first delivered in New York on behalf of a charity at the time of Mr. Thackeray's visit to America in 1852, when he had been giving his series of lectures on the English Humourists. It was subsequently repeated with slight variations in London (once under the title of 'Week-day Preachers') for the benefit of the families of Angus B. Reach and Douglas Jerrold. The lecture on behalf of the Jerrold Fund was given on July 22, 1857, the day after the declaration of the poll on the Oxford Election, when Mr. Thackeray was a candidate for Parliament, and was defeated by Mr. Cardwell. The *Times*, in its account of the lecture, says : 'The opening words of the discourse, uttered with a comical solemnity, of which Mr. Thackeray alone is capable, ran thus :—"Walking yesterday in the High Street of a certain ancient city." So began the lecturer, and was interrupted by a storm of laughter that deferred for some moments the completion of the sentence.'

humourous writers, our gay and kind week-day
preachers, done much in support of that holy cause
which has assembled you in this place; and which
you are all abetting—the cause of love and charity,
the cause of the poor, the weak, and the unhappy;
the sweet mission of love and tenderness, and peace
and goodwill towards men? That same theme
which is urged upon you by the eloquence and
example of good men to whom you are delighted
listeners on Sabbath-days is taught in his way and
according to his power by the humourous writer,
the commentator on every-day life and manners.

And as you are here assembled for a charitable
purpose, giving your contributions at the door to
benefit deserving people who need them, I like to
hope and think that the men of our calling have done
something in aid of the cause of charity, and have
helped, with kind words and kind thoughts at least, to
confer happiness and to do good. If the humourous
writers claim to be week-day preachers, have they
conferred any benefit by their sermons? Are people
happier, better, better disposed to their neighbours,
more inclined to do works of kindness, to love, forbear, forgive, pity, after reading in Addison, in Steele,
in Fielding, in Goldsmith, in Hood, in Dickens? I
hope and believe so, and fancy that in writing they
are also acting charitably, contributing with the
means which heaven supplies them to forward the end
which brings you too together.

A love of the human species is a very vague and
indefinite kind of virtue, sitting very easily on a man,
not confining his actions at all, shining in print, or
exploding in paragraphs, after which efforts of benevolence the philanthropist is sometimes said to go home
and be no better than his neighbours. Tartuffe and
Joseph Surface, Stiggins and Chadband, who are

always preaching fine sentiments, and are no more virtuous than hundreds of those whom they denounce and whom they cheat, are fair objects of mistrust and satire ; but their hypocrisy—the homage, according to the old saying, which vice pays to virtue—has this of good in it, that its fruits are good : a man may preach good morals, though he may be himself but a lax practitioner ; a Pharisee may put pieces of gold into the charity-plate out of mere hypocrisy and ostentation, but the bad man's gold feeds the widow and the fatherless as well as the good man's. The butcher and baker must needs look, not to motives, but to money, in return for their wares.

I am not going to hint that we of the Literary calling resemble Monsieur Tartuffe or Monsieur Stiggins, though there may be such men in our body, as there are in all.

A literary man of the humouristic turn is pretty sure to be of a philanthropic nature, to have a great sensibility, to be easily moved to pain or pleasure, keenly to appreciate the varieties of temper of people round about him, and sympathise in their laughter, love, amusement, tears. Such a man is philanthropic, man-loving by nature, as another is irascible, or red-haired, or six feet high. And so I would arrogate no particular merit to literary men for the possession of this faculty of doing good which some of them enjoy. It costs a gentleman no sacrifice to be benevolent on paper ; and the luxury of indulging in the most beautiful and brilliant sentiments never makes any man a penny the poorer. A literary man is no better than another, as far as my experience goes ; and a man writing a book, no better nor no worse than one who keeps accounts in a ledger, or follows any other occupation. Let us, however, give him credit for the good, at least, which he is the means of doing, as we give credit to a man with a million for the hundred which he puts into the plate at a charity-sermon. He never misses them. He has made them in a moment by a lucky speculation, and parts with them, knowing that he has an almost endless balance at his bank, whence he can call for more. But in esteeming the benefaction, we are grateful to the benefactor, too, somewhat; and so of men of genius, richly endowed, and lavish in parting with their mind's wealth, we may view them at least kindly and favourably, and be thankful for the bounty of which Providence has made them the dispensers.

I have said myself somewhere, I do not know with what correctness (for definitions never are complete), that humour is wit and love; I am sure, at any rate, that the best humour is that which contains most humanity, that which is flavoured throughout with tenderness and kindness. This love does not demand constant utterance or actual expression, as a good father, in conversation with his children or wife, is not perpetually embracing them, or making protestations of his love; as a lover in the society of his mistress is not, at least as far as I am led to believe, for ever squeezing her hand, or sighing in her ear, 'My soul's darling, I adore you!' He shows his love by his conduct, by his fidelity, by his watchful desire to make the beloved person happy; it lightens from his eyes when she appears, though he may not speak it; it fills his heart when she is present or absent; influences all his words and actions; suffuses his whole being; it sets the father cheerily to work through the long day, supports him through the tedious labour of the weary absence or journey, and sends him happy home again, yearning towards the wife and children. This kind of love is not a spasm, but a life. It fondles and caresses at due seasons, no doubt; but the fond heart is always beating fondly and truly, though the wife is not sitting hand-in-hand with him or the children hugging at his knee. And so with a loving humour : I think, it is a genial writer's habit of being ; it is the kind gentle spirit's way of looking out on the world—that sweet friendliness, which fills his heart and his style. You recognise it, even though there may not be a single point of wit, or a single pathetic touch in the page ; though you may not be called upon to salute his genius by a laugh or a tear. That collision of ideas which provokes the one or the other, must be occasional. They must be like papa's embraces, which I spoke of anon, who only delivers them now and again, and cannot be expected to go on kissing the children all night. And so the writer's jokes and sentiment, his ebullitions of feeling, his outbreaks of high spirits, must not be too frequent. One tires of a page of which every sentence sparkles with points, of a sentimentalist who is always pumping the tears from his eyes or your own. One suspects the genuineness of the tear, the naturalness of the humour ; these ought to be true and manly in a man, as everything else in his life should be manly and true ; and he loses his dignity by laughing or weeping out of place, or too often.

When the Reverend Laurence Sterne begins to sentimentalise over the carriage in Monsieur Dessein's courtyard, and pretends to squeeze a tear out of a rickety old shandrydan : when presently he encounters the dead donkey on his road to Paris, and snivels over that asinine corpse, I say : ' Away, you drivelling quack : do not palm off these grimaces of grief upon simple folk who know no better, and cry misled by your hypocrisy.' Tears are sacred. The tributes of kind hearts to misfortune, the mites which gentle souls drop into the collections made for God's

poor and unhappy, are not to be tricked out of them
by a whimpering hypocrite, handing round a begging-
box for your compassion, and asking your pity for a
lie.   When that same man tells me of Lefevre's illness
and Uncle Toby's charity ; of the noble at Rennes
coming home and reclaiming his sword, I thank him
for the generous emotion which, springing genuinely
from his own heart, has caused mine to admire
benevolence and sympathise with honour ; and to feel
love, and kindness, and pity.

If I do not love Swift, as, thank God, I do not,
however immensely I may admire him, it is because I
revolt from the man who placards himself as a
professional hater of his own kind ; because he chisels
his savage indignation on his tombstone, as if to per-
petuate his protest against being born of our race—the
suffering, the weak, the erring, the wicked, if you will,
but still the friendly, the loving children of God our
Father : it is because, as I read through Swift's dark
volumes, I never find the aspect of nature seems to
delight him ; the smiles of children to please him ;
the sight of wedded love to soothe him.   I do not remember in any line of his writing a passing allusion to
a natural scene of beauty.   When he speaks about the
families of his comrades and brother clergymen, it is
to assail them with gibes and scorn, and to laugh at
them brutally for being fathers and for being poor.
He does mention in the Journal to Stella a sick child,
to be sure—a child of Lady Masham, that was ill of
the small-pox—but then it is to confound the brat for
being ill, and the mother for attending to it, when she
should have been busy about a Court intrigue in which
the Dean was deeply engaged.   And he alludes to
a suitor of Stella's, and a match she might have made,
and would have made, very likely, with an honourable
and faithful and attached man, Tisdall, who loved her,

and of whom Swift speaks, in a letter to this lady, in
language so foul that you would not bear to hear it.
In treating of the good the humourists have done,
of the love and kindness they have taught and left
behind them, it is not of this one I dare speak.
Heaven help the lonely misanthrope! be kind to
that multitude of sins, with so little charity to cover
them!

Of Mr. Congreve's contributions to the English
stock of benevolence, I do not speak; for, of any
moral legacy to posterity, I doubt whether that
brilliant man ever thought at all. He had some money,
as I have told; every shilling of which he left to his
friend the Duchess of Marlborough, a lady of great
fortune and the highest fashion. He gave the gold of
his brains to persons of fortune and fashion, too.
There is no more feeling in his comedies than in as
many books of Euclid. He no more pretends to teach
love for the poor, and goodwill for the unfortunate,
than a dancing master does; he teaches pirouettes and
flic-flacs; and how to bow to a lady, and to walk a
minuet. In his private life Congreve was immensely
liked—more so than any man of his age, almost; and,
to have been so liked, must have been kind and good-
natured. His good-nature bore him through extreme
bodily ills and pain, with uncommon cheerfulness and
courage. Being so gay, so bright, so popular, such a
grand seigneur, be sure he was kind to those about
him, generous to his dependants, serviceable to his
friends. Society does not like a man so long as it liked
Congreve, unless he is likeable; it finds out a quack
very soon; it scorns a poltroon or a curmudgeon: we
may be certain that this man was brave, good-tempered,
and liberal; so, very likely, is Monsieur Pirouette, of
whom we spoke; he cuts his capers, he grins, bows,
and dances to his fiddle. In private he may have a

hundred virtues ; in public, he teaches dancing.  His
business is cotillons, not ethics.

As much may be said of those charming and lazy
Epicureans, Gay and Prior, sweet lyric singers, comrades of Anacreon, and disciples of love and the bottle.
' Is there any moral shut within the bosom of the rose ? '
sings our great Tennyson.   Does a nightingale
preach from a bough or the lark from his cloud ?
Not knowingly ;  yet we may be grateful, and love
larks and roses, and the flower-crowned minstrels, too,
who laugh and who sing.

Of Addison's contributions to the charity of the
world I have spoken before, in trying to depict that
noble figure ;  and say now, as then, that we should
thank him as one of the greatest benefactors of that
vast and immeasurably spreading family which speaks
our common tongue.   Wherever it is spoken, there is
no man that does not feel, and understand, and use
the noble English word ' gentleman.'   And there is
no man that teaches us to be gentlemen better than
Joseph Addison.   Gentle in our bearing through life ;
gentle and courteous to our neighbour; gentle in
dealing with his follies and weaknesses ;  gentle in
treating his opposition ;  deferential to the old ;  kindly
to the poor, and those below us in degree ;  for people
above us and below us we must find, in whatever
hemisphere we dwell, whether kings or presidents
govern us ;  and in no republic or monarchy that I
know of is a citizen exempt from the tax of befriending
poverty and weakness, of respecting age, and of
honouring his father and mother.   It has just been
whispered to me—I have not been three months in the
country, and, of course, cannot venture to express an
opinion of my own—that, in regard to paying this
latter tax of respect and honour to age, some very few
of the Republican youths are occasionally a little re-

miss.  I have heard of young Sons of Freedom
publishing their Declaration of Independence before
they could well spell it ; and cutting the connection
with father and mother before they had learned to
shave.  My own time of life having been stated, by
various enlightened organs of public opinion, at almost
any figure from forty-five to sixty, I cheerfully own
that I belong to the Fogy interest, and ask leave to
rank in, and plead for, that respectable class.  Now
a gentleman can but be a gentleman, in Broadway or
the backwoods, in Pall Mall or California ; and where
and whenever he lives, thousands of miles away in the
wilderness, or hundreds of years hence, I am sure that
reading the writings of this true gentleman, this true
Christian, this noble Joseph Addison, must do him
good.  He may take Sir Roger de Coverley to the
diggings with him, and learn to be gentle and good-
humoured, and urbane, and friendly in the midst of
that struggle in which his life is engaged.  I take
leave to say that the most brilliant youth of this
city may read over this delightful memorial of a bygone age, of fashions long passed away ; of manners
long since changed and modified ; of noble gentlemen, and a great and a brilliant and polished
society ; and find in it much to charm and polish, to
refine and instruct him : a courteousness, which can
be out of place at no time, and under no flag ; a politeness and simplicity, a truthful manhood, a gentle
respect and deference, which may be kept as the
unbought grace of life, and cheap defence of mankind,
long after its old artificial distinctions, after periwigs,
and small-swords, and ruffles, and red-heeled shoes,
and titles, and stars and garters have passed away.  I
will tell you when I have been put in mind of two of
the finest gentlemen books bring us any mention of.
I mean *our* books (not books of history, but books of

humour). I will tell you when I have been put in mind of the courteous gallantry of the noble knight, Sir Roger de Coverley of Coverley Manor, of the noble Hidalgo Don Quixote of La Mancha : here in your own omnibus-carriages and railway-cars, when I have seen a woman step in, handsome or not, well dressed or not, and a workman in hobnail shoes, or a dandy in the height of the fashion, rise up and give her his place. I think Mr. Spectator, with his short face, if he had seen such a deed of courtesy, would have smiled a sweet smile to the doer of that gentlemanlike action, and have made him a low bow from under his great periwig, and have gone home and written a pretty paper about him.

I am sure Dick Steele would have hailed him, were he dandy or mechanic, and asked him to a tavern to share a bottle, or perhaps half-a-dozen. Mind, I do not set down the five last flasks to Dick's score for virtue, and look upon them as works of the most questionable supererogation.

Steele, as a literary benefactor to the world's charity, must rank very high, indeed, not merely from his givings, which were abundant, but because his endowments are prodigiously increased in value since he bequeathed them, as the revenues of the lands, bequeathed to our Foundling Hospital at London by honest Captain Coram, its founder, are immensely enhanced by the houses since built upon them. Steele was the founder of sentimental writing in English, and how the land has been since occupied, and what hundreds of us have laid out gardens and built up tenements on Steele's ground! Before his time readers or hearers were never called upon to cry except at a tragedy, and compassion was not expected to express itself otherwise than in blank verse, or for personages much lower in rank than a dethroned monarch, or a widowed or a jilted empress. He stepped off the high-heeled cothurnus, and came down into common life; he held out his great hearty arms, and embraced us all; he had a bow for all women; a kiss for all children; a shake of the hand for all men, high or low; he showed us Heaven's sun shining every day on quiet homes; not gilded palace-roofs only, or Court processions, or heroic warriors fighting for princesses, and pitched battles. He took away comedy from behind the fine lady's alcove, or the screen where the libertine was watching her. He ended all that wretched business of wives jeering at their husbands; of rakes laughing wives, and husbands too, to scorn. That miserable rouged, tawdry, sparkling, hollow-hearted comedy of the Restoration fled before him, and, like the wicked spirit in the Fairy-books, shrank, as Steele let the daylight in, and shrieked, and shuddered, and vanished. The stage of humourists has been common life ever since Steele's and Addison's time; the joys and griefs, the aversions and sympathies, the laughter and tears of nature.

And here, coming off the stage, and throwing aside the motley habit, or satiric disguise, in which he had before entertained you, mingling with the world, and wearing the same coat as his neighbour, the humourist's service became straightway immensely more available; his means of doing good infinitely multiplied; his success, and the esteem in which he was held, proportionately increased. It requires an effort, of which all minds are not capable, to understand 'Don Quixote;' children and common people still read 'Gulliver' for the story merely. Many more persons are sickened by 'Jonathan Wild' than can comprehend the satire of it. Each of the great men who wrote those books was speaking from behind the satiric mask I anon mentioned. Its distortions appal many simple spectators; its settled sneer or laugh is unintelligible to thousands, who have not the wit to interpret the meaning of the vizored satirist preaching from within. Many a man was at fault about Jonathan Wild's greatness, who could feel and relish Allworthy's goodness in 'Tom Jones,' and Doctor Harrison's in 'Amelia,' and dear Parson Adams, and Joseph Andrews. We love to read—we may grow ever so old, but we love to read of them still—of love and beauty, of frankness and bravery and generosity. We hate hypocrites and cowards; we long to defend oppressed innocence, and to soothe and succour gentle women and children. We are glad when vice is foiled and rascals punished; we lend a foot to kick Blifil downstairs; and as we attend the brave bridegroom to his wedding on the happy marriage day, we ask the groomsman's privilege to salute the blushing cheek of Sophia. A lax morality in many a vital point I own in Fielding, but a great hearty sympathy and benevolence; a great kindness for the poor; a great gentleness and pity for the unfortunate; a great love for the pure and good; these are among the contributions to the charity of the world with which this erring but noble creature endowed it.

As for Goldsmith, if the youngest and most unlettered person here has not been happy with the family at Wakefield; has not rejoiced when Olivia returned, and been thankful for her forgiveness and restoration; has not laughed with delighted good-humour over Moses' gross of green spectacles; has not loved with all his heart the good Vicar, and that kind spirit which created these charming figures, and devised the beneficent fiction which speaks to us so tenderly—what call is there for me to speak? In this place and on this occasion, remembering these men, I claim from you your sympathy for the good they have done, and for the sweet charity which they have bestowed on the world.

When humour joins with rhythm and music, and appears in song, its influence is irresistible, its charities are countless, it stirs the feelings to love, peace, friendship, as scarce any moral agent can. The songs of Béranger are hymns of love and tenderness ; I have seen great whiskered Frenchmen warbling the 'Bonne Vieille,' the 'Soldats, au pas, au pas,' with tears rolling down their mustachios. At a Burns's Festival I have seen Scotchmen singing Burns, while the drops twinkled on their furrowed cheeks ; while each rough hand was flung out to grasp its neighbour's ; while early scenes and sacred recollections, and dear and delightful memories of the past came rushing back at the sound of the familiar words and music, and the softened heart was full of love, and friendship, and home. Humour ! if tears are the alms of gentle spirits, and may be counted, as sure they may, among the sweetest of life's charities,—of that kindly sensibility, and sweet sudden emotion, which exhibits itself at the eyes, I know no such provocative as humour. It is an irresistible sympathiser ; it surprises you into compassion : you are laughing and disarmed, and suddenly forced into tears. I heard a humourous balladist not long since, a minstrel with wool on his head, and an ultra-Ethiopian complexion, who performed a negro ballad that I confess moistened these spectacles in the most unexpected manner. They have gazed at dozens of tragedy-queens, dying on the stage, and expiring in appropriate blank verse, and I never wanted to wipe them. They have looked up, with deep respect be it said, at many scores of clergymen in pulpits, and without being dimmed ; and behold a vagabond with a corked face and a banjo sings a little song, strikes a wild note which sets the whole heart thrilling with happy pity. Humour! humour is the mistress of tears; she knows the way to the *fons lachrymarum*, strikes in dry and rugged places with her enchanting wand, and bids the fountain gush and sparkle. She has refreshed myriads more from her natural springs than ever tragedy has watered from her pompous old urn.

Popular humour, and especially modern popular humour, and the writers, its exponents, are always kind and chivalrous, taking the side of the weak against the strong. In our plays, and books, and entertainments for the lower classes in England, I scarce remember a story or theatrical piece in which a wicked aristocrat is not bepummelled by a dashing young champion of the people. There was a book which had an immense popularity in England, and I believe has been greatly read here, in which the Mysteries of the Court of London were said to be unveiled by a gentleman who, I suspect, knows about as much about the Court of London as he does of that of Pekin. Years ago I treated myself to sixpenny-worth of this performance at a railway station, and found poor dear George IV., our late most religious and gracious king, occupied in the most flagitious designs against the tradesmen's families in his metropolitan city. A couple of years after, I took sixpenny-worth more of the same delectable history: George IV. was still at work, still ruining the peace of tradesmen's families; he had been at it for two whole years, and a bookseller at the Brighton station told me that this book was by many many times the most popular of all periodical tales then published, because, says he, 'it lashes the aristocracy!' Not long since I went to two penny theatres in London; immense eager crowds of people thronged the buildings, and the vast masses thrilled and vibrated with the emotion produced

by the piece represented on the stage, and burst into
applause or laughter, such as many a polite actor
would sigh for in vain. In both these pieces there
was a wicked Lord kicked out of the window—there
is always a wicked Lord kicked out of the window.
First piece :—' Domestic drama—Thrilling interest !
—Weaver's family in distress !—Fanny gives away
her bread to little Jacky, and starves !—Enter wicked
Lord : tempts Fanny with offer of Diamond Necklace,
Champagne Suppers, and Coach to ride in !—Enter
sturdy Blacksmith.—Scuffle between Blacksmith and
Aristocratic minion : exit wicked Lord out of the
window.' Fanny, of course, becomes Mrs. Blacksmith.

The second piece was a nautical drama, also of
thrilling interest, consisting chiefly of hornpipes, and
acts of most tremendous oppression on the part of
certain Earls and Magistrates towards the people.
Two wicked Lords were in this piece the atrocious
scoundrels : one Aristocrat, a deep-dyed villain, in
short duck trousers and Berlin cotton gloves ; while
the other minion of wealth enjoyed an eyeglass with a
blue ribbon, and whisked about the stage with a penny
cane. Having made away with Fanny Forester's
lover, Tom Bowling, by means of a press-gang, they
meet her all alone on a common, and subject her to
the most opprobrious language and behaviour : ' Release me, villains !' says Fanny, pulling a brace of
pistols out of her pockets, and crossing them over her
breast so as to cover wicked Lord to the right, wicked
Lord to the left ; and they might have remained in
that position ever so much longer (for the aristocratic
rascals had pistols too), had not Tom Bowling returned
from sea at the very nick of time, armed with a great
marlinespike, with which—whack ! whack ! down
goes wicked Lord No. 1—wicked Lord No. 2.

Fanny rushes into Tom's arms with an hysterical shriek, and I dare say they marry, and are very happy ever after. Popular fun is always kind : it is the champion of the humble against the great. In all popular parables, it is little Jack that conquers, and the Giant that topples down. I think our popular authors are rather hard upon the great folks. Well, well ! their lordships have all the money, and can afford to be laughed at.

In our days, in England, the importance of the humourous preacher has prodigiously increased ; his audiences are enormous ; every week or month his happy congregations flock to him ; they never tire of such sermons. I believe my friend Mr. Punch is as popular to-day as he has been any day since his birth ; I believe that Mr. Dickens's readers are even more numerous than they have ever been since his unrivalled pen commenced to delight the world with its humour. We have among us other literary parties ; we have Punch, as I have said, preaching from his booth ; we have a Jerrold party very numerous and faithful to that acute thinker and distinguished wit ; and we have also—it must be said, and it is still to be hoped—a Vanity-Fair party, the author of which work has lately been described by the London *Times* newspaper as a writer of considerable parts, but a dreary misanthrope, who sees no good anywhere, who sees the sky above him green, I think, instead of blue, and only miserable sinners round about him. So we are ; so is every writer and every reader I ever heard of ; so was every being who ever trod this earth, save One. I cannot help telling the truth as I view it, and describing what I see. To describe it otherwise than it seems to me would be falsehood in that calling in which it has pleased Heaven to place me ; treason to that conscience which says that men are weak ; that truth must be told ; that fault must be owned ; that pardon must be prayed for ; and that love reigns supreme over all.

I look back at the good which of late years the kind English Humourists have done ; and if you are pleased to rank the present speaker among that class, I own to an honest pride at thinking what benefits society has derived from men of our calling. That 'Song of the Shirt,' which *Punch* first published, and the noble, the suffering, the melancholy, the tender Hood sang, may surely rank as a great act of charity to the world, and call from it its thanks and regard for its teacher and benefactor. That astonishing poem, which you all know, of the 'Bridge of Sighs,' who can read it without tenderness, without reverence to Heaven, charity to man, and thanks to the beneficent genius which sang for us nobly ?

I never saw the writer but once ; but shall always be glad to think that some words of mine, printed in a periodical of that day, and in praise of these amazing verses (which, strange to say, appeared almost unnoticed at first in the magazine in which Mr. Hood published them)—I am proud, I say, to think that some words of appreciation of mine reached him on his death-bed, and pleased and soothed him in that hour of manful resignation and pain.

As for the charities of Mr. Dickens, multiplied kindnesses which he has conferred upon us all ; upon our children ; upon people educated and uneducated ; upon the myriads here and at home, who speak our common tongue ; have not you, have not I, all of us reason to be thankful to this kind friend, who soothed and charmed so many hours, brought pleasure and sweet laughter to so many homes ; made such multitudes of children happy ; endowed us with such a sweet store of gracious thoughts, fair fancies, soft sympathies, hearty enjoyments? There are creations of Mr. Dickens's which seem to me to rank as personal benefits; figures so delightful that one feels happier and better for knowing them, as one does for being brought into the society of very good men and women. The atmosphere in which these people live is wholesome to breathe in; you feel that to be allowed to speak to them is a personal kindness; you come away better for your contact with them; your hands seem cleaner from having the privilege of shaking theirs. Was there ever a better charity sermon preached in the world than Dickens's 'Christmas Carol'? I believe it occasioned immense hospitality throughout England; was the means of lighting up hundreds of kind fires at Christmas time; caused a wonderful outpouring of Christmas good feeling; of Christmas punch-brewing; an awful slaughter of Christmas turkeys, and roasting and basting of Christmas beef. As for this man's love of children, that amiable organ at the back of his honest head must be perfectly monstrous. All children ought to love him. I know two that do, and read his books ten times for once that they peruse the dismal preachments of their father. I know one who, when she is happy, reads 'Nicholas Nickleby;' when she is unhappy, reads 'Nicholas Nickleby;' when she is tired, reads 'Nicholas Nickleby;' when she is in bed, reads 'Nicholas Nickleby;' when she has nothing to do, reads 'Nicholas Nickleby;' and when she has finished the book, reads 'Nicholas Nickleby' over again. This candid young critic, at ten years of age, said, 'I like Mr. Dickens's books much better than your books, papa;' and frequently expressed her desire that the latter author should write a book like one of Mr. Dickens's books. Who can? Every man must say his own thoughts in his own voice, in his own way; lucky is he who has such a charming gift of nature as this, which brings all the children in the world trooping to him, and being fond of him.

I remember, when that famous 'Nicholas Nickleby' came out, seeing a letter from a pedagogue in the north of England, which, dismal as it was, was immensely comical. 'Mr. Dickens's ill-advised publication,' wrote the poor schoolmaster, 'has passed like a whirlwind over the schools of the North.' He was a proprietor of a cheap school; Dotheboys Hall was a cheap school. There were many such establishments in the northern counties. Parents were ashamed that never were ashamed before until the kind satirist laughed at them; relatives were frightened; scores of little scholars were taken away; poor schoolmasters had to shut their shops up; every pedagogue was voted a Squeers, and many suffered, no doubt unjustly; but afterwards schoolboys' backs were not so much caned; schoolboys' meat was less tough and more plentiful; and schoolboys' milk was not so sky-blue. What a kind light of benevolence it is that plays round Crummles and the Phenomenon, and all those poor theatre people in that charming book! What a humour! and what a good-humour! I coincide with the youthful critic, whose opinion has just been mentioned, and own to a family admiration for 'Nicholas Nickleby.'

One might go on, though the task would be endless and needless, chronicling the names of kind folk with whom this kind genius has made us familiar. Who does not love the Marchioness, and Mr. Richard Swiveller? Who does not sympathise, not only with Oliver Twist, but his admirable young friend the Artful Dodger? Who has not the inestimable advantage of possessing a Mrs. Nickleby in his own family? Who does not bless Sairey Gamp and wonder at Mrs. Harris? Who does not venerate the chief of that illustrious family who, being stricken by misfortune, wisely and greatly turned his attention to 'coals,' the accomplished, the Epicurean, the dirty, the delightful Micawber?

I may quarrel with Mr. Dickens's art a thousand and a thousand times; I delight and wonder at his genius; I recognise in it—I speak with awe and reverence—a commission from that Divine Beneficence, whose blessed task we know it will one day be to wipe every tear from every eye. Thankfully I take my share of the feast of love and kindness which this gentle, and generous, and charitable soul has contributed to the happiness of the world. I take and enjoy my share, and say a Benediction for the meal.

# THE FOUR GEORGES:

SKETCHES OF MANNERS, MORALS, COURT
AND TOWN LIFE

# GEORGE THE FIRST

A VERY few years since, I knew familiarly a lady who had been asked in marriage by Horace Walpole, who had been patted on the head by George I. This lady had knocked at Doctor Johnson's door; had been intimate with Fox, the beautiful Georgina of Devonshire, and that brilliant Whig society of the reign of George III.; had known the Duchess of Queensberry, the patroness of Gay and Prior, the admired young beauty of the Court of Queen Anne. I often thought as I took my kind old friend's hand, how with it I held on to the old society of wits and men of the world. I could travel back for seven score years of time—have glimpses of Brummel, Selwyn, Chesterfield, and the men of pleasure; of Walpole and Conway; of Johnson, Reynolds, Goldsmith; of North, Chatham, Newcastle; of the fair maids of honour of George II.'s Court; of the German retainers of George I.'s; where Addison was Secretary of State; where Dick Steele held a place; whither the great Marlborough came with his fiery spouse; when Pope, and Swift, and Bolingbroke yet lived and wrote. Of a society so vast, busy, brilliant, it is impossible in four brief chapters to give a complete notion; but we may peep here and there into that bygone world of the Georges, see what they and their Courts were like;

glance at the people round about them ; look at past manners, fashions, pleasures, and contrast them with our own. I have to say thus much by way of preface, because the subject of these lectures has been misunderstood, and I have been taken to task for not having given grave historical treatises, which it never was my intention to attempt. Not about battles, about politics, about statesmen and measures of State, did I ever think to lecture you : but to sketch the manners and life of the old world ; to amuse for a few hours with talk about the old society; and, with the result of many a day's and night's pleasant reading, to try and while away a few winter evenings for my hearers.

Among the German princes who sat under Luther at Wittenberg was Duke Ernest of Celle, whose younger son, William of Lüneburg, was the progenitor of the illustrious Hanoverian House at present reigning in Great Britain. Duke William held his Court at Celle, a little town of ten thousand people that lies on the railway line between Hamburg and Hanover, in the midst of great plains of sand, upon the river Aller. When Duke William had it, it was a very humble wood-built place, with a great brick church, which he sedulously frequented, and in which he and others of his house lie buried. He was a very religious lord, and was called William the Pious by his small circle of subjects, over whom he ruled till fate deprived him both of sight and reason. Sometimes, in his latter days, the good Duke had glimpses of mental light, when he would bid his musicians play the psalm-tunes which he loved. One thinks of a descendant of his, two hundred years afterwards, blind, old, and lost of wits, singing Handel in Windsor Tower.

William the Pious had fifteen children, eight daughters and seven sons, who, as the property left among them was small, drew lots to determine which one of them should marry, and continue the stout race of the Guelphs. The lot fell on Duke George, the sixth brother. The others remained single, or contracted left-handed marriages after the princely fashion of those days. It is a queer picture—that of the old Prince dying in his little wood-built capital, and his seven sons tossing up which should inherit and transmit the crown of Brentford. Duke George, the lucky prizeman, made the tour of Europe, during which he visited the Court of Queen Elizabeth; and in the year 1617, came back and settled at Zell, with a wife out of Darmstadt. His remaining brothers all kept their house at Zell, for economy's sake. And presently, in due course, they all died —all the honest Dukes: Ernest, and Christian, and Augustus, and Magnus, and George, and John—and they are buried in the brick church of Brentford yonder, by the sandy banks of the Aller.

Dr. Vehse gives a pleasant glimpse of the way of life of our Dukes in Zell. 'When the trumpeter on the tower has blown,' Duke Christian orders — viz., at nine o'clock in the morning, and four in the evening—every one must be present at meals, and those who are not must go without. None of the servants, unless it be a knave who has been ordered to ride out, shall eat or drink in the kitchen or cellar; or, without special leave, fodder his horses at the Prince's cost. When the meal is served in the Court-room, a page shall go round and bid every one be quiet and orderly, forbidding all cursing, swearing, and rudeness; all throwing about of bread, bones, or roast, or pocketing of the same. Every morning, at seven, the squires shall have their morning soup, along with which, and dinner, they shall be served with their under-drink—every morning, except Friday morning, when there was sermon, and no drink. Every evening they shall have their beer, and at night their sleep-drink. The butler is especially warned not to allow noble or simple to go into the cellar : wine shall only be served at the Prince's or Councillors' table; and every Monday, the honest old Duke Christian ordains the accounts shall be ready, and the expenses in the kitchen, the wine and beer cellar, the bakehouse, and stable, made out.

Duke George, the marrying Duke, did not stop at home to partake of the beer and wine, and the sermons. He went about fighting wherever there was profit to be had. He served as a general in the army of the circle of Lower Saxony, the Protestant army ; then he went over to the Emperor, and fought in his armies in Germany and Italy ; and when Gustavus Adolphus appeared in Germany, George took service as a Swedish general, and seized the Abbey of Hildesheim, as his share of the plunder. Here, in the year 1641, Duke George died, leaving four sons behind him, from the youngest of whom descend our Royal Georges.

Under these children of Duke George, the old God-fearing simple ways of Zell appear to have gone out of mode. The second brother was constantly visiting Venice, and leading a jolly wicked life there. It was the most jovial of all places at the end of the seventeenth century; and military men, after a campaign, rushed thither, as the warriors of the Allies rushed to Paris in 1814, to gamble, and rejoice, and partake of all sorts of godless delights. This Prince, then, loving Venice, and its pleasures, brought Italian singers and dancers back with him to quiet old Zell ; and, worse still, demeaned himself by marrying a

French lady of birth quite inferior to his own—
Eleanor d'Olbreuse, from whom our Queen is
descended. Eleanor had a pretty daughter, who
inherited a great fortune, which inflamed her cousin,
George Louis of Hanover, with a desire to marry her ;
and so, with her beauty and her riches, she came to
a sad end.

It is too long to tell how the four sons of Duke
George divided his territories amongst them, and
how, finally, they came into possession of the son of
the youngest of the four. In this generation the
Protestant faith was very nearly extinguished in the
family : and then where should we in England have
gone for a king ? The third brother also took delight
in Italy, where the priests converted him and his
Protestant chaplain too. Mass was said in Hanover
once more ; and Italian soprani piped their Latin
rhymes in place of the hymns which William the
Pious and Doctor Luther sang. Louis XIV. gave
this and other converts a splendid pension. Crowds
of Frenchmen and brilliant French fashions came to
his Court. It is incalculable how much that Royal
bigwig cost Germany. Every prince imitated the
French King, and had his Versailles, his Wilhelmshöhe
or Ludwigslust; his Court and its splendours; his
gardens laid out with statues ; his fountains, and
waterworks, and Tritons; his actors, and dancers,
and singers, and fiddlers ; his harem, with its inhabitants ; his diamonds and duchies for these latter ;
his enormous festivities, his gaming-tables, tourna-
ments, masquerades, and banquets lasting a week long,
for which the people paid with their money, when
the poor wretches had it; with their bodies and very
blood when they had none ; being sold in thousands
by their lords and masters, who gaily dealt in soldiers,
staked a regiment upon the red at the gambling-

table; swapped a battalion against a dancing-girl's diamond necklace; and, as it were, pocketed their people.

As one views Europe, through contemporary books of travel, in the early part of the last century, the landscape is awful—wretched wastes, beggarly and plundered; half-burned cottages and trembling peasants gathering piteous harvests; gangs of such tramping along with bayonets behind them, and corporals with canes and cats-of-nine-tails to flog them to barracks. By these passes my Lord's gilt carriage floundering through the ruts, as he swears at the postillions, and toils on to the Residenz. Hard by, but away from the noise and brawling of the citizens and buyers, is Wilhelmslust or Ludwigsruhe, or Monbigou, or Versailles — it scarcely matters which,—near to the city, shut out by woods from the beggared country, the enormous, hideous, gilded, monstrous marble palace, where the Prince is, and the Court, and the trim gardens, and huge fountains, and the forest where the ragged peasants are beating the game in (it is death to them to touch a feather); and the jolly hunt sweeps by with its uniform of crimson and gold; and the Prince gallops ahead puffing his Royal horn; and his lords and mistresses ride after him; and the stag is pulled down; and the grand huntsman gives the knife in the midst of a chorus of bugles; and 'tis time the Court go home to dinner; and our noble traveller, it may be the Baron of Pöllnitz, or the Count de Königsmarck, or the excellent Chevalier de Seingalt, sees the procession gleaming through the trim avenues of the wood, and hastens to the inn, and sends his noble name to the marshal of the Court. Then our nobleman arrays himself in green and gold, or pink and silver, in the richest Paris mode, and is introduced

by the chamberlain, and makes his bow to the jolly
Prince, and the gracious Princess; and is presented
to the chief lords and ladies, and then comes supper
and a bank at Faro, where he loses or wins a
thousand pieces by daylight. If it is a German
Court, you may add not a little drunkenness to this
picture of high life; but German, or French, or Spanish,
if you can see out of your palace windows beyond
the trim-cut forest vistas, misery is lying outside;
hunger is stalking about the bare villages, listlessly
following precarious husbandry; ploughing stony
fields with starved cattle; or fearfully taking in scanty
harvests. Augustus is fat and jolly on his throne;
he can knock down an ox, and eat one almost; his
mistress, Aurora von Königsmarck, is the loveliest,
the wittiest creature; his diamonds are the biggest
and most brilliant in the world, and his feasts as
splendid as those of Versailles. As for Louis the
Great, he is more than mortal. Lift up your glances
respectfully, and mark him eyeing Madame de
Fontanges or Madame de Montespan from under his
sublime periwig, as he passes through the great gallery
where Villars and Vendôme, and Berwick, and Bossuet,
and Massillon are waiting. Can Court be more
splendid; nobles and knights more gallant and
superb; ladies more lovely? A grander monarch,
or a more miserable starved wretch than the peasant
his subject, you cannot look on. Let us bear both
these types in mind, if we wish to estimate the old
society properly. Remember the glory and the
chivalry? Yes! Remember the grace and beauty,
the splendour and lofty politeness; the gallant courtesy
of Fontenoy, where the French line bids the gentlemen of the English guard to fire first; the noble
constancy of the old King and Villars his general,
who fits out the last army with the last crown piece

from the treasury, and goes to meet the enemy and die or conquer for France at Denain. But round all that Royal splendour lies a nation enslaved and ruined: there are people robbed of their rights—communities laid waste—faith, justice, commerce trampled upon, and well-nigh destroyed—nay, in the very centre of Royalty itself, what horrible stains and meanness, crime and shame! It is but to a silly harlot that some of the noblest gentlemen, and some of the proudest women in the world, are bowing down; it is the price of a miserable province that the King ties in diamonds round his mistress's white neck. In the first half of the last century, I say, this is going on all Europe over. Saxony is a waste as well as Picardy or Artois; and Versailles is only larger and not worse than Herrenhausen.

It was the first Elector of Hanover who made the fortunate match which bestowed the race of Hanoverian Sovereigns upon us Britons. Nine years after Charles Stuart lost his head, his niece Sophia, one of many children of another luckless dethroned sovereign, the Elector Palatine, married Ernest Augustus of Brunswick, and brought the reversion to the crown of the three kingdoms in her scanty trousseau.

One of the handsomest, the most cheerful, sensible, shrewd, accomplished of women was Sophia, daughter of poor Frederick, the winter King of Bohemia. The other daughters of lovely unhappy Elizabeth Stuart went off into the Catholic Church; this one, luckily for her family, remained, I cannot say faithful to the Reformed Religion, but at least she adopted no other. An agent of the French King's, Gourville, a convert himself, strove to bring her and her husband to a sense of the truth; and tells us that he one day asked Madame the Duchess of Hanover of what religion her daughter was, then a pretty girl of thirteen years old. The Duchess replied that the Princess *was of no religion as yet*. They were waiting to know of what religion her husband would be, Protestant or Catholic, before instructing her! And the Duke of Hanover having heard all Gourville's proposal, said that a change would be advantageous to his house, but that he himself was too old to change.

This shrewd woman had such keen eyes that she knew how to shut them upon occasion, and was blind to many faults which it appeared that her husband the Bishop of Osnaburg and Duke of Hanover committed. He loved to take his pleasure like other sovereigns—was a merry prince, fond of dinner and the bottle; liked to go to Italy, as his brothers had done before him; and we read how he jovially sold 6700 of his Hanoverians to the Seigniory of Venice. They went bravely off to the Morea, under command of Ernest's son, Prince Max, and only 1400 of them ever came home again. The German princes sold a good deal of this kind of stock. You may remember how George III.'s Government purchased Hessians, and the use we made of them during the War of Independence.

The ducats Duke Ernest got for his soldiers he spent in a series of the most brilliant entertainments. Nevertheless, the jovial Prince was economical, and kept a steady eye upon his own interests. He achieved the electoral dignity for himself: he married his eldest son George to his beautiful cousin of Zell; and sending his sons out in command of armies to fight—now on this side, now on that—he lived on, taking his pleasure, and scheming his schemes, a merry wise prince enough—not, I fear, a moral prince, of which kind we shall have but very few specimens in the course of these lectures.

Ernest Augustus had seven children in all, some of whom were scapegraces, and rebelled against the parental system of primogeniture and non-division of property which the Elector ordained. 'Gustchen,' the Electress writes about her second son :—'Poor Gus is thrust out, and his father will give him no more keep. I laugh in the day, and cry all night about it; for I am a fool with my children.' Three of the six died fighting against Turks, Tartars, Frenchmen. One of them conspired, revolted, fled to Rome, leaving an agent behind him, whose head was taken off. The daughter, of whose early education we have made mention, was married to the Elector of Brandenburg, and so her religion settled finally on the Protestant side.

A niece of the Electress Sophia—who had been made to change her religion, and marry the Duke of Orleans, brother of the French King; a woman whose honest heart was always with her friends and dear old Deutschland, though her fat little body was confined at Paris, or Marly, or Versailles—has left us, in her enormous correspondence (part of which has been printed in German and French), recollections of the Electress, and of George her son. Elizabeth Charlotte was at Osnaburg when George was born (1660). She narrowly escaped a whipping for being in the way on that auspicious day. She seems not to have liked little George, nor George grown up; and represents him as odiously hard, cold, and silent. Silent he may have been: not a jolly prince like his father before him, but a prudent, quiet, selfish potentate, going his own way, managing his own affairs, and understanding his own interests remarkably well.

In his father's lifetime, and at the head of the Hanover forces of 8000 or 10,000 men, George served the Emperor, on the Danube against Turks, at the siege of Vienna, in Italy, and on the Rhine. When he succeeded to the Electorate, he handled its affairs with great prudence and dexterity. He was very much liked by his people of Hanover. He did not show his feelings much, but he cried heartily on leaving them; as they used for joy, when he came back. He showed an uncommon prudence and coolness of behaviour when he came into his kingdom; exhibiting no elation; reasonably doubtful whether he should not be turned out some day; looking upon himself only as a lodger, and making the most of his brief tenure of St. James's and Hampton Court; plundering, it is true, somewhat, and dividing amongst his German followers; but what could be expected of a sovereign who at home could sell his subjects at so many ducats per head, and make no scruple in so disposing of them? I fancy a considerable shrewdness, prudence, and even moderation in his ways. The German Protestant was a cheaper, and better, and kinder king than the Catholic Stuart in whose chair he sat, and so far loyal to England that he let England govern herself.

Having these lectures in view, I made it my business to visit that ugly cradle in which our Georges were nursed. The old town of Hanover must look still pretty much as in the time when George Louis left it. The gardens and pavilions of Herrenhausen are scarce changed since the day when the stout old Electress Sophia fell down in her last walk there, preceding by but a few weeks to the tomb James II.'s daughter, whose death made way for the Brunswick Stuarts in England.

The first two Royal Georges and their father, Ernest Augustus, had quite Royal notions regarding marriage; and Louis XIV. and Charles II. scarce distinguished themselves more at Versailles or Saint James, than these German sultans in their little city on the banks of the Leine. You may see at Herrenhausen the very rustic theatre in which the Platens danced and performed masques, and sang before the Elector and his sons. There are the very fauns and dryads of stone still glimmering through the branches, still grinning and piping their ditties of no tone, as in the days when painted nymphs hung garlands round them ; appeared under their leafy arcades with gilt crooks, guiding rams with gilt horns ; descended from 'machines,' in the guise of Diana or Minerva ; and delivered immense allegorical compliments to the Princes returned home from the campaign.

That was a curious state of morals and politics in Europe ; a queer consequence of the triumph of the monarchical principle. Feudalism was beaten down. The nobility, in its quarrels with the Crown, had pretty well succumbed, and the monarch was all in all. He became almost divine : the proudest and most ancient gentry of the land did menial service for him. Who should carry Louis XIV.'s candle when he went to bed ? what prince of the blood should hold the King's shirt when His Most Christian Majesty changed that garment ?—the French memoirs of the seventeenth century are full of such details and squabbles. The tradition is not yet extinct in Europe. Any of you who were present, as myriads were, at that splendid pageant, the opening of our Crystal Palace in London, must have seen two noble lords, great officers of the household, with ancient pedigrees, with embroidered coats, and stars on their breasts and wands in their hands, walking backwards for near the space of a mile, while the Royal procession made its progress. Shall we wonder—shall we be angry—shall we laugh at these old-world ceremonies? View them as you will, according to your mood; and with scorn or with respect, or with anger and sorrow, as your temper leads you. Up goes Gessler's hat upon the pole. Salute that symbol of sovereignty with heartfelt awe; or with a sulky shrug of acquiescence, or with a grinning obeisance; or with a stout rebellious No—clap your own beaver down on your pate, and refuse to doff it to that spangled velvet and flaunting feather. I make no comment upon the spectators' behaviour; all I say is, that Gessler's cap is still up in the market-place of Europe, and not a few folks are still kneeling to it.

Put clumsy High Dutch statues in place of the marbles of Versailles; fancy Herrenhausen waterworks in place of those of Marly: spread the tables with Schweinskopf, Specksuppe, Leberkuchen, and the like delicacies, in place of the French *cuisine*; and fancy Frau von Kielmansegge dancing with Count Kammerjunker Quirini, or singing French songs with the most awful German accent: imagine a coarse Versailles, and we have a Hanover before us. 'I am now got into the region of beauty,' writes Mary Wortley, from Hanover, in 1716; 'all the women have literally rosy cheeks, snowy foreheads and necks, jet eyebrows, to which may generally be added coal-black hair. These perfections never leave them to the day of their death, and have a very fine effect by candlelight; but I could wish they were handsome with a little variety. They resemble one another as Mrs Salmon's Court of Great Britain, and are in as much danger of melting away by too nearly approaching the fire.' The sly Mary Wortley saw this painted seraglio of the first George at Hanover, the year after his accession to the British throne. There were great doings and feasts there. Here Lady Mary saw George II. too. 'I can tell you, without flattery or partiality,' she says, 'that our young prince has all the accomplishments that it is possible to have at his age, with an air of sprightliness and understanding, and a something so very engaging in his behaviour that needs not the advantage of his rank to appear charming.' I find elsewhere similar panegyrics upon Frederick Prince of Wales, George II.'s son ; and upon George III., of course ; and upon George IV. in an eminent degree. It was the rule to be dazzled by princes, and people's eyes winked quite honestly at that Royal radiance.

The Electoral Court of Hanover was numerous ; pretty well paid, as times went ; above all, paid with a regularity which few other European Courts could boast of. Perhaps you will be amused to know how the Electoral Court was composed. There were the princes of the house in the first class ; in the second, the single field-marshal of the army (the contingent was 18,000, Pöllnitz says, and the Elector had other 14,000 troops in his pay). Then follow, in due order, the authorities civil and military, the working privy councillors, the generals of cavalry and infantry, in the third class ; the high chamberlain, high marshals of the Court, high masters of the horse, the major-generals of cavalry and infantry, in the fourth class ; down to the majors, the hofjunkers or pages, the secretaries or assessors, of the tenth class, of whom all were noble.

We find the master of the horse had 1090 thalers of pay ; the high chamberlain, 2000—a thaler being about three shillings of our money. There were two chamberlains, and one for the Princess ; five gentlemen of the chamber, and five gentlemen ushers ; eleven pages and personages to educate these young noblemen—such as a governor, a preceptor, a fechtmeister or fencing-master, and a dancing ditto, this

latter with a handsome salary of 400 thalers.  There
were three body and Court physicians, with 800 and
500 thalers ; a Court barber, 600 thalers ; a Court
organist ; two musikanten ;  four French fiddlers ;
twelve trumpeters, and a bugler ; so that there was
plenty of music, profane and pious, in Hanover.
There were ten chamber waiters, and twenty-four
lacqueys in livery ; a *maître d'hôtel*, and attendants of
the kitchen ; a French cook, a body cook, ten cooks ;
six cooks' assistants ;  two Braten masters, or masters
of the roast—(one fancies enormous spits turning
slowly, and the honest masters of the roast beladling
the dripping) ; a pastry-baker ; a pie-baker ; and,
finally, three scullions, at the modest remuneration of
eleven thalers.  In the sugar-chamber there were
four pastry cooks (for the ladies, no doubt) ; seven
officers in the wine and beer cellars ;  four bread-
bakers ; and five men in the plate-room.  There
were 600 horses in the Serene stables—no less than
twenty teams of princely carriage horses, eight to a
team ;  sixteen coachmen ;  fourteen postillions ;
nineteen ostlers ;  thirteen helps, besides smiths,
carriage-masters, horse-doctors, and other attendants
of the stable.  The female attendants were not so
numerous : I grieve to find but a dozen or fourteen
of them about the Electoral premises, and only two
washerwomen for all the Court.  These functionaries
had not so much to do as in the present age.  I own
to finding a pleasure in these small-beer chronicles.
I like to people the old world with its every-day
figures and inhabitants—not so much with heroes
fighting immense battles and inspiring repulsed
battalions to engage ; or statesmen locked up in
darkling cabinets and meditating ponderous laws or
dire conspiracies—as with people occupied with their
every-day work or pleasure ; my lord and lady

hunting in the forest, or dancing in the Court, or bowing to their Serene Highnesses as they pass in to dinner ; John Cook and his procession bringing the meal from the kitchen ; the jolly butlers bearing in the flagons from the cellar ; the stout coachman driving the ponderous gilt waggon, with eight cream-coloured horses in housings of scarlet velvet and morocco leather ; a postillion on the leaders, and a pair or a half-dozen of running footmen scudding along by the side of the vehicle, with conical caps, long silver-headed maces, which they poised as they ran, and splendid jackets laced all over with silver and gold. I fancy the citizens' wives and their daughters looking out from the balconies ; and the burghers over their beer and mumm, rising up, cap in hand, as the cavalcade passes through the town with torch-bearers, trumpeters blowing their lusty cheeks out, and squadrons of jack-booted lifeguardsmen, girt with shining cuirasses, and bestriding thundering chargers, escorting his Highness's coach from Hanover to Herrenhausen ; or halting, mayhap, at Madame Platen's country house of Monplaisir, which lies half-way between the summer-palace and the Residenz.

In the good old times of which I am treating, whilst common men were driven off by herds, and sold to fight the Emperor's enemies on the Danube, or to bayonet King Louis's troops of common men on the Rhine, noblemen passed from Court to Court, seeking service with one prince or the other, and naturally taking command of the ignoble vulgar of soldiery which battled and died almost without hope of promotion. Noble adventurers travelled from Court to Court in search of employment ; not merely noble males, but noble females too ; and if these latter were beauties, and obtained the favourable notice of princes, they stopped in the Courts, became the

favourites of their Serene or Royal Highnesses; and
received great sums of money and splendid diamonds;
and were promoted to be duchesses, marchionesses,
and the like; and did not fall much in public esteem
for the manner in which they won their advancement.
In this way Mademoiselle de Quérouailles, a beautiful
French lady, came to London, on a special mission of
Louis XIV., and was adopted by our grateful country
and sovereign, and figured as Duchess of Portsmouth.
In this way the beautiful Aurora of Königsmarck
travelling about found favour in the eyes of Augustus
of Saxony, and became the mother of Marshal Saxe,
who gave us a beating at Fontenoy; and in this
manner the lovely sisters Elizabeth and Melusina of
Meissenbach (who had actually been driven out of
Paris, whither they had travelled on a like errand, by
the wise jealousy of the female favourite there in
possession) journeyed to Hanover, and became
favourites of the Serene house there reigning.

That beautiful Aurora von Königsmarck and her
brother are wonderful as types of bygone manners,
and strange illustrations of the morals of old days.
The Königsmarcks were descended from an ancient
noble family of Brandenburg, a branch of which passed
into Sweden, where it enriched itself and produced
several mighty men of valour.

The founder of the race was Hans Christof, a
famous warrior and plunderer of the Thirty Years'
War. One of Hans's sons, Otto, appeared as ambassador at the Court of Louis XIV., and had to make
a Swedish speech at his reception before the Most
Christian King. Otto was a famous dandy and
warrior, but he forgot the speech, and what do you
think he did? Far from being disconcerted, he re-
cited a portion of the Swedish Catechism to His
Most Christian Majesty and his Court, not one of

whom understood his lingo with the exception of his own suite, who had to keep their gravity as best they might.

Otto's nephew, Aurora's elder brother, Carl Johann of Königsmarck, a favourite of Charles II., a beauty, a dandy, a warrior, a rascal of more than ordinary mark, escaped but deserved being hanged in England, for the murder of Tom Thynne of Longleat. He had a little brother in London with him at this time :— as great a beauty, as great a dandy, as great a villain as his elder. This lad, Philip of Königsmarck, also was implicated in the affair ; and perhaps it is a pity he ever brought his pretty neck out of it. He went over to Hanover, and was soon appointed colonel of a regiment of H.E. Highness's dragoons. In early life he had been page in the Court of Celle ; and it was said that he and the pretty Princess Sophia Dorothea, who by this time was married to her cousin George the Electoral Prince, had been in love with each other as children. Their loves were now to be renewed, not innocently, and to come to a fearful end.

A biography of the wife of George I., by Doctor Doran, has lately appeared, and I confess I am astounded at the verdict which that writer has delivered, and at his acquittal of this most unfortunate lady. That she had a cold selfish libertine of a husband no one can doubt ; but that the bad husband had a bad wife is equally clear. She was married to her cousin for money or convenience, as all princesses were married. She was most beautiful, lively, witty, accomplished : his brutality outraged her ; his silence and coldness chilled her ; his cruelty insulted her. No wonder she did not love him. How could love be a part of the compact in such a marriage as that ? With this unlucky heart to dispose of, the poor creature bestowed it on Philip of Königsmarck, than whom a greater scamp does not walk the history of the seventeenth century. A hundred and eighty years after the fellow was thrust into his unknown grave, a Swedish professor lights upon a box of letters in the University Library at Upsala, written by Philip and Dorothea to each other, and telling their miserble story.

The bewitching Königsmarck had conquered two female hearts in Hanover. Besides the Electoral Prince's lovely young wife Sophia Dorothea, Philip has inspired a passion in a hideous old Court lady, the Countess of Platen. The Princess seems to have pursued him with the fidelity of many years. Heaps of letters followed him on his campaigns, and were answered by the daring adventurer. The Princess wanted to fly with him ; to quit her odious husband at any rate. She besought her parents to receive her back ; had a notion of taking refuge in France, and going over to the Catholic religion ; had absolutely packed her jewels for flight, and very likely arranged its details with her lover, in that last long night's interview, after which Philip of Königsmarck was seen no more.

Königsmarck, inflamed with drink—there is scarcely any vice of which, according to his own showing, this gentleman was not a practitioner—had boasted at a supper at Dresden of his intimacy with the two Hanoverian ladies, not only with the Princess, but with another lady powerful in Hanover. The Countess Platen, the old favourite of the Elector, hated the young Electoral Princess. The young lady had a lively wit, and constantly made fun of the old one. The Princess's jokes were conveyed to the old Platen just as our idle words are carried about at this present day : and so they both hated each other.

The characters in the tragedy, of which the curtain was now about to fall, are about as dark a set as eye ever rested on. There is the jolly Prince, shrewd, selfish, scheming, loving his cups and his ease (I think his good-humour makes the tragedy but darker); his Princess, who speaks little, but observes all; his old painted Jezebel of a mistress; his son, the Electoral Prince, shrewd too, quiet, selfish, not ill-humoured, and generally silent, except when goaded into fury by the intolerable tongue of his lovely wife; there is poor Sophia Dorothea, with her coquetry and her wrongs, and her passionate attachment to her scamp of a lover, and her wild imprudences, and her mad artifices, and her insane fidelity, and her furious jealousy regarding her husband (though she loathed and cheated him), and her prodigious falsehoods; and the confidante, of course, into whose hands the letters are slipped; and there is Lothario, finally, than whom, as I have said, one can't imagine a more handsome, wicked, worthless reprobate.

How that perverse fidelity of passion pursues the villain! How madly true the woman is, and how astoundingly she lies! She has bewitched two or three persons who have taken her up, and they won't believe in her wrong. Like Mary of Scotland, she finds adherents ready to conspire for her even in history, and people who have to deal with her are charmed, and fascinated, and bedevilled. How devotedly Miss Strickland has stood by Mary's innocence! Are there not scores of ladies in this audience who persist in it too? Innocent! I remember as a boy how a great party persisted in declaring Caroline of Brunswick was a martyred angel. So was Helen of Greece innocent. She never ran away with Paris, the dangerous young Trojan. Menelaus, her husband, ill-used her; and there never was any siege of Troy at all. So was Bluebeard's wife innocent. She never peeped into the closet where the other wives were with their heads off. She never dropped the key, or stained it with blood; and her brothers were quite right in finishing Bluebeard, the cowardly brute! Yes, Caroline of Brunswick was innocent; and Madame Laffarge never poisoned her husband; and Mary of Scotland never blew up hers; and poor Sophia Dorothea was never unfaithful; and Eve never took the apple—it was a cowardly fabrication of the serpent's.

George Louis has been held up to execration as a murderous Bluebeard, whereas the Electoral Prince had no share in the transaction in which Philip of Königsmarck was scuffled out of this mortal scene. The Prince was absent when the catastrophe came. The Princess had had a hundred warnings; mild hints from her husband's parents; grim remonstrances from himself—but took no more heed of this advice than such besotted poor wretches do. On the night of Sunday, the 1st of July, 1694, Königsmarck paid a long visit to the Princess, and left her to get ready for flight. Her husband was away at Berlin; her carriages and horses were prepared and ready for the elopement. Meanwhile, the spies of Countess Platen had brought the news to their mistress. She went to Ernest Augustus, and procured from the Elector an order for the arrest of the Swede. On the way by which he was to come, four guards were commissioned to take him. He strove to cut his way through the four men, and wounded more than one of them. They fell upon him; cut him down; and, as he was lying wounded on the ground, the Countess, his enemy, whom he had betrayed and insulted, came out and beheld him prostrate. He cursed her with his dying lips, and the furious woman stamped upon his mouth with her heel. He was despatched presently; his body burnt the next day; and all traces of the man disappeared. The guards who killed him were enjoined silence under severe penalties. The Princess was reported to be ill in her apartments, from which she was taken in October of the same year, being then eight-and-twenty years old, and consigned to the castle of Ahlden, where she remained a prisoner for no less than thirty-two years. A separation had been pronounced previously between her and her husband. She was called henceforth the 'Princess of Ahlden,' and her silent husband no more uttered her name.

Four years after the Königsmarck catastrophe, Ernest Augustus, the first Elector of Hanover, died, and George Louis, his son, reigned in his stead. Sixteen years he reigned in Hanover, after which he became, as we know, King of Great Britain, France, and Ireland, Defender of the Faith. The wicked old Countess Platen died in the year 1706. She had lost her sight, but nevertheless the legend says that she constantly saw Königsmarck's ghost by her wicked old bed. And so there was an end of her.

In the year 1700 the little Duke of Gloucester, the last of poor Queen Anne's children, died, and the folks of Hanover straightway became of prodigious importance in England. The Electress Sophia was declared the next in succession to the English throne. George Louis was created Duke of Cambridge; grand deputations were sent over from our country to Deutschland; but Queen Anne, whose weak heart hankered after her relatives at Saint Germains, never could be got to allow her cousin, the Elector Duke of Cambridge, to come and pay his respects to Her Majesty, and take his seat in her House of Peers. Had the Queen lasted a month longer; had the English Tories been as bold and resolute as they were clever and crafty; had the Prince whom the nation loved and pitied been equal to his fortune, George

Louis had never talked German in Saint James's Chapel Royal.

When the crown did come to George Louis he was in no hurry about putting it on. He waited at home for awhile; took an affecting farewell of his dear Hanover and Herrenhausen; and set out in the most leisurely manner to ascend 'the throne of his ancestors,' as he called it in his first speech to Parliament. He brought with him a compact body of Germans, whose society he loved, and whom he kept round the Royal person. He had his faithful German chamberlains; his German secretaries; his negroes, captives of his bow and spear in Turkish wars; his two ugly elderly German favourites, Mesdames of Kielmansegge and Schulenberg, whom he created respectively Countess of Darlington and Duchess of Kendal. The Duchess was tall, and lean of stature, and hence was irreverently nicknamed the Maypole. The Countess was a large-sized noblewoman, and this elevated personage was denominated the Elephant. Both of these ladies loved Hanover and its delights; clung round the linden trees of the great Herrenhausen avenue, and at first would not quit the place. Schulenberg, in fact, could not come on account of her debts; but finding the Maypole would not come, the Elephant packed up her trunk and slipped out of Hanover, unwieldy as she was. On this the Maypole straightway put herself in motion, and followed her beloved George Louis. One seems to be speaking of Captain Macheath, and Polly, and Lucy. The King we had selected; the courtiers who came in his train; the English nobles who came to welcome him, and on many of whom the shrewd old cynic turned his back—I protest it is a wonderful satirical picture. I am a citizen waiting at Greenwich pier, say, and crying hurrah for King George; and yet I can scarcely keep my countenance, and help laughing at the enormous absurdity of this advent!

Here we are, all on our knees. Here is the Archbishop of Canterbury prostrating himself to the Head of his Church, with Kielmansegge and Schulenberg with their ruddled cheeks grinning behind the Defender of the Faith. Here is my Lord Duke of Marlborough kneeling too, the greatest warrior of all times; he who betrayed King William—betrayed King James II.—betrayed Queen Anne—betrayed England to the French, the Elector to the Pretender, the Pretender to the Elector; and here are my Lords Oxford and Bolingbroke, the latter of whom has just tripped up the heels of the former; and if a month's more time had been allowed him, would have had King James at Westminster. The great Whig gentlemen made their bows and congées with proper decorum and ceremony; but yonder keen old schemer knows the value of their loyalty. 'Loyalty,' he must think, 'as applied to me—it is absurd! There are fifty nearer heirs to the throne than I am. I am but an accident, and you fine Whig gentlemen take me for your own sake, not for mine. You Tories hate me; you archbishop, smirking on your knees, and prating about Heaven, you know I don't care a fig for your Thirty-nine Articles, and can't understand a word of your stupid sermons. You, my Lords Bolingbroke and Oxford—you know you were conspiring against me a month ago; and you, my Lord Duke of Marlborough—you would sell me or any man else, if you found your advantage in it. Come, my good Melusina, come, my honest Sophia, let us go into my private room, and have some oysters and some Rhine wine, and some pipes afterwards: let us make the best of our situation; let us take what we can get, and leave these bawling, brawling, lying English to shout, and fight, and cheat, in their own way!'

If Swift had not been committed to the statesmen of the losing side, what a fine satirical picture we might have had of that general *sauve qui peut* amongst the Tory party! How mum the Tories became; how the House of Lords and House of Commons chopped round; and how decorously the majorities welcomed King George!

Bolingbroke, making his last speech in the House of Lords, pointed out the shame of the Peerage, where several lords concurred to condemn in one general vote all that they had approved in former parliaments by many particular resolutions. And so their conduct was shameful. St. John had the best of the argument, but the worst of the vote. Bad times were come for him. He talked philosophy, and professed innocence. He courted retirement, and was ready to meet persecution; but, hearing that honest Mat Prior, who had been recalled from Paris, was about to peach regarding the past transactions, the philosopher bolted, and took that magnificent head of his out of the ugly reach of the axe. Oxford, the lazy and good-humoured, had more courage, and awaited the storm at home. He and Mat Prior both had lodgings in the Tower, and both brought their heads safe out of that dangerous menagerie. When Atterbury was carried off to the same den a few years afterwards, and it was asked, what next should be done with him? 'Done with him? Fling him to the lions,' Cadogan said, Marlborough's lieutenant. But the British lion of those days did not care much for drinking the blood of peaceful peers and poets, or crunching the bones of bishops. Only four men were executed in London for the rebellion of 1715; and twenty-two in Lancashire. Above a thousand taken in arms submitted to the King's mercy, and petitioned to be transported to His Majesty's colonies in America. I have heard that their descendants took the loyalist side in the disputes which arose sixty years after. It is pleasant to find that a friend of ours, worthy Dick Steele, was for letting off the rebels with their lives.

As one thinks of what might have been, how amusing the speculation is! We know how the doomed Scottish gentlemen came out at Lord Mar's summons, mounted the white cockade, that has been a flower of sad poetry ever since, and rallied round the ill-omened Stuart standard at Braemar. Mar, with 8000 men, and but 1500 opposed to him, might have driven the enemy over the Tweed, and taken possession of the whole of Scotland; but that the Pretender's Duke did not venture to move when the day was his own. Edinburgh Castle might have been in King James's hands; but that the men who were to escalade it stayed to drink his health at the tavern, and arrived two hours too late at the rendezvous under the castle wall. There was sympathy enough in the town—the projected attack seems to have been known there—Lord Mahon quotes Sinclair's account of a gentleman not concerned, who told Sinclair, that he was in a house that evening where eighteen of them were drinking, as the facetious landlady said, 'powdering their hair,' for the attack on the castle. Suppose they had not stopped to powder their hair? Edinburgh Castle, and town, and all Scotland were King James's. The North of England rises, and marches over Barnet Heath upon London. Wyndham is up in Somersetshire; Packington in Worcestershire; and Vivian in Cornwall. The Elector of Hanover and his hideous mistresses pack up the plate, and perhaps the Crown jewels, in London, and are off, *viâ*

Harwich and Helvoetsluys, for dear old Deutschland. The King—God save him!—lands at Dover, with tumultuous applause; shouting multitudes, roaring cannon, the Duke of Marlborough weeping tears of joy, and all the bishops kneeling in the mud. In a few years mass is said in Saint Paul's; matins and vespers are sung in York Minster; and Doctor Swift is turned out of his stall and deanery house at Saint Patrick's to give place to Father Dominic from Salamanca. All these changes were possible then, and once thirty years afterwards—all this we might have had but for the *pulveris exigui jactu*, that little toss of powder for the hair which the Scotch conspirators stopped to take at the tavern.

You understand the distinction I would draw between history—of which I do not aspire to be an expounder—and manners and life such as these sketches would describe. The rebellion breaks out in the North; its story is before you in a hundred volumes, in none more fairly than in the excellent narrative of Lord Mahon. The clans are up in Scotland; Derwentwater, Nithsdale, and Forster are in arms in Northumberland—these are matters of history, for which you are referred to the due chroniclers. The Guards are set to watch the streets, and prevent the people wearing white roses. I read presently of a couple of soldiers almost flogged to death for wearing oak boughs in their hats on the 29th of May—another badge of the beloved Stuarts. It is with these we have to do, rather than the marches and battles of the armies to which the poor fellows belonged —with statesmen, and how they looked, and how they lived, rather than with measures of State, which belong to history alone. For example, at the close of the old Queen's reign, it is known that the Duke of Marlborough left the kingdom—after what menaces, after

what prayers, lies, bribes offered, taken, refused,
accepted; after what dark doubling and tacking, let
history, if she can or dare, say. The Queen dead:
who so eager to return as my Lord Duke? Who
shouts God save the King! so lustily as the great
conqueror of Blenheim and Malplaquet? (By the
way, he will send over some more money for the
Pretender yet, on the sly.)  Who lays his hand on his
blue ribbon, and lifts his eyes more gracefully to
Heaven than this hero?  He makes a quasi-triumphal
entrance into London, by Temple Bar, in his enormous
gilt coach—and the enormous gilt coach breaks down
somewhere by Chancery Lane, and His Highness is
obliged to get another.  There it is we have him.
We are with the mob in the crowd, not with the great
folks in the procession.  We are not the Historic
Muse, but her Ladyship's attendant, tale-bearer—*valet
de chambre*—for whom no man is a hero; and, as
yonder one steps from his carriage to the next handy
conveyance, we take the number of the hack; we
look all over at his stars, ribbons, embroidery; we
think within ourselves, O you unfathomable schemer!
O you warrior invincible!  O you beautiful smiling
Judas!  What master would you not kiss or betray?
What traitor's head, blackening on the spikes on
yonder gate, ever hatched a tithe of the treason which
has worked under your periwig?

We have brought our Georges to London city, and
if we would behold its aspect, may see it in Hogarth's
lively perspective of Cheapside, or read of it in a
hundred contemporary books which paint the manners
of that age.  Our dear old *Spectator* looks smiling
upon the streets, with their innumerable signs, and
describes them with his charming humour. 'Our
streets are filled with Blue Boars, Black Swans, and
Red Lions, not to mention Flying Pigs and Hogs in

Armour, with other creatures more extraordinary than any in the deserts of Africa.' A few of these quaint old figures still remain in London town. You may still see there, and over its old hostel in Ludgate Hill, the 'Belle Sauvage' to whom the *Spectator* so pleasantly alludes in that paper; and who was, probably, no other than the sweet American Pocahontas, who rescued from death the daring Captain Smith. There is the 'Lion's Head,' down whose jaws the *Spectator's* own letters were passed; and over a great banker's in Fleet Street, the effigy of the wallet, which the founder of the firm bore when he came into London a country boy. People this street, so ornamented, with crowds of swinging chairmen, with servants bawling to clear the way, with Mr. Dean in his cassock, his lacquey marching before him; or Mrs. Dinah in her sack, tripping to chapel, her footboy carrying her Ladyship's great prayerbook; with itinerant tradesmen singing their hundred cries (I remember forty years ago, as boy in London City, a score of cheery familiar cries that are silent now). Fancy the beaux thronging to the chocolatehouses, tapping their snuff-boxes as they issue thence, their periwigs appearing over the red curtains. Fancy Saccharissa, beckoning and smiling from the upper windows, and a crowd of soldiers brawling and bustling at the door—gentlemen of the Life Guards, clad in scarlet, with blue facings, and laced with gold at the seams; gentlemen of the Horse Grenadiers, in their caps of sky-blue cloth, with the garter embroidered on the front in gold and silver; men of the Halberdiers, in their long red coats, as bluff Harry left them, with their ruff and velvet flat caps. Perhaps the King's Majesty himself is going to Saint James's as we pass. If he is going to Parliament, he is in his coach-and-eight, surrounded by his guards and the high officers of his crown. Otherwise His Majesty only uses a chair, with six footmen walking before, and six yeomen of the guard at the sides of the sedan. The officers in waiting follow the King in coaches. It must be rather slow work.

Our *Spectator* and *Tatler* are full of delightful glimpses of the town life of those days. In the company of that charming guide, we may go to the opera, the comedy, the puppet-show, the auction, even the cockpit: we can take boat at Temple Stairs, and accompany Sir Roger de Coverley and Mr. Spectator to Spring Garden—it will be called Vauxhall a few years hence, when Hogarth will paint for it. Would you not like to step back into the past, and be introduced to Mr. Addison?—not the Right Honourable Joseph Addison, Esquire, George I.'s Secretary of State, but to the delightful painter of contemporary manners; the man who, when in good-humour himself, was the pleasantest companion in all England. I should like to go into Lockit's with him, and drink a bowl along with Sir R. Steele (who has just been knighted by King George, and who does not happen to have any money to pay his share of the reckoning). I should not care to follow Mr. Addison to his secretary's office in Whitehall. There we get into politics. Our business is pleasure, and the town, and the coffee-house, and the theatre, and the Mall. Delightful Spectator! kind friend of leisure hours! happy companion! true Christian gentleman! How much greater, better, you are than the King Mr. Secretary kneels to!

You can have foreign testimony about old-world London if you like; and my before-quoted friend, Charles Louis, Baron de Pöllnitz, will conduct us to it.

'A man of sense,' says he, 'or a fine gentleman, is never at a loss for company in London, and this is the way the latter passes his time. He rises late, puts on a frock, and, leaving his sword at home, takes his cane, and goes where he pleases. The Park is commonly the place where he walks, because 'tis the Exchange for men of quality. 'Tis the same thing as the Tuileries at Paris, only the Park has a certain beauty of simplicity which cannot be described. The grand walk is called the Mall ; is full of people at every hour of the day, but especially at morning and evening, when their Majesties often walk with the Royal family, who are attended only by half-a-dozen yeomen of the guard, and permit all persons to walk at the same time with them. The ladies and gentlemen always appear in rich dresses, for the English, who, twenty years ago, did not wear gold lace but in their army, are now embroidered and bedaubed as much as the French. I speak of persons of quality ; for the citizen still contents himself with a suit of fine cloth, a good hat and wig, and fine linen. Everybody is well clothed here, and even the beggars don't make so ragged an appearance as they do elsewhere.'

After our friend, the man of quality, has had his morning or undress walk in the Mall, he goes home to dress, and then saunters to some coffee-house or chocolate-house frequented by the persons he would see.

'For 'tis a rule with the English to go once a day at least to houses of this sort, where they talk of business and news, read the papers, and often look at one another without opening their lips. And 'tis very well they are so mute : for were they all as talkative as people of other nations, the coffee-houses would be intolerable, and there would be no hearing what one man said where they are so many. The chocolate-house in Saint James's Street, where I go every morning to pass away the time, is always so full that a man can scarce turn about in it.'

Delightful as London city was, King George I. liked to be out of it as much as ever he could ; and when there, passed all his time with his Germans.  It was with them as with Blucher, a hundred years afterwards, when the bold old Reiter looked down from Saint Paul's and sighed out, 'Was für Plunder !'  The German women plundered ; the German secretaries plundered ; the German cooks and intendants plundered ; even Mustapha and Mahomet, the German negroes, had a share of the booty.  Take what you can get, was the old monarch's maxim. He was not a lofty monarch, certainly : he was not a patron of the fine arts : but he was not a hypocrite, he was not revengeful, he was not extravagant. Though a despot in Hanover, he was a moderate ruler in England.  His aim was to leave it to itself, as much as possible, and to live out of it as much as he could.  His heart was in Hanover.  When taken ill on his last journey, as he was passing through Holland, he thrust his livid head out of the coach-window, and gasped out, 'Osnaburg, Osnaburg !'  He was more than fifty years of age when he came amongst us : we took him because we wanted him, because he served our turn ; we laughed at his uncouth German ways, and sneered at him.  He took our loyalty for what it was worth ; laid hands on what money he could ; kept us assuredly from Popery and wooden shoes.  I, for one, would have been on his side in those days. Cynical and selfish as he was, he was better than a king out of Saint Germains with the French King's orders in his pocket, and a swarm of Jesuits in his train.

The Fates are supposed to interest themselves about Royal personages ; and so this one had omens and prophecies specially regarding him.  He was said to be much disturbed at a prophecy that he should die

very soon after his wife; and sure enough, pallid
Death, having seized upon the luckless Princess in
her castle of Ahlden, presently pounced upon H.M.
King George I., in his travelling chariot, on the
Hanover road.   What postillion can outride that pale
horseman?   It is said, George promised one of his
left-handed widows to come to her after death, if
leave were granted to him to revisit the glimpses of
the moon; and soon after his demise, a great raven
actually flying or hopping in at the Duchess of
Kendal's window at Twickenham, she chose to
imagine the King's spirit inhabited these plumes, and
took special care of her sable visitor.   Affecting
metempsychosis—funereal Royal bird?   How pathetic
is the idea of the Duchess weeping over it!   When
this chaste addition to our English aristocracy died,
all her jewels, her plate, her plunder, went over to her
relations in Hanover.   I wonder whether her heirs
took the bird, and whether it is still flapping its wings
over Herrenhausen!

The days are over in England of that strange
religion of king-worship, when priests flattered princes
in the Temple of God; when servility was held to be
ennobling duty; when beauty and youth tried eagerly
for Royal favour; and woman's shame was held to be
no dishonour.   Mended morals and mended manners
in Courts and people are among the priceless consequences of the freedom which George I. came to
rescue and secure.   He kept his compact with his
English subjects; and if he escaped no more than
other men and monarchs from the vices of his age, at
least we may thank him for preserving and trans-
mitting the liberties of ours.   In our free air, Royal
and humble homes have alike been purified; and
Truth, the birthright of high and low among us,
which quite fearlessly judges our greatest personages,

can only speak of them now in words of respect and regard. There are stains in the portrait of the first George, and traits in it which none of us need admire; but among the nobler features are justice, courage, moderation—and these we may recognise ere we turn the picture to the wall.

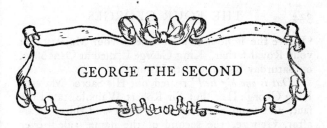

# GEORGE THE SECOND

On the afternoon of the 14th of June, 1727, two horsemen might have been perceived galloping along the road from Chelsea to Richmond. The foremost, cased in the jackboots of the period, was a broad-faced, jolly-looking, and very corpulent cavalier; but, by the manner in which he urged his horse, you might see that he was a bold as well as a skilful rider. Indeed, no man loved sport better; and in the hunting-fields of Norfolk, no squire rode more boldly after the fox, or cheered Ringwood and Sweetlips more lustily, than he who now thundered over the Richmond road.

He speedily reached Richmond Lodge, and asked to see the owner of the mansion. The mistress of the house and her ladies, to whom our friend was admitted, said he could not be introduced to the master, however pressing the business might be. The master was asleep after his dinner; he always slept after his dinner: and woe be to the person who interrupted him! Nevertheless, our stout friend of the jackboots put the affrighted ladies aside, opened the forbidden door of the bedroom, wherein upon the bed lay a little gentleman; and here the eager messenger knelt down in his jackboots.

He on the bed started up, and with many oaths and a strong German accent asked who was there, and who dared to disturb him?

'I am Sir Robert Walpole,' said the messenger. The awakened sleeper hated Sir Robert Walpole.

'I have the honour to announce to your Majesty that your Royal father, King George I., died at Osnaburg, on Saturday last, the 10th instant.'

'*Dat is one big lie!*' roared out His Sacred Majesty King George II.: but Sir Robert Walpole stated the fact, and from that day until three-and-thirty years after, George, the second of the name, ruled over England.

How the King made away with his father's will under the astonished nose of the Archbishop of Canterbury; how he was a choleric little sovereign; how he shook his fist in the face of his father's courtiers; how he kicked his coat and wig about in his rages, and called everybody thief, liar, rascal, with whom he differed,—you will read in all the history books; and how he speedily and shrewdly reconciled himself with the bold Minister, whom he had hated during his father's life, and by whom he was served during fifteen years of his own with admirable prudence, fidelity, and success. But for Sir Robert Walpole, we should have had the Pretender back again. But for his obstinate love of peace, we should have had wars, which the nation was not strong enough nor united enough to endure. But for his resolute counsels and good-humoured resistance, we might have had German despots attempting a Hanoverian regimen over us: we should have had revolt, commotion, want, and tyrannous misrule, in place of a quarter of a century of peace, freedom, and material prosperity, such as the country never enjoyed, until that corrupter of parliaments, that dissolute tipsy cynic, that courageous lover of peace and liberty, that great citizen, patriot, and statesman governed it. In religion he was little better than a heathen; cracked ribald jokes at bigwigs and bishops, and laughed at High Church and Low. In

private life the old pagan revelled in the lowest
pleasures : he passed his Sundays tippling at Richmond ;
and his holidays bawling after dogs, or boozing at
Houghton with boors over beef and punch. He
cared for letters no more than his master did : he
judged human nature so meanly that one is ashamed
to have to own that he was right, and that men
could be corrupted by means so base. But, with his
hireling House of Commons, he defended liberty for
us ; with his incredulity he kept Church-craft down.
There were parsons at Oxford as double-dealing and
dangerous as any priests out of Rome, and he routed
them both. He gave Englishmen no conquests, but
he gave them peace and ease and freedom ; the Three
per Cents nearly at par; and wheat at five and six
and twenty shillings a quarter.

It was lucky for us that our first Georges were not
more high-minded men ; especially fortunate that
they loved Hanover so much as to leave England to
have her own way. Our chief troubles began when
we got a King who gloried in the name of Briton, and,
being born in the country, proposed to rule it. He
was no more fit to govern England than his grandfather and great-grandfather, who did not try. It was
righting itself during their occupation. The dangerous
noble old spirit of Cavalier loyalty was dying out ;
the stately old English High Church was emptying
itself ; the questions dropping which, on one side and
the other—the side of loyalty, prerogative, Church
and king,—the side of right, truth, civil and religious
freedom,—had set generations of brave men in arms.
By the time when George III. came to the throne
the combat between loyalty and liberty was come
to an end ; and Charles Edward, old, tipsy, and
childless, was dying in Italy.

Those who are curious about European Court

history of the last age know the memoirs of the Margravine of Bayreuth, and what a court was that of Berlin, where George II.'s cousins ruled sovereign. Frederick the Great's father knocked down his sons, daughters, officers of state; he kidnapped big men all Europe over to make grenadiers of: his feasts, his parades, his wine-parties, his tobacco-parties, are all described. Jonathan Wild the Great in language, pleasures, and behaviour is scarcely more delicate than this German sovereign. Louis XV., his life, and reign, and doings, are told in a thousand French memoirs. Our George II., at least, was not a worse king than his neighbours. He claimed and took the Royal exemption from doing right which sovereigns assumed. A dull little man of low tastes he appears to us in England; yet Hervey tells us that this choleric prince was a great sentimentalist, and that his letters —of which he wrote prodigious quantities—were quite dangerous in their powers of fascination. He kept his sentimentalities for his Germans and his queen. With us English, he never chose to be familiar. He has been accused of avarice, yet he did not give much money, and did not leave much behind him. He did not love the fine arts, but he did not pretend to love them. He was no more a hypocrite about religion than his father. He judged men by a low standard; yet, with such men as were near him, was he wrong in judging as he did? He readily detected lying and flattery, and liars and flatterers were perforce his companions. Had he been more of a dupe he might have been more amiable. A dismal experience made him cynical. No boon was it to him to be clear-sighted, and see only selfishness and flattery round about him. What could Walpole tell him about his Lords and Commons, but that they were all venal? Did not his clergy, his courtiers, bring him the same story? Dealing with men and women in his rude sceptical way, he came to doubt about honour, male and female, about patriotism, about religion. 'He is wild, but he fights like a man,' George I., the taciturn, said of his son and successor. Courage George II. certainly had. The Electoral Prince, at the head of his father's contingent, had approved himself a good and brave soldier under Eugene and Marlborough. At Oudenarde he specially distinguished himself. At Malplaquet the other claimant to the English throne won but little honour. There was always a question about James's courage. Neither then in Flanders, nor afterwards in his own ancient kingdom of Scotland, did the luckless Pretender show much resolution. But dapper little George had a famous tough spirit of his own, and fought like a Trojan. He called out his brother of Prussia with sword and pistol; and I wish, for the interest of romancers in general, that that famous duel could have taken place. The two sovereigns hated each other with all their might; their seconds were appointed; the place of meeting was settled; and the duel was only prevented by strong representations made to the two, of the European laughter which would have been caused by such a transaction.

Whenever we hear of dapper George at war, it is certain that he demeaned himself like a little man of valour. At Dettingen his horse ran away with him, and with difficulty was stopped from carrying him into the enemy's lines. The King, dismounting from the fiery quadruped, said bravely, 'Now I know I shall not run away;' and placed himself at the head of the foot, drew his sword, brandishing it at the whole of the French army, and calling out to his own men to come on, in bad English, but with the most famous pluck and spirit. In '45, when the Pretender was at Derby, and many people began to look pale, the King never lost his courage—not he. 'Pooh! don't talk to me that stuff!' he said, like a gallant little prince as he was, and never for one moment allowed his equanimity, or his business, or his pleasures, or his travels, to be disturbed. On public festivals he always appeared in the hat and coat he wore on the famous day of Oudenarde; and the people laughed, but kindly, at the odd old garment, for bravery never goes out of fashion.

In private life the Prince showed himself a worthy descendant of his father. In this respect, so much has been said about the First George's manners, that we need not enter into a description of the son's German harem. In 1705 he married a princess remarkable for beauty, for cleverness, for learning, for good temper—one of the truest and fondest wives ever prince was blessed with, and who loved him and was faithful to him, and he, in his coarse fashion, loved her to the last. It must be told to the honour of Caroline of Anspach, that, at the time when German princes thought no more of changing their religion than you of altering your cap, she refused to give up Protestantism for the other creed, although an archduke, afterwards to be an Emperor, was offered to her for a bridegroom. Her Protestant relations in Berlin were angry at her rebellious spirit; it was they who tried to convert her (it is droll to think that Frederick the Great, who had no religion at all, was known for a long time in England as the Protestant hero), and these good Protestants set upon Caroline a certain Father Urban, a very skilful Jesuit, and famous winner of souls. But she routed the Jesuit; and she refused Charles VI.; and she married the little Electoral Prince of Hanover, whom she tended

with love, and with every manner of sacrifice, with
artful kindness, with tender flattery, with entire self-
devotion, thenceforward until her life's end.

When George I. made his first visit to Hanover,
his son was appointed Regent during the Royal
absence. But this honour was never again conferred
on the Prince of Wales; he and his father fell out
presently. On the occasion of the christening of his
second son, a Royal row took place, and the Prince,
shaking his fist in the Duke of Newcastle's face,
called him a rogue, and provoked his august father.
He and his wife were turned out of Saint James's, and
their princely children taken from them, by order of
the Royal head of the family. Father and mother
wept piteously at parting from their little ones. The
young ones sent some cherries, with their love, to
Papa and Mamma; the parents watered the fruit
with tears. They had no tears thirty-five years
afterwards, when Prince Frederick died—their eldest
son, their heir, their enemy.

The King called his daughter-in-law 'cette diablesse
Madame la Princesse.' The frequenters of the latter's
Court were forbidden to appear at the King's: their
Royal Highnesses going to Bath, we read how the
courtiers followed them thither, and paid that homage
in Somersetshire which was forbidden in London.
That phrase of 'cette diablesse Madame la Princesse'
explains one cause of the wrath of her Royal papa.
She was a very clever woman: she had a keen sense
of humour: she had a dreadful tongue: she turned
into ridicule the antiquated sultan and his hideous
harem. She wrote savage letters about him home to
members of her family. So, driven out from the
Royal presence, the Prince and Princess set up for
themselves in Leicester Fields, 'where,' says Walpole,
' the most promising of the young gentlemen of the

next party, and the prettiest and liveliest of the young
ladies, formed the new Court.' Besides Leicester
House, they had their lodge at Richmond, frequented
by some of the pleasantest company of those days.
There were the Herveys, and Chesterfield, and little
Mr. Pope from Twickenham, and with him, sometimes, the savage Dean of Saint Patrick's, and quite a
bevy of young ladies whose pretty faces smile on us
out of history.    There was Lepell, famous in ballad
song ; and the saucy charming Mary Bellenden, who
would have none of the Prince of Wales's fine compliments, who folded her arms across her breast, and
bade H.R.H. keep off; and knocked his purse of
guineas into his face, and told him she was tired of
seeing him count them.    He was not an august
monarch, this Augustus.    Walpole tells how, one
night at the Royal card-table, the playful princesses
pulled a chair away from under Lady Deloraine, who,
in revenge, pulled the King's from under him, so
that His Majesty fell on the carpet.    In whatever
posture one sees this Royal George, he is ludicrous
somehow ; even at Dettingen, where he fought so
bravely, his figure is absurd—calling out in his broken
English, and lunging with his rapier, like a fencing-
master.    In contemporary caricatures, George's son,
'the Hero of Culloden,' is also made an object of
considerable fun.

I refrain to quote from Walpole regarding George
—for those charming volumes are in the hands of all
who love the gossip of the last century.    Nothing
can be more cheery than Horace's letters.    Fiddles
sing all through them : wax-lights, fine dresses, fine
jokes, fine plate, fine equipages, glitter and sparkle
there ; never was such a brilliant, jigging, smirking
Vanity Fair as that through which he leads us.
Hervey, the next great authority, is a darker spirit.

About him there is something frightful : a few years since his heirs opened the lid of the Ickworth box ; it was as if a Pompeii was opened to us—the last century dug up, with its temples and its games, its chariots, its public places—lupanaria. Wandering through that city of the dead, that dreadfully selfish time, through those godless intrigues and feasts, through those crowds, pushing, and eager, and struggling—rouged, and lying, and fawning—I have wanted some one to be friends with. I have said to friends conversant with that history, 'Show me some good person about that Court ; find me, among those selfish courtiers, those dissolute gay people, some one being that I can love and regard.' There is that strutting little sultan George II. ; there is that hunchbacked beetle-browed Lord Chesterfield; there is John Hervey, with his deadly smile, and ghastly painted face—I hate them. There is Hoadly, cringing from one bishopric to another ; yonder comes little Mr. Pope from Twickenham, with his friend the Irish Dean, in his new cassock, bowing, too, but with rage flashing from under his bushy eyebrows, and scorn and hate quivering in his smile. Can you be fond of these ? Of Pope I might : at least I might love his genius, his wit, his greatness, his sensibility— with a certain conviction that at some fancied slight, some sneer which he imagined, he would turn upon me and stab me. Can you trust the Queen ? She is not of our order : their very position makes kings and queens lonely. One inscrutable attachment that inscrutable woman has. To that she is faithful, through all trial, neglect, pain, and time. Save her husband, she really cares for no created being. She is good enough to her children, and even fond enough of them ; but she would chop them all up into little pieces to please him. In her intercourse with all around her she was perfectly kind, gracious, and natural : but friends may die, daughters may depart, she will be as perfectly kind and gracious to the next set. If the King wants her, she will smile upon him, be she ever so sad ; and walk with him, be she ever so weary ; and laugh at his brutal jokes, be she in ever so much pain of body or heart. Caroline's devotion to her husband is a prodigy to read of. What charm had the little man? What was there in those wonderful letters of thirty pages long, which he wrote to her when he was absent, and to his mistresses at Hanover, when he was in London with his wife? Why did Caroline, the most lovely and accomplished princess of Germany, take a little red-faced staring princeling for a husband, and refuse an emperor? Why, to her last hour, did she love him so? She killed herself because she loved him so. She had the gout, and would plunge her feet in cold water in order to walk with him. With the film of death over her eyes, writhing in intolerable pain, she yet had a livid smile and a gentle word for her master. You have read the wonderful history of that death-bed? How she bade him marry again, and the reply the old King blubbered out, 'Non, non : j'aurai des maitresses.' There never was such a ghastly farce. I watch the astonishing scene—I stand by that awful bedside, wondering at the ways in which God has ordained the lives, loves, rewards, successes, passions, actions, ends of His creatures—and can't but laugh, in the presence of death, and with the saddest heart. In that often-quoted passage from Lord Hervey, in which the Queen's death-bed is described, the grotesque horror of the details surpasses all satire : the dreadful humour of the scene is more terrible than Swift's blackest pages or Fielding's fiercest irony. The man who wrote the story had something diabolical about

him : the terrible verses which Pope wrote respecting
Hervey in one of his own moods of almost fiendish
malignity, I fear, are true. I am frightened as I
look back into the past, and fancy I behold that
ghastly beautiful face ; as I think of the Queen
writhing on her death-bed, and crying out, 'Pray !—
pray !'—of the Royal old sinner by her side, who
kisses her dead lips with frantic grief, and leaves her
to sin more ;—of the bevy of courtly clergymen, and
the archbishop, whose prayers she rejects, and who
are obliged for propriety's sake to shuffle off the
anxious inquiries of the public, and vow that Her
Majesty quitted this life 'in a heavenly frame of mind.'
What a life !—to what ends devoted ! What a
vanity of vanities ! It is a theme for another pulpit
than the lecturer's. For a pulpit ?—I think the part
which pulpits play in the deaths of kings is the most
ghastly of all the ceremonial : the lying eulogies, the
blinking of disagreeable truths, the sickening flatteries,
the simulated grief, the falsehood and sycophancies
—all uttered in the name of Heaven in our State
churches : these monstrous threnodies have been sung
from time immemorial over kings and queens, good,
bad, wicked, licentious. The State parson must
bring out his commonplaces ; his apparatus of rhetori-
cal black-hangings. Dead king or live king, the
clergyman must flatter him—announce his piety
whilst living, and when dead perform the obsequies
of 'Our Most Religious and Gracious King.'

I read that Lady Yarmouth (my most religious and
gracious King's favourite) sold a bishopric to a clergyman for £5000. (He betted her £5000 that he
would not be made a bishop, and he lost, and paid
her.) Was he the only prelate of his time led up
by such hands for consecration? As I peep into
George II.'s Saint James's, I see crowds of cassocks

rustling up the back-stairs of the ladies of the Court; stealthy clergy slipping purses into their laps; that godless old King yawning under his canopy in his Chapel Royal, as the chaplain before him is discoursing. Discoursing about what!—about righteousness and judgment? Whilst the chaplain is preaching, the King is chattering in German almost as loud as the preacher; so loud that the clergyman—it may be one Doctor Young, he who wrote 'Night Thoughts,' and discoursed on the splendours of the stars, the glories of Heaven, and utter vanities of this world—actually burst out crying in his pulpit because the Defender of the Faith and dispenser of bishoprics would not listen to him! No wonder that the clergy were corrupt and indifferent amidst this indifference and corruption. No wonder that sceptics multiplied and morals degenerated, so far as they depended on the influence of such a king. No wonder that Whitfield cried out in the wilderness, that Wesley quitted the insulted temple to pray on the hillside. I look with reverence on those men at that time. Which is the sublimer spectacle—the good John Wesley, surrounded by his congregation of miners at the pit's mouth, or the Queen's chaplains mumbling through their morning office in their ante-room, under the picture of the great Venus, with the door opened into the adjoining chamber, where the Queen is dressing, talking scandal to Lord Hervey, or uttering sneers at Lady Suffolk, who is kneeling with the basin at her mistress's side? I say I am scared as I look round at this society—at this King, at these courtiers, at these politicians, at these bishops—at this flaunting vice and levity. Whereabouts in this Court is the honest man? Where is the pure person one may like? The air stifles one with its sickly perfumes. There are some old-world follies and some absurd ceremonials about our Court of the present day, which I laugh at, but as an Englishman, contrasting it with the past, shall I not acknowledge the change of to-day. As the mistress of Saint James's passes me now, I salute the Sovereign, wise, moderate, exemplary of life; the good mother; the good wife; the accomplished lady; the enlightened friend of art; the tender sympathiser in her people's glories and sorrows.

Of all the Court of George and Caroline, I find no one but Lady Suffolk with whom it seems pleasant and kindly to hold converse. Even the misogynist Croker, who edited her letters, loves her, and has that regard for her with which her sweet graciousness seems to have inspired almost all men and some women who came near her. I have noted many little traits which go to prove the charms of her character (it is not merely because she is charming, but because she is characteristic, that I allude to her). She writes delightfully sober letters. Addressing Mr. Gay at Tunbridge (he was, you know, a poet, penniless and in disgrace), she says: 'The place you are in has strangely filled your head with physicians and cures; but, take my word for it, many a fine lady has gone there to drink the waters without being sick; and many a man has complained of the loss of his heart, who had it in his own possession. I desire you will keep yours; for I shall not be very fond of a friend without one, and I have a great mind you should be in the number of mine.'

When Lord Peterborough was seventy years old, that indomitable youth addressed some flaming love, or rather gallantry, letters to Mrs. Howard—curious relics they are of the romantic manner of wooing sometimes in use in those days. It is not passion; it is not love; it is gallantry: a mixture of earnest and acting: high-flown compliments, profound bows, vows, sighs and ogles, in the manner of the Clélie romances, and Millamont and Doricourt in the comedy. There was a vast elaboration of ceremonies and etiquette, of raptures—a regulated form for kneeling and wooing which has quite passed out of our downright manners. Henrietta Howard accepted the noble old Earl's philandering; answered the queer love-letters with due acknowledgment; made a profound curtsey to Peterborough's profound bow; and got John Gay to help her in the composition of her letters in reply to her old knight. He wrote her charming verses, in which there was truth as well as grace. 'O wonderful creature!' he writes :—

'O wonderful creature, a woman of reason !
  Never grave out of pride, never gay out of season !
  When so easy to guess who this angel should be,
  Who would think Mrs. Howard ne'er dreamt it was
    she ?'

The great Mr. Pope also celebrated her in lines not less pleasant, and painted a portrait of what must certainly have been a delightful lady :—

    'I know a thing that's most uncommon—
        Envy, be silent and attend !
    I know a reasonable woman,
        Handsome, yet witty, and a friend :

    Not warp'd by passion, aw'd by rumour,
        Not grave through pride, or gay through folly :
    An equal mixture of good-humour
        And exquisite soft melancholy.

    Has she no faults, then (Envy says), sir ?
        Yes, she has one, I must aver—
    When all the world conspires to praise her,
        The woman's deaf, and does not hear !'

Even the women concurred in praising and loving her. The Duchess of Queensberry bears testimony to her amiable qualities, and writes to her : 'I tell you so and so, because you love children, and to have children love you.' The beautiful jolly Mary Bellenden, represented by contemporaries as ' the most perfect creature ever known,' writes very pleasantly to her ' dear Howard,' her ' dear Swiss,' from the country, whither Mary had retired after her marriage, and when she gave up being a maid of honour. ' How do you do, Mrs. Howard ? ' Mary breaks out. ' How do you do, Mrs. Howard ? that is all I have to say. This afternoon I am taken with a fit of writing ; but as to matter, I have nothing better to entertain you, than news of my farm. I therefore give you the following list of the stock of eatables that I am fatting for my private tooth. It is well known to the whole county of Kent, that I have four fat calves, two fat hogs, fit for killing, twelve promising black pigs, two young chickens, three fine geese, with thirteen eggs under each (several being duck-eggs, else the others do not come to maturity) ; all this, with rabbits, and pigeons, and carp in plenty, beef and mutton at reasonable rates. Now, Howard, if you have a mind to stick a knife into anything I have named, say so !'

A jolly set must they have been, those maids of honour. Pope introduces us to a whole bevy of them, in a pleasant letter. 'I went,' he says, ' by water to Hampton Court, and met the Prince, with all his ladies, on horseback, coming from hunting. Mrs. Bellenden and Mrs. Lepell took me into protection, contrary to the laws against harbouring Papists, and gave me a dinner, with something I liked better, an opportunity of conversation with Mrs. Howard. We all agreed that the life of a maid of honour was of all things the most miserable, and wished that all women who envied it had a specimen of it. To eat West-phalia ham of a morning, ride over hedges and ditches on borrowed hacks, come home in the heat of the day with a fever, and (what is worse a hundred times) with a red mark on the forehead from an uneasy hat—all this may qualify them to make excellent wives for hunters. As soon as they wipe off the heat of the day they must simper an hour and catch cold in the Princess's apartment; from thence to dinner with what appetite they may; and after that till midnight, work, walk, or think which way they please. No lone house in Wales, with a mountain and rookery, is more contemplative than this Court. Miss Lepell walked with me three or four hours by moonlight, and we met no creature of any quality but the King, who gave audience to the Vice-chamberlain all alone under the garden wall.'

I fancy it was a merrier England, that of our ancestors, than the island which we inhabit. People high and low amused themselves very much more. I have calculated the manner in which statesmen and persons of condition passed their time—and what with drinking, and dining, and supping, and cards, wonder how they got through their business at all. They played all sorts of games, which, with the exception of cricket and tennis, have quite gone out of our manners now. In the old prints of Saint James's Park, you will see the marks along the walk, to note the balls when the Court played at Mall. Fancy Birdcage Walk now so laid out, and Lord John and Lord Palmerston knocking balls up and down the avenue! Most of those jolly sports belong to the past, and the good old games of England are only to be found in old novels, in old ballads, or the columns of dingy old newspapers, which say how a main of cocks is to be fought at Winchester between the Winchester men and the Hampton men ; or how the Cornwall men and the Devon men are going to hold a great wrestling-match at Totnes, and so on.

A hundred and twenty years ago there were not only country towns in England, but people who inhabited them. We were very much more gregarious ; we were amused by very simple pleasures. Every town had its fair, every village its wake. The old poets have sung a hundred jolly ditties about great cudgel-playings, famous grinning through horse-collars, great maypole meetings, and morris-dances. The girls used to run races clad in very light attire ; and the kind gentry and good parsons thought no shame in looking on. Dancing bears went about the country with pipe and tabor. Certain well-known tunes were sung all over the land for hundreds of years, and high and low rejoiced in that simple music. Gentlemen who wished to entertain their female friends constantly sent for a band. When Beau Fielding, a mighty fine gentleman, was courting the lady whom he married, he treated her and her companion at his lodgings to a supper from the tavern, and after supper they sent out for a fiddler—three of them. Fancy the three, in a great wainscoted room, in Covent Garden or Soho, lighted by two or three candles in silver sconces, some grapes, and a bottle of Florence wine on the table, and the honest fiddler playing old tunes in quaint old minor keys, as the Beau takes out one lady after the other, and solemnly dances with her !

The very great folks, young noblemen, with their governors, and the like, went abroad and made the great tour ; the home satirists jeered at the Frenchified and Italian ways which they brought back ; but the greater number of people never left the country. The jolly squire often had never been twenty miles

from home. Those who did go went to the baths, to
Harrogate, or Scarborough, or Bath, or Epsom. Old
letters are full of these places of pleasure. Gay writes
to us about the fiddlers at Tunbridge; of the ladies
having merry little private balls amongst themselves;
and the gentlemen entertaining them by turns with
tea and music. One of the young beauties whom he
met did not care for tea.

'We have a young lady here,' he says, 'that is very particular in her desires. I have known some young ladies,
who, if ever they prayed, would ask for some equipage or
title, a husband or matadores: but this lady, who is but
seventeen, and has £30,000 to her fortune, places all her
wishes on a pot of good ale. When her friends, for the
sake of her shape and complexion, would dissuade her from
it, she answers, with the truest sincerity, that by the loss
of shape and complexion she could only lose a husband,
whereas ale is her passion.'

Every country town had its assembly-room —
mouldy old tenements, which we may still see in
deserted inn-yards, in decayed provincial cities, out of
which the great wen of London has sucked all the
life. York, at assize-times, and throughout the
winter, harboured a large society of northern gentry.
Shrewsbury was celebrated for its festivities. At
Newmarket, I read of 'a vast deal of good company,
besides rogues and blacklegs;' at Norwich, of two
assemblies, with a prodigious crowd in the hall, the
rooms, and the gallery. In Cheshire (it is a maid of
honour of Queen Caroline who writes, and who is
longing to be back at Hampton Court, and the fun
there) I peep into a country-house, and see a very
merry party :—

'We meet in the work-room before nine, eat, and break

a joke or two till twelve, then we repair to our own chambers and make ourselves ready, for it cannot be called dressing. At noon the great bell fetches us into a parlour, adorned with all sorts of fine arms, poisoned darts, several pair of old boots and shoes worn by men of might, with the stirrups of King Charles I., taken from him at Edgehill.'

And there they have their dinner, after which comes dancing and supper.

As for Bath, all history went and bathed and drank there. George II. and his Queen, Prince Frederick and his Court, scarce a character one can mention of the early last century but was seen in that famous Pump Room where Beau Nash presided, and his picture hung between the busts of Newton and Pope—

> 'This picture, placed these busts between,
>     Gives satire all its strength :
> Wisdom and Wit are little seen,
>     But Folly at full length.'

I should like to have seen the Folly. It was a splendid, embroidered, beruffled, snuff-boxed, red-heeled, impertinent Folly, and knew how to make itself respected. I should like to have seen that noble old madcap Peterborough in his boots (he actually had the audacity to walk about Bath in boots !), with his blue ribbon and stars, and a cabbage under each arm, and a chicken in his hand, which he had been cheapening for his dinner. Chesterfield came there many a time and gambled for hundreds, and grinned through his gout. Mary Wortley was there, young and beautiful ; and Mary Wortley, old, hideous, and snuffy. Miss Chudleigh came there, slipping away from one husband, and on the look-out for another. Walpole passed many a day there ; sickly, supercilious, absurdly dandified, and affected; with a brilliant wit, a delightful sensibility; and for his friends, a most tender, generous, and faithful heart. And if you and I had been alive then, and strolling down Milsom Street—hush! we should have taken our hats off, as an awful, long, lean, gaunt figure, swathed in flannels passed by in its chair, and a livid face looked out from the window—great fierce eyes staring from under a bushy powdered wig, a terrible frown, a terrible Roman nose—and we whisper to one another, 'There he is! There's the great commoner! There is Mr. Pitt!' As we walk away, the abbey bells are set a-ringing; and we meet our testy friend Toby Smollett, on the arm of James Quin the actor, who tells us that the bells ring for Mr. Bullock, an eminent cow-keeper from Tottenham, who has just arrived to drink the waters; and Toby shakes his cane at the door of Colonel Ringworm—the Creole gentleman's lodgings next his own—where the colonel's two negroes are practising on the French horn.

When we try to recall social England, we must fancy it playing at cards for many hours every day. The custom is well-nigh gone out among us now, but fifty years ago was general, fifty years before that almost universal, in the country. 'Gaming has become so much the fashion,' writes Seymour, the author of the 'Court Gamester,' 'that he who in company should be ignorant of the games in vogue would be reckoned low-bred, and hardly fit for conversation.' There were cards everywhere. It was considered ill-bred to read in company. 'Books were not fit articles for drawing-rooms,' old ladies used to say. People were jealous, as it were, and angry with them. You will find in Hervey that George II. was always furious at the sight of books; and his Queen, who loved reading, had to practise it in secret in her

closet. But cards were the resource of all the world.
Every night for hours, kings and queens of England
sat down and handled their majesties of spades and
diamonds. In European Courts I believe the practice
still remains, not for gambling, but for pastime. Our
ancestors generally adopted it. 'Books! prithee,
don't talk to me about books,' said old Sarah
Marlborough. 'The only books I know are men and
cards.' 'Dear old Sir Roger de Coverley sent all his
tenants a string of hogs' puddings and a pack of cards
at Christmas,' says the *Spectator*, wishing to depict a
kind landlord. One of the good old lady writers in
whose letters I have been dipping cries out, 'Sure,
cards have kept us women from a great deal of
scandal!' Wise old Johnson regretted that he had
not learnt to play. 'It is very useful in life,' he says;
'it generates kindness, and consolidates society.'
David Hume never went to bed without his whist.
We have Walpole, in one of his letters, in a transport
of gratitude for the cards. 'I shall build an altar to
Pam,' says he, in his pleasant dandified way, 'for the
escape of my charming Duchess of Grafton.' The
Duchess had been playing cards at Rome, when she
ought to have been at a cardinal's concert, where the
floor fell in, and all the monsignors were precipitated
into the cellar. Even the Nonconformist clergy
looked not unkindly on the practice. 'I do not
think,' says one of them, 'that honest Martin Luther
committed sin by playing at backgammon for an hour
or two after dinner, in order by unbending his mind
to promote digestion.' As for the High Church
parsons, they all played, bishops and all. On
Twelfth-day the Court used to play in state.

'This being Twelfth-day, His Majesty, the Prince of
Wales, and the Knights Companions of the Garter,

Thistle, and Bath, appeared in the collars of their respective orders. Their Majesties, the Prince of Wales, and three eldest Princesses, went to the Chapel Royal, preceded by the heralds. The Duke of Manchester carried the sword of State. The King and Prince made offering at the altar of gold, frankincense, and myrrh, according to the annual custom. At night their Majesties played at hazard with the nobility, for the benefit of the groom-porter; and 'twas said the King won 600 guineas; the Queen 360; Princess Amelia, 20; Princess Caroline, 10; the Duke of Grafton and the Earl of Portmore, several thousands.'

Let us glance at the same chronicle, which is of the year 1731, and see how others of our forefathers were engaged.

'*Cork, 15th January.*—This day, one Tim Croneen was, for the murder and robbery of Mr. St. Leger and his wife, sentenced to be hanged two minutes, then his head to be cut off, and his body divided into four quarters, to be placed in four crossways. He was servant to Mr. St. Leger, and committed the murder with the privity of the servant maid, who was sentenced to be burned; also of the gardener, whom he knocked on the head, to deprive him of his share of the booty.'

'*January 3rd.*—A postboy was shot by an Irish gentleman on the road near Stone, in Staffordshire, who died in two days, for which the gentleman was imprisoned.'

'A poor man was found hanging in a gentleman's stables at Bungay, in Suffolk, by a person who cut him down, and running for assistance, left his penknife behind him. The poor man recovering, cut his throat with the knife; and a river being nigh, jumped into it; but company coming, he was dragged out alive, and was like to remain so.'

'The Honourable Thomas Finch, brother to the Earl of Nottingham, is appointed Ambassador at the Hague, in the room of the Earl of Chesterfield, who is on his return home.'

'William Cowper, Esq., and the Rev. Mr. John Cowper, chaplain in ordinary to Her Majesty, and rector of Great Berkhampstead, in the county of Hertford, are appointed clerks of the Commissioners of Bankruptcy.'

'Charles Creagh, Esq., and —— Macnamara, Esq., between whom an old grudge of three years had subsisted, which had occasioned their being bound over about fifty times for breaking the peace, meeting in company with Mr. Eyres, of Galloway, they discharged their pistols, and all three were killed on the spot—to the great joy of their peaceful neighbours, say the Irish papers.'

'Wheat is 26s. to 28s., and barley 20s. to 22s. a quarter; three per cents, 92; best loaf sugar, 9¼d.; Bohea, 12s. to 14s.; Pekoe, 18s.; and Hyson, 35s. per pound.

'At Exon was celebrated with great magnificence the birthday of the son of Sir W. Courtney, Bart., at which more than 1000 persons were present. A bullock was roasted whole; a butt of wine and several tuns of beer and cider were given to the populace. At the same time Sir William delivered to his son, then of age, Powdram Castle, and a great estate.'

'Charlesworth and Cox, two solicitors, convicted of forgery, stood on the pillory at the Royal Exchange. The first was severely handled by the populace, but the other was very much favoured, and protected by six or seven fellows who got on the pillory to protect him from the insults of the mob.'

'A boy killed by falling upon iron spikes, from a lamp-post, which he climbed to see Mother Needham stand in the pillory.'

'Mary Lynn was burned to ashes at the stake for being concerned in the murder of her mistress.'

'Alexander Russell, the foot soldier, who was capitally convicted for a street robbery in January sessions, was reprieved for transportation; but having an estate fallen to him, obtained a free pardon.'

'The Lord John Russell married to the Lady Diana Spencer, at Marlborough House. He has a fortune of £30,000 down, and is to have £100,000 at the death of the Duchess Dowager of Marlborough, his grandmother.'

'March 1 being the anniversary of the Queen's birthday, when Her Majesty entered the forty-ninth year of her age, there was a splendid appearance of nobility at St. James's. Her Majesty was magnificently dressed, and wore a flowered muslin head-edging, as did also Her Royal Highness. The Lord Portmore was said to have had the richest dress, though an Italian Count had twenty-four diamonds instead of buttons.'

New clothes on the birthday were the fashion for all loyal people. Swift mentions the custom several times. Walpole is constantly speaking of it; laughing at the practice, but having the very finest clothes from Paris, nevertheless. If the King and Queen were unpopular, there were very few new clothes at the drawing-room. In a paper in the *True Patriot*, No. 3, written to attack the Pretender, the Scotch, French, and Popery, Fielding supposes the Scotch and the Pretender in possession of London, and himself about to be hanged for loyalty,—when, just as the rope is round his neck, he says : 'My little girl entered my bed-chamber, and put an end to my dream by pulling open my eyes, and telling me that the tailor had just brought home my clothes for His Majesty's birthday.' In his 'Temple Beau,' the beau is dunned 'for a birthday suit of velvet, £40.' Be sure that Mr. Harry Fielding was dunned too.

The public days, no doubt, were splendid, but the private Court life must have been awfully wearisome.

'I will not trouble you,' writes Hervey to Lady Sundon, 'with any account of our occupations at

Hampton Court. No mill-horse ever went in a more constant track, or a more unchanging circle; so that, by the assistance of an almanack for the day of the week, and a watch for the hour of the day, you may inform yourself fully, without any other intelligence but your memory, of every transaction within the verge of the Court. Walking, chaises, levées, and audiences fill the morning. At night the King plays at commerce and backgammon, and the Queen at quadrille, where poor Lady Charlotte runs her usual nightly gauntlet, the Queen pulling her hood, and the Princess Royal rapping her knuckles. The Duke of Grafton takes his nightly opiate of lottery, and sleeps as usual between the Princesses Amelia and Caroline. Lord Grantham strolls from one room to another (as Dryden says), like some discontented ghost that oft appears, and is forbid to speak; and stirs himself about as people stir a fire, not with any design, but in hopes to make it burn brisker. At last the King gets up; the pool finishes; and everybody has their dismission. Their Majesties retire to Lady Charlotte and my Lord Lifford; my Lord Grantham, to Lady Frances and Mr. Clark: some to supper, some to bed; and thus the evening and the morning make the day.'

The King's fondness for Hanover occasioned all sorts of rough jokes among his English subjects, to whom *sauerkraut* and sausages have ever been ridiculous objects. When our present Prince Consort came among us, the people bawled out songs in the streets, indicative of the absurdity of Germany in general. The sausage-shops produced enormous sausages which we might suppose were the daily food and delight of German Princes. I remember the caricatures at the marriage of Prince Leopold with the Princess Charlotte. The bridegroom was drawn in rags. George III.'s wife was called by the people a beggarly German duchess; the British idea being that all princes were beggarly except British princes. King George paid us back. He thought there were no manners out of Germany. Sarah Marlborough once coming to visit the Princess, whilst Her Royal Highness was whipping one of the roaring Royal children, 'Ah!' says George, who was standing by, 'you have no good manners in England, because you are not properly brought up when you are young.' He insisted that no English cook could roast, no English coachman could drive : he actually questioned the superiority of our nobility, our horses, and our roast beef !

Whilst he was away from his beloved Hanover, everything remained there exactly as in the Prince's presence. There were eight hundred horses in the stables, there was all the apparatus of chamberlains, Court-marshals, and equerries ; and Court assemblies were held every Saturday, where all the nobility of Hanover assembled at what I can't but think a fine and touching ceremony. A large arm-chair was placed in the assembly room, and on it the King's portrait. The nobility advanced, and made a bow to the arm-chair, and to the image which Nebuchadnezzar the King had set up ; and spoke under their voices before the august picture, just as they would have done had the King Churfürst been present himself.

He was always going back to Hanover. In the year 1729, he went for two whole years, during which Caroline reigned for him in England, and he was not in the least missed by his British subjects. He went again in '35 and '36 ; and between the years 1740 and 1755 was no less than eight times on the Continent, which amusement he was obliged to give up at the outbreak of the Seven Years' War. Here every day's amusement was the same. 'Our life is as uniform as that of a monastery,' writes a courtier whom Vehse quotes. 'Every morning at eleven, and every evening at six, we drive in the heat to Herrenhausen, through an enormous linden avenue; and twice a day cover our coats and coaches with dust. In the King's society there never is the least change. At table, and at cards, he sees always the same faces, and at the end of the game retires into his chamber. Twice a week there is a French theatre; the other days there is play in the gallery. In this way, were the King always to stop in Hanover, one could make a ten years' calendar of his proceedings; and settle beforehand what his time of business, meals, and pleasure would be.'

The old pagan kept his promise to his dying wife. Lady Yarmouth was now in full favour, and treated with profound respect by the Hanover society, though it appears rather neglected in England when she came among us. In 1740, a couple of the King's daughters went to see him at Hanover; Anna, the Princess of Orange (about whom, and whose husband and marriage-day, Walpole and Hervey have left us the most ludicrous descriptions), and Maria of Hesse-Cassel, with their respective lords. This made the Hanover Court very brilliant. In honour of his high guests, the King gave several *fêtes*; among others, a magnificent masked ball, in the green theatre at Herrenhausen—the garden theatre, with linden and box for screen, and grass for a carpet, where the Platens had danced to George and his father the late sultan. The stage and a great part of the garden were illuminated with coloured lamps. Almost the whole Court appeared in white dominoes, 'like,' says the describer of the scene, 'like spirits in the Elysian fields.' At night, supper was served in the gallery with three great tables, and the King was very merry.

After supper dancing was resumed, and I did not get home till five o'clock by full daylight to Hanover. Some days afterwards we had, in the opera-house at Hanover, a great assembly. The King appeared in a Turkish dress; his turban was ornamented with a magnificent *agrafe* of diamonds; the Lady Yarmouth was dressed as a sultana; nobody was more beautiful than the Princess of Hesse.' So, while poor Caroline is resting in her coffin, dapper little George, with his red face and his white eyebrows and goggle-eyes, at sixty years of age, is dancing a pretty dance with Madame Walmoden, and capering about dressed up like a Turk! For twenty years more, that little old Bajazet went on in this Turkish fashion, until the fit came which choked the old man, when he ordered the side of his coffin to be taken out, as well as that of poor Caroline's who had preceded him, so that his sinful old bones and ashes might mingle with those of the faithful creature. O strutting Turkey-cock of Herrenhausen! O naughty little Mahomet! in what Turkish paradise are you now, and where be your painted houris? So Countess Yarmouth appeared as a sultana, and His Majesty in a Turkish dress wore an *agrafe* of diamonds, and was very merry, was he? Friends! he was your fathers' King as well as mine—let us drop a respectful tear over his grave.

He said of his wife that he never knew a woman who was worthy to buckle her shoe: he would sit alone weeping before her portrait, and when he had dried his eyes, he would go off to his Walmoden and talk of her. On the 25th day of October, 1760, he being then in the seventy-seventh year of his age, and the thirty-fourth of his reign, his page went to take him his Royal chocolate, and behold! the Most Religious and Gracious King was lying dead on the floor. They went and fetched Walmoden; but

Walmoden could not wake him. The Sacred
Majesty was but a lifeless corpse. The King was
dead; God save the King! But, of course, poets and
clergymen decorously bewailed the late one. Here
are some artless verses, in which an English divine
deplored the famous departed hero, and over which
you may cry or you may laugh, exactly as your
humour suits :—

'While at his feet expiring Faction lay,
   No contest left but who should best obey ;
 Saw in his offspring all himself renewed ;
 The same fair path of glory still pursued ;
 Saw to young George Augusta's care impart
 Whate'er could raise and humanise the heart ;
 Blend all his grandsire's virtues with his own,
 And form their mingled radiance for the throne—
 No farther blessing could on earth be given—
 The next degree of happiness was—heaven !'

If he had been good, if he had been just, if he had
been pure in life, and wise in council, could the poet
have said much more? It was a parson who came
and wept over this grave, with Walmoden sitting on
it, and claimed heaven for the poor old man slumbering
below. Here was one who had neither dignity,
learning, morals, nor wit—who tainted a great society
by a bad example ; who, in youth, manhood, old age,
was gross, low, and sensual ; and Mr. Porteous, afterwards my Lord Bishop Porteous, says the earth was
not good enough for him, and that his only place was
heaven ! Bravo, Mr. Porteous ! The divine who
wept these tears over George the Second's memory
wore George the Third's lawn. I don't know
whether people still admire his poetry or his sermons.

# GEORGE THE THIRD

We have to glance over sixty years in as many minutes. To read the mere catalogue of characters who figured during that long period would occupy our allotted time, and we should have all text and no sermon. England has to undergo the revolt of the American colonies; to submit to defeat and separation; to shake under the volcano of the French Revolution; to grapple and fight for the life with her gigantic enemy Napoleon; to gasp and rally after that tremendous struggle. The old society, with its courtly splendours, has to pass away; generations of statesmen to rise and disappear; Pitt to follow Chatham to the tomb; the memory of Rodney and Wolfe to be superseded by Nelson's and Wellington's glory; the old poets who unite us to Queen Anne's time to sink into their graves; Johnson to die, and Scott and Byron to arise; Garrick to delight the world with his dazzling dramatic genius, and Kean to leap on the stage and take possession of the astonished theatre. Steam has to be invented; kings to be beheaded, banished, deposed, restored. Napoleon is to be but an episode, and George III. is to be alive through all these varied changes, to accompany his people through all these revolutions of thought, government, society; to survive out of the old world into ours.

When I first saw England, she was in mourning
for the young Princess Charlotte, the hope of the
empire. I came from India as a child, and our ship
touched at an island on the way home, where my
black servant took me a long walk over rocks and hills
until we reached a garden, where we saw a man
walking. 'That is he,' said the black man : 'that is
Bonaparte ! He eats three sheep every day, and all
the little children he can lay hands on !' There
were people in the British dominions besides that poor
Calcutta serving-man, with an equal horror of the
Corsican ogre.

With the same childish attendant, I remember
peeping through the colonnade at Carlton House,
and seeing the abode of the great Prince Regent. I
can see yet the guards pacing before the gates of
the place. The place ! What place ? The palace
exists no more than the palace of Nebuchadnezzar.
It is but a name now. Where be the sentries who
used to salute as the Royal chariots drove in and out ?
The chariots, with the kings inside, have driven to
the realms of Pluto ; the tall Guards have marched
into darkness, and the echoes of their drums are
rolling in Hades. Where the palace once stood, a
hundred little children are paddling up and down the
steps to Saint James's Park. A score of grave gentlemen are taking their tea at the 'Athenæum Club ;'
as many grisly warriors are garrisoning the 'United
Service Club,' opposite. Pall Mall is the great social
Exchange of London now—the mart of news, of
politics, of scandal, of rumour—the English Forum,
so to speak, where men discuss the last despatch from
the Crimea, the last speech of Lord Derby, the next
move of Lord John. And, now and then, to a few
antiquarians whose thoughts are with the past rather
than with the present, it is a memorial of old times

and old people, and Pall Mall is our Palmyra. Look!
About this spot Tom of Ten Thousand was killed
by Königsmarck's gang. In that great red house
Gainsborough lived, and Culloden Cumberland,
George III.'s uncle. Yonder is Sarah Marlborough's
palace, just as it stood when that termagant occupied
it. At 25, Walter Scott used to live; at the house,
now No. 79,* and occupied by the society for the
Propagation of the Gospel in Foreign Parts, resided
Mistress Eleanor Gwynn, comedian. How often has
Queen Caroline's chair issued from under yonder
arch! All the men of the Georges have passed up
and down the street. It has seen Walpole's chariot
and Chatham's sedan; and Fox, Gibbon, Sheridan,
on their way to Brooks's; and stately William Pitt
stalking on the arm of Dundas; and Hanger and Tom
Sheridan reeling out of Raggett's; and Byron limping
into Wattier's; and Swift striding out of Bury Street;
and Mr. Addison and Dick Steele, both perhaps a
little the better for liquor; and the Prince of Wales
and the Duke of York clattering over the pavement;
and Johnson counting the posts along the streets,
after dawdling before Dodsley's window; and Horry
Walpole hobbling into his carriage, with a gimcrack
just bought at Christie's; and George Selwyn
sauntering into White's.

In the published letters to George Selwyn we get a
mass of correspondence by no means so brilliant and
witty as Walpole's, or so bitter and bright as Hervey's,
but as interesting, and even more descriptive of the
time, because the letters are the work of many hands.
You hear more voices speaking, as it were, and more
natural than Horace's dandified treble, and Sporus's
malignant whisper. As one reads the Selwyn letters
—as one looks at Reynolds's noble pictures illustrative

* 1856.

of those magnificent times and voluptuous people—
one almost hears the voice of the dead past; the
laughter and the chorus; the toast called over the
brimming cups; the shout at the race-course or the
gaming-table; the merry joke frankly spoken to the
laughing fine lady. How fine those ladies were, those
ladies who heard and spoke such coarse jokes; how
grand those gentlemen!

I fancy that peculiar product of the past, the fine
gentleman, has almost vanished off the face of the
earth, and is disappearing like the beaver or the Red
Indian. We can't have fine gentlemen any more,
because we can't have the society in which they lived.
The people will not obey: the parasites will not be
as obsequious as formerly: children do not go down
on their knees to beg their parents' blessing: chaplains
do not say grace and retire before the pudding:
servants do not say 'your honour' and 'your worship'
at every moment: tradesmen do not stand hat in
hand as the gentleman passes: authors do not wait
for hours in gentlemen's anterooms with a fulsome
dedication, for which they hope to get five guineas
from his Lordship. In the days when there were
fine gentlemen, Mr. Secretary Pitt's under-secretaries
did not dare to sit down before him; but Mr. Pitt, in
his turn, went down on his gouty knees to George II.;
and when George III. spoke a few kind words to him,
Lord Chatham burst into tears of reverential joy and
gratitude; so awful was the idea of the monarch, and
so great the distinctions of rank. Fancy Lord John
Russell or Lord Palmerston on their knees whilst the
Sovereign was reading a despatch, or beginning to
cry because Prince Albert said something civil!

At the accession of George III., the patricians were
yet at the height of their good fortune. Society
recognised their superiority, which they themselves

pretty calmly took for granted. They inherited not only titles and estates, and seats in the House of Peers, but seats in the House of Commons. There were a multitude of Government places, and not merely these, but bribes of actual £500 notes, which members of the House took not much shame in receiving. Fox went into Parliament at twenty : Pitt when just of age : his father when not much older. It was the good time for patricians. Small blame to them if they took and enjoyed, and over-enjoyed, the prizes of politics, the pleasures of social life.

In these letters to Selwyn, we are made acquainted with a whole society of these defunct fine gentlemen : and can watch with a curious interest a life which the novel-writers of that time, I think, have scarce touched upon. To Smollett, to Fielding even, a lord was a lord : a gorgeous being with a blue ribbon, a coroneted chair, and an immense star on his bosom, to whom commoners paid reverence. Richardson, a man of humbler birth than either of the above two, owned that he was ignorant regarding the manners of the aristocracy, and besought Mrs. Donnellan, a lady who had lived in the great world, to examine a volume of Sir Charles Grandison, and point out any errors which she might see in this particular. Mrs. Donnellan found so many faults, that Richardson changed colour ; shut up the book ; and muttered that it were best to throw it in the fire. Here, in Selwyn, we have the real original men and women of fashion of the early time of George III. We can follow them to the new club at Almack's : we can travel over Europe with them : we can accompany them not only to the public places, but to their country-houses and private society. Here is a whole company of them ; wits and prodigals ; some persevering in their bad ways ; some repentant, but relapsing ; beautiful ladies, parasites, humble chaplains, led captains. Those fair creatures whom we love in Reynolds's portraits, and who still look out on us from his canvases with their sweet calm faces and gracious smiles—those fine gentlemen who did us the honour to govern us ; who inherited their boroughs ; took their ease in their patent places ; and slipped Lord North's bribes so elegantly under their ruffles—we make acquaintance with a hundred of these fine folks, hear their talk and laughter, read of their loves, quarrels, intrigues, debts, duels, divorces ; can fancy them alive if we read the book long enough. We can attend at Duke Hamilton's wedding, and behold him marry his bride with the curtain-ring : we can peep into her poor sister's death-bed : we can see Charles Fox cursing over the cards, or March bawling out the odds at Newmarket : we can imagine Burgoyne tripping off from St. James's Street to conquer the Americans, and slinking back into the club somewhat crestfallen after his beating ; we can see the young King dressing himself for the drawing-room and asking ten thousand questions regarding all the gentlemen : we can have high life or low, the struggle at the Opera to behold the Violetta or the Zamperini—the Macaronis and fine ladies in their chairs trooping to the masquerade or Madame Cornelys's—the crowd at Drury Lane to look at the body of Miss Ray, whom Parson Hackman has just pistolled—or we can peep into Newgate, where poor Mr. Rice the forger is waiting his fate and his supper. 'You need not be particular about the sauce for his fowl,' says one turnkey to another ; 'for you know he is to be hanged in the morning.' 'Yes,' replies the second janitor, 'but the chaplain sups with him, and he is a terrible fellow for melted butter.'

Selwyn has a chaplain and parasite, one Doctor

Warner, than whom Plautus, or Ben Jonson, or
Hogarth, never painted a better character. In letter
after letter he adds fresh strokes to the portrait of
himself, and completes a portrait not a little curious
to look at now that the man has passed away ; all the
foul pleasures and gambols in which he revelled, played
out ; all the rouged faces into which he leered,
worms and skulls ; all the fine gentlemen whose shoe-
buckles he kissed, laid in their coffins. This worthy
clergyman takes care to tell us that he does not
believe in his religion, though, thank Heaven, he is
not so great a rogue as a lawyer. He goes on Mr.
Selwyn's errands, any errands, and is proud, he says, to
be that gentleman's proveditor. He waits upon the
Duke of Queensberry—old Q.—and exchanges pretty
stories with that aristocrat. He comes home 'after a
hard day's christening,' as he says, and writes to his
patron before sitting down to whist and partridges for
supper. He revels in the thoughts of ox-cheek and
burgundy—he is a boisterous, uproarious parasite,
licks his master's shoes with explosions of laughter and
cunning smack and gusto, and likes the taste of that
blacking as much as the best claret in old Q.'s cellar.
He has Rabelais and Horace at his greasy fingers'
ends. He is inexpressibly mean, curiously jolly ; kindly
and good-natured in secret—a tender-hearted knave,
not a venomous lickspittle. Jesse says, that at his
chapel in Long Acre, 'he attained a considerable
popularity by the pleasing, manly, and eloquent style
of his delivery.' Was infidelity endemic, and corruption in the air ? Around a young King, himself
of the most exemplary life and undoubted piety, lived
a Court society as dissolute as our country ever knew.
George II.'s bad morals bore their fruit in George III.'s
early years ; as I believe that a knowledge of that
good man's example, his moderation, his frugal

simplicity, and God-fearing life, tended infinitely to improve the morals of the country and purify the whole nation.

After Warner, the most interesting of Selwyn's correspondents is the Earl of Carlisle, grandfather of the amiable nobleman at present* Viceroy in Ireland. The grandfather, too, was Irish Viceroy, having previously been treasurer of the King's household; and, in 1778, the principal Commissioner for treating, consulting, and agreeing upon the means of quieting the divisions subsisting in His Majesty's colonies, plantations, and possessions in North America. You may read his Lordship's manifestoes in the *Royal New York Gazette*. He returned to England, having by no means quieted the colonies; and speedily afterwards the *Royal New York Gazette* somehow ceased to be published.

This good, clever, kind, highly-bred Lord Carlisle was one of the English fine gentlemen who was well-nigh ruined by the awful debauchery and extravagance which prevailed in the great English society of those days. Its dissoluteness was awful: it had swarmed over Europe after the Peace; it had danced, and raced, and gambled in all the Courts. It had made its bow at Versailles; it had run its horses on the plain of Sablons, near Paris, and created the Anglo-mania there: it had exported vast quantities of pictures and marbles from Rome and Florence: it had ruined itself by building great galleries and palaces for the reception of the statues and pictures: it had brought over singing-women and dancing-women from all the operas of Europe, on whom my Lords lavished their thousands, whilst they left their honest wives and honest children languishing in the lonely deserted splendours of the castle and park at home.

* 1856.

Besides the great London society of those days, there was another unacknowledged world, extravagant beyond measure, tearing about in the pursuit of pleasure; dancing, gambling, drinking, singing; meeting the real society in the public places (at Ranelaghs, Vauxhalls, and Ridottos, about which our old novelists talk so constantly), and outvying the real leaders of fashion in luxury, and splendour, and beauty. For instance, when the famous Miss Gunning visited Paris as Lady Coventry, where she expected that her beauty would meet with the applause which had followed her and her sister through England, it appears she was put to flight by an English lady still more lovely in the eyes of the Parisians. A certain Mrs. Pitt took a box at the opera opposite the Countess; and was so much handsomer than her Ladyship, that the parterre cried out that this was the real English angel, whereupon Lady Coventry quitted Paris in a huff. The poor thing died presently of consumption, accelerated, it was said, by the red and white paint with which she plastered those luckless charms of hers. (We must represent to ourselves all fashionable female Europe, at that time, as plastered with white, and raddled with red.) She left two daughters behind her, whom George Selwyn loved (he was curiously fond of little children), and who are described very drolly and pathetically in these letters, in their little nursery, where passionate little Lady Fanny, if she had not good cards, flung hers into Lady Mary's face; and where they sat conspiring how they should receive a mother-in-law whom their papa presently brought home. They got on very well with their mother-in-law, who was very kind to them; and they grew up, and they were married, and they were both divorced afterwards—poor little souls! Poor painted mother, poor society, ghastly in its pleasures, its loves, its revelries!

As for my Lord Commissioner, we can afford to speak about him; because, though he was a wild and weak Commissioner at one time, though he hurt his estate, though he gambled and lost ten thousand pounds at a sitting—'five times more,' says the unlucky gentleman, 'than I ever lost before;' though he swore he never would touch a card again; and yet, strange to say, went back to the table and lost still more; yet he repented of his errors, sobered down, and became a worthy peer and a good country gentleman, and returned to the good wife and the good children whom he had always loved with the best part of his heart. He had married at one-and-twenty. He found himself, in the midst of a dissolute society, at the head of a great fortune. Forced into luxury, and obliged to be a great lord and a great idler, he yielded to some temptations, and paid for them a bitter penalty of manly remorse; from some others he fled wisely, and ended by conquering them nobly. But he always had the good wife and children in his mind, and they saved him. 'I am very glad you did not come to me the morning I left London,' he writes to G. Selwyn, as he is embarking for America. 'I can only say, I never knew till that moment of parting, what grief was.' There is no parting now, where they are. The faithful wife, the kind generous gentleman, have left a noble race behind them; an inheritor of his name and titles, who is beloved as widely as he is known; a man most kind, accomplished, gentle, friendly, and pure; and female descendants occupying high stations and embellishing great names; some renowned for beauty, and all for spotless lives, and pious matronly virtues.

Another of Selwyn's correspondents is the Earl of

March, afterwards Duke of Queensberry, whose life lasted into this century ; and who certainly as earl or duke, young man or greybeard, was not an ornament to any possible society. The legends about old Q. are awful. In Selwyn, in Wraxall, and contemporary chronicles, the observer of human nature may follow him, drinking, gambling, intriguing to the end of his career ; when the wrinkled, palsied, toothless old Don Juan died, as wicked and unrepentant as he had been at the hottest season of youth and passion. There is a house in Piccadilly, where they used to show a certain low window at which old Q. sat to his very last days, ogling through his senile glasses the women as they passed by.

There must have been a great deal of good about this lazy sleepy George Selwyn, which, no doubt, is set to his present credit. 'Your friendship,' writes Carlisle to him, 'is so different from anything I have ever met with or seen in the world, that when I recollect the extraordinary proofs of your kindness, it seems to me like a dream.' 'I have lost my oldest friend and acquaintance, G. Selwyn,' writes Walpole to Miss Berry : 'I really loved him, not only for his infinite wit, but for a thousand good qualities.' I am glad, for my part, that such a lover of cakes and ale should have had a thousand good qualities—that he should have been friendly, generous, warm-hearted, trustworthy. 'I rise at six,' writes Carlisle to him, from Spa (a great resort of fashionable people in our ancestors' days), 'play at cricket till dinner, and dance in the evening, till I can scarcely crawl to bed at eleven. There is a life for you ! You get up at nine ; play with Raton your dog till twelve, in your dressing-gown ; then creep down to "White's" ; are five hours at table ; sleep till supper-time ; and then make two wretches carry you in a sedan-chair, with three pints of claret in you, three miles for a shilling.' Occasionally, instead of sleeping at 'White's,' George went down and snoozed in the House of Commons by the side of Lord North. He represented Gloucester for many years, and had a borough of his own, Ludgershall, for which, when he was too lazy to contest Gloucester, he sat himself. 'I have given directions for the election of Ludgershall to be of Lord Melbourne and myself,' he writes to the Premier, whose friend he was, and who was himself as sleepy, as witty, and as good-natured as George.

If, in looking at the lives of princes, courtiers, men of rank and fashion, we must perforce depict them as idle, profligate, and criminal, we must make allowances for the rich men's failings, and recollect that we, too, were very likely indolent and voluptuous, had we no motive for work, a mortal's natural taste for pleasure, and the daily temptation of a large income. What could a great peer, with a great castle and park, and a great fortune, do but be splendid and idle? In these letters of Lord Carlisle's from which I have been quoting, there is many a just complaint made by the kind-hearted young nobleman of the state which he is obliged to keep; the magnificence in which he must live; the idleness to which his position as a peer of England bound him. Better for him had he been a lawyer at his desk, or a clerk in his office;—a thousand times better chance for happiness, education, employment, security from temptation. A few years since the profession of arms was the only one which our nobles could follow. The Church, the Bar, medicine, literature, the arts, commerce, were below them. It is to the middle class we must look for the safety of England : the working educated men, away from Lord North's bribery in the senate ; the good clergy not corrupted into parasites by hopes of preferment ; the tradesmen rising into manly opulence ; the painters pursuing their gentle calling ; the men of letters in their quiet studies : these are the men whom we love and like to read of in the last age. How small the grandees and the men of pleasure look beside them ! how contemptible the stories of the George III. Court squabbles are beside the recorded talk of dear old Johnson ! What is the grandest entertainment at Windsor, compared to a night at the club over its modest cups, with Percy and Langton, and Goldsmith and poor Bozzy at the table ! I declare I think, of all the polite men of that age, Joshua Reynolds was the finest gentleman. And they were good, as well as witty and wise, those dear old friends of the past. Their minds were not debauched by excess, or effeminate with luxury. They toiled their noble day's labour : they rested, and took their kindly pleasure : they cheered their holiday meetings with generous wit and hearty interchange of thought : they were no prudes, but no blush need follow their conversation : they were merry, but no riot came out of their cups. Ah ! I would have liked a night at the 'Turk's Head,' even though bad news had arrived from the colonies, and Doctor Johnson was growling against the rebels ; to have sat with him and Goldy ; and to have heard Burke, the finest talker in the world ; and to have had Garrick flashing in with a story from his theatre !—I like, I say, to think of that society ; and not merely how pleasant and how wise, but how *good* they were. I think it was on going home one night from the club that Edmund Burke— his noble soul full of great thoughts, be sure, for they never left him ; his heart full of gentleness—was accosted by a poor wandering woman, to whom he spoke words of kindness ; and moved by the tears of this Magdalen, perhaps having caused them by the

good words he spoke to her, he took her home to the
house of his wife and children, and never left her
until he had found the means of restoring her to
honesty and labour.  O you fine gentlemen! you
Marches, and Selwyns, and Chesterfields, how small
you look by the side of these great men!  Good-
natured Carlisle plays at cricket all day, and dances in
the evening 'till he can scarcely crawl,' gaily
contrasting his superior virtue with George Selwyn's,
' carried to bed by two wretches at midnight with
three pints of claret in him.'   Do you remember the
verses—the sacred verses—which Johnson wrote on
the death of his humble friend Levett?

> ' Well tried through many a varying year,
>     See Levett to the grave descend ;
> Officious, innocent, sincere,
>     Of every friendless name the friend.
>
> In misery's darkest cavern known,
>     His useful care was ever nigh,
> Where hopeless anguish poured the groan,
>     And lonely want retired to die.
>
> No summons mocked by chill delay,
>     No petty gain disdained by pride,
> The modest wants of every day
>     The toil of every day supplied.
>
> His virtues walked their narrow round,
>     Nor made a pause, nor left a void ;
> And sure the Eternal Master found
>     His single talent well employed.'

Whose name looks the brightest now, that of Queensberry the wealthy duke, or Selwyn the wit, or Levett
the poor physician ?
  I hold old Johnson (and shall we not pardon James

Boswell some errors for embalming him for us?) to be
the great supporter of the British monarchy and
Church during the last age—better than whole benches
of bishops, better than Pitts, Norths, and the great
Burke himself. Johnson had the ear of the nation:
his immense authority reconciled it to loyalty, and
shamed it out of irreligion. When George III. talked
with him, and the people heard the great author's good
opinion of the Sovereign, whole generations rallied to
the King. Johnson was revered as a sort of oracle;
and the oracle declared for Church and King. What
a humanity the old man had! He was a kindly
partaker of all honest pleasures: a fierce foe to all sin,
but a gentle enemy to all sinners. 'What, boys, are
you for a frolic?' he cries, when Topham Beauclerc
comes and wakes him up at midnight: 'I'm with you.'
And away he goes, tumbles on his homely old clothes,
and trundles through Covent Garden with the young
fellows. When he used to frequent Garrick's theatre,
and had 'the liberty of the scenes,' he says, 'All the
actresses knew me, and dropped me a curtsey as they
passed to the stage.' That would make a pretty
picture: it is a pretty picture, in my mind, of youth,
folly, gaiety, tenderly surveyed by wisdom's merciful
pure eyes.

George III. and his Queen lived in a very unpretending but elegant-looking house, on the site of the
hideous pile under which his granddaughter at present
reposes. The King's mother inhabited Carlton House,
which contemporary prints represent with a perfect
paradise of a garden, with trim lawns, green arcades,
and vistas of classic statues. She admired these in
company with my Lord Bute, who had a fine classic
taste, and sometimes counsel took and sometimes tea
in the pleasant green arbours along with that polite
nobleman. Bute was hated with a rage of which there

have been few examples in English history. He was the butt for everybody's abuse; for Wilkes's devilish mischief; for Churchill's slashing satire; for the hooting of the mob that roasted the boot, his emblem, in a thousand bonfires; that hated him because he was a favourite and a Scotchman, calling him 'Mortimer,' 'Lothario,' I know not what names, and accusing his Royal mistress of all sorts of crimes—the grave, lean, demure elderly woman, who, I dare say, was quite as good as her neighbours. Chatham lent the aid of his great malice to influence the popular sentiment against her. He assailed, in the House of Lords, 'the secret influence, more mighty than the throne itself, which betrayed and clogged every administration.' The most furious pamphlets echoed the cry. 'Impeach the King's mother,' was scribbled over every wall at the Court end of the town, Walpole tell us. What had she done? What had Frederick, Prince of Wales, George's father, done, that he was so loathed by George II. and never mentioned by George III.? Let us not seek for stones to batter that forgotten grave, but acquiesce in the contemporary epitaph over him :—

> 'Here lies Fred,
> Who was alive, and is dead.
> Had it been his father,
> I had much rather.
> Had it been his brother,
> Still better than another.
> Had it been his sister,
> No one would have missed her.
> Had it been the whole generation,
> Still better for the nation.
> But since 'tis only Fred,
> Who was alive, and is dead,
> There's no more to be said.'

The widow with eight children round her prudently
reconciled herself with the King, and won the old
man's confidence and good-will.  A shrewd, hard,
domineering, narrow-minded woman, she educated
her children according to her lights, and spoke of the
eldest as a dull good boy : she kept him very close :
she held the tightest rein over him : she had curious
prejudices and bigotries.   His uncle, the burly Cumberland, taking down a sabre once, and drawing it to amuse
the child—the boy started back and turned pale.  The
Prince felt a generous shock : 'What must they
have told him about me ?' he asked.

His mother's bigotry and hatred he inherited with
the courageous obstinacy of his own race ; but he was
a firm believer where his fathers had been freethinkers,
and a true and fond supporter of the Church, of which
he was the titular defender.  Like other dull men, the
King was all his life suspicious of superior people.
He did not like Fox ; he did not like Reynolds ; he
did not like Nelson, Chatham, Burke ; he was testy
at the idea of all innovations, and suspicious of all
innovators.  He loved mediocrities ; Benjamin West
was his favourite painter ; Beattie was his poet.  The
King lamented, not without pathos, in his after life,
that his education had been neglected.  He was a dull
lad brought up by narrow-minded people.  The
cleverest tutors in the world could have done little
probably to expand that small intellect, though they
might have improved his taste, and taught his percep-
tions some generosity.

But he admired as well as he could.  There is little
doubt that a letter, written by the little Princess
Charlotte of Mecklenburg-Strelitz,—a letter containing the most feeble commonplaces about the horrors
of war, and the most trivial remarks on the blessings
of peace—struck the young monarch greatly, and

decided him upon selecting the young princess as the
sharer of his throne.  I pass over the stories of his
juvenile loves—of Hannah Lightfoot, the Quakeress,
to whom they say he was actually married (though I
don't know who has ever seen the register)—of lovely
black-haired Sarah Lennox, about whose beauty
Walpole has written in raptures, and who used to lie
in wait for the young Prince, and make hay at him on
the lawn of Holland House.  He sighed and he longed,
but he rode away from her.  Her picture still hangs
in Holland House, a magnificent masterpiece of
Reynolds, a canvas worthy of Titian.  She looks from
the castle window, holding a bird in her hand, at
black-eyed young Charles Fox, her nephew.  The
Royal bird flew away from lovely Sarah.  She had to
figure as bridesmaid at her little Mecklenburg rival's
wedding, and died in our own time a quiet old lady,
who had become the mother of the heroic Napiers.
    They say the little Princess who had written the
fine letter about the horrors of war —a beautiful
letter without a single blot, for which she was to be
rewarded, like the heroine of the old spelling-book
story—was at play one day with some of her young
companions in the gardens of Strelitz, and that the
young ladies' conversation was, strange to say, about
husbands.  'Who will take such a poor little princess
as me?'  Charlotte said to her friend, Ida von Bulow,
and at that very moment the postman's horn sounded,
and Ida said, 'Princess! there is the sweetheart.'  As
she said, so it actually turned out.  The postman
brought letters from the splendid young King of all
England, who said, 'Princess! because you have
written such a beautiful letter, which does credit to
your head and heart, come and be Queen of Great
Britain, France, and Ireland, and the true wife of your
most obedient servant, George!'  So she jumped for

joy ; and went upstairs and packed all her little trunks ; and set off straightway for her kingdom in a beautiful yacht, with a harpsichord on board for her to play upon, and around her a beautiful fleet, all covered with flags and streamers : and the distinguished Madame Auerbach complimented her with an ode, a translation of which may be read in the *Gentleman's Magazine* to the present day :—

> 'Her gallant navy through the main
>   Now cleaves its liquid way.
> There to their queen a chosen train
>   Of nymphs due reverence pay.
>
> Europa, when conveyed by Jove
>   To Crete's distinguished shore,
> Greater attention scarce could prove,
>   Or be respected more.'

They met, and they were married, and for years they led the happiest simplest lives sure ever led by married couple. It is said the King winced when he first saw his homely little bride ; but, however that may be, he was a true and faithful husband to her, as she was a faithful and loving wife. They had the simplest pleasures—the very mildest and simplest— little country dances, to which a dozen couples were invited, and where the honest King would stand up and dance for three hours at a time to one tune ; after which delicious excitement they would go to bed without any supper (the Court people grumbling sadly at that absence of supper), and get up quite early the next morning, and perhaps the next night have another dance ; or the Queen would play on the spinet—she played pretty well, Haydn said—or the King would read to her a paper out of the *Spectator*, or perhaps one of Ogden's sermons. O Arcadia !

what a life it must have been! There used to be
Sunday drawing-rooms at Court; but the young King
stopped these, as he stopped all that godless gambling
whereof we have made mention. Not that George
was averse to any innocent pleasures, or pleasures
which he thought innocent. He was a patron of the
arts, after his fashion; kind and gracious to the artists
whom he favoured, and respectful to their calling. He
wanted once to establish an Order of Minerva for
literary and scientific characters; the knights were to
take rank after the Knights of the Bath, and to sport
a straw-coloured ribbon and a star of sixteen points.
But there was such a row among the *literati* as to the
persons who should be appointed, that the plan was
given up, and Minerva and her star never came down
amongst us.

He objected to painting St. Paul's, as Popish
practice; accordingly, the most clumsy heathen
sculptures decorate that edifice at present. It is
fortunate that the paintings, too, were spared, for
painting and drawing were woefully unsound at the
close of the last century; and it is far better for our
eyes to contemplate whitewash (when we turn them
away from the clergyman) than to look at Opie's
pitchy canvases, or Fuseli's livid monsters.

And yet there is one day in the year—a day when
old George loved with all his heart to attend it—when
I think St. Paul's presents the noblest sight in the
whole world: when five thousand charity children
with cheeks like nosegays, and sweet fresh voices, sing
the hymn which makes every heart thrill with praise
and happiness. I have seen a hundred grand sights in
the world—coronations, Parisian splendours, Crystal
Palace openings, Pope's chapels with their processions
of long-tailed cardinals and quavering choirs of fat
soprani—but think in all Christendom there is no such

sight as Charity Children's Day. *Non Angli, sed angeli.* As one looks at that beautiful multitude of innocents : as the first note strikes : indeed one may almost fancy that cherubs are singing.

Of Church music the King was always very fond, showing skill in it both as a critic and as a performer. Many stories, mirthful and affecting, are told of his behaviour at the concerts which he ordered. When he was blind and ill he chose the music for the Ancient Concerts once, and the music and words which he selected were from 'Samson Agonistes,' and all had reference to his blindness, his captivity, and his affliction. He would beat time with his music-roll as they sang the anthem in the Chapel Royal. If the page below was talkative or inattentive, down would come the music-roll on young scapegrace's powdered head. The theatre was always his delight. His bishops and clergy used to attend it, thinking it no shame to appear where that good man was seen. He is said not to have cared for Shakespeare or tragedy much ; farces and pantomimes were his joy ; and especially when clown swallowed a carrot or a string of sausages, he would laugh so outrageously that the lovely Princess by his side would have to say, 'My gracious monarch, do compose yourself.' But he continued to laugh, and at the very smallest farces, as long as his poor wits were left him.

There is something to me exceedingly touching in that simple early life of the King's. As long as his mother lived—a dozen years after his marriage with the little spinet-player—he was a great shy awkward boy under the tutelage of that hard parent. She must have been a clever, domineering, cruel woman. She kept her household lonely and in gloom, mistrusting almost all people who came about her children. Seeing the young Duke of Gloucester silent and unhappy once, she sharply asked him the cause of his silence. 'I am thinking,' said the poor child. 'Thinking, sir! and of what?' 'I am thinking if ever I have a son I will not make him so unhappy as you make me.' The other sons were all wild, except George. Dutifully every evening George and Charlotte paid their visit to the King's mother at Carlton House. She had a throat-complaint, of which she died; but to the last persisted in driving about the streets to show she was alive. The night before her death the resolute woman talked with her son and daughter-in-law as usual, went to bed, and was found dead there in the morning. 'George, be a king!' were the words which she was for ever croaking in the ears of her son: and a king the simple, stubborn, affectionate, bigoted man tried to be.

He did his best; he worked according to his lights; what virtue he knew, he tried to practise; what knowledge he could master, he strove to acquire. He was for ever drawing maps, for example, and learned geography with no small care and industry. He knew all about the family histories and genealogies of his gentry, and pretty histories he must have known. He knew the whole *Army List*; and all the facings, and the exact number of the buttons, and all the tags and laces, and the cut of all the cocked-hats, pigtails, and gaiters in his army. He knew the *personnel* of the Universities; what doctors were inclined to Socinianism, and who were sound Churchmen; he knew the etiquettes of his own and his grandfather's Courts to a nicety, and the smallest particulars regarding the routine of ministers, secretaries, embassies, audiences; the humblest page in the anteroom, or the meanest helper in the stables or kitchen. These parts of the Royal business he was capable of learning, and he learned. But, as one thinks of an office, almost divine, performed by any mortal man—of any single being pretending to control the thoughts, to direct the faith, to order the implicit obedience of brother millions, to compel them into war at his offence or quarrel; to command, 'in this way you shall trade, in this way you shall think; these neighbours shall be your allies whom you shall help, these others your enemies whom you shall slay at my orders; in this way you shall worship God;'—who can wonder that, when such a man as George took such an office on himself, punishment and humiliation should fall upon people and chief?

Yet there is something grand about his courage. The battle of the King with his aristocracy remains yet to be told by the historian who shall view the reign of George more justly than the trumpery panegyrists who wrote immediately after his decease. It was he, with the people to back him, who made the war with America; it was he and the people who refused justice to the Roman Catholics; and on both questions he beat the patricians. He bribed: he bullied: he darkly dissembled on occasion: he exercised a slippery perseverance, and a vindictive resolution, which one almost admires as one thinks his character over. His courage was never to be beat. It trampled North under foot: it bent the stiff neck of the younger Pitt: even his illness never conquered that indomitable spirit. As soon as his brain was clear, it resumed the scheme, only laid aside when his reason left him: as soon as his hands were out of the strait-waistcoat, they took up the pen and the plan which had engaged him up to the moment of his malady. I believe it is by persons believing themselves in the right that nine-tenths of the tyranny of this world has been perpetrated. Arguing on that convenient premiss, the Dey of Algiers would cut off twenty heads of a morning; Father Dominic would burn a score of Jews in the presence of the Most Catholic King, and the Archbishops of Toledo and Salamanca sing Amen. Protestants were roasted, Jesuits hung and quartered at Smithfield, and witches burned at Salem, and all by worthy people, who believed they had the best authority for their actions.

And so, with respect to old George, even Americans, whom he hated and who conquered him, may give him credit for having quite honest reasons for oppressing them. Appended to Lord Brougham's biographical sketch of Lord North are some autograph notes of the King, which let us most curiously into the state of his mind. 'The times certainly require,' says he, 'the concurrence of all who wish to prevent anarchy. I have no wish but the prosperity of my own dominions, therefore I must look upon all who would not heartily assist me as bad men, as well as bad subjects.' That is the way he reasoned. 'I wish nothing but good, therefore every man who does not agree with me is a traitor and a scoundrel.' Remember that he believed himself anointed by a Divine commission; remember that he was a man of slow parts and imperfect education; that the same awful will of Heaven which placed a crown upon his head, which made him tender to his family, pure in his life, courageous and honest, made him dull of comprehension, obstinate of will, and at many times deprived him of reason. He was the father of his people; his rebellious children must be flogged into obedience. He was the defender of the Protestant faith; he would rather lay that stout head upon the block than that Catholics should have a share in the government of England. And you do not suppose that there are not honest bigots enough in all countries to back kings in this kind of statesmanship? Without doubt the American war was popular in England. In 1775 the address in favour of coercing the colonies was carried by 304 to 105 in the Commons, by 104 to 29 in the House of Lords. Popular?—so was the Revocation of the Edict of Nantes popular in France: so was the Massacre of Saint Bartholomew: so was the Inquisition exceedingly popular in Spain.

Wars and revolutions are, however, the politician's province. The great events of this long reign, the statesmen and orators who illustrated it, I do not pretend to make the subjects of an hour's light talk. Let us return to our humbler duty of Court gossip. Yonder sits our little Queen, surrounded by many stout sons and fair daughters whom she bore to her faithful George. The history of the daughters, as little Miss Burney has painted them to us, is delightful. They were handsome—she calls them beautiful; they were most kind, loving, and ladylike; they were gracious to every person, high and low, who served them. They had many little accomplishments of their own. This one drew: that one played the piano: they all worked most prodigiously, and fitted up whole suites of rooms—pretty smiling Penelopes—with their busy little needles. As we picture to ourselves the society of eighty years ago, we must imagine hundreds of thousands of groups of women in great high caps, tight bodies and full skirts, needling away, whilst one of the number, or perhaps a favoured gentleman in a pigtail, reads out a novel to the company. Peep into the cottage at Olney, for example, and see there Mrs. Unwin and Lady Hesketh, those high-bred ladies, those sweet pious women, and William Cowper, that delicate wit, that trembling pietist, that refined gentleman, absolutely reading out

'Jonathan Wild' to the ladies! What a change in our manners, in our amusements, since then!

King George's household was a model of an English gentleman's household. It was early; it was kindly; it was charitable; it was frugal; it was orderly; it must have been stupid to a degree which I shudder now to contemplate. No wonder all the Princes ran away from the lap of that dreary domestic virtue. It always rose, rode, dined at stated intervals. Day after day was the same. At the same hour at night the King kissed his daughters' jolly cheeks; the Princesses kissed their mother's hand; and Madame Thielke brought the Royal night-cap. At the same hour the equerries and women in waiting had their little dinner, and cackled over their tea. The King had his back-gammon or his evening concert; the equerries yawned themselves to death in the anteroom; or the King and his family walked on Windsor slopes, the King holding his darling little Princess Amelia by the hand; and the people crowded round quite good-naturedly; and the Eton boys thrust their chubby cheeks under the crowd's elbows; and the concert over, the King never failed to take his enormous cocked-hat off, and salute his band, and say, 'Thank you, gentlemen.'

A quieter household, a more prosaic life than this of Kew or Windsor, cannot be imagined. Rain or shine, the King rode every day for hours; poked his red face into hundreds of cottages round about, and showed that shovel hat and Windsor uniform to farmers, to pig-boys, to old women making apple-dumplings; to all sorts of people, gentle and simple, about whom countless stories are told. Nothing can be more un-dignified than these stories. When Haroun Alraschid visits a subject incog., the latter is sure to be very much the better for the caliph's magnificence. Old George showed no such Royal splendour. He used to give a guinea sometimes : sometimes feel in his pockets and find he had no money : often ask a man a hundred questions : about the number of his family, about his oats and beans, about the rent he paid for his house, and ride on. On one occasion he played the part of King Alfred, and turned a piece of meat with a string at a cottager's house. When the old woman came home, she found a paper with an enclosure of money, and a note written by the Royal pencil : 'Five guineas to buy a jack.' It was not splendid, but it was kind and worthy of Farmer George. One day, when the King and Queen were walking together, they met a little boy—they were always fond of children, the good folk—and patted the little white head. 'Whose little boy are you ?' asks the Windsor uniform. 'I am the King's beefeater's little boy,' replied the child. On which the King said, 'Then kneel down, and kiss the Queen's hand.' But the innocent offspring of the beefeater declined this treat. 'No,' said he, 'I won't kneel, for if I do, I shall spoil my new breeches.' The thrifty King ought to have hugged him and knighted him on the spot. George's admirers wrote pages and pages of such stories about him. One morning, before anybody else was up, the King walked about Gloucester town ; pushed over Molly the housemaid with her pail, who was scrubbing the doorsteps ; ran upstairs and woke all the equerries in their bedrooms ; and then trotted down to the bridge, where, by this time, a dozen of louts were assembled. 'What ! is this Gloucester New Bridge ?' asked our gracious monarch ; and the people answered him, 'Yes, your Majesty.' 'Why, then, my boys,' said he, 'let us have a huzzay !' After giving them which intellectual gratification, he went home to breakfast. Our fathers read these simple tales with fond pleasure ; laughed at these very small jokes ; liked the old man

who poked his nose into every cottage; who lived on
plain wholesome roast and boiled; who despised your
French kickshaws; who was a true hearty old English
gentleman. You may have seen Gilray's famous
print of him—in the old wig, in the stout old hideous
Windsor uniform—as the King of Brobdingnag,
peering at a little Gulliver, whom he holds up in his
hand, whilst in the other he has an opera-glass,
through which he surveys the pigmy? Our fathers
chose to set up George as the type of a great king;
and the little Gulliver was the great Napoleon. We
prided ourselves on our prejudices; we blustered and
bragged with absurd vainglory; we dealt to our enemy
a monstrous injustice of contempt and scorn; we
fought him with all weapons, mean as well as heroic.
There was no lie we would not believe; no charge of
crime which our furious prejudice would not credit.
I thought at one time of making a collection of the
lies which the French had written against us, and we
had published against them during the war: it would
be a strange memorial of popular falsehood.

Their Majesties were very sociable potentates: and
the Court Chronicler tells of numerous visits which
they paid to their subjects, gentle and simple: with
whom they dined; at whose great country-houses
they stopped; or at whose poorer lodgings they affably
partook of tea and bread-and-butter. Some of the
great folk spent enormous sums in entertaining their
sovereigns. As marks of special favour, the King and
Queen sometimes stood as sponsors for the children of
the nobility. We find Lady Salisbury was so honoured
in the year 1786; and in the year 1802, Lady Chesterfield. The *Court News* relates how her Ladyship
received their Majesties on a state bed 'dressed with
white satin and a profusion of lace: the counterpane
of white satin embroidered with gold, and the bed of

crimson satin lined with white.' The child was first
brought by the nurse to the Marchioness of Bath,
who presided as chief nurse. Then the Marchioness
handed baby to the Queen. Then the Queen handed
the little darling to the Bishop of Norwich, the
officiating clergyman ; and, the ceremony over, a cup
of caudle was presented by the Earl to His Majesty on
one knee, on a large gold waiter, placed on a crimson
velvet cushion. Misfortunes would occur in these
interesting genuflectory ceremonies of Royal worship.
Bubb Doddington, Lord Melcombe, a very fat, puffy
man, in a most gorgeous Court-suit, had to kneel,
Cumberland says, and was so fat and so tight that he
could not get up again. 'Kneel, sir, kneel !' cried my
Lord-in-waiting to a country mayor who had to read
an address, but who went on with his compliment
standing. 'Kneel, sir, kneel !' cries my Lord, in
dreadful alarm. 'I can't !' says the Mayor, turning
round ; 'don't you see I have got a wooden leg ?'
In the capital 'Burney Diary and Letters,' the home
and Court life of good old King George and good old
Queen Charlotte are presented at portentous length.
The King rose every morning at six : and had two
hours to himself. He thought it effeminate to have a
carpet in his bedroom. Shortly before eight, the
Queen and the Royal family were always ready for
him, and they proceeded to the King's chapel in the
castle. There were no fires in the passages : the
chapel was scarcely alight ; princesses, governesses,
equerries grumbled and caught cold : but cold or hot,
it was their duty to go : and, wet or dry, light or
dark, the stout old George was always in his place to
say amen to the chaplain.

The Queen's character is represented in 'Burney'
at full length. She was a sensible, most decorous
woman ; a very grand lady on State occasions, simple

enough in ordinary life; well read as times went, and giving shrewd opinions about books; stingy, but not unjust; not generally unkind to her dependants, but invincible in her notions of etiquette, and quite angry if her people suffered ill-health in her service. She gave Miss Burney a shabby pittance, and led the poor young woman a life which well-nigh killed her. She never thought but that she was doing Burney the greatest favour, in taking her from freedom, fame, and competence, and killing her off with languor in that dreary Court. It was not dreary to her. Had she been servant instead of mistress, her spirit would never have broken down: she never would have put a pin out of place, or been a moment from her duty. *She* was not weak, and she could not pardon those who were. She was perfectly correct in life, and she hated poor sinners with a rancour such as virtue sometimes has. She must have had awful private trials of her own: not merely with her children, but with her husband, in those long days about which nobody will ever know anything now; when he was not quite insane; when his incessant tongue was babbling folly, rage, persecution; and she had to smile and be respectful and attentive under this intolerable ennui. The Queen bore all her duties stoutly, as she expected others to bear them. At a State christening, the lady who held the infant was tired and looked unwell, and the Princess of Wales asked permission for her to sit down. 'Let her stand,' said the Queen, flicking the snuff off her sleeve. *She* would have stood, the resolute old woman, if she had had to hold the child till his beard was grown. 'I am seventy years of age,' the Queen said, facing a mob of ruffians who stopped her sedan: 'I have been fifty years Queen of England, and I never was insulted before.' Fearless, rigid, unforgiving little Queen! I don't wonder that her sons revolted from her.

Of all the figures in that large family group which surrounds George and his Queen, the prettiest, I think, is the father's darling, the Princess Amelia, pathetic for her beauty, her sweetness, her early death, and for the extreme passionate tenderness with which her father loved her. This was his favourite amongst all the children: of his sons, he loved the Duke of York best. Burney tells a sad story of the poor old man at Weymouth, and how eager he was to have this darling son with him. The King's house was not big enough to hold the Prince; and his father had a portable house erected close to his own, and at huge pains, so that his dear Frederick should be near him. He clung on his arm all the time of his visit: talked to no one else; had talked of no one else for some time before. The Prince, so long expected, stayed but a single night. He had business in London the next day, he said. The dulness of the old King's Court stupefied York and the other big sons of George III. They scared equerries and ladies, frightened the modest little circle, with their coarse spirits and loud talk. Of little comfort, indeed, were the King's sons to the King.

But the pretty Amelia was his darling; and the little maiden, prattling and smiling in the fond arms of that old father, is a sweet image to look on. There is a family picture in 'Burney,' which a man must be very hard-hearted not to like. She describes an after-dinner walk of the Royal family at Windsor.

'It was really a mighty pretty procession,' she says. 'The little Princess, just turned of three years old, in a robe-coat covered with fine muslin, a dressed close cap, white gloves, and fan, walked on alone and first,

highly delighted with the parade, and turning from side
to side to see everybody as she passed ; for all the terracers
stand up against the walls, to make a clear passage for
the Royal family the moment they come in sight.   Then
followed the King and Queen, no less delighted with
the joy of their little darling.   The Princess Royal
leaning on Lady Elizabeth Waldegrave, the Princess
Augusta holding by the Duchess of Ancaster, the Princess
Elizabeth led by Lady Charlotte Bertie, followed.'

'Office here takes place of rank,' says Burney,—
to explain how it was that Lady Elizabeth Waldegrave, as lady of the bedchamber, walked before a
duchess.

'General Bude, and the Duke of Montague, and Major
Price as equerry, brought up the rear of the procession.'

One sees it : the band playing its old music, the
sun shining on the happy loyal crowd, and lighting
the ancient battlements, the rich elms, and purple
landscape, and bright greensward ; the Royal standard
drooping from the great tower yonder ; as old George
passes, followed by his race, preceded by the charming
infant, who caresses the crowd with her innocent
smiles.

'On sight of Mrs. Delany, the King instantly stopped
to speak to her ; the Queen, of course, and the little
Princess, and all the rest, stood still.   They talked a
good while with the sweet old lady, during which time
the King once or twice addressed himself to me.   I
caught the Queen's eye, and saw in it a little surprise,
but by no means any displeasure, to see me of the party.
The little Princess went up to Mrs. Delany, of whom
she is very fond, and behaved like a little angel to her.
She then, with a look of inquiry and recollection, came
behind Mrs. Delany to look at me.   "I am afraid," said

I, in a whisper, and stooping down, "your Royal Highness does not remember me?" Her answer was an arch little smile, and a nearer approach, with her lips pouted out to kiss me.'

The Princess wrote verses herself, and there are some pretty plaintive lines attributed to her, which are more touching than better poetry :—

> 'Unthinking, idle, wild, and young,
> I laughed, and danced, and talked, and sung:
> And, proud of health, of freedom vain,
> Dreamed not of sorrow, care, or pain;
> Concluding, in those hours of glee,
> That all the world was made for me.
>
> But when the hour of trial came,
> When sickness shook this trembling frame,
> When folly's gay pursuits were o'er,
> And I could sing and dance no more,
> It then occurred, how sad 'twould be,
> Were this world only made for me.'

The poor soul quitted it—and ere yet she was dead the agonised father was in such a state, that the officers round about him were obliged to set watchers over him, and from November 1810 George III. ceased to reign. All the world knows the story of his malady: all history presents no sadder figure than that of the old man, blind and deprived of reason, wandering through the rooms of his palace, addressing imaginary parliaments, reviewing fancied troops, holding ghostly Courts. I have seen his picture as it was taken at this time, hanging in the apartment of his daughter, the Landgravine of Hesse Hombourg —amidst books and Windsor furniture, and a hundred

fond reminiscences of her English home.  The poor
old father is represented in a purple gown, his snowy
beard falling over his breast—the star of his famous
Order still idly shining on it.  He was not only
sightless : he became utterly deaf.  All light, all
reason, all sound of human voices, all the pleasures
of this world of God, were taken from him.  Some
slight lucid moments he had ; in one of which the
Queen, desiring to see him, entered the room, and
found him singing a hymn, and accompanying himself at the harpsichord.  When he had finished he
knelt down and prayed aloud for her, and then for
his family, and then for the nation, concluding with
a prayer for himself, that it might please God to avert
his heavy calamity from him, but if not, to give him
resignation to submit.    He then burst into tears,
and his reason again fled.

What preacher need moralise on this story ; what
words save the simplest are requisite to tell it ?  It
is too terrible for tears.  The thought of such
a misery smites me down in submission before the
Ruler of kings and men, the Monarch Supreme over
empires and republics, the inscrutable Dispenser of
life, death, happiness, victory.  'O brothers,' I said
to those who heard me first in America — 'O
brothers !  speaking the same dear mother-tongue—
O comrades ! enemies no more, let us take a mournful
hand together as we stand by this Royal corpse, and
call a truce to battle !  Low he lies, to whom the
proudest used to kneel once, and who was cast lower
than the poorest : dead, whom millions prayed for in
vain.    Driven off his throne ; buffeted by rude
hands ; with his children in revolt ; the darling of
his old age killed before him untimely ; our Lear
hangs over her breathless lips and cries, " Cordelia,
Cordelia, stay a little ! "

"Vex not his ghost—oh! let him pass—he hates him
 That would upon the rack of this tough world
 Stretch him out longer!"

Hush! Strife and Quarrel, over the solemn grave!
Sound, trumpets, a mournful march! Fall, dark
curtain, upon his pageant, his pride, his grief, his
awful tragedy!'

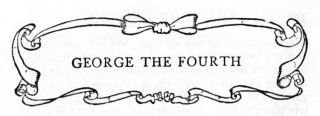

# GEORGE THE FOURTH

In Twiss's amusing 'Life of Eldon,' we read how, on the death of the Duke of York, the old chancellor became possessed of a lock of the defunct Prince's hair ; and so careful was he respecting the authenticity of the relic, that Bessy Eldon his wife sat in the room with the young man from Hamlet's who distributed the ringlet into separate lockets, which each of the Eldon family afterwards wore. You know how, when George IV. came to Edinburgh, a better man than he went on board the Royal yacht to welcome the King to his kingdom of Scotland, seized a goblet from which His Majesty had just drunk, vowed it should remain for ever as an heirloom in his family, clapped the precious glass in his pocket, and sat down on it and broke it when he got home. Suppose the good sheriff's prize unbroken now at Abbotsford, should we not smile with something like pity as we beheld it ? Suppose one of those lockets of the no-Popery Prince's hair offered for sale at Christie's, *quot libras e duce summo invenies?* how many pounds would you find for the illustrious Duke ? Madame Tussaud has got King George's coronation robes : is there any man now alive who would kiss the hem of that trumpery ? He sleeps since thirty years : do not any of you, who remember him, wonder that you once respected and huzza'd and admired him ?

To make a portrait of him at first seemed a matter of small difficulty. There is his coat, his star, his wig, his countenance simpering under it : with a slate and a piece of chalk, I could at this very a desk perform

a recognisable likeness of him. And yet after reading
of him in scores of volumes, hunting him through old
magazines and newspapers, having him here at a ball,
there at a public dinner, there at races and so forth,
you find you have nothing—nothing but a coat and a
wig and a mask smiling below it—nothing but a great
simulacrum. His sire and grandsires were men. One
knows what they were like: what they would do in
given circumstances: that on occasion they fought
and demeaned themselves like tough good soldiers.
They had friends whom they liked according to their
natures; enemies whom they hated fiercely; passions,
and actions, and individualities of their own. The
sailor King who came after George was a man: the
Duke of York was a man, big, burly, loud, jolly, cursing, courageous. But this George, what was he? I
look through all his life, and recognise but a bow and
a grin. I try and take him to pieces, and find silk
stockings, padding, stays, a coat with frogs and a fur
collar, a star and blue ribbon, a pocket-handkerchief
prodigiously scented, one of Truefitt's best nutty-
brown wigs reeking with oil, a set of teeth and a huge
black stock, underwaistcoats, more underwaistcoats,
and then nothing. I know of no sentiment that he
ever distinctly uttered. Documents are published
under his name, but people wrote them—private
letters, but people spelt them. He put a great George
P. or George R. at the bottom of the page and fancied
he had written the paper; some bookseller's clerk,
some poor author, some *man* did the work; saw to
the spelling, cleaned up the slovenly sentences, and
gave the lax maudlin slipslop a sort of consistency.
He must have had an individuality: the dancing-
master whom he emulated, nay, surpassed—the wig-
maker who curled his toupee for him—the tailor who
cut his coats, had that. But, about George, one can

get at nothing actual. The outside, I am certain, is
pad and tailor's work; there may be something behind, but what? We cannot get at the character;
no doubt never shall. Will men of the future have
nothing better to do than to unswathe and interpret
that Royal old mummy? I own I once used to think
it would be good sport to pursue him, fasten on him,
and pull him down. But now I am ashamed to mount
and lay good dogs on, to summon a full field, and then
to hunt the poor game.

On the 12th August, 1762, the forty-seventh anniversary of the accession of the House of Brunswick to
the English throne, all the bells in London pealed in
gratulation, and announced that an heir to George
III. was born. Five days afterwards the King was
pleased to pass letters patent under the great seal,
creating H.R.H. the Prince of Great Britain,
Electoral Prince of Brunswick Lüneburg, Duke
of Cornwall and Rothesay, Earl of Carrick, Baron
of Renfrew, Lord of the Isles, and Great Steward
of Scotland, Prince of Wales, and Earl of Chester.

All the people at his birth thronged to see this
lovely child; and behind a gilt china-screen railing in
Saint James's Palace, in a cradle surmounted by the
three princely ostrich feathers, the Royal infant was
laid to delight the eyes of the lieges. Among the
earliest instances of homage paid to him, I read that
'a curious Indian bow and arrows were sent to the
Prince from his father's faithful subjects in New
York.' He was fond of playing with these toys: an
old statesman, orator, and wit of his grandfather's and
great-grandfather's time, never tired of his business,
still eager in his old age to be well at Court, used to
play with the little Prince, and pretend to fall down
dead when the Prince shot at him with his toy bow
and arrows—and get up and fall down dead over and

over again—to the increased delight of the child.  So
that he was flattered from his cradle upwards; and
before his little feet could walk, statesmen and
courtiers were busy kissing them.

There is a pretty picture of the Royal infant—a
beautiful buxom child—asleep in his mother's lap;
who turns round and holds a finger to her lip, as if she
would bid the courtiers around respect the baby's
slumbers.  From that day until his decease, sixty-eight
years after, I suppose there were more pictures taken
of that personage than of any other human being who
ever was born and died—in every kind of uniform and
every possible Court-dress—in long fair hair, with
powder, with and without a pigtail—in every conceiv-
able cocked-hat—in dragoon uniform—in Windsor
uniform—in a field-marshal's clothes—in a Scotch
kilt and tartans, with dirk and claymore (a stupendous
figure)—in a frogged frock-coat with a fur-collar and
tight breeches and silk stockings—in wigs of every
colour, fair, brown, and black—in his famous coronation robes finally, with which performance he was so
much in love that he distributed copies of the picture
to all the Courts and British embassies in Europe, and
to numberless clubs, town-halls, and private friends.
I remember as a young man how almost every dining-
room had his portrait.

There is plenty of biographical tattle about the
Prince's boyhood.  It is told with what astonishing
rapidity he learned all languages, ancient and modern;
how he rode beautifully, sang charmingly, and played
elegantly on the violoncello.  That he was beautiful
was patent to all eyes.  He had a high spirit; and
once, when he had had a difference with his father,
burst into the Royal closet and called out, 'Wilkes
and liberty for ever!'  He was so clever, that he
confounded his very governors in learning; and one

of them, Lord Bruce, having made a false quantity in
quoting Greek, the admirable young Prince instantly
corrected him.   Lord Bruce could not remain a
governor after this humiliation ; resigned his office,
and, to soothe his feelings, was actually promoted to
be an earl ! It is the most wonderful reason for promoting a man that ever I heard.   Lord Bruce was made
an earl for a blunder in prosody : and Nelson was
made a baron for the victory of the Nile.

Lovers of long sums have added up the millions
and millions which in the course of his brilliant existence this single Prince consumed.   Besides his income
of £50,000, £70,000, £100,000, £120,000 a year,
we read of three applications to Parliament ; debts
to the amount of £160,000, of £650,000 ; besides
mysterious foreign loans, whereof he pocketed the
proceeds.   What did he do for all this money ?   Why
was he to have it ?   If he had been a manufacturing
town, or a populous rural district, or an army of five
thousand men, he would not have cost more.   He,
one solitary stout man, who did not toil, nor spin,
nor fight,—what had any mortal done that he should
be pampered so ?

In 1784, when he was twenty-one years of age,
Carlton Palace was given to him, and furnished by
the nation with as much luxury as could be devised.
His pockets were filled with money : he said it was
not enough ; he flung it out of window : he spent
£10,000 a year for the coats on his back.   The
nation gave him more money, and more, and more.
The sum was past counting.   He was a prince most
lovely to look on, and was christened Prince Florizel
on his first appearance in the world.   That he was
the handsomest prince in the whole world was agreed
by men, and alas ! by many women.

I suppose he must have been very graceful.   There

are so many testimonies to the charm of his manner,
that we must allow him great elegance and powers
of fascination. He, and the King of France's
brother, the Count d'Artois, a charming young
Prince who danced deliciously on the tight-rope—a
poor old tottering exiled King, who asked hospitality
of King George's successor, and lived awhile in the
palace of Mary Stuart—divided in their youth the title
of first gentleman of Europe. We in England of course
gave the prize to *our* gentleman. Until George's death
the propriety of that award was scarce questioned,
or the doubters voted rebels and traitors. Only
the other day I was reading in the reprint of the
delightful 'Noctes' of Christopher North. The
health of THE KING is drunk in large capitals by
the loyal Scotsman. You would fancy him a hero,
a sage, a statesman, a pattern for kings and men. It
was Walter Scott who had that accident with the
broken glass I spoke of anon. He was the King's
Scottish champion, rallied all Scotland to him, made
loyalty the fashion, and laid about him fiercely with
his claymore upon all the Prince's enemies. The
Brunswicks had no such defenders as those two
Jacobite commoners, old Sam Johnson, the Lichfield
chapman's son, and Walter Scott, the Edinburgh
lawyer's.

Nature and circumstance had done their utmost to
prepare the Prince for being spoiled : the dreadful dulness of Papa's Court, its stupid amusements, its dreary
occupations, the maddening humdrum, the stifling
sobriety of its routine, would have made a scapegrace
of a much less lively prince. All the big princes
bolted from that castle of ennui where old King
George sat, posting up his books and droning over
his Handel ; and old Queen Charlotte over her
snuff and her tambour-frame. Most of the sturdy

gallant sons settled down after sowing their wild
oats, and became sober subjects of their father and
brother—not ill liked by the nation, which pardons
youthful irregularities readily enough, for the sake
of pluck, and unaffectedness, and good-humour.

The boy is father of the man. Our Prince
signalised his entrance into the world by a feat
worthy of his future life. He invented a new shoe-
buckle. It was an inch long and five inches broad.
'It covered almost the whole instep, reaching down
to the ground on either side of the foot.' A sweet
invention ! lovely and useful as the Prince on whose
foot it sparkled. At his first appearance at a Court
ball, we read that 'his coat was pink silk, with white
cuffs ; his waistcoat white silk, embroidered with
various coloured foil, and adorned with a profusion of
French paste. And his hat was ornamented with
two rows of steel beads, five thousand in number,
with a button and loop of the same metal, and cocked
in a new military style.' What a Florizel ! Do
these details seem trivial ? They are the grave
incidents of his life. His biographers say that when
he commenced housekeeping in that splendid new
palace of his, the Prince of Wales had some windy
projects of encouraging literature, science, and the
arts ; of having assemblies of literary characters ;
and societies for the encouragement of geography,
astronomy, and botany. Astronomy, geography,
and botany ! Fiddlesticks ! French ballet-dancers,
French cooks, horse-jockeys, buffoons, procurers,
tailors, boxers, fencing-masters, china, jewel, and
gimcrack merchants—these were his real companions.
At first he made a pretence of having Burke and Fox
and Sheridan for his friends. But how could such
men be serious before such an empty scapegrace as
this lad ? Fox might talk dice with him, and Sheridan

wine; but what else had these men of genius in common with their tawdry young host of Carlton House? That fribble the leader of such men as Fox and Burke! That man's opinions about the Constitution, the India Bill, justice to the Catholics—about any question graver than the button for a waistcoat or the sauce for a partridge—worth anything! The friendship between the Prince and the Whig chiefs was impossible. They were hypocrites in pretending to respect him, and if he broke the hollow compact between them, who shall blame him? His natural companions were dandies and parasites. He could talk to a tailor or a cook; but, as the equal of great statesmen, to set up a creature, lazy, weak, indolent, besotted, of monstrous vanity, and levity incurable—it is absurd. They thought to use him, and did for awhile; but they must have known how timid he was; how entirely heartless and treacherous, and have expected his desertion. His next set of friends were mere table companions, of whom he grew tired too; then we hear of him with a very few select toadies, mere boys from school or the Guards, whose sprightliness tickled the fancy of the worn-out voluptuary. What matters what friends he had? He dropped all his friends; he never could have real friends. An heir to the throne has flatterers, adventurers who hang about him, ambitious men who use him; but friendship is denied him.

And women, I suppose, are as false and selfish in their dealings with such a character as men. Shall we take the Leporello part, flourish a catalogue of the conquests of this Royal Don Juan, and tell the names of the favourites to whom, one after the other, George Prince flung his pocket-handkerchief? What purpose would it answer to say how Perdita was pursued, won, deserted, and by whom succeeded? What good in

knowing that he did actually marry Mrs. Fitz-Herbert
according to the rites of the Roman Catholic Church ;
that her marriage settlements have been seen in
London ; that the names of the witnesses to her
marriage are known ?  This sort of vice that we are
now come to presents no new or fleeting trait of
manners.  Debauchees, dissolute, heartless, fickle,
cowardly, have been ever since the world began.
This one had more temptations than most, and so
much may be said in extenuation for him.

It was an unlucky thing for this doomed one,
and tending to lead him yet farther on the road to the
deuce, that, besides being lovely, so that women were
fascinated by him ; and heir-apparent, so that all the
world flattered him ; he should have had a beautiful
voice, which led him directly in the way of drink :
and thus all the pleasant devils were coaxing on poor
Florizel ; desire, and idleness, and vanity, and drunkenness, all clashing their merry cymbals and bidding
him come on.

We first hear of his warbling sentimental ditties
under the walls of Kew Palace by the moonlit banks
of Thames, with Lord Viscount Leporello keeping
watch lest the music should be disturbed.

Singing after dinner and supper was the universal
fashion of the day.  You may fancy all England
sounding with choruses, but some ribald, some harmless, all occasioning the consumption of a prodigious
deal of fermented liquor.

> ' The jolly Muse her wings to try no frolic flights
>     need take,
>   But round the bowl would dip and fly, like swallows
>     round a lake,'

sang Morris in one of his gallant Anacreontics, to

which the Prince many a time joined in chorus, and of which the burden is,—

'And that I think's a reason fair to drink and fill again.'

This delightful boon companion of the Prince's found 'a reason fair' to forego filling and drinking, saw the error of his ways, gave up the bowl and chorus, and died retired and religious. The Prince's table no doubt was a very tempting one. The wits came and did their utmost to amuse him. It is wonderful how the spirits rise, the wit brightens, the wine has an aroma, when a great man is at the head of the table. Scott, the loyal Cavalier, the King's true liegeman, the very best *raconteur* of his time, poured out with an endless generosity his store of old-world learning, kindness, and humour. Grattan contributed to it his wondrous eloquence, fancy, feeling. Tom Moore perched upon it for awhile, and piped his most exquisite little love-tunes on it, flying away in a twitter of indignation afterwards, and attacking the Prince with bill and claw. In such society, no wonder the sitting was long, and the butler tired of drawing corks. Remember what the usages of the time were, and that William Pitt, coming to the House of Commons after having drunk a bottle of port-wine at his own house, would go into Bellamy's with Dundas, and help finish a couple more.

You peruse volumes after volumes about our Prince, and find some half-dozen stock stories—indeed not many more—common to all the histories. He was good-natured; an indolent voluptuous prince, not unkindly. One story, the most favourable to him of all, perhaps, is that as Prince Regent he was eager to hear all that could be said in behalf of prisoners condemned to death, and anxious, if possible, to remit the capital sentence. He was kind to his servants.

There is a story common to all the biographies, of Molly the housemaid, who, when his household was to be broken up, owing to some reforms which he tried absurdly to practise, was discovered crying as she dusted the chairs because she was to leave a master who had a kind word for all his servants. Another tale is that of a groom of the Prince's being discovered in corn and oat peculations, and dismissed by the personage at the head of the stables; the Prince had word of John's disgrace, remonstrated with him very kindly, generously reinstated him, and bade him promise to sin no more—a promise which John kept. Another story is very fondly told of the Prince as a young man hearing of an officer's family in distress, and how he straightway borrowed six or eight hundred pounds, put his long fair hair under his hat, and so disguised carried the money to the starving family. He sent money, too, to Sheridan on his death-bed, and would have sent more had not death ended the career of that man of genius. Besides these, there are a few pretty speeches, kind and graceful, to persons with whom he was brought in contact. But he turned upon twenty friends. He was fond and familiar with them one day, and he passed them on the next without recognition. He used them, liked them, loved them perhaps, in his way, and then separated from them. On Monday he kissed and fondled poor Perdita, and on Tuesday he met her and did not know her. On Wednesday he was very affectionate with that wretched Brummell, and on Thursday forgot him; cheated him even out of a snuff-box which he owed the poor dandy; saw him years afterwards in his downfall and poverty, when the bankrupt Beau sent him another snuff-box with some of the snuff he used to love, as a piteous token of remembrance and submission; and the King took the snuff, and ordered his horses, and drove on, and had not the grace to notice his old companion, favourite, rival, enemy, superior. In Wraxall there is some gossip about him. When the charming, beautiful, generous Duchess of Devonshire died—the lovely lady whom he used to call his dearest duchess once, and pretend to admire as all English society admired her—he said, 'Then we have lost the best-bred woman in England.' 'Then we have lost the kindest heart in England,' said noble Charles Fox. On another occasion, when three noblemen were to receive the Garter, says Wraxall, 'A great personage observed that never did three men receive the order in so characteristic a manner. The Duke of A. advanced to the sovereign with a phlegmatic, cold, awkward air like a clown; Lord B. came forward fawning and smiling like a courtier; Lord C. presented himself easy, unembarrassed, like a gentleman!' These are the stories one has to recall about the Prince and King —kindness to a housemaid, generosity to a groom, criticism on a bow. There *are* no better stories about him : they are mean and trivial, and they characterise him. The great war of empires and giants goes on. Day by day victories are won and lost by the brave. Torn smoky flags and battered eagles are wrenched from the heroic enemy and laid at his feet ; and he sits there on his throne and smiles, and gives the guerdon of valour to the conqueror. He ! Elliston the actor, when the *Coronation* was performed, in which he took the principal part, used to fancy himself the King, burst into tears, and hiccup a blessing on the people. I believe it is certain about George IV., that he had heard so much of the war, knighted so many people, and worn such a prodigious quantity of marshal's uniforms, cocked-hats, cock's feathers, scarlet and bullion in general, that he actually fancied he had been present in some campaigns, and, under the name of General Brock, led a tremendous charge of the German legion at Waterloo.

He is dead but thirty years, and one asks how a great society could have tolerated him? Would we bear him now? In this quarter of a century, what a silent revolution has been working! how it has separated us from old times and manners! How it has changed men themselves! I can see old gentlemen now among us, of perfect good breeding, of quiet lives, with venerable grey heads, fondling their grandchildren; and look at them, and wonder what they were once. That gentleman of the grand old school, when he was in the 10th Hussars, and dined at the Prince's table, would fall under it night after night. Night after night that gentleman sat at Brooks's or Raggett's over the dice. If, in the petulance of play or drink, that gentleman spoke a sharp word to his neighbour, he and the other would infallibly go out and try to shoot each other the next morning. That gentleman would drive his friend Richmond, the black boxer, down to Moulsey, and hold his coat, and shout and swear, and hurrah with delight whilst the black man was beating Dutch Sam the Jew. That gentleman would take a manly pleasure in pulling his own coat off, and thrashing a bargeman in a street row. That gentleman has been in a watch-house. That gentleman, so exquisitely polite with ladies in a drawing-room, so loftily courteous, if he talked now as he used among men in his youth, would swear so as to make your hair stand on end. I met lately a very old German gentleman, who had served in our army at the beginning of the century. Since then he has lived on his own estate, but rarely meeting with an Englishman, whose language—the language of fifty years ago, that is—he possesses perfectly. When this highly-bred old man began to speak English to me almost every other word he uttered was an oath : as they used (they swore dreadfully in Flanders) with the Duke of York before Valenciennes, or at Carlton House over the supper and cards. Read Byron's letters. So accustomed is the young man to oaths that he employs them even in writing to his friends, and swears by the post. Read his account of the doings of the young men at Cambridge, of the ribald professors, 'one of whom could pour out Greek like a drunken Helot,' and whose excesses surpassed even those of the young men. Read Matthew's description of the boyish lordling's housekeeping at Newstead, the skull-cup passed round, the monks' dresses from the masquerade warehouse, in which the young scapegraces used to sit until daylight, chanting appropriate songs round their wine. 'We come to breakfast at two or three o'olock,' Matthews says. 'There are gloves and foils for those who like to amuse themselves, or we fire pistols at a mark in the hall, or we worry the wolf.' A jolly life truly! The noble young owner of the mansion writes about such affairs himself in letters to his friend, Mr. John Jackson, pugilist in London.

All the Prince's time tells a similar strange story of manners and pleasure. In Wraxall we find the Prime Minister himself, the redoubted William Pitt, engaged in high jinks with personages of no less importance than Lord Thurlow the Lord Chancellor, and Mr. Dundas the Treasurer of the Navy. Wraxall relates how these three statesmen, returning after dinner from Addiscombe, found a turnpike open and galloped through it without paying the toll. The turnpike-man, fancying they were highwaymen, fired a blunderbuss after them, but missed them ; and the poet sang,—

> 'How as Pitt wandered darkling o'er the plain,
> His reason drown'd in Jenkinson's champagne,
> A rustic's hand, but righteous Fate withstood,
> Had shed a Premier's for a robber's blood.'

Here we have the Treasurer of the Navy, the Lord High Chancellor, and the Prime Minister, all engaged in a most undoubted lark. In Eldon's 'Memoirs,' about the very same time, I read that the bar loved wine, as well as the woolsack. Not John Scott himself; he was a good boy always; and though he loved port-wine, loved his business and his duty and his fees a great deal better.

He has a Northern Circuit story of those days, about a party at the house of a certain Lawyer Fawcett, who gave a dinner every year to the counsel.

'On one occasion,' related Lord Eldon, 'I heard Lee say, "I cannot leave Fawcett's wine. Mind, Davenport, you will go home immediately after dinner, to read the brief in that cause that we have to conduct to-morrow."

'"Not I," said Davenport. "Leave my dinner and my wine to read a brief! No, no, Lee; that won't do."

'"Then," said Lee, "what is to be done? Who else is employed?"

'*Davenport.* "Oh! young Scott."

'*Lee.* "Oh! he must go. Mr. Scott, you must go home immediately, and make yourself acquainted with that cause, before our consultation this evening."

'This was very hard upon me; but I did go, and there was an attorney from Cumberland, and one from Northumberland, and I do not know how many other persons. Pretty late, in came Jack Lee, as drunk as he could be.

'"I cannot consult to-night; I must go to bed," he exclaimed, and away he went. Then came Sir Thomas Davenport.

'"We cannot have a consultation to-night, Mr. Wordsworth" (Wordsworth, I think, was the name; it was a Cumberland name), shouted Davenport. "Don't you see how drunk Mr. Scott is? it is impossible to consult." Poor me! who had scarce had any dinner, and lost all my wine—I was so drunk that I could not consult! Well, a verdict was given against us, and it was all owing to Lawyer Fawcett's dinner. We moved for a new trial; and I must say, for the honour of the bar, that those two gentlemen, Jack Lee and Sir Thomas Davenport, paid all the expenses between them of the first trial. It is the only instance I ever knew; but they did. We moved for a new trial (on the ground, I suppose, of the counsel not being in their senses), and it was granted. When it came on, the following year, the judge rose and said,—

'"Gentlemen, did any of you dine with Lawyer Fawcett yesterday? for, if you did, I will not hear this cause till next year."

'There was great laughter. We gained the cause that time.'

On another occasion, at Lancaster, where poor Bozzy must needs be going the Northern Circuit, 'we found him,' says Mr. Scott, 'lying upon the pavement inebriated. We subscribed a guinea at supper for him, and a half-crown for his clerk '—(no doubt there was a large bar, so that Scott's joke did not cost him much)—'and sent him, when he waked next morning, a brief, with instructions to move for what we denominated the writ of *quare adhæsit pavimento*; with observations duly calculated to induce him to think that it required great learning to explain the necessity of granting it, to the judge before whom he was to move.' Boswell sent all round the town to attorneys for books that might enable him to distinguish himself—but in vain. He moved, however, for the writ, making the best use he could of the observations in the brief. The judge was perfectly astonished, and the audience amazed. The judge said, 'I never heard of such a writ—what can it be that adheres *pavimento?* Are any of you gentlemen at the bar able to explain this?'

The bar laughed. At last one of them said—

'My Lord, Mr. Boswell last night *adhæsit pavimento.* There was no moving him for some time. At last he was carried to bed, and he has been dreaming about himself and the pavement.'

The canny old gentleman relishes these jokes. When the Bishop of Lincoln was moving from the deanery of Saint Paul's, he says he asked a learned friend of his, by name Will Hay, how he should move some especially fine claret, about which he was anxious.

'Pray, my Lord Bishop,' says Hay, 'how much of the wine have you?'

The Bishop said six dozen.

'If that is all,' Hay answered, 'you have but to ask me six times to dinner, and I will carry it all away myself.'

There were giants in those days; but this joke about wine is not so fearful as one perpetrated by Orator Thelwall, in the heat of the French Revolution, ten years later, over a frothing pot of porter. He blew the head off, and said, 'This is the way I would serve all kings.'

Now we come to yet higher personages, and find their doings recorded in the blushing pages of timid little Miss Burney's 'Memoirs.' She represents a Prince of the Blood in quite a Royal condition. The loudness, the bigness, boisterousness, creaking boots and rattling oaths of the young princes appear to have frightened the prim household of Windsor, and set all the teacups twittering on the tray. On the night of a ball and birthday, when one of the pretty kind princesses was to come out, it was agreed that her brother, Prince William Henry, should dance the opening minuet with her, and he came to visit the household at their dinner.

'At dinner, Mrs. Schwellenberg presided, attired magnificently; Miss Goldsworthy, Mrs. Stanford, Messrs. Du Luc and Stanhope dined with us; and while we were still eating fruit, the Duke of Clarence entered.

'He was just risen from the King's table, and waiting for his equipage to go home and prepare for the ball. To give you an idea of the energy of His Royal Highness's language, I ought to set apart an objection to writing, or rather intimating, certain forcible words, and beg leave to show you in genuine colours a Royal sailor.

'We all rose, of course, upon his entrance, and the two gentlemen placed themselves behind their chairs, while the footmen left the room. But he ordered us all to sit down, and called the men back to hand about some wine. He was in exceeding high spirits, and in the utmost good-humour. He placed himself at the head of the table, next Mrs. Schwellenberg, and looked remarkably well, gay, and full of sport and mischief; yet clever withal, as well as comical.

'"Well, this is the first day I have ever dined with the King at Saint James's on his birthday. Pray, have you all drunk His Majesty's health?"

'"No, your Royal Highness; your Royal Highness might make dem do dat," said Mrs. Schwellenberg.

'"Oh, by ——, I will! Here, you" (to the footman), "bring champagne; I'll drink the King's health again, if I die for it. Yes, I have done it pretty well already; so has the King, I promise you! I believe His Majesty was never taken such good care of before; we have kept his spirits up, I promise you; we have enabled him to go through his fatigues; and I should have done more still, but for the ball and Mary;—I have promised to dance with Mary. I must keep sober for Mary."'

Indefatigable Miss Burney continues for a dozen pages reporting H.R.H.'s conversation, and indicating, with a humour not unworthy of the clever little author of 'Evelina,' the increasing state of excitement of the young sailor Prince, who drank more and more champagne, stopped old Mrs. Schwellenberg's remonstrances by giving the old lady a kiss, and telling her to hold her potato-trap, and who did not 'keep sober for Mary.' Mary had to find another partner that night, for the Royal William Henry could not keep his legs.

Will you have a picture of the amusements of another Royal Prince? It is the Duke of York, the blundering general, the beloved Commander-in-chief of the army, the brother with whom George IV. had had many a midnight carouse, and who continued his habits of pleasure almost till death seized his stout body.

In Pückler Muskau's 'Letters,' that German Prince describes a bout with H.R.H., who in his best time was such a powerful toper that 'six bottles of claret after dinner scarce made a perceptible change in his countenance.'

'I remember,' says Pückler, 'that one evening—indeed, it was past midnight—he took some of his guests, among whom were the Austrian Ambassador, Count Meervelt, Count Beroldingen, and myself, into his beautiful armoury. We tried to swing several Turkish sabres, but none of us had a very firm grasp; whence it happened that the Duke and Meervelt both scratched themselves with a sort of straight Indian sword so as to draw blood. Meervelt then wished to try if the sword cut as well as a Damascus, and attempted to cut through one of the wax candles that stood on the table. The experiment answered so ill, that both the candles, candlesticks and all, fell to the ground and were extinguished. While we were groping in the dark and trying to find the door, the Duke's aide-de-camp stammered out in great agitation, "By G——, sir, I remember the sword is poisoned!"

'You may conceive the agreeable feelings of the wounded at this intelligence! Happily, on further examination, it appeared that claret, and not poison, was at the bottom of the colonel's exclamation.'

And now I have one more story of the Bacchanalian sort, in which Clarence and York, and the very highest personage of the realm, the great Prince Regent, all play parts. The feast took place at the Pavilion at Brighton, and was described to me by a gentleman who was present at the scene. In Gilray's caricatures, and amongst Fox's jolly associates, there figures a great nobleman, the Duke of Norfolk, called Jockey of Norfolk in his time, and celebrated for his table exploits. He had quarrelled with the Prince, like the rest of the Whigs; but a sort of reconciliation had taken place; and now, being a very old man, the Prince invited him to dine and sleep at the Pavilion, and the old Duke drove over from his Castle of Arundel with his famous equipage of grey horses, still remembered in Sussex.

The Prince of Wales had concocted with his Royal brothers a notable scheme for making the old man drunk. Every person at table was enjoined to drink wine with the Duke—a challenge which the old toper did not refuse. He soon began to see that there was a conspiracy against him; he drank glass for glass; he overthrew many of the brave. At last the First Gentleman of Europe proposed bumpers of brandy. One of the Royal brothers filled a great glass for the Duke. He stood up and tossed off the drink. 'Now,' says he, 'I will have my carriage, and go home.' The Prince urged upon him his previous promise to sleep under the roof where he had been so generously entertained. 'No,' he said; he had had enough of such hospitality. A trap had been set for him; he would leave the place at once and never enter its doors more.

The carriage was called, and came; but, in the half-hour's interval, the liquor had proved too potent for the old man; his host's generous purpose was answered, and the Duke's old grey head lay stupefied on the table. Nevertheless, when his post-chaise was announced, he staggered to it as well as he could, and stumbling in, bade the postillions drive to Arundel. They drove him for half-an-hour round and round the Pavilion lawn; the poor old man fancied he was going home. When he awoke that morning he was in bed at the Prince's hideous house at Brighton. You may see the place now for sixpence: they have fiddlers there every day; and sometimes buffoons and mountebanks hire the Riding House and do their tricks and tumbling there. The trees are still there, and the gravel walks round which the poor old sinner was trotted. I can fancy the flushed faces of the Royal Princes as they support themselves at the portico pillars, and look on at old Norfolk's disgrace; but I can't fancy how the man who perpetrated it continued to be called a gentleman.

From drinking, the pleased Muse now turns to gambling, of which in his youth our Prince was a great practitioner. He was a famous pigeon for the play-men; they lived upon him. Egalité Orleans, it was believed, punished him severely. A noble lord, whom we shall call the Marquis of Steyne, is said to have mulcted him in immense sums. He frequented the clubs, where play was then almost universal; and, as it was known his debts of honour were sacred, whilst he was gambling Jews waited outside to purchase his notes of hand. His transactions on the turf

were unlucky as well as discreditable : though I believe he, and his jockey, and his horse, Escape, were
all innocent in that affair which created so much
scandal.

Arthur's, Almack's, Boodle's, and White's were the
chief clubs of the young men of fashion.  There was
play at all, and decayed noblemen and broken-down
senators fleeced the unwary there.  In Selwyn's
'Letters' we find Carlisle, Devonshire, Coventry,
Queensberry, all undergoing the probation.  Charles
Fox, a dreadful gambler, was cheated in very late
times—lost £200,000 at play.  Gibbon tells of his
playing for twenty-two hours at a sitting, and losing
£500 an hour.  That indomitable punter said that
the greatest pleasure in life, after winning, was
losing.  What hours, what nights, what health did
he waste over the devil's books !  I was going to say
what peace of mind ; but he took his losses very
philosophically.  After an awful night's play, and
the enjoyment of the greatest pleasure but *one* in life,
he was found on a sofa tranquilly reading an Eclogue
of Virgil.

Play survived long after the wild Prince and Fox
had given up the dice-box.  The dandies continued
it.  Byron, Brummell—how many names could I
mention of men of the world who have suffered by it !
In 1837 occurred a famous trial which pretty nigh
put an end to gambling in England.  A peer of the
realm was found cheating at whist, and repeatedly
seen to practise the trick called *sauter la coupe*.  His
friends at the clubs saw him cheat, and went on
playing with him.  One greenhorn, who had discovered his foul play, asked an old hand what he
should do.  'Do !' said the Mammon of Unrighteous-
ness.  '*Back him, you fool !*'  The best efforts were
made to screen him.  People wrote him anonymous

letters and warned him ; but he would cheat, and
they were obliged to find him out.  Since that day,
when my Lord's shame was made public, the gaming-
table has lost all its splendour.  Shabby Jews and
blacklegs prowl about racecourses and tavern parlours,
and now and then inveigle silly yokels with greasy
packs of cards in railroad cars ; but Play is a deposed
goddess, her worshippers bankrupt, and her table in
rags.

So is another famous British institution gone to
decay—the Ring : the noble practice of British boxing, which in my youth was still almost flourishing.

The Prince, in his early days, was a great patron of
this national sport, as his grand-uncle Culloden
Cumberland had been before him ; but, being present
at a fight at Brighton, where one of the combatants
was killed, the Prince pensioned the boxer's widow,
and declared he never would attend another battle.
' But, nevertheless '—I read in the noble language of
Pierce Egan (whose smaller work on Pugilism I have
the honour to possess)—' he thought it a manly and
decided English feature, which ought not to be
destroyed.  His Majesty had a drawing of the sport-
ing characters in the Fives Court placed in his
boudoir, to remind him of his former attachment and
support of true courage ; and when any fight of note
occurred after he was King, accounts of it were read
to him by his desire.'  That gives one a fine image of
a king taking his recreation ;—at ease in a Royal
dressing-gown ;—too majestic to read himself, order-
ing the Prime Minister to read him accounts of
battles : how Cribb punched Molyneux's eye, or Jack
Randal thrashed the Game Chicken.

Where my Prince *did* actually distinguish himself
was in driving.  He drove once in four hours and a
half from Brighton to Carlton House—fifty-six miles.

All the young men of that day were fond of that sport. But the fashion of rapid driving deserted England; and, I believe, trotted over to America. Where are the amusements of our youth? I hear of no gambling now but amongst obscure ruffians; of no boxing but amongst the lowest rabble. One solitary four-in-hand still drove round the parks in London last year; but that charioteer must soon disappear. He was very old; he was attired after the fashion of the year 1825. He must drive to the banks of Styx ere long,—where the ferry-boat waits to carry him over to the defunct revellers who boxed and gambled and drank and drove with King George.

The bravery of the Brunswicks, that all the family must have it, that George possessed it, are points which all English writers have agreed to admit; and yet I cannot see how George IV. should have been endowed with this quality. Swaddled in feather-beds all his life, lazy, obese, perpetually eating and drinking, his education was quite unlike that of his tough old progenitors. His grandsires had confronted hardship and war, and ridden up and fired their pistols undaunted into the face of death. His father had conquered luxury and overcome indolence. Here was one who never resisted any temptation; never had a desire but he coddled and pampered it; if ever he had any nerve, frittered it away among cooks, and tailors, and barbers, and furniture-mongers, and opera-dancers. What muscle would not grow flaccid in such a life— a life that was never strung up to any action—an endless Capua without any campaign—all fiddling and flowers, and feasting, and flattery, and folly? When George III. was pressed by the Catholic Question and the India Bill, he said he would retire to Hanover rather than yield upon either point; and he would have done what he said. But, before yield-

ing, he was determined to fight his Ministers and
Parliament; and he did, and he beat them. The
time came when George IV. was pressed too upon
the Catholic claims; the cautious Peel had slipped
over to that side; the grim old Wellington had joined
it; and Peel tells us, in his 'Memoirs,' what was the
conduct of the King. He at first refused to submit;
whereupon Peel and the Duke offered their resigna-
tions, which their gracious master accepted. He did
these two gentlemen the honour, Peel says, to kiss
them both when they went away. (Fancy old
Arthur's grim countenance and eagle beak as the
monarch kisses it!) When they were gone he sent
after them, surrendered, and wrote to them a letter
begging them to remain in office, and allowing them
to have their way. Then His Majesty had a meeting
with Eldon, which is related at curious length in the
latter's 'Memoirs.' He told Eldon what was not
true about his interview with the new Catholic
converts; utterly misled the old ex-Chancellor; cried,
whimpered, fell on his neck, and kissed him too. We
know old Eldon's own tears were pumped very freely.
Did these two fountains gush together? I can't fancy
a behaviour more unmanly, imbecile, pitiable. This
a defender of the faith! This a chief in the crisis of
a great nation! This an inheritor of the courage of
the Georges!

Many of my hearers no doubt have journeyed to
the pretty old town of Brunswick, in company with
that most worthy, prudent, and polite gentleman, the
Earl of Malmesbury, and fetched away Princess
Caroline, for her longing husband, the Prince of
Wales. Old Queen Charlotte would have had her
eldest son marry a niece of her own, that famous
Louisa of Strelitz, afterwards Queen of Prussia, and
who shares with Marie Antoinette in the last age the

sad pre-eminence of beauty and misfortune. But George III. had a niece at Brunswick; she was a richer Princess than Her Serene Highness of Strelitz: —in fine, the Princess Caroline was selected to marry the heir to the English throne. We follow my Lord Malmesbury in quest of her; we are introduced to her illustrious father and Royal mother; we witness the balls and fêtes of the old Court; we are presented to the Princess herself, with her fair hair, her blue eyes, and her impertinent shoulders — a lively, bouncing, romping Princess, who takes the advice of her courtly English mentor most generously and kindly. We can be present at her very toilette, if we like; regarding which, and for very good reasons, the British courtier implores her to be particular. What a strange Court! What a queer privacy of morals and manners do we look into! Shall we regard it as preachers and moralists, and cry Woe, against the open vice and selfishness and corruption; or look at it as we do at the king in the pantomime, with his pantomime wife and pantomime courtiers, whose big heads he knocks together, whom he pokes with his pantomime sceptre, whom he orders to prison under the guard of his pantomime beefeaters, as he sits down to dine on his pantomime pudding? It is grave, it is sad: it is theme most curious for moral and political speculation; it is monstrous, grotesque, laughable, with its prodigious littlenesses, etiquettes, ceremonials, sham moralities; it is as serious as a sermon; and as absurd and outrageous as Punch's puppet show.

Malmesbury tells us of the private life of the Duke, Princess Caroline's father, who was to die, like his warlike son, in arms against the French; presents us to his courtiers, his favourite; his Duchess, George III.'s sister, a grim old Princess, who took the British envoy aside and told him wicked old stories of wicked old dead people and times; who came to England afterwards when her nephew was Regent, and lived in a shabby furnished lodging, old and dingy, and deserted, and grotesque, but somehow Royal. And we go with him to the Duke to demand the Princess's hand in form, and we hear the Brunswick guns fire their adieux of salute, as H.R.H. the Princess of Wales departs in the frost and snow; and we visit the domains of the Prince Bishop of Osnaburg—the Duke of York of our early time; and we dodge about from the French revolutionists, whose ragged legions are pouring over Holland and Germany and gaily trampling down the old world to the tune of 'Ça ira;' and we take shipping at Stade, and we land at Greenwich, where the Princess's ladies and the Prince's ladies are in waiting to receive Her Royal Highness.

What a history follows! Arrived in London, the bridegroom hastened eagerly to receive his bride. When she was first presented to him, Lord Malmesbury says she very properly attempted to kneel. 'He raised her gracefully enough, embraced her, and turning round to me, said,—

'"Harris, I am not well; pray get me a glass of brandy."

'I said, "Sir, had you not better have a glass of water?"

'Upon which, much out of humour, he said, with an oath, "No; I will go to the Queen."'

What could be expected from a wedding which had such a beginning—from such a bridegroom and such a bride? I am not going to carry you through the scandal of that story, or follow the poor Princess through all her vagaries; her balls and her dances, her travels to Jerusalem and Naples, her jigs, and her junketings, and her tears. As I read her trial in history, I vote she is not guilty. I don't say it is an

impartial verdict; but as one reads her story the heart
bleeds for the kindly, generous, outraged creature. If
wrong there be, let it lie at his door who wickedly
thrust her from it. Spite of her follies, the great
hearty people of England loved, and protected, and
pitied her. 'God bless you! we will bring your
husband back to you,' said a mechanic one day, as she
told Lady Charlotte Bury with tears streaming down
her cheeks. They could not bring that husband back;
they could not cleanse that selfish heart. Was hers
the only one he had wounded? Steeped in selfishness,
inpotent for faithful attachment and manly enduring
love,—had it not survived remorse, was it not
accustomed to desertion?

Malmesbury gives us the beginning of the marriage
story;—how the Prince reeled into chapel to be
married; how he hiccupped out his vows of fidelity—
you know how he kept them: how he pursued the
woman whom he had married; to what a state he
brought her; with what blows he struck her; with
what malignity he pursued her; what his treatment
of his daughter was; and what his own life. *He* the
first gentleman of Europe! There is no stronger
satire on the proud English society of that day, than
that they admired George.

No, thank God, we can tell of better gentlemen:
and whilst our eyes turn away, shocked, from this
monstrous image of pride, vanity, weakness, they may
see in that England over which the last George pretended to reign, some who merit indeed the title of
gentlemen, some who make our hearts beat when we
hear their names, and whose memory we fondly salute
when that of yonder imperial mannikin is tumbled
into oblivion. I will take men of my own profession
of letters. I will take Walter Scott, who loved the
King, and who was his sword and buckler, and

championed him like that brave Highlander in his own story, who fights round his craven chief. What a good gentleman! What a friendly soul, what a generous hand, what an amiable life was that of the noble Sir Walter! I will take another man of letters, whose life I admire even more,—an English worthy, doing his duty for fifty noble years of labour, day by day storing up learning, day by day working for scant wages, most charitable out of his small means, bravely faithful to the calling which he had chosen, refusing to turn from his path, for popular praise or prince's favour;—I mean *Robert Southey*. We have left his old political landmarks miles and miles behind; we protest against his dogmatism; nay, we begin to forget it and his politics: but I hope his life will not be forgotten, for it is sublime in its simplicity, its energy, its honour, its affection. In the combat between Time and Thalaba, I suspect the former destroyer has conquered. Kehama's Curse frightens very few readers now; but Southey's private letters are worth piles of epics, and are sure to last among us as long as kind hearts like to sympathise with goodness and purity, and love and upright life.

'If your feelings are like mine,' he writes to his wife, 'I will not go to Lisbon without you, or I will stay at home, and not part from you. For though not unhappy when away, still without you I am not happy. For your sake, as well as my own and little Edith's, I will not consent to any separation; the growth of a year's love between her and me, if it please God she should live, is a thing too delightful in itself, and too valuable in its consequences, to be given up for any light inconvenience on your part or mine. . . . On these things we will talk at leisure; only, dear dear Edith, *we must not part!*'

This was a poor literary gentleman. The First

Gentleman in Europe had a wife and daughter too. Did he love them so? Was he faithful to them? Did he sacrifice ease for them, or show them the sacred examples of religion and honour? Heaven gave the Great English Prodigal no such good fortune. Peel proposed to make a baronet of Southey; and to this advancement the King agreed. The poet nobly rejected the offered promotion.

'I have,' he wrote, 'a pension of £200 a year, conferred upon me by the good offices of my old friend C. Wynn, and I have the laureateship. The salary of the latter was immediately appropriated, as far as it went, to a life insurance for £3000, which, with an earlier insurance, is the sole provision I have made for my family. All beyond must be derived from my own industry. Writing for a livelihood, a livelihood is all that I have gained; for, having also something better in view, and never, therefore, having courted popularity, nor written for the mere sake of gain, it has not been possible for me to lay by anything. Last year, for the first time in my life, I was provided with a year's expenditure beforehand. This exposition may show how unbecoming and unwise it would be to accept the rank which, so greatly to my honour, you have solicited for me.'

How noble his poverty is, compared to the wealth of his master! His acceptance even of a pension was made the object of his opponents' satire: but think of the merit and modesty of this State pensioner; and that other enormous drawer of public money, who receives £100,000 a year, and comes to Parliament with a request for £650,000 more.

Another true knight of those days was Cuthbert Collingwood; and I think, since Heaven made gentlemen, there is no record of a better one than that. Of brighter deeds, I grant you, we may read performed by others ; but where of a nobler, kinder, more beautiful life of duty, of a gentler, truer heart? Beyond dazzle of success and blaze of genius, I fancy shining a hundred and a hundred times higher the sublime purity of Collingwood's gentle glory. His heroism stirs British hearts when we recall it. His love, and goodness, and piety make one thrill with happy emotion. As one reads of him and his great comrade going into the victory with which their names are immortally connected, how the old English word comes up, and that old English feeling of what I should like to call Christian honour! What gentlemen they were, what great hearts they had ! 'We can, my dear Coll,' writes Nelson to him, 'have no little jealousies ; we have only one great object in view,—that of meeting the enemy, and getting a glorious peace for our country.' At Trafalgar, when the 'Royal Sovereign' was pressing alone into the midst of the combined fleets, Lord Nelson said to Captain Blackwood : 'See how that noble fellow, Collingwood, takes his ship into action ! How I envy him !' The very same throb and impulse of heroic generosity was beating in Collingwood's honest bosom. As he led into the fight, he said—'What would Nelson give to be here !'

After the action of the 1st of June, he writes :—

'We cruised for a few days, like disappointed people looking for what they could not find, *until the morning of little Sarah's birthday*, between eight and nine o'clock, when the French fleet, of twenty-five sail of the line, was discovered to windward. We chased them, and they bore down within about five miles of us. The night was spent in watching and preparation for the succeeding day ; and many a blessing did I send forth to my Sarah, lest I should never bless her more. At dawn, we made our approach on the enemy, then drew up, dressed our ranks, and it was about eight when the admiral made the signal for each ship to engage her opponent, and bring her to close action ; and then down we went under a crowd of sail, and in a manner that would have animated the coldest heart, and struck terror into the most intrepid enemy. The ship we were to engage was two ahead of the French admiral, so we had to go through his fire and that of two ships next to him, and received all their broadsides two or three times before we fired a gun. It was then near ten o'clock. I observed to the admiral that about that time our wives were going to church, but that I thought the peal we should ring about the Frenchman's ear would outdo their parish bells.'

There are no words to tell what the heart feels in reading the simple phrases of such a hero. Here is victory and courage, but love sublimer and superior. Here is a Christian soldier spending the night before battle in watching and preparing for the succeeding day, thinking of his dearest home, and sending many blessings forth to his Sarah, 'lest he should never bless her more.' Who would not say Amen to his supplication ? It was a benediction to his country— the prayer of that intrepid loving heart.

We have spoken of a good soldier and good men of letters as specimens of English gentlemen of the age just past : may we not also—many of my elder hearers, I am sure, have read, and fondly remember, his delightful story—speak of a good divine, and mention Reginald Heber as one of the best of English gentlemen ? The charming poet, the happy possessor of all sorts of gifts and accomplishments, birth, wit, fame, high character, competence—he was the beloved parish priest in his own home of Hodnet, 'counselling his people in their troubles, advising them in their difficulties,

comforting them in distress, kneeling often at their
sick beds at the hazard of his own life; exhorting,
encouraging where there was need : where there
was strife the peacemaker; where there was want
the free giver.'

When the Indian bishopric was offered to him he
refused at first; but after communing with himself
(and committing his case to the quarter whither such
pious men are wont to carry their doubts), he withdrew his refusal, and prepared himself for his mission
and to leave his beloved parish. 'Little children,
love one another, and forgive one another,' were the
last sacred words he said to his weeping people. He
parted with them, knowing, perhaps, he should see
them no more. Like those other good men of whom
we have just spoken, love and duty were his life's
aim. Happy he, happy they who were so gloriously
faithful to both! He writes to his wife those
charming lines on his journey :—

'If thou, my love, wert by my side, my babies at my knee,
How gladly would our pinnace glide o'er Gunga's mimic
    sea!

I miss thee at the dawning grey, when, on our deck
    reclined,
In careless ease my limbs I lay and woo the cooler wind.

I miss thee when by Gunga's stream my twilight steps I
    guide ;
But most beneath the lamp's pale beam I miss thee by
    my side.

I spread my books, my pencil try, the lingering noon to
    cheer ;
But miss thy kind approving eye, thy meek attentive
    ear.

But when of morn and eve the star beholds me on my
  knee,
I feel, though thou art distant far, thy prayers ascend for
  me.

Then on! then on! where duty leads my course be
  onward still—
O'er broad Hindostan's sultry meads, or bleak Almorah's
  hill.

That course nor Delhi's kingly gates, nor wild Malwah
  detain,
For sweet the bliss us both awaits by yonder western
  main.

Thy towers, Bombay, gleam bright, they say, across the
  dark blue sea:
But ne'er were hearts so blithe and gay as then shall
  meet in thee!'

Is it not Collingwood and Sarah, and Southey and
Edith? His affection is part of his life. What were life
without it? Without love, I can fancy no gentleman.

How touching is a remark Heber makes in his
'Travels through India,' that on inquiring of the
natives at a town, which of the governors of India
stood highest in the opinion of the people, he found
that, though Lord Wellesley and Warren Hastings
were honoured as the two greatest men who had
ever ruled this part of the world, the people spoke
with chief affection of Judge Cleveland, who had died,
aged twenty-nine, in 1784. The people have built
a monument over him, and still hold a religious feast
in his memory. So does his own country still tend
with a heart's regard the memory of the gentle Heber.

And Cleveland died in 1784, and is still loved by
the heathen, is he? Why, that year 1784 was
remarkable in the life of our friend the First
Gentleman of Europe. Do you not know that he

was twenty-one in that year, and opened Carlton House with a grand ball to the nobility and gentry, and doubtless wore that lovely pink coat which we have described. I was eager to read about the ball, and looked to the old magazines for information. The entertainment took place on the 10th February. In the *European Magazine* of March 1784 I came straightway upon it :—

'The alterations at Carlton House being finished, we lay before our readers a description of the State apartments as they appeared on the 10th instant, when H.R.H. gave a grand ball to the principal nobility and gentry. . . . The entrance to the State room fills the mind with an inexpressible idea of greatness and splendour.

'The State chair is of a gold frame, covered with crimson damask ; on each corner of the feet is a lion's head, expressive of fortitude and strength ; the feet of the chair have serpents twining round them, to denote wisdom. Facing the throne, appears the helmet of Minerva ; and over the windows, glory is represented by Saint George with a superb gloria.

'But the saloon may be styled the *chef d'œuvre*, and in every ornament discovers great invention. It is hung with a figured lemon satin. The window-curtains, sofas, and chairs are of the same colour. The ceiling is ornamented with emblematical paintings, representing the Graces and Muses, together with Jupiter, Mercury, Apollo, and Paris. Two *ormolu* chandeliers are placed here. It is impossible by expression to do justice to the extraordinary workmanship, as well as design, of the ornaments. They each consist of a palm, branching out in five directions for the reception of lights. A beautiful figure of a rural nymph is represented entwining the stems of the tree with wreaths of flowers. In the centre of the room is a rich chandelier. To see this apartment *dans son plus beau jour*, it should be viewed in the glass over the chimney-piece. The range of apartments from the saloon to the ballroom, when the doors are open, formed one of the grandest spectacles that ever was beheld.'

In the *Gentleman's Magazine*, for the very same month and year—March 1784—is an account of another festival, in which another great gentleman of English extraction is represented as taking a principal share :—

'According to order, H.E. the Commander-in-Chief was admitted to a public audience of Congress ; and, being seated, the President, after a pause, informed him that the United States assembled were ready to receive his communications. Whereupon he arose, and spoke as follows :—

'"Mr. President,—The great events on which my resignation depended having at length taken place, I present myself before Congress to surrender into their hands the trust committed to me, and to claim the indulgence of retiring from the service of my country.

'"Happy in the confirmation of our independence and sovereignty, I resign the appointment I accepted with diffidence ; which, however, was superseded by a confidence in the rectitude of our cause, the support of the supreme power of the nation, and the patronage of Heaven. I close this last act of my official life by commending the interests of our dearest country to the protection of Almighty God, and those who have the superintendence of them to His holy keeping. Having finished the work assigned me, I retire from the great theatre of action ; and, bidding an affectionate farewell to this august body, under whose orders I have so long acted, I here offer my commission and take my leave of the employments of my public life."

'To which the President replied :—

'"Sir, having defended the standard of liberty in the New World, having taught a lesson useful to those who inflict and those who feel oppression, you retire with the blessings of your fellow-citizens ; though the glory of your virtues will not terminate with your military command, but will descend to remotest ages." '

Which was the most splendid spectacle ever witnessed,—the opening feast of Prince George in London, or the resignation of Washington ? Which is the noble character for after ages to admire,—yon fribble dancing in lace and spangles, or yonder hero who sheaths his sword after a life of spotless honour, a purity unreproached, a courage indomitable, and a consummate victory ? Which of these is the true gentleman ? What is it to be a gentleman ? Is it to have lofty aims, to lead a pure life, to keep your honour virgin ; to have the esteem of your fellow-citizens, and the love of your fireside ; to bear good fortune meekly ; to suffer evil with constancy; and through evil or good to maintain truth always ? Show me the happy man whose life exhibits these qualities, and him we will salute as gentleman, whatever his rank may be ; show me the prince who possesses them, and he may be sure of our love and loyalty. The heart of Britain still beats kindly for George III., not because he was wise and just, but because he was pure in life, honest in intent, and because according to his lights he worshipped Heaven. I think we acknowledge in the inheritrix of his sceptre a wiser rule and a life as honourable and pure ; and I am sure the future painter of our manners will pay a willing allegiance to that good life, and be loyal to the memory of that unsullied virtue.

**THE END.**